There wasn't much space between them. A metre… maybe a little less.

Mila still held his gaze. He wished hers was unreadable, but it wasn't—not any more. He was sure his wasn't either.

All he had to do was reach for her…

And that would be it.

And it would change everything.

Their friendship—the friendship that was so important to him, that he needed so badly— would be altered for ever.

And Mila…

Was this really what *she* wanted?

'I just want tonight,' Mila whispered, reading his mind.

And with that he was losing himself in those eyes, falling into their depths.

He needed to touch her. He needed Mila. There was no going back.

THE BILLIONAIRE
FROM HER PAST

BY
LEAH ASHTON

MILLS & BOON

First Published in Great Britain 2016
By Mills & Boon, an imprint of HarperCollins*Publishers*
1 London Bridge Street, London, SE1 9GF

© 2016 Leah Ashton

ISBN: 978-0-263-92018-5

23-0916

Our policy is to use papers that are natural, renewable and recyclable products and made from wood grown in sustainable forests. The logging and manufacturing processes conform to the legal environmental regulations of the country of origin.

Printed and bound in Spain
by CPI, Barcelona

RITA® Award-winning author **Leah Ashton** never expected to write books. She grew up reading everything she could lay her hands on—from pony books to the backs of cereal boxes at breakfast. One day she discovered the page-turning, happy-sigh-inducing world of romance novels… and one day, much later, wondered if maybe she could write one too.

Leah now lives in Perth, Western Australia, and writes happy-ever-afters for heroines who definitely *don't* need saving. She has a gorgeous husband, two amazing daughters and the best intentions to plan meals and maintain an effortlessly tidy home. When she's not writing, Leah loves all-day breakfast, rambling conversations and laughing until she cries. She really hates cucumber. And scary movies. You can visit Leah at www.leah-ashton.com or Facebook.com/leahashtonauthor.

For my dad, Jeff.

Whether it be for a tennis match, dressage test,
job interview or career decision, you have always
supported me with your wisdom, your positivity,
your love—and your ability to reverse a horse-float.
Thank you for always being there for me. I love you.
Go Freo!

PROLOGUE

PURPLE.

That was what Mila Molyneux remembered.

And bubblegum-pink. Crocodile-green. Little-boy-blue.

So many colours: primary and pastels, and in stripes and polka dots. Everywhere. On party dresses, balloons and pointed party hats. Or scrunched and forgotten in the mountains of desperately ripped and dismissed wrapping paper that wafted across the lawn.

A rainbow of happy, excited eight-year-olds beneath a perfect Perth sky.

But Stephanie had definitely worn purple to her birthday party all those years ago. Purple tights, purple dress and glittering purple cowboy boots.

Mila remembered how excited her best friend had been that day. She remembered how excited she'd been, too—what eight-year-old girl wasn't excited by a birthday party? It had been years before their dreary Gothic black high school days, so Mila guessed she'd been wearing some shade of red—her favourite colour—but that detail of her memories had faded. As had the memory of what Seb had worn, but he'd been there, too. Three friends, neighbours all in a row, although back then Seb had most definitely still had 'boy germs'.

But that had changed later.

As had Stephanie's backyard.

Today there were no balloons in Mr and Mrs van Berlo's garden. No patchwork of forgotten wrapping paper. No mountain of presents or shrieking of excited children.

And definitely no purple, nor even the tiniest hint of a rainbow.

Instead the guests wore black as they mingled amongst

tall tables topped with elegant white flower arrangements. In this same garden, where Stephanie and Mila had played hide and seek hundreds of times, it just didn't seem real. Didn't seem possible.

But then—none of this did, did it?

'If anyone else tells me how lucky we are to have such *amazing* weather today I'm going to—'

Sebastian Fyfe stood beside her, staring out at the monochrome guests beneath the unseasonably perfect winter sky. His voice was strong and deep, as it always was.

It had been years since they'd spoken face to face. Almost as long since their emails and social media messages had dribbled out into nothing.

'If anyone else tells you how lucky we are to have such *amazing* weather today you're going to nod politely—because you get how no one has a clue what to say to a man at his wife's funeral,' Mila finished for him.

Seb raised his untouched beer in Mila's direction. 'Correct,' he conceded. His tone was as tired as his grey-blue eyes. '*I* don't know what to say at my wife's funeral either. Maybe I should steal their material and start the weather conversation myself.'

Mila managed a small smile. 'Do whatever you have to do to get through this,' she said. 'Personally, I'm just not talking to anybody.'

Even her mother and two sisters were giving her the space she needed. But they stood nearby, in a neat half-circle, just in case she changed her mind.

'Is Ben here?' Seb asked, not really looking at her.

Mila shook her head. 'No,' she said. 'We broke up.'

A few months ago now. Steph had known, but obviously she hadn't passed on the news to Seb. Not that long ago Mila would've told Seb herself—but things had changed.

For a long while they just stood together silently, Seb was tall and stiff and stoic in his perfectly tailored suit, looking like the successful businessman he was—but it was impossible to ignore the flatness of his expression and the emptiness in his eyes. His dark hair was rumpled—it always was—but today it looked too long, as if he'd missed a haircut. Or two.

A waitress offered canapés, which they both refused. Mila swirled her remaining Shiraz in its glass, but didn't drink.

She desperately wanted to say something. To ask how Seb was—how he *really* was. To wrap her arms around him and hold on tight. To cry tears for Stephanie that only Seb could understand. But it had been too long since their friendship had been like that.

It had been six years since Seb and Stephanie had moved to London, and maybe they should have expected things to change with so much distance between them.

'Did Steph—?' Seb began, then stopped.

'Did she what?'

He turned to meet Mila's gaze. 'Did you know?' he said. 'What she was doing?'

Did you know about the drugs?

Mila shook her head. 'No,' she said.

Something shifted in his eyes. Relief?

'Me either,' he said. 'I hate myself every day for not knowing. But it helps—in a way—that she hid it from you, too.'

Mila blinked, confused. 'I wouldn't say she *hid* it from me, Seb,' she said gently, not really wanting to disagree with him on a day like today, but also knowing he deserved her honesty. 'The last time I spoke to Steph was her birthday.' Almost six months ago. 'And we weren't really talking regularly before that. Not for a long time.'

Seb's expression hardened. 'But you're her best friend.'

Mila nodded. 'Of course. It's just…'

'You should've been there for her.'

His words were clipped and brutal. His abrupt anger— evident in every line of his face and posture—shocked her.

'Seb, Steph always knew I was there for her, but our lives were so different. We were both busy...'

It sounded as awful and lame an excuse as it was. Mila knew it. Seb knew it.

Maybe everything had changed when they'd moved to London. Maybe it had been earlier. Not that it *really* mattered. No matter how rarely they'd spoken recently, Stephanie had been her Best Friend. A proper noun, with capital letters. Always and for ever.

Until death do us part.

Tears prickled, threatened.

She looked at Seb through blurry eyes. The sunlight was still inappropriately glorious, dappling Seb's shoulders through the trees. He was angry, but not with her. Or at least not *just* with her. She knew him well enough, even now, to know that he was simply *angry*. With everything.

So she wasn't going to try to defend herself with words she didn't even believe. Instead she could only attempt to turn back the clock—to be the type of friend none of them had been to each other for this past half decade and more.

She reached for him, laying her hand on his arm. 'Seb—if I can do anything...'

He shrugged, dislodging her hand. His gaze remained unyielding. 'Now you just sound like all the others. You've just skipped the bit about the weather.'

And as he walked away her tears trickled free.

CHAPTER ONE

Eighteen months later

MILA TOOK A step backwards and crossed her arms as she surveyed the sea of figurines before her.

Fresh from the kiln, the small army of dragons and other mythical creatures stood in neat rows, their colourful glazes reflecting the last of the sun filtering through the single window in the back room of Mila's pottery workshop.

There was a red dragon with only three legs. A beautifully wonky centaur. A winged beast with dramatically disproportionate wings.

Plus many other creations that Mila now knew she must wait for the children in her class to describe.

It had only taken one offended ten-year-old for Mila to learn that it was best *not* to mention the name of the creation she was complimenting. Now she went with, *That is amazing!* Rather than: *What an amazing tiger!* Because, as it turned out, sometimes what appeared to be a *tiger* was actually a *zebra*.

Whoops.

But here she was, surveying the results of her beginners' class for primary school age children—a new venture for Mila's Nest—and, to her, the table of imperfect sculptures was absolutely beautiful. She couldn't wait for the kids' reactions when they saw their creatures dressed in their brilliant glazes—such a change from the muted colours they'd worn prior to being fired in the kiln.

A tinkling bell signalled that someone had entered the shop. Mila's gaze darted to the oversized clock on the wall—it was well after five, but she'd forgotten to put up her *'Closed'* sign.

With a sigh, Mila stepped out of her workshop. Mila's Nest was one of a small group of four double-storey terrace-style shops on a busy Claremont Street, each with living accommodation upstairs. Mila had split the downstairs area into two: a small shop near the street, and a larger workshop behind, where she ran her pottery classes.

The shop displayed Mila's own work, which tended towards usable objects—vases, platters, bowls, jugs and the like. Mila had always been interested in making the functional beautiful and the mundane unique.

The man who'd entered her shop stood with his back towards her, perusing the display in her shop window. He was tall, and dressed as if he'd just walked off a building site, with steel-capped boots, sturdy-looking knee-length shorts and a plaster-dusted shirt covering his broad shoulders.

He must have come from the shop next door. Vacant for years, it had been on the verge of collapse, and Mila had been seriously relieved when its renovation had begun only a week or so ago. Even teaching above the shriek of power tools, hammering and banging had been preferable to the potential risk of her own little shop being damaged by its derelict neighbour.

The man picked up a small decorative bowl, cradling it carefully in the palm of one large hand.

'That piece has a lustre glaze,' Mila said, stepping closer so she could trace a finger across the layered metallic design. 'If you're after something larger, I have—'

But by now Mila's gaze had travelled from the workman's strong hands to his face. His extremely familiar and completely unexpected face.

'Seb!' she said on a gasp, her hands flying to her mouth in surprise.

Unfortunately her fingers momentarily caught on the rim of the tiny bowl and it crashed to the jarrah floor, immediately shattering into a myriad of blue and silver pieces.

* * *

'Dammit!' Mila said, dropping to her knees.

Seb swore under his breath, and dropped to his haunches beside her. 'Sorry,' he said, inadequately.

This wasn't the way he'd planned for things to go.

Mila looked up, meeting his gaze through her brunette curls. Her hair was shorter than it had been at the funeral and it suited her, making her big blue eyes appear even larger and highlighting the famous cheekbones she'd inherited from her movie star father.

'It wasn't your fault,' she said. 'You just surprised me'.

She piled the largest pieces of the bowl into a small heap, then stood and strode over to the shop's front door, flipping the red and white sign to *'Closed'*. When she turned back to face him she'd crossed her arms in front of the paint-splattered apron she wore.

Her expression had shifted, too. He'd thought, just for a second, that maybe she was glad to see him. But, no, that moment had gone.

'Yes?' she prompted.

He had a speech planned, of sorts. An explanation of why he'd hadn't returned her many phone calls, or her emails, or her social media messages in the months after Steph's funeral—before she'd clearly given up on ever receiving a response.

It wasn't a very good speech, or a good explanation.

Explaining something that he didn't really understand was difficult, he'd discovered.

'I stuffed up,' he said, finally. Short and to the point.

Mila raised her eyebrows, but he could see some of the tension leave her shoulders. Not all of it, though.

'I wasn't contacting you to make myself feel better, like you said,' Mila said. 'Or out of guilt.' Another pause. 'I was worried about you.'

Ah. Yes, he had replied to one email. He remembered typing it, with angry, careless keystrokes. He didn't remember the content—he didn't want to. It wouldn't have been nice. It would have been cruel.

'I wasn't in a good place,' he said.

Mila nodded. 'I know. I wish you'd let me be there for you. Steph was my best friend, but she was your *wife*. I can't imagine how difficult this has been for you.'

She stepped towards him now, reaching out a hand before letting it drop away against her hip, not having touched him at all. He realised, belatedly, that she wasn't angry with him. That he'd misinterpreted the narrowing of her eyes, the tension in her muscles...

She was guarded, not angry. As if she was protecting herself.

He'd known he'd hurt her at the funeral. Not straight away—it had taken months for his brain to function properly again—but eventually. And she was still hurt, now.

That was difficult for Seb to acknowledge. The Mila he knew was always so together. So tough. So assured. She didn't sweat the small things. Didn't put up with nonsense.

But he'd hurt her—and he was supposed to be her friend. Once he'd been one of her closest friends—and the last person in the world who would want to cause her pain. And yet he had. He didn't like that at all.

'You didn't stuff up,' she said after a long silence. 'I mean, I don't think there are really rules in this situation. When a man loses his wife. But I think lashing out occasionally is allowed.' She shrugged. 'I'm a big girl. I can deal with it.'

She was being too kind, too understanding. 'I can still apologise,' he said. 'That's why I'm here. To say sorry. For what I said at the funeral and for everything afterwards. We both lost Steph. I should've been there for you, too. I should've been a better friend.'

He could see her ready to argue again, to attempt to absolve him of all guilt—but he didn't want that. And maybe she understood.

'Okay.'

But he could see she wasn't entirely comfortable.

'I accept your apology. But only if you promise not to send any more mean emails. Deal?'

There it was—the spark in her gaze. The sparkle he remembered from the strong, cheeky, stubborn teenage version of Mila. And the strong, cheeky, stubborn early-twenty-something version, too.

'Deal,' he said, with a relieved smile.

She was twenty-nine, now. A year younger than Seb. She'd matured and lost that lanky teenage look, but she was still very much the Mila Molyneux who featured in so many of his childhood memories. He'd lived two houses down from her in their exclusive Peppermint Grove neighbourhood—although at first they'd had no idea of their privileged upbringing. All the three of them—Steph, Mila and Seb—had cared about was their next adventure. Building forts, riding their bikes, clandestine trips to the shops for overstuffed bags of lollies… And then, once they were older, they'd somehow maintained their friendship despite being split into separate gender-specific high schools. All three had studied together, hung out together. Had fun.

Mila had even been the first girl he'd kissed.

He hadn't thought about that in years. It had, it turned out, been a disaster. He'd misread the situation, embarrassed them both.

Mila was looking at him curiously.

'So, any chance of a tour?' he asked, dragging himself back into the present.

Mila shook her head firmly. 'Not until you tell me why on earth you're wearing *that*,' she said, with a pointed look at his work clothes.

Seb grinned. 'Ah,' he said. 'Long story. How about you give me the tour of your shop first? Then I'll give you a tour of next door and explain.'

'Nope,' Mila said firmly. 'You're giving me your tour

first—because I *need* to find out how an international IT consultant has ended up renovating the shop next door.'

'Well,' Seb said, smiling fully now, 'that's kind of all your fault, Mila.'

'*My* fault?' Mila said, tapping her chest as if to confirm who he was referring to.

'Most definitely,' he said. Then he grabbed her hand and tugged her towards her front door. 'Come on, then.'

And, for one of the very few times he could remember, Mila Molyneux looked less than in control of a situation.

Seb decided he liked that.

CHAPTER TWO

SEB'S HAND FELT DIFFERENT.

Not rough, or anything. Just… Mila didn't know how to describe it. Tougher? As if this utterly unexpected transformation from brilliant IT geek into rugged workman had not happened recently.

But then—how did she even *know* it felt different? How long had it been since he'd held her hand? Or even touched her?

Years.

For ever.

She gave her head a little shake as Seb led her through the entrance of the shop next door. This was just silly. She'd let go of thinking about Seb's touch years ago—or reacting in any way. She wasn't about to start again now.

Especially not now.

'I promise, Steph, I don't like *him, like him. It's okay.'*

Thirteen-year-old Mila had managed a wide smile, even if her gaze hadn't quite met her best friend's.

They'd sat cross-legged on Steph's bed, a small mountain of rented VHS tapes between them, awaiting their planned sleepover movie marathon.

'Are you sure?' Steph had asked. *'Because—'*

'Yes!' Mila had said emphatically. *'He's just my friend. I don't have like…romantic feelings for him. I never have and I never will. I promise…'*

He'd dropped her hand now, anyway, oblivious. He'd taken a few steps into the gutted shop and now spread his arms out wide to encompass the cavernous double-height space, pivoting to look at her expectantly.

Mila needed a moment to take it all in. To take *Seb* in.

It had been more than six months since his email—

since he'd so unequivocally told Mila never to contact him again. He'd then blocked her and unfollowed her on all social media. Set all of his accounts to private.

Effectively, he'd erased himself from Mila's life. And, on the other side of the world, she'd been helpless to do one thing about it.

Rationally, she'd understood that he was in a dark place, and that his behaviour was not about *her*. That he wasn't deliberately trying to hurt *her*. But it had still hurt.

So she hadn't expected to see Seb again. At least, not like this. Certainly not dressed like a builder, proudly showing off the elderly, crumbling building next door.

She wasn't sure how she felt about it. After shock, her immediate reaction on seeing Seb had been joy—maybe a Pavlovian reaction to seeing her once-so-close childhood friend. But now she wasn't so sure. She felt confused. And cautious, too. His apology, his earnestness… It was such a contrast to what she'd believed to be her last ever interaction with Seb Fyfe.

Mila surveyed the dilapidated space. It was the exact external dimensions of her own place, and it was interesting to see how her shop would look without necessities like a staircase or—well, the entire first floor. The walls had been stripped of plaster, leaving bare brick, and there was absolutely no lighting. Now, at dusk, little light pushed through the dirty, cracked shop windows and the open doorway behind her.

Basically—it was a big, dark, empty, filthy room.

'Well,' she began, 'I may need to hear a bit more of your plans before I can be appropriately impressed.'

Seb's lips quirked upwards. God, it was so *weird*, seeing her old friend dressed like this. He'd always had lovely shoulders, but now they were muscled. And, yes, of course he'd always been unavoidably handsome. But more in a lean, very slightly geeky way—befitting his career in IT consulting and her memories of him tinkering with hard drives and other computer paraphernalia.

Now he looked like a *man*. A proper, grown-up man—not an oversized version of the teenage Seb she remembered. And not even one per cent geek.

Seb had always been self-assured, always had that innate confidence—probably partly because he had enough family money behind him to know it was nearly impossible for him to fail in anything—but mainly, Mila felt, because that was the kind of guy he was. But now there was something more. Something beyond the confidence she recognised. An...*ease*.

And it was an ease he had now, in his tradesman's outfit, that she hadn't even realised he'd lacked in a five-thousand-dollar suit.

'Fair enough. There's not a lot to see just yet.' He pointed to the far wall, where a large poster-sized plan was taped to the bricks. 'The details are there, but really it's nothing too exciting. It'll be fitted out for a fashion retailer I've got lined up—a good fit for the other shops in the terrace.'

'Fashion? So this isn't some new obscure location for Fyfe Technology?'

That was about as far as Mila had got in trying to work out what this was all about. A trendy suburban location for a multinational company with offices across Europe, the US and Australia and an office already in the Perth CBD? It didn't actually make any sense. But then, she was still trying to process Seb's new shoulders...

Another shake of her head—mentally, this time.

'I sold Fyfe,' Seb said simply.

It was so nonchalantly delivered that it took Mila a long moment to comprehend what he'd just told her.

'Pardon me?'

He watched her steadily. 'It was a difficult decision. Dad wasn't happy at first—I mean, in many ways it was still his company, even though he's been retired for years. But eventually he understood where I was coming from. Why I needed to do this.'

Again his arms spread out to take in the building site.

'And *this* is…?'

Seb shrugged. 'To do what you do. Follow my dreams without just sliding down my family's mountain of money.'

Mila twisted her fingers together, suddenly uncomfortable. 'I don't think anyone should ever use *me* as a good example for anything.'

'Why not?' Seb said. 'You're doing exactly what you want to do—earning your own income and treading your own path. What's not great about that?'

Mila laughed. 'You're skipping the bit where I dropped out of two different universities, at least four different vocational courses, and completely ignored the advice of basically everyone who cares about me.'

'Exactly,' he said, with a truly gorgeous smile. 'And how awesome is *that*?'

Mila ran her hands through her hair. Yes, she was proud of what she'd achieved, and proud that she lived completely independently of her frankly obscene trust fund, but that was her… Seb was… Seb wasn't like that. Seb had taken his family's already successful business and blown it out of the water. He'd expanded Fyfe throughout Europe, stayed one step ahead of new technologies and made a multi-million-dollar empire a multi-*billion*-dollar one.

'I'm confused,' Mila said. 'Steph always told me how much you loved your work. How excited you were about the company's expansion, about—'

'How I loved my work more than my wife?' he said.

The sudden horrible, harsh words hung in the air between them.

'No,' she said softly. 'She never said that.'

'Not to you,' Seb said.

Mila didn't know what to do with what he'd said. She

didn't know what to do with *any* of this. It was all so unexpected, and it had been so long.

This Seb before her was such an odd combination of the boy she'd thought she'd known and this man she barely recognised. The Seb she'd known would never have sold his father's company. But then, the Steph and Seb she'd known had been deliriously happily married. The Steph she'd known would never have taken drugs.

Emotion hung in the air between them.

'What's going on here, Seb?' Mila said, suddenly frustrated. She'd never thought she'd see or hear from Seb again. And now here he was, with unexpected apologies and painful memories. 'Because I don't for a minute believe that your new dream just coincidentally started with the shop next door to mine.'

A small but humourless smile. Then Seb rubbed his forehead. 'Okay—here's the deal. I sold the company, donated a big chunk of the proceeds to addiction-related charities and then put some aside for the children I have no intention of having—that would require a wife—but my lawyer still insisted I provide for. Then I gave myself a relatively modest loan—' he named an amount that would buy the row of shops many several times over '—which I will pay back once my new venture takes off. And the new venture is a building company. I've started with smaller developments, like this one, although already I'm starting on bigger projects: think entire apartment blocks, maybe office towers one day.'

'So your dream wasn't to play with computers all day but to build skyscrapers?'

Seb shook his head. 'No, my dream was to do exactly what my dad did, but better. Which was the problem. I've spent my whole life deliberately walking in my father's footsteps. I've finally realised that I'm more than that. That I can build a company from the ground up myself.' He paused for a long moment. 'When my acquisitions team recommended I buy this place I didn't know it was next to your shop,' he said. 'But obviously it came up in the research. I should've known, really—I remember the photos you sent through to us when you first bought it.' His lips quirked. 'And that was really what sealed it—'

'So you bought this place because of *me*?'

'No,' Seb said. 'I was always going to buy it for the right price—which I had no problem negotiating.'

There it was—a glimpse of the ruthless businessman Mila remembered. Just this time without the suit.

'The question was whether I'd let you *know* I'd bought it.'

Mila looked again at the building plan. In the corner was the company logo and its name: Heliotrope Construction.

'Steph…' Mila breathed.

'It's not that original,' Seb said. 'But if Steph could call her fashion label Violet, I figured…'

Shades of purple—Steph's favourite colour.

'I like it,' Mila said.

But Seb was moving the conversation along. 'I did consider not being hands-on with this place, to reduce the chances that we'd bump into each other. But that would have been pretty gutless. I've been back in Perth a few months now. I couldn't avoid you for ever.'

Months? Seb's email had been six months ago, and she'd dealt with his rejection then. Even so, it stung to realise he'd been back home for so long. Somehow rejection had hurt less when he was a million miles away.

'I thought about calling. I knew I couldn't email you.' He shoved his hands into his pockets. 'But I had to apologise in person. Buying this place just forced me into action. I'm sorry,' he said again. 'For waiting this long. Since Steph… everything's been messed up. *I've* been messed up…'

'I know,' Mila said. She got it. Or at least some of it. She *did*.

They were both silent for a while. Mila didn't quite know what to think—she'd mentally classified Seb as part of her past. And now here he was—so different—in her present.

'I hope I'm not too late,' Seb said.

'For what?' Mila asked, confused.

'To fix things.' He was watching her steadily, his gaze exploring her face. 'To fix *us*. I'd hoped—'

Maybe he'd seen something in her expression, because for once Seb looked less than completely assured.

'You and Steph were my closest friends. Steph's gone for ever, but *we* still have each other. I want you in my life again, Mila. If you'll let me.'

Part of Mila wanted to smile and laugh, tell Seb *Of course!* And in so many ways that was the obvious answer.

She'd told him she'd forgiven him for his behaviour amidst his grief. But it had still hurt. A lot. Because she'd certainly had enough rejection in her life—her ex-fiancé being the latest purveyor of rejection. And part of her—the pragmatic side—just wondered what the point actually was.

Had too much time passed? Was it better that their friendship remained a fond memory? Limited only to the occasional catch-up message on social media?

Remembering how she'd felt when he'd held her hand before—the warmth and strength of his fingers and the echoing, unwanted warmth in her belly—Mila thought she definitely knew the answer.

Seb had just lost his wife. And he'd been Steph's *husband*. She had no place considering the breadth of his shoulders or the strength of his hands.

She should keep her distance. Be his friend, but acknowledge that things could never be as they had been. They could never have the connection of their childhood again. It was too complicated. The emotions too intense.

And yet—here he was. Right in front of her. This strange, compelling mix of the cute boy next door and this handsome almost-stranger next door.

Seb must have seen the conflict in her gaze.

'Well,' he said, 'maybe I am too late.'

He was looking straight at her, but his eyes now gave nothing away. Gone was all that emotion, shuttered away.

He really wanted this, Mila realised. This was more than an extended apology or an attempt to make amends. And what was she worried about, anyway? *Really?*

So what if Seb still had the smile that had made her teenage self weak at the knees? She'd dealt with all that years ago. All that messy unrequited love and the whole heap of angst that came with your best friend marrying the first boy you'd fallen in love with. The first boy you'd kissed.

That had been for ever ago.

Today the butterflies in her tummy meant nothing. She was being silly. Right now Seb didn't need her pushing him away for no apparent reason. And—frankly—she didn't really want to push him away. She'd missed him.

'So, do you honestly want a tour of my pottery studio?' she asked.

Seb grinned triumphantly. 'Lead on, Ms Molyneux!'

And of course Mila found herself smiling back.

CHAPTER THREE

'KNOCK, KNOCK!'

The familiar female voice floated through to Mila's shop and was promptly followed by an impatient rattling of the workshop's back door.

'Mila!' Ivy called out. 'Could you hurry, please? I really need to pee.'

Mila grinned as she hurried to greet her sister. Her nephew, Nate, was fast asleep in his pram on the other side of the fly screen, looking exactly as angelic as Ivy said he was *not*.

'Mila? I mean it. I have about fifteen seconds.'

Mila dragged her gaze away from Nate to glance at her sister.

'Maybe ten,' Ivy clarified.

Quickly Mila flicked open the lock, and Ivy sprinted past her to the small powder room in the corner of the workshop used by Mila's students.

'You'll understand one day,' Ivy said as she slammed the toilet door, muttering something about eight-and-a-half-pound babies.

Mila stepped outside, then squatted in front of Nate's pram. There wasn't much space behind Mila's shop—enough for Mila's car, her bins, and a large collection of enthusiastically growing pot plants—all planted in an eclectic mix of pots and vessels that Mila had decided unfit for sale after firing.

Nate held Mila's mail in his chubby fist, collected by Ivy from the letterbox beside the rear courtyard gate. Nate loved junk mail, and he was happily gazing at the lurid colours of a discount store brochure with intent.

She wasn't exactly sure how old Nate was—nine months,

maybe? He'd just started crawling, anyway, and talking in musical meaningless tones. He was so beautiful, with long eyelashes that brushed his cheeks and thick, curly blond hair. Both from his father, apparently—although Mila couldn't yet see even a hint of Ivy's hulking SAS soldier husband in delicate, picture-perfect Nate.

Ivy had taken to dropping by regularly—a result of Nate's unwillingness to nap in his cot and, Mila thought, a latent 'big sister' instinct for Ivy to check up on her that had begun just after Steph had died. Originally it had taken the form of daily phone calls from Ivy's office at Molyneux Tower, and had only metamorphosed into actual visits when Nate had come along and so adamantly refused to sleep.

Mila had always been close to both her sisters—but she hadn't seen workaholic Ivy so often since they were kids living at home. And for that Mila figured she owed Nate one.

She leaned in closed to kiss his velvety cheek. 'Nice work, kid.'

'You know what I wish?' Ivy asked a few minutes later, when they were settled with cups of tea on the old wooden church pew that edged one wall of the workshop. 'That I could have banked all those hours of time I wasted over the years so I could have them now. Because, honestly, I don't know how I ever thought I was busy before. This mum stuff is *nuts*.'

Mila raised her eyebrows. 'You didn't have any spare time to bank,' she pointed out. Her big sister had always been the high-flying, high-achieving child in the family—groomed practically from birth to take over the Molyneux mining empire.

Ivy shrugged. 'Maybe.'

Mila smiled. Ivy had never been good at acknowledging her obsession with work.

Her sister leant closer and spoke in a hushed tone. 'This is going to sound terrible, but I'm really enjoying being back at work a few days a week. I can actually get stuff *done*.

Yesterday I committed Molyneux Mining to a joint venture project with a British conglomerate. Today I've discovered that Nate no longer likes peas.'

'Don't worry,' Mila said with a grin. 'There isn't actually a Mum Police.'

Ivy sighed. 'Yeah, I know. There is definitely Mum Guilt, though.'

'Hey,' Mila said, catching Ivy's gaze. 'Don't feel bad for enjoying the career you loved before Nate came along. He knows you love him.'

'Words can't describe how much.' A long pause, then a wobbly bottom lip. 'Oh, God, I'm going to blub. Now I can't even blame breastfeeding hormones.'

Mila scooted closer to her sister so she could press her shoulder against Ivy's as they sat together quietly with their now empty teacups.

'Cake?' Mila asked. 'One of my students baked—'

The tinkling sound of the shop door being opened had Mila on her feet, giving a vague gesture towards the small fridge in the workshop kitchenette as she hurried out of the room.

'Good morning—' she began, then stopped. It was Seb. 'Hi!' she said, with a wide smile. Mila still wasn't sure if reconnecting with Seb was a good idea—but she couldn't deny that she was pleased to see him.

Seb lips quirked as he glanced at the forgotten teacup in her hand. 'Busy day?' he teased.

Mila shrugged. 'I've had a flood of online orders this morning, actually, after one of my pieces was used in a feature in the latest *Home + Home* mag.' She'd swallowed her pride over a year ago and accepted her sister April's offer to feature one of her indoor planters on her hugely popular lifestyle blog. The subsequent interest from stylists and interior decorators hadn't abated. 'The store makes up a pretty small amount of my income,' she continued, pointedly, 'leaving plenty of time for guilt-free tea.'

'That's my favourite type of anything.' He grinned. 'And, really? "A pretty small amount"?'

'Eighteen point two-three per cent. Down one point nine per cent from the previous quarter.'

'There you go. Mila and her numbers.'

'I had to be halfway decent at *something* at school, otherwise Mum would've completely disowned me.' She hadn't had much interest in anything other than maths, and had been truly terrible at pretending.

'She probably wouldn't have, you know.' Ivy leant casually against the workshop doorframe, her eyes sparkling with curiosity as she glanced between Mila and Seb. 'Probably.'

A pause, and Mila knew her sister had taken in Seb's unfamiliar work clothes. 'I didn't realise you were visiting Perth. It's good to see you.'

Under better circumstances. It went unsaid, but the fleeting reference to Stephanie still made Mila's heart ache.

'Not visiting,' Seb said. 'Back. For good.'

Those last two words he directed at Mila, and her awful, disloyal heart flipped over.

No. In the same minute her throat constricted at the memory of her friend. She was *not* allowed to get all fluttery about Sebastian. She crossed her arms in front of her chest, but that was completely ineffective. Instead, while Seb filled Ivy in on his new business venture, she deposited her teacup on the counter, then needlessly wiped a cloth over the vases in shades of teal and grey that were silhouetted like a skyline in her shop window.

'Mila?'

She didn't even look up at Seb's voice, instead focusing her attention on a non-existent mark on a blue-green glaze.

'I'm sorry—now isn't really a good time,' she said. Maybe if she appeared suitably busy he'd go away—and so would her inappropriate heart-flipping.

'For what?'

She straightened to face him, once again crossing her

arms. Aware that Ivy was watching, Mila didn't really know what to say. What *could* she say? *It's not a good time for me to still be attracted to my best friend's husband?*

Accurate, but never, *ever* to be articulated.

At her continued silence, Seb leant a little closer. That didn't help anything.

'I thought you were okay with us being friends again?'

'I am,' she said. And she was. It wasn't Seb's fault she had faulty hormones—or whatever it was inside her that just *would not quit* when it came to Seb Fyfe.

Seb needed her right now. But she needed space. More time, maybe? To recalibrate to a world where she co-existed with Seb without the fact of his being her best friend's husband to stall any heart-flipping or tingling of skin.

He will always be Steph's husband.

She'd been a terrible friend to Steph for too long. That stopped *now*.

'Do you still play tennis?' she said, a bit more loudly than she would have liked.

'On occasion.'

'Great!' she said, even louder. *Dammit.* 'Let's hire a court later this week. Have a hit.'

This was a genius plan. Physical distance. Smacking of objects.

'Sure…' he said, sounding a little confused.

'Great!' she repeated. *'Great!'*

Then finally he left, with a tinkling of the doorbell, and from Mila a significant sigh of relief.

Ivy marched over, every inch the billionaire business-woman demanding to know exactly what was going on. But before she could open her mouth a low, sleepy cry reverberated from the workshop.

'Later,' Ivy threw over her shoulder as she jogged back to Nate.

Seemed Mila owed Nate another one: *Nice work, Nate.*

Now she had time to work out something to tell Ivy—to

explain whatever her sister had thought she'd witnessed. Because Ivy had never known about Mila's unrequited teenage crush. Nor April, for that matter.

And no one was ever going to find out about this silly adult version either.

Seb propped his shoulder against the front wall of his shop. Inside, the sounds of building activity thumped and buzzed through the open door, and a lanky apprentice chippy carted rubble in white plastic buckets to the large skip that hunkered at the kerb.

His meeting with the foreman had gone well. So well, in fact, that Seb knew it wasn't even close to necessary that he checked in with the man each day. Richard had thirty years' experience and knew exactly what he was doing. He knew more than Seb, actually—although to be perfectly honest that wasn't particularly hard for anyone in the construction industry.

This bothered Seb. He'd known from a very young age that he would one day own his father's company. Just like for Mila's older sister Ivy it had been his destiny, and he'd done everything in his power to be worthy of following in his dad's footsteps.

That had included actually knowing what his staff did.

He'd graduated with honours in his Computer Science degree so he could write code like his developers. Then he'd done an MBA as he'd begun taking over from his father. And he'd attended each and every course before he'd sent his staff —whether it be marketing, customer service, project management or system development. He'd known that he didn't get to stop learning just because he was the boss, and he hadn't been about to waste his team's time on a course he wasn't prepared to do himself.

He hadn't pretended he could do *every* job in his mammoth company—and he hadn't needed to—but he'd figured he should be able to walk into any meeting, at any Fyfe office in the world, and not feel as if his staff were talking in a foreign language.

He still had a long way to go when it came to his new venture.

It bothered him that he didn't know enough about joists and sub-floors and ceiling-fixing and roofing and I-beams and…

In fact, his entire prior experience in the building industry involved demoing the bathroom of the London flat he'd owned with Steph prior to its—outsourced—renovation, a disproportionate interest in power tools for a man who didn't have a shed—or a back garden to put one in—and many good intentions to attend a tiling/carpentry/plastering workshop one day.

He'd always been interested in tools and building things. He'd just funnelled it in a technological direction. Steph had encouraged him to take some time off—to do a weekend course, to paint their home rather than having professional decorators return three separate times to get the flawless finish he'd demanded. But that was the problem with being a work-obsessed perfectionist—he hadn't been about to take time off from Fyfe.

Nothing had been worth that. Certainly not a bit of DIY.

'Not me,' Steph had told him more than once. *'Not even me.'*

Seb drained the last of his coffee, his fingernails digging ever so slightly into the takeaway cup's corrugated cardboard outer shell. He stared at nothing—at the sky, at the passing traffic—and finally at the stencilled company name on the side of the battered skip, letting his gaze lose focus.

He'd read somewhere—or heard, maybe, on a podcast or something—that grief hit you like a wave. At first the waves just kept on pounding. Pounding you down and down, with barely a breath of air before you were sucked back under again. But then, over time, the gaps between the waves would grow. They would still hit just as hard—and be just as shocking—but in between you could begin to breathe. To exist again.

Sometimes you even got better at handling the waves, at bracing yourself and swimming back up to the surface. Not every wave though. Some would always sneak up on you and drown you as brutally as the first.

Every memory of Steph…every reminder of his many mistakes…what he could have done…should have done… It wasn't getting easier.

Seb had discovered that the waves didn't stop coming. He had just got better at swimming.

Footsteps drew his attention back to his surroundings. He looked up to see Mila striding along the footpath, her gaze on the screen of her phone. Her eyes flicked upwards as she approached, and the moment her gaze locked on his it skittered away again.

It was just like yesterday: that same unexpected and suddenly closed expression. He had absolutely no idea why.

But then her gaze swung back, as if she was *really* looking at him now, and her long strides came to a halt in front of him.

'I didn't see you there,' she said.

He had a feeling if she had she would have exited via the rear of her shop. The realisation frustrated him. Why was she keeping her distance?

But now she was studying him carefully, as if attempting to translate what the sum total of his face and posture actually meant.

He pushed away from the wall and rolled his shoulders back, uncomfortable with whatever Mila might have thought she'd seen.

'Are you okay?'

He nodded sharply, not quite meeting her eyes. 'Of course.'

'You don't look okay,' she said—which shouldn't have surprised him. Mila wasn't one to accept anything at surface value.

She took a step closer, trying to catch his gaze.

He knew he was just being stupid now, but for some reason he just couldn't quite look at her—the knife-edged echo of Steph's remembered words was still yet to be washed out to sea.

She reached out, resting her fingers just above his wrist. Her hand was cool against his sun-warmed skin.

'Last night,' she said, as he focused on the deep red shade of her nail polish, 'do you know what I did? I found that photobook Steph made after our trip to Bali when we were about twenty. Remember? Our first holiday without our parents. We thought we were so grown-up.'

He nodded. They'd gone with a group of his and Steph's friends from uni. Mila had just dropped out of her umpteenth course, but that had been back when she and Steph had done everything together. There'd never been any question—of course Mila would go with them.

'Do you remember that guy I met? From Melbourne?' She laughed. 'Oh, God. What a loser.' She shook her head. 'Anyway, last night I wanted to *see* Steph—see her happy—with you and...uh...me, of course.'

Her words had become a little faster, and he was finally able to drag his gaze to hers. She must be wearing boots with a heel, as she looked taller than he'd expected—actually, simply closer to him than he'd expected.

'It made me smile,' she said. 'And cry.'

Her hand was still on his arm, but she'd shifted her fingers to grip harder—as if she was desperately holding on.

'What I'm trying to say,' she said, her big blue eyes earnest and unwavering, 'is that I get it. These moments. Minutes. Hours.'

'Days...'

But he stopped himself saying the rest: *weeks, months...* Because he'd realised it wasn't true. Not now.

Mila realised it too—he could tell. They stood there on the street, staring at each other with a strange mix of sadness for the beautiful, smart, funny, flawed Stephanie they so missed and relief that their lives continued onwards.

'Are you okay?' Mila asked again.

He nodded. The ocean had stilled. The wave of grief and guilt and loss had receded.

She still gripped his arm. They both seemed to realise it at the same time. Her touch felt different now. No longer cool or simply comforting. Her fingers loosened, but didn't fall away. She didn't step back—but then neither did he.

Her gaze seemed to flicker slightly, darting about his face to land nowhere in particular.

When they'd been about fifteen, Mila had successfully dragged Steph into her Goth phase. Seb couldn't remember what the actual point of it all had been, but he did remember a lot of depressing music and heavy eyeliner.

'You have incredible eyes,' he said, without thinking.

Those incredible eyes widened—and they *were* incredible…he'd always thought so—and Mila took an abrupt step back, snatched her hand away.

'What?'

He instantly missed her touch—enough that it bothered him. Although he couldn't have explained why.

'I was thinking of all that eye make-up you used to wear towards the end of high school. I hated it. You look perfect just like this.'

Mila's cheeks might have pinkened—it was hard to tell in the sunlight—but her eyes had definitely narrowed. 'I didn't ask for your approval of my make-up choices.'

He'd stuffed up. There it was—that shuttered, defensive expression.

'That wasn't what I meant. I—'

'Look, I really have to go.' She'd already taken a handful of steps along the footpath.

'See you at tennis?' he said. They'd organised it via text for the following evening.

Mila didn't look back. 'Yes,' she said, sounding about as excited as if he'd reminded her of a dental appointment.

Sebastian tossed his empty coffee cup in the skip, then headed back to the building site. He might not need to be here daily to speak to the project manager, but he could find other ways to make himself useful—ideally in usefulness that involved swinging a sledgehammer.

CHAPTER FOUR

THE VERY LAST glimmers of sun were fading as Mila pulled into the Nedlands Tennis Club car park. A moment after she'd hooked her tennis bag over her shoulder floodlights came on, illuminating the navy blue hard courts and their border of forest-green.

The car park was nearly empty. An elderly-looking sedan with probationary 'P' plates most likely belonged to one of the teenage girls warming up very seriously for a doubles match, while the top-of-the-range blood-red sports utility had to belong to one of the two guys around Mila's age who were laughing as they very casually lobbed a ball back and forth.

Judging by the fluorescent workwear tossed in the tray of the ute, Mila could almost guarantee those guys were wealthy FIFO workers: men—generally—who flew in to work at one of Western Australia's isolated mines in the Pilbara for weeks at a time, living in 'dongas'—basic, transportable single rooms—and then flying out for a week or more off, back home in Perth. It was a brutal, but extremely well-paid lifestyle—providing blue collar workers with incomes unheard of before the mining boom.

Mila could never have done it. She'd visited the Molyneux-owned mines many times in her youth, and while she could appreciate the ancient, spectacular beauty of the Pilbara, the complete isolation somehow got to her. Out there you were over one thousand five hundred kilometres from Perth, and not much closer to anything else.

Ivy loved it—she'd married her new husband there, after all. And April did, too, regularly 'glamping' with her husband in remote Outback locations and posting dreamy, impossibly perfect photos on social media. But Mila always felt that she must be missing some essential Molyneux genes. The mining gene, or the iron ore gene, or even the red dust and boab tree gene.

Because Mila was never going to follow in her big sisters' footsteps. Regardless of her uninterest in her education for all of her childhood and the early part of her twenties, it just wasn't who she was. The industry and the land—that was *everything* to the Molyneux empire… Mila just didn't *fit*.

Seb still hadn't arrived, so Mila leant back against the driver's side of her modest little hatchback, the door still warm from the day's glorious spring sun. The two probable FIFO guys had become more serious, and their banter and laughter was now only between points. She vaguely watched the ball ping between them without really following what was going on.

Mila had long believed that there was a lot more of her father in her than her mother. She even *looked* like Blaine Spencer—except without the blond hair. She definitely—or so she'd been told—had her father's intense blue eyes. *'Eyes that'll make the world fall in love with him'*—that was what a film reviewer had said, in the ancient newspaper cutting that Mila had found in a book years after he'd walked out on them when she was only a toddler.

She'd burnt that review—at an angry sixteen—when her father had once again let her down. Not that it mattered. She could still recall every word.

A car slid into the parking spot directly beside her—a sleek, low, luxury vehicle in the darkest shade of grey. Seb climbed out, turning as he shut the car door to rest his forearms on its roof.

He grinned as he looked at Mila across the gleaming paintwork. 'Ready to be run off your feet?' he asked.

The lights in the car park were dim, leaving his face in both light and shadow. Even so, Mila could *feel* his gaze on her like a physical touch. She shivered as his gaze flicked downwards, taking in her outfit of pale pink tank top and black shorts, and then down again to her white ankle socks and sneakers.

Did his gaze slow on her legs?

She squeezed her eyes shut for a moment. Nope. It did *not*.

Just as he'd definitely meant nothing when he'd said *incredible* and *perfect* yesterday.

Mila forced a laugh. 'Last time I checked I still lead in our head-to-head.'

His laugh was genuine as he reached into his car for his tennis bag. He tossed it over his shoulder as he walked around the car to her. 'That doesn't sound right to me.'

He was dressed casually, all in black: long baggy running shorts and a fitted T-shirt in some type of sporty material. It revealed all sorts of somehow unexpectedly generous muscles: biceps and triceps and trapeziums…

The genius of her idea was now clearly questionable.

'Trust me—' Her voice sounded high and unlike her own. She cleared her throat. 'Trust me—you know how good I am with numbers.'

He shrugged and smiled again, and the instant warmth that little quirk of his lips triggered was unbelievably frustrating.

Mila strode towards the courts, opening the door within the tall cyclone fence and barely waiting for Seb to step through before walking briskly to the court they'd hired.

To be honest, she didn't remember the exact head-to-head score between them. When they'd started lessons together in primary school Mila had been the stronger player. She probably still was—it was just that eventually Seb had become *actually* stronger than her. And significantly taller.

At some point she'd known exactly how many sets she'd won against Seb—she'd kept a tally all the way through high school and into uni, enjoying their semi-regular matches because, if she was truthful, it had been the one thing she'd done just with Seb. For Steph had been many things, but definitely *not* an athlete.

But somewhere along the line Mila had forgotten her hard-earned leading score against Seb. Now, as she dropped her bag at the side of the net, and then fished out her water, racquet and a skinny can of new tennis balls, she searched her memory for a hint—but there was nothing. She might be leading by one or a hundred—she had no idea.

Like so much that had once been important to her when it came to Sebastian and Stephanie, over time she'd allowed it to become less important. And eventually to fade completely away.

Seb stood on the opposite side of the net, his racquet extended, the strings flat, ready for Mila to place a couple of tennis balls on its surface.

He raised an eyebrow. 'You all right?' he asked.

She nodded firmly. 'Yes,' she said—and she was, she realised. 'But I was thinking…let's wipe our scores. Start with a clean slate.'

She couldn't change the past—and, while it might be complicated, she *did* have this second chance with Seb.

His smile was wide. 'I like the sound of that,' he said.

Mila dropped the tennis balls onto his racquet, then stuffed two in her pockets as she headed for the baseline.

'Although,' he called out as she pivoted to face him, 'it's pretty sad that you can't just admit I was winning.'

And Mila laughed as she smacked a forehand in his direction to start their warm-up.

Maybe this wasn't such a terrible idea, after all.

This had been a *terrible* idea.

'Three-love,' Mila announced gleefully as they changed ends. Her eyes sparkled beneath the floodlights as they crossed paths at the net.

From now on all efforts related to repairing his friendship with Mila would definitely require more clothing.

How had he ever forgotten those legs? They went on and on…

Well, no, he hadn't forgotten them. He was human, after all. He hadn't married Stephanie and then instantly become blind to beautiful women. Certainly not to Mila. But before it had been an objective realisation: *Mila Molyneux has rather nice legs.* Kind of like: *The sky is blue. I don't like raw tomato. My mum cooks the world's best spaghetti and meatballs.* That type of thing.

Certainly nothing more.

Certainly not this…this *visceral* reaction to the curve of thigh and calf. This tightening in his belly…this heat to his skin. As sudden and as unexpected as a punch to his stomach.

It was his serve. He took a deep breath as he bounced the ball a handful of times before rocking back onto his heel as he tossed the ball high into the night sky.

Thwack.

Ace. Good.

'Fifteen-love.'

But *was* it sudden? This reaction?

He hadn't let himself analyse what he'd said yesterday, or questioned his choice of words. He'd told himself he'd just been speaking the truth when he'd told Mila her eyes were incredible. That she was perfect.

Hadn't he always thought so? Objectively, of course. So why verbalise those facts now? Especially when she'd been standing so close to him. Close enough that it had only been after she'd walked away that he'd realised his heart-rate was decelerating, that his body had registered more than simple comfort in her proximity.

Thwack.

The ball landed so far past the service line that Mila didn't bother calling it. Instead she grinned, catching his eye as she took a couple of steps forward, ready for a less powerful second serve.

Thwack.

He'd hit it even harder than his first serve, his tennis tactics being the furthest thing from his mind.

'Out!' Mila said, as it landed a ball-width too wide of the centreline.

She still hit it back, and he blocked it with his racquet, bouncing it a few times before shoving the ball in his pocket.

'Fifteen-all.'

Mila held up her hand before he went to serve again, to indicate that he should wait. He watched as she fussed with her hair, pushing it behind her ears and sliding in the clips that kept it out of her eyes. There was absolutely nothing provocative about what she was doing—if he ignored the pull of her singlet against her skin as she raised her arms. And the shape of her waist and breasts that the thin material so relentlessly clung to.

Which, despite his best efforts, he could not.

He turned away abruptly, and for the first time in his life smashing his racquet into the unforgiving surface of the court seemed an excellent option. He could almost feel it—the satisfaction of channelling his body into destroying something rather than generating seriously inappropriate thoughts about Mila.

His friend. His *friend*.

Stephanie's *best* friend.

No, he wasn't going to ruin his racquet—just as he would never allow himself to ruin things with Mila. He would not and he could not.

Not much was clear to him any more except two things: his new business and his need to have Mila back in his life. Platonically. Because even if Mila saw him as more than the once awkward, occasionally pimply teenage nerd who had lived next door—which seemed unlikely—a relationship was not an option anyway.

With Mila or with anyone.

He stepped back to the baseline.

Thwack.

Ace.

'Thirty-fifteen.'

There had been women since Stephanie. Two, to be exact. Meaningless, nothingness. Found in a fog of grief in London bars without even the decency to remember their names. He'd woken up alone and even emptier—so he'd stopped.

It had been months since the last. Almost a year.

Thwack. Thwack. Thwack.

Winner—down the line.

'Forty-fifteen.'

So he'd failed at casual sex and he'd clearly failed at marriage. He could barely remember the last time he'd slept with Stephanie—he'd always been working away, or late. *Too* late. And when he *had* been home there had still been distance between them. He'd fobbed Steph off when she'd attempted to address it. He couldn't remember how many times.

He did remember the shape of her body as she'd slept alone in their bed, her back towards his side. Always.

He'd refused to make time for Steph and he'd stubbornly ignored—or at best minimised—her concerns about their relationship. The lack of communication. The lack of intimacy. Their effectively separate lives.

The concerns of the woman he was supposed to love.

What sort of man did that make him?

A man who hurt the people he loved. A man who shouldn't *do* relationships. A man who'd driven his wife to make catastrophic choices.

Thwack. Thwack. Thwack. Thwack.

Mila had chased his cross-court forehand down and thrown up a high lob. He ran to the net, waiting for the ball to fall and for the opportunity to smash that ball into oblivion. He had his racquet up, ready.

Up, up, up…

Down, down, down…

And then, powered by every single uncomfortable, unpleasant, unwanted emotion inside him…*thwack*.

It was the perfect smash—right in the corner on the baseline. Mila had no chance to reach it but she tried anyway, stretching her legs and arms and her racquet to their absolute limit.

Then somehow all those outstretched limbs tripped and tangled, and with a terrible hard thump Mila tumbled to the ground, skidding a little on the court's unforgiving surface.

Sebastian was in motion before she'd come to a stop, his feet pounding as he ran to her.

Mila had levered herself so she was sitting. She held up her palms, all red and scratched.

'Ow,' she said simply, with half a smile.

Seb dropped down beside her. 'Are you okay?' It took everything he had not to gather her in his arms. He worriedly ran his gaze over her, searching for any sign of injury.

Mila stretched out both her legs experimentally, then wiggled her ankles in a circle.

'All seems to be in order,' she said, looking up at him.

'Not quite,' he said, and it was impossible to stop himself from reaching out and turning her arm gently, so Mila could see the shallow scratches that tracked their way along the length of her arm. Tiny pinpricks of blood decorated the ugly red lines.

'That looks worse than it feels.'

'You are one tough cookie, Mila Molyneux,' he said.

She smiled—just a little. 'Sometimes.'

Like yesterday, their eyes met. And once again Seb found himself lost in her incredible blue eyes. This time there was no pretending he was being objective, that he was admiring Mila simply as his strong, beautiful friend.

No, the way he felt right now had more in common with his fourteen-year-old self. Like then, his hormones were wreaking havoc on his body, his brain firmly relegated in the pecking order.

He'd forgotten. Forgotten what it was like to look at Mila

this way, to see her this way—to *want* her this way. It had been so long.

But how was she looking at *him*? Not with the disgust he'd expected, that he deserved for ogling his *friend*. More like—

A loud whoop from the neighbouring court ended the moment before it had fully formed. Seb looked up. The two young guys had finished their match, and the shorter of the two was completing a victory lap around the net.

Meanwhile Mila had climbed to her feet.

'Three-one,' she said firmly, with not a hint of whatever he might have just seen in her eyes. 'My serve.'

CHAPTER FIVE

MILA'S PHONE VIBRATED quietly beneath the shop counter as she carefully wrapped a customer's purchase in tissue paper.

The older gentleman had bought a quite extravagant salad bowl, with an asymmetrical rim and splashes of luminous cerulean glaze. For his granddaughter, he'd said, who had just moved out of home along with a mountain of the family's hand-me-down everything. *'I want her to have a few special things that are just hers alone.'*

After he'd left, Mila retrieved her phone and propped her hip against the counter. It had been a busy Friday, with a flurry of customers searching for the perfect gift for the weekend. She still had half an hour before Sheri arrived to take over the shop while Mila taught her afternoon classes— and so half an hour before she'd get to eat, as her rumbling tummy reminded her.

Lunch?

The text was from Seb, as she'd expected.

Sure. Pedro's?

Text messages from Seb had become routine in the two weeks since their… Mila didn't even know how to describe it.

Strained? Tense? Awkward?

Charged.

Yes, that was probably the correct word to describe their tennis match.

Fortunately Sebastian seemed equally as determined as she was to pretend nothing *charged* had happened, and instead had determinedly progressed his quest to repair their friendship.

That, it would seem, involved regular deliveries of her favourite coffee —double-shot large flat white—and just a few days ago had escalated to a lunch date.

They'd had lunch at a noisy, crowded, trendy Brazilian café—Pedro's—a short walk from her shop and his building site, and the impossibility of deep conversation or privacy had seemed to suit them both just fine.

Not that Seb showed *any* hint that there was anything more to their friendship than…well, friendship. And a pretty superficial friendship, if Mila was honest. They weren't quite spending their time discussing the weather…but it wasn't much more, either.

At times there was the tiniest suggestion of their old friendship—they'd laugh at each other's slightly off-kilter jokes, or share a look or a smile the way that only very old friends could. But those moments were rare. Mostly there was a subtle tension between them. As if they had more of those close moments either one of them might read more into it. As if maybe their friendly looks would morph into something like what had happened when she'd fallen playing tennis. When she'd seen something in Seb's gaze that had made her insides melt and her skin heat.

And as by unspoken consensus that hadn't been a *good* thing, a slightly tense and superficial friendship was what they had.

Which was good, of course. It meant that once Seb had processed his tumult of grief and guilt and loss their rehashed friendship would drift again. There would be no more tension and no more confusing, conflicting—definitely unwanted—emotions.

And her life would go back to normal.

Her phone rang, vibrating in her hand as it was still on silent. It wasn't a number she recognised.

'Hello?'

'Mila Molyneux?' asked a female voice with a heavy American accent.

Mila's stomach instantly went south. She knew exactly who this was.

'Speaking,' she told her father's personal assistant.

For a moment—a long moment—she considered hanging up. It was exactly what her sisters would do. But then Blaine Spencer wouldn't bother calling *them*, would he? He knew which daughter put up with his lies and broken promises.

'Just put my dad on,' said Mila.

This one. This gutless, hopeful, stupid daughter.

'La-la!'

'*Mila*,' she corrected, as she did every time. 'I'm not three, Dad.'

The age she'd been when he'd left.

'You still are to *me*, darling girl!'

Every muscle in her body tightened just that little bit more.

'Any chance you could call me yourself, one time?' she asked, not bothering to hide her frustration. 'You know— find my name in your contacts, push the call button. It's not difficult.'

'Now, don't be like that, *Mila*, you know how hard I work.'

There it was: The Justification. Mila always capitalised it in her mind.

Why didn't you call for <insert significant life event>?
But you said you'd come to <insert significant life event>.
And then The Justification.
You know how hard I work.
Or its many variations.
You can't just pass up opportunities in this industry.
Work has been crazy!
This director is a hard-ass. I'm working fourteen-hour days...
But always: *You know I love you, right?*
Right.

'So you've been working hard for the past three months, then?'

She'd done the calculations. In fact, this was pretty good for him. Normally his calls were biannual. Maybe that was why she hadn't hung up on him.

'I have, indeed,' he said, either missing or ignoring Mila's sarcasm.

To be honest, Mila didn't know him well enough to say which. Maybe that was the problem—she clung to the possibility that he was just thoughtless, not a selfish waste of a father who knew exactly how much pain he caused.

'I've just landed in Sydney for the premiere of my latest.' He always expected Mila to know everything about him.

'Latest what, Dad?'

'Movie,' he said, all incredulous.

Mila rolled her eyes.

'*Tsunami*. The director's from Perth, so the Australian premiere is over there tomorrow night. I'm doing a few cast interviews in Sydney today, then hopping on a plane tonight. You won't believe it, but I'm booked on a late flight because Serena has no concept of how far away bloody Perth is…'

Blaine Spencer just kept on talking, but Mila wasn't paying attention any more. 'Wait—Dad. You're coming *here*?'

'Seriously, I wouldn't be surprised if she'd booked us a hotel in Melbourne instead of Perth. All the capital cities are the same to her—' He finally registered that Mila had spoken. 'Yes,' he said, as if seeing his daughter for the first time in six years was something totally normal to drop obliquely into conversation. 'Just for the night,' he clarified, because bothering to extend his stay to visit with his daughter would never occur to him.

'Okay…' Mila said—just to say something.

'If you want to catch up you'll have to come to the premiere,' he said. 'I'm doing radio interviews tomorrow morning and then I'll have to sleep most of the day. You know I can never sleep on a plane.'

She didn't. She didn't know him at all.

'So if I can't make it to the premiere I won't see you?'

'No. Sorry, darling. Can't stay this time.'

Here it comes.

'Pre-production has already started on my next. Got to get to work!'

It took Mila another long moment to respond. All the words she wanted to say—to spew at him—teetered on her tongue.

There was nothing unusual about this phone call. The last-minute nature of his invitation, the way he'd somehow shifted the responsibility for them seeing each other onto her, his total lack of awareness or consideration for her own plans for the weekend. Or for her *life*, really.

No, nothing unusual.

If—somehow—Blaine got Ivy's phone number, or April's, and either woman allowed the conversation to continue beyond the time it took to hang up on him, Mila knew how her sisters would respond to what was hardly an invitation.

With a *no*. A very clear, very definite, I'd-rather-scrub-the-toilet-than-waste-my-time-on-you *no*.

They would each be furious with Mila for even considering seeing him. For even answering this phone call.

The little tinkling sound of the doorbell drew Mila's attention away from her father for a moment.

It was Seb. Of course.

He gestured that he'd wait outside, but Mila held up a hand so he'd stay. This wouldn't take long.

'Just get Serena to email me the details,' she said.

'So you'll come?'

And there it was. The reason why she had always been going to go to her father's premiere. That slightest of suggestions that maybe her dad had been worried she'd refuse to see him. The hint that he was genuine about this—that he really *did* want to see his youngest daughter.

After all, why else would he invite her?

Ugh, she should know better.

But she just couldn't stop herself:

'I'll see you tomorrow,' Mila began, but her dad had already handed his phone back to his assistant. Such typical casual thoughtlessness made her shake her head, but smile despite herself.

'Who was that?' Seb asked as he approached the counter.

Behind them, Mila heard the familiar creak and bang of the workshop's back door that heralded Sheri's arrival.

'Dad,' Mila said simply. She'd considered lying to Seb—broken families and deadbeat parents were certainly not *de rigueur* for their superficial conversations of late. But then—it was *Seb.*

Even so, her lips formed a perfectly straight line as she waited for his reaction. Would he be angry that she still spoke to her Dad? The way that Ivy and April were?

Seb knew the whole story. He'd experienced the fall-out of typical Blaine Spencer incidents, he'd listened to many Mila rants, and once—on that terrible sixteenth birthday—let her heavy tears and Gothic eyeliner soak into his T-shirt as she'd clung to him and Steph.

So maybe she'd see pity. Pity for the woman who—at almost thirty—wasn't all that further along in her emotional development than her sixteen-year-old self. At least, not when it came to her father.

He'd be right to be angry, or to pity her. Or both.

Hell. Mila was angry with *herself.* If she was her own friend she'd definitely pity herself, too. *I mean...how pathetic! Keeping that little hopeful wretched flame burning for a dad who doesn't deserve it...*

'You ready to go?' he said instead. 'I'm starving.'

Then he smiled. And in that smile there was understanding and acknowledgement of all Seb knew about her relationship with Blaine Spencer. But there was no judgement, no anger. Certainly no pity. Just support and a gorgeous, heavenly Sebastian Fyfe smile.

It was *exactly* what she needed.

As was a lunch, spent window shopping as they walked and ate their Brazilian *choripán* hot dogs, talking about absolutely nothing important.

Until they arrived back at the rear entrance to Mila's shop, where a handful of her students were already chattering loudly inside.

'I'm coming with you,' he said, firmly and abruptly. 'I have no idea where you're meeting him, or what your plans are, but I'm coming. At least until I'm sure that idiot actually turns up to see the daughter he doesn't deserve.'

Mila blinked. 'You are?'

'I am. Text me the details once the selfish moron's assistant sends them.'

Mila found herself laughing rather than arguing—and then Sebastian was walking away, before she had a chance to say anything anyway. Although any argument would have rung hollow. Seb had known she needed him tomorrow night, even if she hadn't.

And right now she didn't care about anything else that might or might not be complicating things between them. She was just glad Seb was here.

'Ivy has instructed me to convey her disapproval,' April said as she opened her front door. 'However, Nate has just vomited all over her, so she's taking him to the doctor instead of telling you personally.'

'Is he okay?' Mila asked as she followed April down her hallway. Her sister lived with her husband in an airy, modern home close to Cottesloe Beach, with heaps of windows and moody, muted artwork on the walls.

'Ivy thinks so. She suspects he's eaten one of the older kid's crayons at playgroup, given his vomit is blue, but she's just making sure.'

'Gross,' Mila said.

'I can't wait,' said April, deadpan.

She and Evan were actively trying for a baby. April even said it like that—*'We're actively trying'*—if anyone was dense enough to ask that intensely personal question. April said it made it sound as if they were having sex hanging from a chandelier.

They actually *did* have a chandelier—a modern version— and it was under all its sparkling refracted daylight that April had laid out a selection of evening gowns on her dining table.

'Just to be clear,' she said, 'I disapprove as well. He'll make you cry, and he's not worth it.'

That wasn't entirely accurate. Mila hadn't wasted her tears on her father for at least a decade. But she understood what April meant.

'I thought you'd be angrier,' Mila said.

April shrugged. 'You were wise to tell me via text. I got to be angry at you via Evan.'

'I'm sorry.'

'For Evan? Or for going to see Dad?'

'For Evan,' Mila clarified. 'Not for Dad. I *have* to see him. I can't not.'

April tilted her head. Her long blonde hair was piled up in high bun. 'Hmm… I've been there. You'll grow out of it.'

Mila's jaw clenched, but there was no point in arguing. Although she was less than two years younger than April, and five years younger than Ivy, they both definitely suffered from an ingrained belief that they knew best when it came to Mila's life. The fact that they both resented similar behaviour from their mother when it came to *their* lives was utterly lost on them.

Fortunately their mother had long ago given up advising Mila on anything. They'd become much closer since Irene Molyneux had let go of her ill-fitting dreams for her youngest daughter and accepted that Mila would be creating art with earth's natural materials—not mining them.

April was rattling off the names of dress designers, not that any of them were meaningful to Mila. Her eye was drawn to the darkest fabric—a deep, deep navy—a welcome contrast amongst the frothy pastels.

It fitted well, and Mila felt good as she twisted and turned in front of the mirror in April's spare room.

Her sister poked her head inside the door. 'Oh, that's *lovely*,' she breathed, and Mila smiled. 'Can I post a photo to—?'

'*No,*' Mila said, and laughed.

Seb hadn't been upstairs to Mila's apartment before. It was nice. Small—a single open-plan living area—with the kitchen positioned in front of a large window that overlooked the tree-lined street. Mila had muttered something about making himself at home as she'd raced up the stairs ahead of him, her hair still damp around her shoulders and a bathrobe knotted at her waist.

He walked over to the kitchen, running a hand aimlessly along the pale granite countertop. Mila had obviously renovated. The kitchen was simple but modern, sitting comfortably amongst the original wide timber floorboards, tall skirtings and ornate cornices. The wall the apartment shared with his own shop was exposed—a mix of red brick and mortar and patches of artfully remaining patches of plaster—as it was on the floor below. From the ceiling hung a simple black industrial light fitting, and the living area was furnished with mid-century low-line pieces in a style that had recently become fashionable again. But, knowing Mila, the rich tan leather couch and the elegant, spindly dining suite would be the real deal, not replicas. Seb could just imagine Mila busily searching for treasures in some dusty old antique furniture store.

It was almost dark outside, the street light outside the kitchen window already softly lit. He checked his watch.

'We're going to be late,' Mila said, behind him.

Seb pivoted to face her—and whatever he'd been about to say froze on his lips.

Somehow he hadn't thought ahead to this part—to the reality of escorting Mila to her father's film premiere. His focus had been on just *being* there, and nothing else—certainly not on what Mila would wear, or how she might look. Or that it might suddenly—shockingly—as he stood in her kitchen in a charcoal suit, feel like a date.

She wore a dress of navy blue, in some soft, draping material that wrapped around her waist and the curve of her breasts, leaving her shoulders bare and falling straight from her hips. Her hair was different—smooth and sleek and pushed back from her face—so that all the focus was on her brilliant blue eyes and the ruby-red of her lips.

Those brilliant blue eyes met his gaze, steady and sure. 'It's April's,' she said, her hand casually smoothing the fabric against her hip. 'I thought it looked all right.'

'An understatement,' he said, and he didn't miss the hint of a blush that warmed her cheeks, although she didn't look away.

'Thanks,' she said, very matter-of-fact.

Mila was equally businesslike as she located her clutch bag and he ordered a taxi. And as she marched down the steps ahead of him and locked up the shop. Then all the way to the small theatre near the beach which had apparently inspired the film—thankfully without *any* history of apocalyptic tsunamis—and as they approached the red carpet.

It was there that she went still. That her confident stride and chatter spluttered away to nothing.

Parked along the street was a van for each of the local television stations. A large crowd had gathered behind the cameras to watch the arrivals. Blaine Spencer might not be an A-lister, but the large posters flanking the entrance revealed that the movie's star was an up-and-coming Australian actress—famous enough that even Seb had heard of her.

Automatically Seb reached for Mila, aiming to put his hand at her elbow, but she shook him off.

'I'm fine,' she said, very firmly.

They hadn't quite reached the bright lights that lit the red carpet, but Seb could still see well enough to read Mila's expression.

Was she fine? Mila had always been good at relaying her father's latest example of uselessness when they were teenagers. But, looking back now, he realised she'd done so with a large truckload of bravado—she'd been simply telling a story. It was only that one time, when Blaine hadn't turned up at her sixteenth birthday party, that she'd shown any emotion.

He remembered how awkward he'd felt as she'd sobbed into his shoulder, sure he was being of no help at all, but also certain that he wasn't going anywhere.

He didn't feel all that different now.

Mila raised an eyebrow. 'Really,' she said. 'I'm not going to blubber all over you again. Don't panic.'

His lip quirked upwards. He was not surprised she'd referenced the same memory. 'My shoulder remains available if needed. Both of them, actually.'

'Noted,' she said, smiling now. 'But I'm not an angsty teenager any more. I'm an adult with possibly the most selfishly unreliable parent in history. I know what I'm doing.'

He opened his mouth—before snapping it shut again.

'Then why am I doing it?' she said, reading his mind. 'I suspect when I work that out I'll finally stop answering his calls.'

Seb nodded, even though he didn't really understand. 'So, let's do this?'

Mila's smile had fallen away, and something had shifted in her strong, determined gaze. But still, ever Mila, she straightened her shoulders, and he watched her take a long, deep breath.

'Let's go,' she said.

Without Ivy, April or her mother by her side, not one of the photographers or reporters along the red carpet recognised

Mila as a Molyneux. That suited her just fine—she'd never had any aspirations to embrace the quasi-celebrity that her family name might give her.

Ivy's job meant she had no choice but to network with the rich and famous, and April had always loved that scene—and in recent years had certainly grown her status as a society darling. Both would've been at home on the red carpet, would've known exactly what to say, how to smile, how to pose for photographs.

Although, her father wasn't famous enough that even if an enterprising paparazzo *had* recognised her it would have mattered.

Her mother had never spoken much about Blaine. Mila knew they'd had a whirlwind romance and a turbulent relationship, and that it had been somewhat of a scandal at the time—the billionaire mining heiress and the Hollywood heartthrob. But that had been more than thirty-five years ago. Old news. Plus none of them—not her mother nor her sisters—had ever breathed a word about their fractured relationship with their father to the media. To anyone, really.

Even at that sixteenth birthday party, when against her own judgement she'd agreed to an elaborate, expensive celebration inviting everyone she knew—and many she didn't—the only guests who'd known of her devastation at her father's absence had been Seb and Stephanie.

And even then she hadn't been stupid enough to tell anyone that her father was coming. Even then she'd suspected he'd let her down.

Tonight, she could almost guarantee he would. Yet here she was. Letting that minuscule tendril of hope drag her down a red carpet.

'Sebastian!'

The shout came from within the throng of reporters. Mila glanced up at Seb.

'Must be a famous Sebastian here,' he said, and kept on walking.

'Sebastian Fyfe!'

Now there was no mistake.

'Keep on walking,' Seb said, stepping closer and leaning inwards. 'Tonight isn't about me.'

They were almost at the entrance to the theatre, but were stalled by a group who were posing for photographs: a single woman in a gold-spangled dress flanked by men in matching tuxedos.

'Why?' Mila asked, confused.

'Didn't I tell you I've taken up a career in film?' he said, with a smile that looked forced. 'In between my building projects, of course.'

The joke fell pancake-flat.

'Give us a photo with your new girl!' that single voice shouted, explaining everything.

'Oh,' Mila said, unnecessarily.

Seb just clenched his jaw.

'Should we explain?' Mila said. 'That we're just friends?'

'It's none of their business,' Seb said, his gaze directed straight ahead, as if he was willing the people blocking their path to move.

'I think we should,' Mila said. 'I don't want anyone to think—'

'What?' Seb said, his voice suddenly harsh. 'That I've moved on? I think it's allowed. I'm sure I've met society's rules about appropriate mourning periods.'

He looked down at her now, his eyes revealing that awful emptiness she remembered from the funeral.

'And, of course,' he continued, 'what everyone thinks is *always* my number one priority.'

'Of course you're allowed to move on,' Mila said, annoyed now. 'You know that's not what I meant.'

Cameras continued to flash ahead of them.

'Look,' he said, '*we* know we're not together. That we're friends—we've only ever been friends, and will only ever be friends.'

The nonchalantly spoken words shouldn't have landed so heavily, but they did. Heavily enough that Mila flinched.

'That's all that matters,' Seb continued. 'What *we* know. What *we* think. You know that—you've never cared about what anyone else thinks about you.'

That earlier moment had passed, and that emptiness was gone from his gaze. Now he just looked at her curiously.

'You're right,' she said, reminding herself as well. 'I've always thought all this stuff is total nonsense.'

'Exactly,' he said.

Finally the traffic on the red carpet was flowing again, and they quickly put distance between themselves and that lone, determined reporter, making it into the relative calm of the bustling theatre foyer.

'Mila!'

This time the voice came from ahead of them, thick with an American accent.

Seb stepped closer, his shoulder bumping against hers. Without a word she pressed back against him, just for a moment, her bare arm against the subtle texture of his suit. His warmth, his strength.

'In case I forget later,' she said softly, 'thank you.'

He tilted his head in subtle acknowledgement. 'You've got this,' he said.

CHAPTER SIX

SEBASTIAN FIGURED IT was just his luck that a reporter who read the business pages was at the premiere.

Steph had always enjoyed these types of events. As Fyfe Technology had grown they'd found themselves invited to all manner of charity balls, or museum openings or exclusive cocktail evenings. For a long time Seb had enjoyed them too. It had been part of their big move to London, after all—an opportunity to network in international circles both for Seb and also for Steph and her fledgling fashion label.

He could still remember how they'd worked as a team. Stephanie had always been so charming and so beautiful. She'd drawn people to her, in a natural way that Seb had always admired. For Seb, networking had been more of an effort—a successful one, but an effort nonetheless. It had been Steph who was in her element—smart, sexy and cheeky. He remembered how she'd meet his gaze during those interminably pointless conversations that seemed a given at every event—with a subtle quirk to her eyebrow, the barest roll of her eyes...

Or maybe they hadn't been as clever as they'd thought—maybe everyone had seen through the young, ambitious couple in their early twenties with huge dreams, equally huge determination and really no idea how to succeed on a global stage. Not that it really mattered.

Fyfe Technology's growth had been explosive—far greater than Seb had forecast—and Steph's designs had soon been stocked in major department stores. They'd both been so busy, and soon they'd been declining more invitations than they'd accepted.

Or rather Seb had.

'Babe, I told you about this weeks ago. The ball is this Friday.'

A shrug.

'I'm sorry. I need to stay on in Berlin. Go without me. I'd just get in the way.'

How many times had he done that?

'So, Seb,' Blaine Spencer asked now, 'what do you do for a living?'

They'd met once before—one year when Blaine *had* visited for Mila's birthday. Unsurprisingly, Mila's dad did not remember him.

They stood in the foyer, where the crowd was beginning to thin as guests filtered into the theatre. Mila stood beside Blaine. She'd gravitated closer to her father as they'd been speaking, and now it was Seb who remained on his own.

Seb watched Mila as he spoke to Blaine. She stood with her standard excellent posture, her chin slightly tilted upwards as she studied her dad. Her expression was completely unreadable.

She looked stunning. Exactly the kind of woman any sensible man would want on his arm as he walked a red carpet.

He had to forcibly drag his gaze away from her, at least pretend he was engaged in this conversation.

What had he told her? *We're friends—we've only ever been friends, and we'll only ever be friends.*

He'd said the words easily—after all he'd been silently shouting them at himself all night.

A woman with a tight ponytail sidled up beside them, talking to Blaine in a low tone before glancing at Mila and Seb.

'Time to take your seats,' she said, with an accent that twanged.

'I'll sit with the cast,' Blaine said, 'But dinner after?'

Mila nodded. 'That would be great,' she said, her tone even.

It wasn't until Blaine had stepped away that Mila met his gaze. Her smile was blinding.

'Seriously—I thought he'd consider this five-minute chat *it*,' she said. 'I'm shocked.'

'Me too.'

Mila grinned. 'Guess I didn't need reinforcements to-night.'

'You never did,' Seb said. 'I'm just here for the free movie.'

Mila shoved him in the shoulder. 'Dork,' she said.

And then they headed into the theatre.

The movie was actually pretty good. Mila rarely watched her father's films. She figured if he couldn't make the time to see her, then she wouldn't bother to see *him*—even if on celluloid. Kind of like her own silent protest. Plus, she knew her dad hated it when he inevitably asked if she'd seen his latest movie and she always said no.

Petty, yes. Immature, yes. But that simply reflected the depths her relationship with her father had reached. Too far gone ever to come back from—or so she'd thought. Tonight had Mila questioning that, and she was glad. Very glad.

At about the time the movie's first skyscraper-sized wave crashed down on the fictional metropolis, Mila nudged Seb with her clutch.

'Guess what's in here,' she whispered.

Seb tilted his head close. Close enough for Mila to feel his breath against her cheek.

'You're kidding me?' he said, before she'd even opened her bag.

She grinned. 'Nope.'

Together they tried, and failed, to silently open their individual bags of brightly coloured sherbet, and then ate them with tiny plastic spoons. Just as they had at many movies, many years ago.

It was a memory from even before he'd started going out with Steph—this was from when they'd walked to the local deli to spend their parents' spare change on bags of lollies before catching the bus to the cinema. All three of them had always each had a bag of sherbet. In their twelve-year-olds' logic it had seemed a very grown-up choice—equally as grown-up as seeing a movie without their parents.

Of course now they were *really* all grown-up. In the darkness, Mila was particularly aware of all-grown-up Seb's size. The way his shoulders seemed to overlap into her space. The way it seemed quite an effort for Seb to keep his legs an acceptable distance from hers. And how they both seemed to have come to the decision that neither of them would use their dividing armrest. Which was uncomfortable—both literally and otherwise. After all, if they were just friends for all eternity what would it matter if their arms accidentally touched?

Fortunately the movie had enough loud bangs and impressive special effects to distract Mila from thinking too much about Seb, or about anything else. At least until after the movie. Then, back in the foyer, she couldn't help but acknowledge—again—how truly excellent he looked in a suit. As she sipped from the Champagne she'd plucked from a passing tray, she decided she was simply being objective.

So objective, in fact, that she told him.

'I didn't say earlier, but you look great. Nice suit.'

Seb's grin was wicked. 'Well,' he said, 'I—'

'Ms Molyneux!'

The voice was unmistakably Blaine's assistant. She hurried over in her sky-high heels, managing to appear both harried and rather bored.

For the first time Mila noticed that even though much of the crowd had dispersed, she hadn't yet spotted Blaine.

'Are we meeting Dad at the restaurant?'

Serena's head-shake was nearly imperceptible. 'No. He sends his apologies. He now has other plans.'

Suddenly Seb was standing right beside her. Close enough that she could lean into him if she needed to.

She didn't.

'I see,' Mila said.

Blaine's assistant waited a beat, as if for a longer message to relay back to Blaine. Eventually the silence *became* that message, and Serena nodded briskly.

Then—just a moment before she went on her efficient, busy way—Serena stepped closer to Mila. 'I'm sorry,' she said, ever so softly.

Then she was gone.

And somehow it was *that* that made the difference. That overloaded the scales, that pushed her over the edge…beyond dealing with this in a reasonable manner. Reasonable because this was not unexpected. None of this was without precedent. *None.*

But rather than just roll her eyes, or make some pithy comment to Seb, Serena's words—Serena's *pity*—made that impossible.

Standing still was no longer an option. Remaining calm was not an option. Pretending she was okay was *not* an option.

Mila didn't remember leaving the theatre, although she *did* remember the sharp, satisfying click of her heels on the footpath as she strode away.

And then the clicking stopped, abruptly, as her feet sank into sand. Beach sand.

She stopped, turning around on the spot to take in where she was.

She stood at the top of a sandy pathway down to the beach. The street lights lit the way somewhat, identifying scrubby plants growing right up to the pine railings.

'Mila!'

It was Seb—and it wasn't the first time he'd called her name, she was certain.

Instead of answering, Mila kicked off her shoes and swung them in her fingers as she headed with purpose towards the beach.

She heard the rustle of Seb removing his own shoes behind her, but didn't slow her pace. He'd follow her—she knew that.

She stopped when the sand became damp beneath her feet. There was enough moonlight that she could watch the small waves stretching towards the empty beach, although it wasn't warm enough that the brush of the water against her skin was anything but extremely cold. She didn't care.

Seb was now beside her, his feet also sinking into the sodden sand.

'Well,' he said, 'that sucks.'

A short laugh burst from Mila's lungs.

'Maybe I should tell myself *I told you so*,' she said. 'Because I did.'

'That doesn't matter.'

'No,' she said. 'My continued delusions when it comes to my father are of absolutely *no* cause for concern.'

'This isn't your mistake,' Seb said. 'Not at all.'

Mila shook her head, staring out at the total blackness of the horizon. 'Of course it is. You've heard the saying, right? Fool me once, shame on you. Fool me twice…' She laughed harshly. 'Fool me a hundred times. Shame on me.'

'Your dad should be ashamed—not you.'

She wrapped her arms around herself, holding tight. 'He should be a lot of things,' Mila said. But, really, she'd only ever wanted him to be one thing.

'He's an idiot for not realising how lucky he is to have you.'

'He doesn't *have* me,' she said. A sharp breeze whipped over the waves, dragging tendrils of her hair out of place. 'I'm done.'

As she said it she realised it was true. Even silly, hopeful Mila had a limit. This, it would seem, was it.

'You sure?' Seb asked.

Mila was so surprised that she finally turned to face him. His dark suit was stark against the pale sand, even in the moonlight. His face was shadowed.

'Why did you give him so many chances?'

Her gaze dropped. His white shirt was bright in the gloom. 'I just said why. I'm delusional—obviously.'

'No, you're not. I'd say you're the least delusional person I know.'

'You don't know me all that well, then. Not any more.'

There was a bit more bite in her words then she'd intended. But it was the truth.

'Maybe,' he conceded. 'But I remember a Mila Molyneux who never let herself be stomped on.'

He was right. Maybe that was the part of her mother she *had* inherited—an accurate radar for all things deceitful and fickle. An intolerance for pretence. It had served her well in business, although clearly it had taken her a little longer to learn to apply it to her relationships. But now she knew exactly how important it was to walk away before she was walked all over.

'My father is my blind spot,' she said. A pause. '*Was*, I mean.'

Her throat felt tight, but she wasn't able to concede to the tears April had forecast.

'Ivy told me that he wasn't all that great a dad when he was around,' Mila said, hoping that talking might help. 'That he wasn't all that interested in us. That he was away a lot. But I was too young when he left. I only remembered the good bits—big bear hugs, stories in bed. I can't remember how often they happened.' She turned back to the ocean again, closing her eyes and focusing on the sensation of the breeze against her cheeks. 'You know, I've asked myself the same question. A hundred times. Ivy and April keep on asking, too.' Another pause. 'Not Mum, though. Maybe she gets it—she seemed to persist with Dad…with Blaine…for a really long time, too.'

It was completely silent except for the soft little rumble of waves.

'It doesn't make any sense. This isn't who I am. I don't

like this person. This needy person.' *This vulnerable person.* She *never* let herself feel like this.

'I think it's understandable to wish you had a great dad,' Seb said.

'That's the thing,' Mila said. 'It *was* just a wish. A dream. A fantasy. And when he did deign to involve me in his life it was only an illusion. He doesn't really care about me.'

'No,' Seb agreed. 'I don't think he does.'

Oh, that hurt.

'That's rich,' Mila said, knowing she was being incredibly unfair but not caring. 'Coming from you. Where have *you* been when I needed you?'

'You know how sorry I am for the way I behaved after Steph—'

'You left. You *and* Steph. You got married and—*poof!* You were gone.'

She was directing her anger at the wrong target, but she couldn't stop. She needed an outlet for all this emotion. A target who would actually care.

'You wanted us to stay in Perth for the rest of our lives?' he asked, incredulous.

Mila shook her head. 'No, don't go and be all calm and sensible on me. You had a new and exciting life and you forgot about me.'

'I never forgot about you,' he said.

She never forgot about him, either. Some part of her knew that was the problem.

'I forgot about you,' she said, more quietly now. 'At least I thought I had.'

'I'm sorry—' Seb began.

'No,' she said, quite loudly. 'Don't. I was busy too. I got lazy about staying in touch, too. I know I'm not being fair.'

'Someone told me that it's allowed to be like that sometimes.'

But it was easier when it was other people.

'This was a mistake,' she said abruptly.

'Tonight?' Seb sounded confused.

'No,' she said. 'I mean, yes—of course tonight was always going to be a farce. But I mean…' She faced him, gesturing towards Seb and then herself. '*This*. This is a mistake.'

'Me coming tonight?'

'No, you coming back into my life. I'm sorry, I shouldn't have agreed to it. If we really mattered to each other we would've tried harder to stay in touch. Tonight has just made it clear that some things are better left as memories.'

Memories always benefited from a glorious rose-coloured haze. Reality was complicated.

'You sent me messages for almost a year, Mila. Why would you do that if you thought our friendship was a mistake?'

Mila shook her head. 'Because that wasn't about *us*—that was about Steph. That was about my concern for you.' She paused, trying to organise her rioting thoughts. 'And, besides, you were on the other side of the world. You weren't supposed to go and buy the shop next door.'

'That's nice. So you were only there for me if I remained at an acceptable distance?'

Yes. No. *No*.

They both knew that wasn't true.

And Mila also knew that she'd *never* expected Seb to come home. Or that if he did she'd feel…

Feel what? She couldn't even describe it.

Off-balance?

Confused?

Uncomfortable?

And worse. Breathless, warm…tingly. Dammit. *Tingly*. She didn't want this. Not with Seb.

'This isn't a mistake,' Seb said, his voice low but with a hint of something far from calm in his tone.

'Go ahead,' Mila said simply. 'Disagree away. It doesn't change anything. We were always going to end up friendly acquaintances once we'd finished this charade of vaguely awkward lunches and tennis and talking about the weather. Let's just fast-track it.'

'I don't want to talk about the weather with you.'

She'd deliberately referenced his words at the funeral, not caring any more.

'Then what *do* you want from me?' she said. 'Someone to reminisce with about lolly bags at the movies? We can do that on social media. Tag each other in old photos or something.'

'That isn't what I want.'

'We can even make pithy comments and subtle references that no one else on our friends list will understand!' Her voice was gloriously false. 'It will be *so* fun!'

She was done with this now. Her dad was permanently gone from her life, and now Seb was relegated to a category only marginally more intimate.

She had to learn from what had happened with her dad. You couldn't force relationships. And her friendship with Seb—through time and distance and neglect—had been over long ago.

So shouldn't she be feeling good? Relieved?

She refused to think about that.

'That isn't what I want,' Seb repeated.

'I understand,' she said. Mila knew all about not getting what she wanted.

She turned, feeling the sand rough between her toes. She was a few steps into the dry sand beyond the waves when Seb spoke again.

'Is that it?' he said.

Tears threatened again, from nowhere. Desperately unwanted.

'I thought it was pretty clear,' she said, and kept on walking.

'It's not to me,' he said.

If he'd touched her, physically tried to make her stop,

she would have shoved him away. But instead he took big strides in the deep sand to overtake her, to stand in her path.

Now she had to walk around him. That was harder than it should have been, even though she knew he'd never stop her.

For a moment it seemed impossible. She just stood there, her eyes trained on the knot of his tie.

'What *do* you want?' she said finally.

'I want you in my life.'

She made herself meet his gaze, annoyed that it was so difficult to do so.

Even in the moonlight she felt too exposed. As if he could see something inside her that even she didn't know about.

'Why?'

'Because you used to be my best friend,' he said.

Mila shook her head. 'Not enough. I'm not living in the past any more.'

No longer would she grasp onto childish hopes and dreams built on snatches of memories. Not with her father, and not with Seb.

'I'm not a substitute for Stephanie,' Mila said suddenly.

'I never thought you were,' Seb said.

Finally she'd made him angry. She'd cracked the veneer of calm he'd been so careful to maintain. Now on the beach. Before on the red carpet. Maybe the whole time he'd been back in her life.

But why did she even want to do that? She had no idea.

'But I am…kind of,' she said gently. Now it was her turn to be calm. 'You lost the woman you loved. I'm part of your same shared memories. It makes sense you'd want to reconnect. And we tried. But it's not working.'

'No,' he said. '*No.*'

'*Yes,*' Mila said, warming to this theory. 'Don't feel bad about it. It's okay.'

Now she should just walk past him. Or at the very least fish her phone out of her bag and call a taxi. This was over.

But instead she wiggled her toes in the sand. Beneath the

relative warmth of the surface the tiny grains were freezing, just a few inches below. Her feet felt heavy, as if the sand was setting around them like concrete.

'Stop it, Mila,' Seb said.

He stepped closer, and it was impossible to move.

'Don't you dare reduce yourself to a variation of someone else.'

Something in the atmosphere had shifted, triggering an uncomfortable tension.

Mila shook her head, as if that would fix it.

Seb stepped closer again.

'Maybe I would be better off as a different variety of Mila,' she said, trying to recall the false levity she'd voiced before. She failed, and simply sounded breathless. 'You know—like a new, improved version? Mila two point zero.'

Now he touched her. His fingers brushed against her wrist, his hand gently circling it, his thumb sliding over her furiously beating pulse.

'You don't have to change a thing.'

Mila could barely think with Seb so close to her. She seemed to be leaning towards him. His tie was still her focus, but it was much closer now.

'My mum thinks I should eat more salad,' she managed.

Seb's laugh was sudden and loud, whipped about in the sea breeze.

'I can accept that,' he said. 'But only if you want to.'

'I will if there's no coriander. That stuff is—'

But her words stopped forming as Seb's hand shifted, his fingers meshing with hers. She held on tight as she finally lifted her gaze.

The street lights were all behind him, up above the beach, so his face was in almost total darkness. She could just make out the shape of his cheekbones, the strong line of his nose.

And his mouth.

She definitely knew where his mouth was. It was as if every sensation in her body was focused upon it, as if nothing else existed beyond Seb, Mila, this cloaking darkness… and his mouth.

Her shoes dropped from her fingers to the sand with a soft thud, seemingly releasing her feet from their concrete-like shackles. She stepped closer, because she was helpless to do anything else.

She closed her eyes, trying to gather her thoughts…or something. His breath was warm, soft against her eyelashes.

Snippets of common sense did flitter within her, but with no success. Her body was awash with too many emotions right now for her to pay attention: her father's rejection, the loss of the man she'd always so badly wanted him to be.

Plus the awful emptiness that her attempts to remove this man right before her from her life had triggered. Even despite her maddening inability to do so.

With all this whirling loss and confusion all Mila knew was that she wanted to feel good. She wanted to feel close to someone—to anyone.

No.

Not anyone. *This* man.

Right now this man felt right. More right than anything else that had happened tonight. That had happened in for ever.

'Mila…'

Oh, God, his voice was low and rough. The voice of a man barely in control.

Seb *wanted* her. He wanted *her*.

Tonight that was what she needed more than absolutely everything.

Mila's eyes snapped open. It was far too dark to read anything in Seb's eyes, but that really didn't matter.

If anything, it helped. It reduced everything down to what she wanted and what he wanted. Which was to touch much more than just their hands.

Mila gripped his hand tighter and then, her gaze dropping to his lips, tugged, pulled him towards her.

Their lips met a split second before their bodies—chest to breast, hips to hips. Seb's hand dropped hers, only to appear near her waist, his other hand at her lower back, drawing her even closer.

Mila's hand curled up and behind his neck, her fingers combing into his hair.

Their mouths were momentarily as cool as the breeze, but as they kissed there was nothing but heat.

Seb showed no caution. He kissed her with the confidence of a man who knew what they both wanted—and he was right. All Mila wanted was to be closer, closer—luxuriating in the sensation of lips and teeth and tongue.

This was *all* want and *all* need. As wild as the ocean and as uncontrollable.

Mila slid her hand towards Seb's tie, tugging at it, and then at the top buttons of his shirt, frustrated that so much of him was covered in linen and silk. His skin felt impossibly hot beneath her fingertips, and then against her back, as Seb's hand searched for its own bare skin, finding it at her shoulder.

They barely broke apart for air, every kiss just fuelling the next. Their mouths and their bodies working together in search of that same goal of delicious sensation. Of heat and of need and of want.

But then it was over. As abruptly as it had begun and so suddenly that Mila reached for Seb automatically, her body refusing to accept the space now between them.

But the space was there, and her fingertips held nothing but thin air.

'We can't do this,' said Seb.

'Why not?'

It seemed the only possible question. There was nothing more right, right now, than that kiss. Mila was absolutely sure of that.

'This is wrong,' Seb said, and his unknowing contradiction was like a punch to her gut.

Reality descended.

'You've had a tough night. I shouldn't have done this.'

'*We* did this,' Mila said.

He shook his head. 'No. This is my mistake. This wasn't supposed to happen.'

'I didn't plan this either,' she said, but he wasn't really listening.

Instead he ran his hands through his hair, staring up at the sky.

As every second passed the *rightness* of what had just happened became less tangible.

'This can't happen,' Seb said, but Mila had the sense that he wasn't really speaking to her. 'It would change everything.'

He'd walked a few steps away, but now came closer again, focusing again on Mila. Again the lack of light was frustrating. It was impossible to read whatever was in his eyes.

'I need you,' he said, rough and earnest. 'In my life. As my *friend*. *Not* like this. I won't risk our friendship. Not for a kiss. Not for anything.' A pause. 'I don't want this.'

A car drove past along the road above them, its lights briefly revealing Seb's gaze.

But Mila could see nothing. He'd retreated, shut up shop, boarded up his windows.

It took a few seconds for his words to start hurting. Maybe she'd already felt too much tonight. Surely soon she would run out of space.

But, no—the pain found a way. Alongside her father's rejection now lay Seb's. And beside that the faintest echo of Seb's very first rejection, all those years ago. When a teenage Mila's raw heart had first begun to build its armour.

Now she had fifteen years of further reinforcements, but tonight she'd let Blaine *and* Seb step right through.

That wouldn't happen again.

Mila retrieved her shoes and finally stepped around Seb, as she should have done what now felt a million hours ago.

She'd already ordered a taxi on her phone by the time Seb joined her on the footpath a few minutes later.

He talked a bit, tried to get Mila to respond, but she just couldn't pay attention. Instead, with a frustration so intense it made her want to scream, she focused on doing everything in her power not to cry.

CHAPTER SEVEN

ON MONDAY, SEBASTIAN pushed open the door to Mila's shop with one shoulder, a takeaway coffee tray in his hand. Sheri was at the counter, looking every inch the university arts student that Seb knew her to be, complete with vintage eyeliner and purple Bettie Page-style hair.

She smiled as he approached her, and more broadly when he placed her coffee in front of her.

'Awesome,' she said. 'Thanks. Mila's out the back.'

Mila was carefully sliding a tray of pottery into the large kiln that hunkered against the side wall. She glanced at him, but for such a brief second that he had no chance to register if she was glad to see him or otherwise.

He suspected otherwise.

Her tone—if there *was* such a thing in text messages—had been terse over the weekend. She hadn't answered his calls.

'Mila—' he began, but she held up a hand.

'Give me a sec,' she said.

He waited as she swung the heavy door shut and then pushed a series of buttons on an electronic screen. The kiln beeped happily in response.

'Yes?' she asked, once she was done.

But she still didn't really look at him, instead walking over to the sink to wash her hands.

'I'm not happy with how things ended on Friday.'

Mila shrugged. 'That's a shame.' Her gaze zeroed in on the coffee tray. 'What do I owe you for the coffee?'

'*Nothing*,' he said. 'I'm not here just to bring you coffee.'

'Really?' she said. She turned, propping her butt against the sink cabinet. She wore skinny black jeans beneath a long artist's smock, liberally splashed with what he assumed was clay and glaze.

Her feet were clad only in flip flops, her toenails painted a vivid red. They drew his eye, and also drew an unwanted memory of bare feet on the beach, sinking into sand as he and Mila sank into each other.

'So what *do* you want, then?'

Mila's voice dragged him back to the present. Her tone was strong and direct—like the Mila he was used too. Not fractured or abandoned. He'd never seen Mila like she'd been on that beach, even as a teenager. Friday had been something else—a different level.

He'd hated to see Mila in pain. He'd hated to cause her pain.

'I want to fix this,' he said.

'I thought I'd made it clear how our relationship would progress from now on,' she said.

She was meeting his gaze now. Her big blue eyes were luminous.

'I don't want to just be another forgotten acquaintance on your friends list.'

'You want me to be a real friend?' Mila said, very calmly. 'Who you can have lunch with and buy coffee for—' she nodded at the cups he still held '—and chat about current events and our lives and stuff?'

He nodded, but he knew this wasn't headed anywhere good.

'But not to kiss on the beach under any circumstances, right? Just so we're both crystal-clear.'

He couldn't read her at all now. He didn't know what she meant.

'Did you want that to happen?' he asked, genuinely surprised. Although he wasn't sure if he was surprised by what she'd said or the fact that she'd said it.

He hadn't allowed himself to reflect on what had happened, and the tension between them well before that kiss.

He'd only focused on the fact that it shouldn't have happened at all.

'No,' Mila said. 'I didn't.'

She said the words firmly, her gaze equally firm. But there was still something wrong. Something in the way she held herself and the way she looked at him. A vulnerability, perhaps, that made Seb want to fill the air with explanations.

'I just can't do this, Mila. And not just with you—this isn't about you. This is about *me*, and what a crappy husband I was, and how that proves I shouldn't do relationships, that I'm terrible at them. I'd just screw things up and hurt you like I hurt Steph. And I just can't face hurting you, and losing you, too—'

'It was a kiss, Seb, nothing more,' Mila said, again with that relentless calm. 'There's no need to talk about relationships.'

'Mila—'

She shook her head. 'You were right. It was a mistake.'

'So why—?'

'Can't we be friends?' she said. 'Because it's a waste of time. Just like it's a waste of time whenever I answer a call from my dad. Or am stupid enough to agree to see him. People make time for those who are important to them. Neither of us did that—for *years*. You know what? I can't be bothered with subterfuge.'

'I'm *not* like your father, Mila,' Seb said, his jaw tight.

'You're right,' Mila said simply. 'You have absolutely no reason to feel guilty for walking away.'

'I'm not walking away.'

Mila smiled sadly. 'You already did. So did I. Can't you see?'

It felt as if a hand was inside his chest, relentlessly smothering his heart. Until now Seb had refused to believe this could happen. This was fixable. It *had* to be. He *couldn't* lose Mila as well. He couldn't.

'For more than fifteen years we were almost inseparable.

So what if we got busy and distracted and lazy—and if I've been a grieving, selfish ass? That doesn't erase our friendship. I don't believe you ever thought our friendship was over before Steph died. So why is it over now?'

He just didn't get it. He knew he'd stuffed up. He knew he'd hurt her. But he'd apologised. Even Mila had acknowledged the role that grief had played in his still unacceptable behaviour.

'Why do you want this so badly?' Mila asked.

She hadn't answered his question, but he was hardly in a position to push. Seb knew it would take only the slightest of nudges to lose her for ever.

It would be easy for him to repeat what he'd told her that first day—that he'd lost Steph and simply wanted Mila back in his life. But the way he felt right now: his throat tight, his shoulders thick with tension... It was more than that.

The idea of not seeing Mila again... It was causing him pain. Literal, physical pain.

'I need you, Mila.' His voice cracked. He hated that. *Hated* that.

He gave no further explanation. He didn't have one. He hated himself for delaying seeing Mila when he'd returned to Perth, for delaying his apology. But he'd been arrogant enough to believe that—beyond his own guilt—time wouldn't matter. That Mila would always be there. That they'd just step back into the easy friendship of the past.

He'd been wrong.

It hadn't happened. Their friendship was certainly no longer easy.

But that didn't change what he knew, unequivocally: he needed her.

Mila stepped closer, reaching towards the coffee tray he'd forgotten he was still holding. The tall cardboard cups leant precariously, but Mila plucked them to safety, then nodded somewhere behind him.

'You can chuck the tray in the recycling bin over there.'

He did so, obediently, unable to interpret Mila's expression. When he turned back Mila hadn't moved. But now she held out his coffee as she licked milk foam from her lips.

He took it and drank, but didn't taste the strong black liquid, still hot against his tongue. Every sense in his body was too busy waiting for Mila. He swallowed the coffee, but it didn't ease the suffocating tightness of his throat.

'Okay,' Mila said. 'Okay.'

They both stood in silence for a little while longer.

Eventually Mila smiled.

And finally Seb could breathe.

Later that week they played tennis again.

It had been Mila's idea, but she couldn't say she'd been looking forward to it.

Seb had arrived first. He was already out on court, but he was facing away from the car park when Mila's car pulled in, his phone pressed to his ear.

He wore similar attire to the last time they'd played and, like the last time they'd played, Mila was unable to do anything but admire his muscular form.

Mila also wore the same outfit as she had last time: a singlet, and tennis shorts that hit mid-thigh. For a moment at home she'd held a pair of old, long baggy shorts in her hands—before deciding she was being ridiculous. Her outfit was practical and sporty. Nothing more. And if they were to continue their friendship, then showing a bit of skin was *not* allowed to be an issue.

That was how Mila was approaching this. This situation with Seb. She would simply disallow any complications.

Mila and Seb were friends. Only. It was that simple.

It had to be.

Mila grabbed her tennis bag from her back seat before climbing out of her car and beginning her walk to the court.

On Monday, in the face of Seb's pain and unexpected desperation, it had suddenly become impossible for Mila to walk away from him. So that meant she needed to work out a plan. A plan to be there for Seb in his obvious time of need—and a way to move on from this unwanted, uncomfortable attraction.

On her own terms.

She hadn't answered Seb's question then—the reason why they simply couldn't continue their friendship. But that wasn't because the reason was unclear. The reasons, really.

Partly—there was guilt. There was still her loyalty to Stephanie, and the fact that even after all these years her promise to Steph still resonated somewhere inside her. But mainly the reason was that all that guilt wouldn't have mattered if Seb hadn't labelled their kiss as wrong, but had instead kissed her again, and again...

She wouldn't have cared. She would have thrown her promise to the wind and plummeted into wherever that kiss had taken them.

And that realisation was both galling and terrifying.

For her attraction to Seb was so intense—and so very, very, real—that she would have allowed herself to forget everything she'd learned. That her father had taught her— that her ex-fiancé had taught her. That even fourteen-year-old Seb had taught her.

Rejection hurt. Bone-deep.

How many times had she told herself not to put herself in that situation again? *Every* time her father had let her down. The time when Ben had...

'Mila!'

Seb's smile was wide as he dropped his phone to his side. 'Sorry,' he said. 'Work call.'

Mila smiled back at him. It wasn't forced—being around Seb *did* make her smile. She just needed to ensure that it was always in a determinedly *friends only* type of way.

'How was your day?' Seb asked as Mila dropped her bag beside the net.

For the next few minutes they chatted casually—the latest

on Seb's apartment block development, how quickly Mila's latest class had filled up. It was all very pleasant. As pleasant as their occasional texts over the past few days.

Seb hadn't dropped by with any more coffee. Maybe he'd guessed—rightly—that Mila needed some distance. But he'd stayed in touch, and been keen to catch up.

So here they were. Once again with the protection of the tennis net between them.

One set later Mila had started to relax. She'd won a tie-breaker—*convincingly*, she'd said. *Narrowly*, Seb had insisted, with a smile.

It was fun, she'd decided. Maybe this was what their 'thing' could be. Weekly tennis. She could do that.

Later Seb had break point on Mila's serve. A deep ground stroke had sent Mila scrambling after the ball, and she'd managed only the weakest defensive lob in return. As the ball floated up and up Seb raced to the net, his racquet up and ready to hit a smash.

Just for a split second he glanced at Mila and winked—and that was just so one hundred per cent assured, cheeky Seb that Mila laughed out loud.

And then laughed even harder when his pre-emptive smugness led to his racquet hitting nothing but fresh air and the ball landing safely within the court—too far away, despite Seb's very best efforts to reach it.

He stood, bemused, hands on hips. 'I've got nothing,' he said, his eyes sparkling.

'Deuce,' Mila replied happily, then went on to win the game.

They laughed again when Mila feigned a racquet-throwing tantrum after a silly double fault, and Seb laughed at Mila's whoop of victory when a lucky net cord fell her way.

Mila won in straight sets, and they both jogged to the net to shake hands—an old habit that Mila didn't think twice about.

Until, that was, Seb actually held her hand in his. Warm, big, strong.

And just like that all the camaraderie, all the *friendship* of the past ninety minutes, evaporated. All that remained was the reality that for the first time since they'd kissed amongst the sand dunes they were touching. Skin to skin.

Electricity shot up Mila's arm, so shocking that for a moment, her brain went blank.

She couldn't remember any of the reasons why they were only friends. She couldn't remember why leaping over the net and into his arms would be a truly terrible idea.

But then Seb let go.

'You're very fit,' he said quickly. Randomly.

'Pardon me?' she said, although she'd heard him. She needed a moment to locate her thoughts.

He'd taken a step back and rubbed his hand down his thigh, as if wiping away Mila's touch. Irrationally, that stung.

'You barely raised a sweat,' he said, trying again.

That wasn't even close to true. 'I'm a sporadic gym-user,' Mila said, keen for pointless conversation to ease the sudden tension between them. 'I got into it a bit when I was with Ben. Now I go when I remember. Or just go for walks with Ivy and Nate. Mostly that, actually.'

Perfect—another man, her sister and a baby were the perfect topics to divert attention.

'What happened with Ben?' Seb asked.

Mila had been looking into the darkness beyond Seb's shoulder and the court fencing, but now she forced herself to meet his gaze.

Maybe Seb was grasping at the opportunity to talk about absolutely anything. Or more likely he felt nothing when they touched and was simply having a perfectly reasonable conversation.

'He cheated on me,' Mila said baldly. There was really no other way to say it.

'Oh, Mila—' Seb began.

But Mila wasn't about to let him continue. She didn't need to see the pity in his gaze as he realised that—yes—yet another man had *not* chosen Mila.

'It's old news, Seb, I'd rather not talk about it.'

She grabbed her water bottle from beside her bag and took a long, long drink. She made sure she was smiling by the time she packed her racquet back in its bag and as they walked together back to their cars. Their conversation moved on to the trivial, and by the time Mila was in her car and driving home she'd just about convinced herself that she'd imagined her reaction to Seb's touch.

And besides—it didn't really matter, did it? They were just friends.

It was the perfect summer evening—warm, but with a sea breeze cooling their skin. The Fremantle beach was dotted with open-sided tents and food trucks, and a busker sang beneath a zig-zag of festoon lights—although the sun was still yet to complete its descent. Beneath the purple and red sky children ran and laughed, and their parents held cardboard trays piled high with food. Tourists took photos with bulky cameras and teenagers took phone selfies against the backdrop of surf and sand and towering Norfolk pines.

'Cool, huh?' Mila smiled up at Seb, her lovely eyes covered by her oversized sunglasses.

Seb nodded his agreement. He'd invited her for a drink after work, but Mila had suggested the beach markets instead. It was a good idea—more casual, more people.

Although that had been why Seb had suggested a drink in the first place: because it *shouldn't* matter if he and Mila had a drink in a bar—it shouldn't feel like anything but two friends catching up after work. It shouldn't feel private, or intimate, or date-like.

But it seemed that maybe Mila had thought it would. Maybe Seb did, too. It didn't really matter—the important thing was that he and Mila were hanging out together, just as he'd wanted. As friends.

Over the past couple of weeks, since the film premiere, it had become clear that they were both on the same page, that they wanted to remain within firm 'friends only' boundaries. There'd been a few blips—that first, post-kiss tennis game, for example.

He'd been quite pleased at how well that match had gone, despite the distraction of Mila, and her obvious gorgeousness in her tennis gear, and her legs that went on for ever. He'd just about convinced himself that he was back to being objective Seb, capable of simply admiring the attractiveness of his *friend* without it meaning anything more, and then they'd shaken hands...

How stupid that such a G-rated touch had robbed him of his ability to think. For long moments, Seb hadn't been able to grasp at even one reason why he and Mila couldn't be much, much more than friends.

Fortunately he'd come to his senses, and Mila had seemed utterly unaware. But Seb had made sure there'd been no handshake at the end of their match the following week, though—just to be safe.

And now here they were, on a postcard-perfect beach, surrounded by the scents of falafel and satay and pizza. Mila was a few steps ahead, scouting out their dinner options. It was exactly what he wanted—the easy, comfortable, reliable friendship of his past.

Because he'd realised, when faced with losing Mila, that she was the only constant in his now topsy-turvy life. Everything had changed, Everything was no longer how it was meant to be. His friendships—in London and at Fyfe Technology—had drifted, and floated away, not strong enough to sustain his international relocation. He didn't mind—he'd eventually make new friends, find new mates to go cycling with, to invite over for a beer. But he wasn't ready for that yet. He wasn't ready to share his history with just anyone, or to invite others into this new and uncertain phase of his life.

Mila already knew him. Not the details of the past few years—and certainly not the mess of his marriage—but she did know *him*. He didn't have to explain himself to her. He didn't have to be anyone else for her. He just got to *be* with her.

Except when he was derailed by this continued, unwanted attraction.

But he could handle it. Surely it would pass with time.

Mila pointed at a tent to their right, then looked back at Seb over her shoulder. She wore a pale blue summer dress, her shoulders golden in the setting sun.

'Oh, *look*—crêpes!'

They ended up completing a full lap of all the food options before spotting a park bench, shaded by the outstretched boughs of a Norfolk pine, which they promptly claimed. In order to sample most of the food up for offer, they'd agreed to share—with one of them heading out for food while the other saved the seat.

Seb set out, returning with a shredded beef burger, topped with a shiny brioche bun. Mila finished her half first, and headed back out into the crowd for their second course.

The sun continued its gradual fall into the ocean, where two container ships interrupted the perfect line of the horizon. As Seb sat there, wiping barbecue sauce from his fingers with a napkin, he felt for the first time as if...

'Is this seat taken?'

Seb looked up at the sound of a soft, very female voice. The woman was short, blonde, and very pretty, with long tumbling hair and warm brown eyes.

Unthinkingly, he ran his thumb over the place where his wedding band had once been—but of course it wasn't there.

'Oh,' he said, wondering if he was jumping to conclusions. Maybe she genuinely just needed somewhere to sit?

'Seb?'

It was Mila, cradling a neatly closed white cardboard box and a tray with two forks stabbed into a mound of paella.

'Oh!' the blonde woman said. 'I'm so sorry. I thought—' She was blushing, her gaze darting to her feet. 'Have a lovely day!'

Then she was gone.

'Who was that?' Mila asked, settling onto the bench. She put the box down beside her—away from Seb. 'Dessert,' she said with a grin. 'It's a surprise.'

Then she carefully served out the paella into the second tray that had been hiding beneath the first.

'I have no idea,' Seb said, and then had his first mouthful of paella—all spicy and delicious.

'So she was hitting on you?'

Seb coughed, a piece of rice stuck in his throat. 'I guess,' he said, really not wanting to have this conversation with Mila.

'She was pretty. Do you want to go talk to her? I won't mind.'

'What?'

Mila shrugged, waving a piece of chorizo on the end of her fork. 'Go on. Don't let me stop you.'

She was still wearing her sunglasses, so it was impossible to read her expression.

'Don't you remember what I said? About how I'm terrible at relationships?'

'That was just to make me feel—' But she didn't finish the sentence, instead taking off her sunglasses and meeting his gaze. '*That* wasn't a relationship. That was a woman angling to ask you out. You could do that.'

'No,' he said, unequivocally. 'I could not.'

'Why not?'

Mila was focused on her paella now, chasing pieces of meat and vegetables about in the rice. She sounded completely relaxed.

Seb had lost his appetite.

'I wasn't a very good husband, Mila. I don't want to put someone else through that again.'

'That doesn't mean you can't date again. Have some fun.'

He honestly hadn't really thought about it. In London, his one-night stands had left him empty. And now, back in Perth, there was Mila…

No. He simply wasn't ready.

He said so.

'I get that,' Mila said. 'That's understandable. I just wanted to make sure your decision wasn't anything to do with me.'

She met his gaze now, absolutely direct. It was almost as if she was daring him to agree. Or disagree. Seb had no idea.

'It isn't,' Seb said.

'Good,' she said, looking out to the ocean. 'You know, I kind of get it… After what happened with Ben I didn't think I ever wanted to do that again.' A pause. '*Ever.*' She finished her paella. 'But, you know, that is pretty unrealistic. I've been to both my sisters' weddings over the past couple of years. I know I want that too. To be in love like that. To be loved like that. I think the trick will be to work out a way to protect myself.'

'From what?' he said.

'You know…' she said, with half a smile. 'The messy bits that hurt. Like your ex-fiancé hooking up with a girl from work. They're engaged now.'

'Ouch,' Seb said.

'Yup.' A grin. 'But that's okay. I think I fought too long for that relationship to work. The signs were there. Kind of like my dad, in a way. I let hope drive my delusions…illusions…whatever. I won't do *that* again.'

'So how will you do it? How will you protect yourself?'

Mila shook her head. 'I'm working on it,' she said.

They were both quiet for a while. Two little girls with fairies painted on their cheeks came running past them, squealing and waving sequined wands.

'Can you hurry up and finish your dinner, Seb?' Mila said suddenly—and brightly. 'Because we *have* to try these cupcakes. One is triple choc *and* salted caramel. How is that even *possible*?'

CHAPTER EIGHT

SEB WAS ON the phone when Mila walked into his shop on Tuesday.

He stood at the back, a shoulder propped against the bare brick wall. The new first floor was in, although the rafters were still exposed. Mila could hear the activity of tradesmen upstairs: the murmur of conversation punctuated by the occasional whir of a drill.

Aaron, one of the labourers, was sweeping up a pile of rubble and sawdust near the shop window. He smiled a greeting. He was young and tall, with his red-blond hair arranged in a man bun and a cheeky glint to his eye.

They'd spoken once before, when Mila had asked if she could retrieve some old coloured glass bottles from the skip. She'd thought maybe she could use the glass in some of her pieces. Or just use them as skinny vases. She wasn't sure— she just thought they were pretty.

Mila found herself smoothing her T-shirt against her hips as she walked towards Seb, but she stopped herself. She didn't have to worry about looking nice for Seb. Besides, she was wearing a variation of what she wore every day— skinny jeans and a loose T-shirt with a loud print. Today the print was of nasturtiums. She wasn't trying to impress *anyone*. Certainly not Seb.

He'd seen her as soon as she'd walked in, his smile wide and welcoming. Mila grinned back. *See. This was nice.*

She'd popped over to see if he was free for lunch. She'd made too much pasta last night, so thought she'd invite him up to her place for leftovers. Surely you couldn't get more relaxed and friend-like than *that*.

Although with the way her heart accelerated as she took in his work shirt, shorts and heavy boots...which she still wasn't used to and still really rather liked…she decided that maybe she'd bring their bowls of penne downstairs, and they could eat in the workshop—with Sheri as a chaperon, of sorts.

Oh, God. She was being ridiculous. Because what had happened on Friday at the beach markets had been a *good* thing. She was at pains to remind herself of that. Was there any better way to define their friendship then to bring another women into the equation? Seb should have gone after her, and spoken to her. She'd looked nice. Very pretty, too.

There was simply no reason why he shouldn't have. Least of all because of the way Mila had felt when she'd spotted them, her arms full with paella and a box of cupcakes.

She should probably have expected that seeing Seb with another woman would feel like a knife to her heart. That seemed dramatic now, but it was how she'd felt. She'd stood there for a moment, utterly still, her insides all sliced up with pain.

Which was silly. She had no right.

Seb had made it clear—for him, being with Mila was wrong, even though for her it had felt right. And she just couldn't argue with that. He could wrap it up in talk of being *'terrible at relationships'*, blah-blah-blah. But how stupid—as if Seb would never be with anyone else after Steph.

He just didn't want to be with *her*.

Seb asked the person on the phone to hold on for a moment, before holding his phone against his chest. 'Sorry, Mila, I'll only be another minute. I'm having a major issue with this supplier—'

'That's fine,' she said with another smile. She wasn't in a hurry.

'How are you, Mila?' Aaron asked, behind her.

Glad for something to do, she turned to face him. He really was quite handsome, although in a surfer, music festival kind of way.

'I'm good,' she said. 'Busy day?'

They chatted for a few minutes. Aaron had recently bought a new car that he described enthusiastically. Cars weren't really Mila's thing, but then she'd told all and sundry when she'd first got her new kiln, so she understood the excitement of a big, shiny toy.

From the corner of her eye Mila saw Seb turn slightly away from them. His words were still calm, but there was definitely a layer of steel in what he said.

'So I was wondering…would you like to go see it? With me?'

'Pardon me?' Mila said, suddenly realising the conversation had moved on from cars and their stereo systems.

Aaron's gaze was confident and his lips quirked upwards. 'I asked if you wanted to see *Agent X*—you know, that spy movie? It's cheap night tonight.' He paused. 'Not that I'd mind paying for full-priced tickets for you, of course.'

Mila laughed at his aplomb, then realised he was being serious.

'Oh,' she said.

'Unless,' Aaron said, 'you've got something going with my boss? Only I heard him tell one of the other guys you were just friends, so I thought—'

Ouch.

But it was true—once again, she really had nothing to be upset about.

'No,' she said. 'We *are* just friends.'

Aaron grinned.

Mila was flattered, and Aaron did seem very nice—if young—but…

'Thanks for the invite, but—'

Seb had finished his call and turned back to face them. She couldn't read his expression—not at all. He was just watching them. Waiting for Mila to finish her conversation.

What had she expected? Jealousy?

'Actually,' Mila said, 'that sounds great. What time?'

They swapped phone numbers before Aaron went back to his work and Mila walked over to Seb.

'Hot date?' he asked with a grin.

Maybe his smile was forced. *Maybe* he didn't meet her gaze. Or maybe he was simply pleased for her.

It didn't matter.

'Something like that,' she said, with a deliberately broad smile. 'So, do you feel like some penne marinara? I made it and, without a word of a lie, it's awesome.'

Seb went for a really long walk after dinner. His apartment was in East Perth, so he went past the cricket ground and down to the Swan River. He shared the path with late-night dog walkers, joggers and cyclists—the latter's headlights blinding in the darkness.

He hadn't bothered to dress appropriately, so he was still wearing what he'd changed into after work—jeans, flip flops, a faded old T-shirt. So he didn't really fit in with all the Lycra and the neon running shoes—but then, he wasn't here to exercise. Although his pace wasn't completely sedate. He found himself walking faster and faster, his shoes slapping on the bitumen in an attempt to outpace his thoughts.

Maybe.

Until now it had been easy to fill his brain and his day with stuff that didn't involve Mila. With work, mostly. A new site purchase, an investor meeting, a marketing consultant. Then, later, with food. He must have perused every possible home delivery option, and then spent way too long reading online reviews before finally ordering. When his food had eventually arrived he hadn't been hungry. Instead he'd just pushed it around with a fork before eventually conceding defeat and constructing a little tower of plastic containers in his fridge.

So now he'd run out of things to distract his brain with. All that was left was Mila. Mila on her date. With Aaron.

He thought he'd handled things quite well in his shop.

He'd teased her, as was appropriate given he was her *friend*. And Aaron seemed to be a good guy. He was hard-working, reliable and enthusiastic about his job—all reasons why Seb should like him. Until today he had. Tonight…he didn't.

He didn't like him at all.

He'd tried telling himself that he was worried about Mila. That after Ben cheating on her, and her father letting her down—after losing Steph—the last thing she needed was to be hurt again.

After all, that was why he'd ended their kiss. Why he'd realised it was wrong. He just couldn't be responsible for Mila being hurt again. He would not allow it.

But that wasn't the only reason he didn't like Mila's date. This wasn't brotherly-type concern.

Far from it.

Maybe Mila was okay with him talking to other women—as she'd said at the markets. With him having relationships with other women.

As they'd talked that night he'd agreed with everything she'd said: in theory.

Because it was one thing for them both to talk about their hypothetical relationships in a hypothetical future. It was another for the future to be here right now.

And right this instant Mila was on a date with another man. A man who wasn't him.

He *hated* that.

The sea breeze was cool against Seb's skin. He headed towards the new Elizabeth Quay and the bell tower, where restaurants perched along the water. Even on a Tuesday night people bustled about—it was a perfect early summer evening, before the weather became too hot to do anything but swim.

Seb slowed his pace to a dawdle, and then came to a complete stop just to the side of the footpath. He stood on the grass, watching the small white caps on the river's tiny waves.

He wanted Mila.

But he couldn't have her.

He couldn't risk hurting her and losing her.

Because she was all he had left.

He couldn't face the idea of his world without Mila.

On the beach, she'd been so very wrong to label herself a substitute for Steph. That was doing a disservice to both women. Steph had irreplaceably been Steph, while Mila was irreplaceably Mila.

He'd never imagined a world without either of them—even as he'd known his marriage was failing and that his relationship with Steph had become irreparable.

For Steph to be gone was still impossible—she'd been so full of life, so full of dreams. She'd deserved a future no longer married to him. She'd deserved a future, full stop.

But Mila was still here. She was real, alive, and still part of his world. He was not going to ruin that. He *would* not.

A splash in the inky black river drew Seb's attention. But the river was calm. Then again—a subtle splash, this time in Seb's line of vision, a shift in the shadows beneath the moonlight.

A dolphin. Two. Swimming together, their fins appearing and disappearing amongst the waves, a pair perfectly in sync.

His phone vibrated in his back pocket, and by the time he'd retrieved it the dolphins were gone.

A text message—from Mila.

I need to see you.

CHAPTER NINE

BY THE TIME Seb had walked back to his apartment block Mila was already there. She was waiting in the foyer, pacing a short path in front of the mirrored lifts.

She paused the instant Seb stepped through the automatic doors, making as if to hurry towards him—but then she stopped. Instead she waited for him to approach her.

'Nice place,' Mila said, meeting his gaze.

He shrugged. 'It's fine,' he said. 'I plan to build something like this—but better—some day soon.'

She nodded sharply. 'You will.'

She'd wrapped her arms around herself even though it was perfectly temperature-controlled in here—not too hot, not too cold. She wore skinny blue jeans and spiky heels. Her jacket was of some type of faded grey linen, with sections of a silky pink camisole top visible where her arms weren't gripping herself tightly. She looked fantastic.

He wasn't being objective.

'Can I come up?' she asked.

There was no point acknowledging that it was a bad idea—to himself or to Mila. 'Sure,' he said.

He reached past her to push the elevator's 'up' button, then when the doors opened gestured for Mila to walk into the small space before him. Her heels clattered loudly on the marble floor as she fidgeted inside the elevator—walking over to the back to run a finger along the railing, then over to the side, and then simply standing almost exactly in the middle, shifting her weight from foot to foot.

Seb scanned his access key and pressed the button for his floor. He didn't move as the doors swished shut, not sure what to do. Keeping his distance from Mila seemed the best idea. He didn't know why she was here.

'Not the penthouse?' Mila asked as they stepped onto his floor.

'No,' he said with a shrug. 'New business. New priorities.'

Not that he was exactly slumming it. He still had half of the entire floor to himself. Unlocking his front door revealed a tastefully decorated, luxury serviced apartment—and, more importantly, the view across the river he'd just walked beside to the twinkling lights of the South Perth foreshore.

'Nice,' Mila said simply, walking before him into the main living space.

It was an open-plan conglomeration of gourmet kitchen, dining room and living room, looking out over a wide her-ringbone-paved balcony complete with a barbecue he never used and an outdoor setting he used nearly every day. He was definitely taking advantage of the Perth sun after years in far less sunny London.

'Can we go outside?' Mila said. 'It's a bit stuffy in here.'

It wasn't, but he followed her onto the balcony. Since she'd greeted him she hadn't met his gaze at all. He didn't think he'd ever seen her so highly strung. She was constantly moving—crossing and uncrossing her arms, lacing her fingers together, touching every different texture she found: the grain of the jarrah outdoor table, the shine of the stain-less steel barbecue lid, the rough surface of the stone-hewn abstract sculpture in one corner.

'This is really ugly,' she said.

It was, but that wasn't the point. 'What's going on, Mila?' Seb asked. 'Why do you need to see me?'

Finally she turned to look at him—to *really* look at him. He stood in front of the still open sliding door. Mila was metres away from him, near the balcony railing.

'Aaron kissed me,' she said.

Seb simply had no words.

Mila filled up the silence. 'He's a really nice guy, it turns out. And he's tall. And hot. In a really, really young kind of way...'

'Am I supposed to offer you congratulations?'

'No,' Mila said. '*No*. That's the point. I wanted to kiss him. I think so, anyway. Or maybe I just wanted to *want* to kiss him. I don't know.' She pivoted on her heel to face out towards the river. 'But kissing him wasn't great. Wasn't even good. It was awful, actually. And awfully quick. It was over in seconds—I just couldn't do it. I knew it was wrong. Really wrong.'

Seb walked up to stand beside her, also leaning against the rail.

Mila ran her hands through her hair, her fingers leaving it all haphazard. 'It was wrong, totally wrong, because…'

And now her avalanche of words ended.

She turned again, propping her hip against the rail so she faced Seb. He did the same, although their casual poses were failing in any attempt to relax the growing tension between them.

Mila met his gaze and held it. He could practically see it—that one last boulder, teetering at the top, waiting for Mila to open her mouth again.

'Why was it wrong, Mila?'

She glared at him. 'You *know*. You do—and don't pretend you don't.'

But he really wanted to pretend. Everything would be simpler if he did.

Yet they both just stood there.

'It was wrong because of you,' Mila said eventually, unnecessarily. 'It was wrong because of this. Because of us.'

She gestured between them, pointing to Seb and then to herself.

'I hate this,' Mila said, very softly.

'Why did you come here?' Seb asked.

'Because I was angry. At myself. At you.'

'Why are you angry?'

'Because this shouldn't be happening.'

'I know,' he said. But he needed to know her reasons. 'Why not?'

'Because it isn't how it's supposed to be. I'm not supposed to feel this way about you. You're *Seb*—you're Steph's husband. You're my best friend's husband.'

'Not any more.'

'I know,' she said. She ran a hand through her hair, looking past him towards that ugly sculpture. 'And that isn't even really the reason. I just don't want to feel this way. Because I know what will happen. I know—' She stopped abruptly, then looked straight at him. 'And I'm angry at *you*. For not walking away when I told you to. I needed you to walk away, Seb…'

'I could never walk away from you, Mila.'

She looked up at the sky, rolling her eyes.

He didn't understand—how could she not believe him? 'Why did you need to see me, Mila?' he asked again, this time with a hard edge. 'What did you want to happen?'

He couldn't work it out—what she was thinking, what she wanted. But he did understand the tension between them.

'I don't know,' she said, but Seb didn't really believe her.

She shouldn't have come. And he definitely shouldn't be glad she was here. But she had, and he was.

'What do *you* want to happen?' she asked.

'I don't know,' he said, lying too.

There wasn't much space between them. A metre… maybe a little less.

Mila still held his gaze. He wished hers was unreadable, but it wasn't—not any more. He was sure his wasn't either.

All he had to do was reach for her…

And that would be it.

It would change everything. Their friendship—the friendship that was so important to him, that he needed so badly—would be altered for ever.

And Mila… Was this really what she wanted?

'I just want tonight,' Mila whispered, reading his mind.

And with that he was losing himself in those eyes, falling into their depths. He needed to touch her. He needed Mila. There was no going back.

He shifted his weight, pushing himself away from the railing. Mila remained still, but watched him. He stepped closer, with plans to drag her into his arms. But then he paused.

Instead he leant forward, bending closer, until her breath was against his lips. Her breath hitched.

Heat flooded Seb's body. He wasn't even touching her, yet every cell in his body was on high alert, desperate for Mila.

Then, finally, he kissed her. It just seemed fitting for their lips to meet first, for their kiss to be their focus—maybe to give Mila that one last chance to back away from the point of no return.

Because Seb knew he didn't have the strength to do it himself.

Her lips were plump, soft. Their kiss was intimate. Different from that kiss on the beach. More considered, more knowing. This was a kiss without a question—this was a kiss with a destination.

And Mila was definitely coming along for the ride.

Mila's hands were suddenly behind his neck; his were at her waist. And then she was in his arms, pressed as close as she could be.

Their kiss deepened as Seb's hand slid beneath Mila's camisole top, finding warm, smooth skin at her back. Mila slid her hands downwards, greedily discovering the shape of his shoulders and his chest.

His lips moved from her mouth to her jaw, to her neck—desperate to explore all of her, to taste all of her.

Mila continued her own exploration, her hands shoving up his T-shirt, feeling his skin hot beneath her touch.

Somehow they were back inside. Seb was backing her against the nearest wall. Mila was smiling and sighing against his mouth as they kissed.

But even now—even as his whole world was focused on Mila and how she felt, how *this* felt—Seb knew what he was doing. Knew what he was risking.

But he couldn't make himself stop. He couldn't walk away from this—this maelstrom of need and desire. He needed this. Needed her. Needed tonight.

It would have to be enough.

When Mila woke it was still dark.

She rolled over in Seb's bed, hoping for an alarm clock or something that would tell her the time, but there was none.

Her phone was in her bag, abandoned somewhere in Seb's cavernous living area, so that couldn't help her.

Not that the time really mattered. What would she do with the information, anyway? Work out if it was an acceptable time to call a taxi and make a run for it back to her place? Or maybe, if it was still truly the middle of the night, use the time as an excuse to simply close her eyes again and snuggle closer to Seb's gorgeous warmth?

She didn't really need to know the time to do either of those things. Mila knew that. Either were viable options, regardless of the time.

One was the better option, of course. She should go. But instead she stayed exactly where she was. Naked, but not quite touching Seb, a thin expensive-feeling sheet covering them both.

Her eyes had adjusted to the darkness. It was a nice room, although understandably devoid of any personality. The large bed had a stitched fabric buttoned headboard, and the bedside tables were spindly and clutter-free. Where Mila lay, she faced the door to the hallway. A large abstract canvas decorated the wall immediately opposite her, aligned with the door. It was too dark to work out the colours—they were simply dark splashes and swirls against a pale background. Mila had been too wrapped up in Seb to notice it when the lights had still been on.

She smiled at the memory.

Maybe she didn't need to know the time. Without it the night remained unanchored to reality. Like a dream. Perfect, with no regrets.

Seb shifted behind her, breathing with the steady, deep pattern of sleep.

Mila rolled over so she faced Seb again. He was also on his side, but it was impossible to make out any details in the darkness. She could watch his shoulders lift with his breathing, the shape of his body silhouetted against the window in the almost blackness...

'Mila...' he said, after a while.

'Sebastian.'

She never said his full name. Tonight, the longer word sounded like an endearment.

He reached out, drawing a finger along her jaw. 'You are so beautiful,' he said, very softly.

His thumb brushed against her bottom lip, and she couldn't have spoken if she'd wanted to. She realised she'd been restraining herself from touching Seb. Whatever reason she'd had for doing that instantly evaporated and became impossible to justify. Why, oh, why would she want to do anything *but* touch Sebastian Fyfe?

And so she did—exploring his face the way he'd explored hers, delicately tracing his eyebrows, his cheekbones, his nose, his lips.

She was rediscovering a face she'd known almost her whole life. But it was not the face of a boy any longer. Tonight it was almost unfamiliar—foreign to her. But then, that made sense, didn't it? Yesterday Seb had been a lifelong friend. Tonight he was her lover.

Mila waited for regret to descend.

But it didn't.

It would.

But right now that didn't matter. Right now it was dark. Right now time stood still.

Mila leant closer and kissed him.

* * *

She was having a shower. Seb was awake, sitting up in bed, reading some emails on his phone. From the shower Mila could see him through the open en-suite bathroom door, the shape of one propped knee tenting the sheet, his bare chest golden in the lamplight. He could probably turn the light off now, though. It was morning.

Mila turned her face upwards, directly into the spray of water, her eyes tight shut. This was all very domestic. Not quite comfortable, but not entirely awkward either.

She hadn't left as she'd intended, in yesterday's clothes under the cover of darkness. He hadn't asked her to, either. Although maybe he was just being polite.

She didn't know what the rules were in this situation. How did you have a one-night stand with a friend? Or someone who had once been a friend? Mila didn't know how to define Seb in her life any more. The definition had changed too much recently. A few weeks ago she'd thought she'd never see him again. Then suddenly he was a daily presence in her life, and recently there'd been glimpses of the friendship they'd once had. But now—now she didn't know what to call Seb.

Ex-something, though. Ex-friend…ex-lover. Because this was it, of course. After last night and this morning they were done.

She'd known it last night—known exactly what she was doing when she'd come to Seb's apartment. She'd just focused on her need to see him—on her need *for* him—and allowed herself to do so: just for one night.

Seb had asked her at the beach markets how she would protect herself. Well, when it came to Seb and her decision to see him last night her plan had been simple.

It would only be one night.

I just want tonight.

One night she could handle. One night would not create expectations of a future and those delusions she was so apt to create.

And so she was safe, within her self-determined, one-night-only time box. Ivy had told her about time boxes, although she suspected they were rather different for mining project management. And in her time box Mila had been able to kiss Seb again, to discover his body, to sleep with him. Despite all the reasons why she shouldn't.

And it had been amazing. Incredible. Better than she could have imagined. So good that she couldn't regret it. She just couldn't.

But now that it was morning, and she had reached the end of her time box, reality was starting to descend even if regret did not. And the most obvious reality—the most important—was that she'd just slept with her best friend's husband.

Oh, she knew that wasn't strictly true any longer. She even knew that Steph would be the last person to expect Mila to stand by a teenage promise from beyond the grave. And, truth be told, Mila didn't *truly* feel guilty, as such.

But she did feel intensely aware, right now, of Steph. Suddenly Steph's loss felt raw. Raw in a way it hadn't for many months.

Mila turned beneath the water, bowing her head forward as her throat tightened. Water gushed over her hair, pushing it forward and into her eyes, but she didn't care. Silent tears mingled amongst the spray.

Seb's feet came into her watery view, just outside the shower. She lifted her gaze, then ran her fingers through her hair, pushing it back from her forehead.

'You okay?' he asked.

He'd been about to join her—his nakedness made that obvious. The last time Mila had seen Seb completely naked—in the daylight—would be twenty or more years ago. Amongst twirling sprinkler heads and shrieks of laughter.

Now he looked utterly different. And not the way she'd expected Seb to grow up. This Seb had all the extra muscles of a man with a physical job, not the lanky geekiness of the adult Seb she remembered. His shoulders were broad, his pectorals and stomach muscles defined, his legs powerful.

He was gorgeous—that was a fact. Strong. The tradesman's tan—where his olive skin abruptly became paler in the shape of a T-shirt and work shorts—did not even slightly distract from his perfection.

'Mila?'

She shook her head.

'You're not okay?' he asked. He stepped closer, as if to join her—or to check on her. Who knew?

'No, no,' she said firmly. 'I'm fine. Just getting out, though. It's all yours.'

He blinked, clearly confused.

Mila stepped aside, leaving the water running so he could step immediately beneath its warmth. She kept her distance, knowing that if she touched him she wouldn't be leaving the shower.

She felt his eyes on her as she grabbed a fluffy white towel and dried herself. For the first time she was aware of *her* nakedness. Was he reflecting, as well, on how her body had changed now that she was all grown-up? Or was he thinking of the other girl who'd run shrieking through those sprinklers all those years ago? Whose grown-up body he'd been far more familiar with. That he would've known almost as well as his own.

Suddenly it was all too much.

Her grief. Steph. Her time box. Seb.

Her procrastination was definitely over. She needed to leave. Not to be there any more.

I need to go.

So she did.

In his kitchen, she scrawled a note on the back of a takeaway menu. Seb hadn't noticed her retreat. Or maybe he was just more *au fait* with how one should behave the morning after.

It didn't matter—what he thought, what we would have said if she'd given him the chance to say goodbye.

Why would it? She'd been crystal-clear: *I just want tonight.*

And the night was over.

CHAPTER TEN

EACH WEEK SEB caught up with his parents for dinner.

Usually it was at a nice restaurant—his mum was a bit of a foodie, and took a lot of joy in sharing her favourite meals with her 'favourite child'. He was also her *only* child, although that didn't really lessen the sentiment. In the months he'd been back in Perth he'd yet to eat dinner at his parents' place. He'd barely visited, actually. Deliberately. And this hadn't gone unnoticed by his always shrewd parents.

They never said anything—they were good like that—but his mum would invite him over occasionally. Never with any pressure, never with any questions as to why he consistently declined—but she'd still ask him. As if prodding a bruise: *Does this still hurt too much, darling?*

As luck would have it, this week his mum, Monique, had invited him over for Sunday dinner. And she hadn't been at all successful in hiding her surprise when he'd accepted.

Seb parked his car in front of the four-car garage located just to the side of his parents' mammoth home. It had been his mum and dad's dream home when it had been built—Seb still remembered the excitement of the day they'd moved in, when his parents had run around exploring the rooms as excited as the pre-school-age Seb had been.

Over the years the house had been modernised, its exterior rendered to hide all that once fashionable feature brick, and Seb's old bedroom converted to a guest room many moons ago. But it would always feel like home to Seb—the place intrinsically linked with so many of his childhood memories.

He'd had the best pool in the street, for example—complete with a slide and a small diving board—which had just been *the coolest thing ever*. It had been a hub for his friends—and the backdrop to many of Mila, Steph and Seb's adventures.

They'd played Marco Polo, they'd hosted pool parties, and they'd even shared a bottle of peach schnapps in the small pool house, aged fifteen and sixteen. That hadn't ended well—with sore heads and furious parents.

But it was his memories with Steph—just Steph—that made it so hard for Seb to visit this place.

Laughing together in his bedroom as they'd studied—with parent-prescribed door open, of course. Steph joining his family for dinner, charming his parents. That one night after Steph's Year Twelve ball in the pool house...

Seb climbed out of his car, slamming the door harder than he'd intended. It was dusk, and huge jacaranda trees were throwing long shadows across the Fyfe mansion. Twin jacarandas also stood outside the mansion to the left: the mansion that had once belonged to Steph's parents. Not any more, though. They'd sold up shortly after the funeral. Now a millionaire mobile app entrepreneur lived there, his mum had said. Complete with the sunshine-yellow Lamborghini parked in the drive.

While he understood why her parents had moved, it didn't seem possible that it was no longer 'Steph's place'. He'd always thought of it that way, even when they'd been living together in London.

He'd loved Steph. Really loved her. Once they'd been inseparable: that annoyingly happy couple that never argued. But as things had begun to fracture in their relationship Seb had wondered if maybe they'd married too young. They'd grown up together—but maybe they'd still had some growing up to do after they'd become husband and wife. Maybe if they hadn't both got caught up in their London dreams—if marriage hadn't conveniently provided Seb with the visa that Steph had by default through her mum's British heritage...

Maybe, maybe, maybe. Maybe they shouldn't have got married.

No.

Seb couldn't wish away his marriage. He couldn't regret what they'd had. Once it had been special.

But he *could* regret his single-minded refusal to address the cracks—and later canyons—that had appeared between them.

He'd failed Stephanie. Driven her away, and driven her to—

'Honey?'

His mother stood at the top of the limestone steps before the grand front door, a short distance away. Seb realised he hadn't moved, had simply been standing beside his car, staring blankly out at the street he'd grown up on.

'Mum!' he said with a big smile, striding towards her.

She watched him carefully, not bothering to conceal her 'worried parent' expression.

'I'm okay,' Seb said, pre-empting her question as he sprang up the oversized steps. 'Really.'

He followed his mum indoors. She talked about dinner as she led him down the hallway: she'd cooked something new, with salmon and something fancy that possibly sounded French.

His dad was in the kitchen, his hip propped against the large granite-topped island, a beer in his hand. The huge space faced a dining and living area of similar scale, and beyond that were large picture windows overlooking the glass-fenced pool and a spacious grassed area beyond.

'You finally made it,' his dad said.

'Kevin,' his mum said. 'Don't be so insensitive.'

He shrugged. 'It's an observation—nothing more.'

Seb nodded. Once he would have been equally matter-of-fact. He'd learnt a lot about life's shades of grey in the past eighteen months.

'I thought there might be too many memories here,' he said. He might as well be matter-of-fact about that too.

'Are there?' his mum asked. She retrieved a bottle of wine from the fridge and held it up—a second unspoken question.

'Yes, to the wine,' he said, 'and I'm not sure about the memories. Not yet.' So far the house didn't feel at all as he'd expected.

Conversation moved on as Seb's dad set the table and Seb and his mother stood together by the stove as the salmon sizzled and spat. They talked about Seb's new business, about his parents' travel plans, the baby news of someone Seb had once gone to school with who Monique had bumped into at the supermarket...

Why had he come here? Why tonight, after he'd avoided it for so long?

Earlier, beside his car, Steph had been all he'd been able to think about. He'd expected to step inside the front door and for the emotion to be overwhelming: for the walls and floors to release his memories, for that familiar wave of grief to drown him again.

But it hadn't happened.

It had been five days since he'd seen Mila—since she'd silently exited his apartment without even a goodbye. Instead she'd left the briefest of notes.

We can't be friends any more.

That had been it.

It hadn't been unexpected—after all, that had been her response after their kiss. And their night together had been so much more. More...*everything.*

But at the time he'd hoped that *'I just want tonight'* meant that the next morning they'd return to their regular friendship.

Or maybe that was just what he'd told himself to justify something he'd known was a truly terrible idea.

But—regardless—Seb still thought Mila's decision made no sense. Even less so now than after their kiss. Before, she'd argued that his attempts to reinvigorate their friendship were pointless because they'd both—according to Mila—neglected it for far too long. But surely the past few weeks had proved her theory wrong?

His attempts to contact her to discover the real problem had proved fruitless. She'd simply repeated her note, with slight variations, in her text messages, or simply not answered his calls at all.

It was frustrating.

But mostly it hurt like hell.

He missed Mila.

So for five days he'd worked like a man possessed—both in the Heliotrope offices and on site. Although not at the shop beside Mila's—instinctively he knew that now was not the time to push her. After nearly twenty-five years of friendship he at least knew that.

What he *didn't* know was how he felt about that night, aside from the fact it had led to Mila's removal from his life. He wasn't allowing himself to think about it—and his extreme work habits had allowed him to achieve that goal.

His priority was somehow getting Mila back in his life. That was all that mattered.

He looked down at his plate. He'd cleared it of every morsel, but had no recollection of actually eating it.

'Dessert?' his mum asked.

He nodded.

So why come here tonight? To this house chock full of memories of Steph *and* of Mila? With every minute he was here—and with every disjointed thought that careened through his brain—it became clearer to him that it was not a coincidence.

He'd been wary of this place for so long. Wary of the pain he was so sure it would trigger. But he'd been wrong. In this house he felt comforted by history. By memories of giggling games of hide and seek and bowls of salty popcorn in front of the VCR.

Was that it? After five days without Mila he wanted to be near her—no matter how obliquely?

No. Not even close.

Finally he realised this had nothing to do with Mila.

This had everything to do with Steph.

Slowly he tuned back in to the conversation. His mum served up a still steaming apple pie, placing perfect little scoops of vanilla bean ice cream beside each piece.

'Did you see it?' his mum asked.

Belatedly Seb realised she was talking to him.

'Pardon me?'

'The photo in that magazine. You know—the one that comes in the weekend paper.' She paused as she pressed the lid back onto the ice cream carton. 'The photo of you and Mila Molyneux. At a film premiere.'

'I didn't know you were seeing her,' said his dad. 'I've always liked her—a straight talker, that girl.'

'She does something crafty now,' his mum said, all conversationally. 'Pots, is it?'

Seb shoved back his seat, needing to stand up. 'I'm not seeing her,' he said.

But once he was standing he had no further plan. Just for something to do, he grabbed his empty wine glass and put it in the dishwasher.

Ah. *This* was it. This feeling when his parents mentioned Mila. That little leap in his pulse, the instant flashback to memories he'd not allowed himself to reflect upon.

That was why he wanted to come here tonight. That was why he'd wanted to feel close to Steph…

Because Mila wasn't like the women he'd slept with in London.

Mila wasn't the first woman he'd slept with after Steph, but she was the first who mattered.

He didn't feel guilty—as if he'd cheated on Steph or anything. But it did feel significant. As significant as the day he'd stopped wearing his wedding band.

Does this mean I'm really moving on, Steph?

And was that also why he'd embargoed his own memories of that night? Had he hoped, somehow, that Mila *had* been like the others? Out of some form of misplaced loyalty to Steph?

Possibly. But that was stupid.

Had he hoped that because then it would be easy? Then he could easily argue to Mila that it had just been a bit of meaningless fun and there was no reason why their friendship couldn't go straight back to the way it had been.

She was the first one who mattered. What did that even mean?

Seb had walked back to the table now and he ate his pie mindlessly, watching his ice cream become a puddle.

After dessert he stood up again. This time he ended up at the window. Outside it was now dark, the tall trees that lined the rear fence merging into the black sky.

'Honey, is there anything you want to talk about?'

His mum's voice was gentle, her tone reassuring.

Seb ran his hands through his hair. 'No.'

This definitely wasn't something he wanted to share with his parents: his brain full of Steph and Mila and messy confusion. He didn't want to share it with anybody. He wasn't good at talking about this stuff.

After Steph's death he'd had his PA back at Fyfe Technology find him a counsellor to talk to—it had seemed the sensible thing to do. What he would have organised for any member of his staff.

Besides, he'd hardly had other options. With Steph's death had come an ugly truth: not only had he not truly known his wife any more, but he was surrounded by a crowd of people who either worked for him or were nothing but the most superficial of acquaintances. His work had become his wife, his friend, his family.

He'd had nobody to talk to—except maybe his parents. And, as desperate as they'd been to help, he just hadn't been capable of revealing how pathetic he was, how little he'd known about the woman he'd once loved.

There'd been Mila, too—with her regular and then more intermittent emails and social media messages. She'd been the only one who'd persisted for more than a few weeks— she tried for months until he'd eventually driven her away with his calculated rudeness.

But he just hadn't been able to talk to her—not then.

He'd been broken, grief-stricken.

Ashamed.

So he'd gone to the counsellor his PA had booked. He'd sat in the waiting room. And then left without seeing her.

In the end, talking had seemed impossible. So he'd remained alone and silent.

Eventually—and it had come gradually, with no epiphany or any particular day he could remember—he hadn't wanted to be alone any more. So he'd sold Fyfe, despite its success, because of all it had represented and reminded him of. His flaws, his mistakes, those wasted years.

And he'd come home to be close to those who still truly cared for him. His parents. Mila.

One night *could not* be the end of his friendship with Mila.

It could *not*.

He pushed open the sliding door and stepped out onto the deck. A few metres away was the glass pool fence, twinkling in the light reflected from the house. It was cool, but still, outside.

Seb had walked a few steps when he heard movement behind him. He looked over his shoulder—his father had slid the door shut and, with a nod, left Seb alone.

To his right was the pool house, and it felt natural that Seb went there. The wooden bi-fold doors that made up two of the walls were pushed partly open, so Seb opened one of them the rest of the way, before collapsing onto a large day bed, his legs stretched out before him.

For a long while he just lay there, staring at the raked ceiling. He didn't really understand what he was doing, or what he was thinking. Out here—more so than in the house—snippets of memories whizzed through his brain. Most were almost too quick to grasp—vignettes of a primary school age birthday party, Christmas lunches his parents had hosted, water bomb competitions off the diving board.

But others lingered: Mila suggesting they jump off his mum's exercise trampoline and into the pool. Steph claiming she could hold her breath underwater *'waaaayyy'* longer than Seb could. The afternoons they'd been supposed to study together but had instead sprawled in the pool house, discussing everything and anything—with the earnestness and intensity of teenagers who thought they knew it all.

In the end calling Mila seemed the only possible thing to do.

She didn't answer his first call, but she picked up after what seemed like infinite rings on his second.

'I told you, Seb—'

'I'm at the pool house,' Seb said, interrupting. 'Can you come over?'

Saying no hadn't been an option.

In fact it hadn't even been a consideration. Which should've been weird, given Mila had literally been in the process of telling Seb never to contact her again when he'd asked her.

But it was the pool house. *The pool house.*

So she'd come straight over. After a quick visit to the bottle shop.

Monique and Kevin had simply ushered her through when she'd arrived.

She wore jeans and a singlet, and her flip flops were loud against the merbau decking, the evening air cool against her skin.

Seb was sprawled across the day bed in almost darkness, the pool house lit only by the light from the main house.

'I brought your favourite,' Mila called out.

He propped himself up on one elbow as she approached. 'You drink schnapps?' he asked, incredulous.

'Only on special occasions,' Mila said, handing him the bottle.

She walked over to the small bar that still occupied the corner of the pool house. In the limited light she grabbed a couple of shot glasses, and noted that the alcohol was no longer locked away in some undisclosed location in Seb's house. Instead the bottles lined a couple of shelves along the wall, no longer vulnerable to curious teenagers. No peach schnapps, though.

Seb pulled himself up, propping his back against the plush cushions that edged the day bed. Mila crawled across the mattress to sit beside him. But not touching.

Seb was staring straight ahead, across the pool. Silently, she handed the glasses to him and then poured them both a drink.

'Why did you invite me over?' Mila asked, then immediately downed her drink.

Seb followed her lead, then grimaced. 'How on earth did we drink a bottle of this?'

'Why did you invite me over?' Mila repeated, ignoring him.

Seb finally held her gaze. She could tell he was, despite the darkness, simply by the intensity of him doing so.

Now that her eyes had adjusted to the mix of moon and ambient light she could make out more details of his face: a few days' worth of stubble on his jaw, lines of tension etched about his eyes and mouth.

'I need to talk,' he said. 'About Steph.' He swallowed. 'I want you to talk about Steph, too.'

The request was not unexpected, Mila knew the significance of the pool house. Knew the hundreds of memories the three of them had shared here. And of course knew the memories that should have been between only Seb and Steph.

She'd been Steph's best friend and they'd been seventeen. She *knew* Steph had lost her virginity here. She knew more details than she'd probably needed to—but then, she'd been seventeen and curious too.

Back then she'd felt occasional flutters of jealousy—she'd carried a little torch for Seb through numerous boyfriends of her own. But she'd simply boxed up her crush, not allowing it to impact on her friendship with Steph or with Seb. It had been simply what it was. Nothing more. She'd been happy for them both.

But now, only days after sleeping naked beside this man…days since he'd been inside her…it was hard. To be here beside this man and beside the memory of Steph.

'Mila?'

At some point her gaze had dropped to her hands. She'd knotted her fingers together, but now she disentangled them, laying her hands flat against her thighs.

But wasn't *all* of this hard? For both of them? She'd known that when Seb had asked her to come here. She'd known what she was doing, and she'd also known she needed to do it.

For Seb and for herself.

'When we were thirteen, I dared Steph to steal a bottle of purple glitter nail polish from that chemist near Teli's Deli. Remember it?'

Mila looked up, at Seb watching her. He nodded.

'I never thought she'd do it, but she did. No one noticed… no one knew. For about five minutes we thought we were the biggest, coolest rebels ever. And then we felt terrible. Steph started crying.'

Mila's lips quirked upwards. She was remembering how they'd sat under the shade of a Moreton Bay Fig at a park nearby, their ill-gotten contraband lying on the grass between them.

'Then I started crying too, and we ended up going home and telling Ivy. Ivy made us go back to the chemist, tell the manager what we did, and pay for it. She never told our parents, never told anyone. We didn't tell anyone, either.'

'Not even me?'

Mila shook her head. 'No.'

Seb smiled. 'Steph told me that story.'

'No!' Mila said, genuinely shocked. 'We had a *pact*!' She said it with all the latent indignation of her thirteen-year-old self.

He shrugged. 'We'd had too much to drink at a party in London one night. I can't remember why it came up. She made me promise never to tell you I knew, and she was mortified she'd told me.' He smiled. 'But I always did wonder— why didn't you tell me back then?'

'There were always some things that were just between Steph and me.'

For a while they sat in silence. Long enough for Mila to tune in to the sounds around them: the regular chirp of crickets, hidden somewhere in the lush gardens, Rustling leaves. And, further away, the muffled sounds of the occasional car travelling down the street.

'Did she tell you about us?' Seb said, then cleared his throat. 'That she wasn't happy?'

Automatically Mila went to shake her head—but then she realised that a denial would not be entirely truthful. 'We didn't speak often over the past few years,' she said. She'd do anything to turn back time and change that. 'But when we did we used to talk for hours. She'd talk about her business, about where you were living, about all the new people she was meeting. And about you. A lot. She was so proud of your success.'

Mila paused. Although they sat side by side Mila was looking straight ahead, her gaze focused on the perfect glass-like surface of the pool.

'But our conversations became shorter as they became

further apart. And I started to notice that I had to ask about you. You didn't seem to be such a large part of the life that she was sharing with me. I noticed that, but I didn't question it.'

'Why not?' Seb asked, but with only curiosity, not censure.

'Because she sounded happy. Maybe I thought she would mention it herself if there was a problem—or a problem she wanted me to know about.' Now Mila turned towards Seb, tucking her legs beneath her. 'I guess that says a lot about how our relationship changed. I was only sharing the highlights of *my* life, too. Not the messy bits.'

Seb just watched silently as she spoke, his expression unreadable.

'But mostly,' Mila said, 'I don't think I really believed it. I mean—you were both so happy. So perfect together.'

'We were far from perfect.'

'I should've asked her—'

'You wouldn't have had anything to ask if I'd been a better husband.'

'I'm sure it wasn't all your fault,' Mila said gently.

'Based on all the conversations you had with Steph about our relationship?' His words were flat. Brutal.

'Ouch.'

Seb ran his hands through his hair. Now he was looking out at the pool. 'I'm sorry. I'm being unfair.' He sighed. 'Objective me can quote all sorts of clichés about relationships being a two-way street, or say that it takes two to tango… But I was there and I knew things were breaking—that they were broken. And I did nothing. I just went to work each day, carrying on like normal.'

'What did Steph do to try and save your relationship?'

Seb didn't like that question. It was apparent in every instantly tense line of his body.

'She tried harder than me. She tried to talk about it, but I didn't want to know. She organised counselling, but I'd always cancel.'

'Why?'

'I've asked myself that a million times,' he said, with a rough facsimile of a laugh. 'At the time it was basic denial. I just didn't want to deal with it. But obviously it was more than that. Of course I knew that it was over. But I didn't want to think about what that meant. Steph and I had set up a life together. We'd left our families behind. And we'd been more successful than in our wildest dreams. If we broke up, what would happen to the perfect life we had? If the relationship that had been core to our success failed, what did that mean for everything else? I'd been with Steph for half my life. My success seemed intrinsically tied up with hers and with *her*.' He sighed. 'So that's what it came down to. Fear of failure. Pretty pathetic, huh?'

Mila didn't say a word, just allowed Seb's words to keep on flowing.

'When I noticed how much she was going out, how many nights she'd get home at crazy hours, I did ask what she was doing, but she assured me all was well. I knew it wasn't, but she was still going to work each day, her business was still doing so well...' He shook his head. 'What does that say about me? That I'd use capability for work as an indicator she was okay? Part of me knew it was destructive behaviour, knew that we were in the death throes of our marriage. I think she knew, too. But we were both just too busy to get around to ending it, to dealing with the end of Stephanie and Sebastian. It seemed impossible.'

He swallowed.

'I think she might have been seeing someone, actually. We had a memorial service in London, and there were a group of friends there I didn't recognise. I hated them instantly, because I associated them with what her life had become—the parties, the drugs. But they weren't what I expected—they looked like professionals. Young, financially secure. Which made sense. Steph overdosed in a penthouse in South Kensington, not in a gutter.'

Mila realised she was crying. Silent tears were sliding down her cheeks and dripping from her chin.

'One guy... I don't know... I just *knew*. He wouldn't look at me. And he was pretty cut up. His friends seemed to be rallying around him.'

Mila had to touch him so she slid closer, holding his hand.

'Steph's choices were not your responsibility,' Mila said softly.

'I failed her, Mila—can't you see that?' Seb said, his words firm. 'It doesn't make any difference who introduced her to her dealer, or what happened next. All that matters is that I was supposed to be there for her—more than anyone else in the world. And I wasn't. I was distant—emotionally, geographically. I was too obsessed with my company and its continued success to make time for our relationship. I even made sure I was too busy to end our relationship—to let her move on with her life. I was selfish and I was scared. I failed her.'

Mila gripped his fingers harder. 'I failed her too,' she said. 'I wasn't the best friend I was supposed to be. I let time and time zones transform us into being little more than ac- quaintances, always with the best of intentions to reignite our friendship "one day".' She wiped at her eyes ineffectively, leaving her palm damp with tears. 'One day...' she repeated.

For a long while they both sat in silence, surrounded by their choices, their mistakes, their regrets.

A leaf had marred the perfect surface of the pool, and Mila watched its slow, directionless journey across the water.

'Do you remember when Steph was going to make her fortune baking Steph's special mint slice?' Seb said, after an eternity. 'How old were you? Twelve? She even made a website on one of those awful free site-builders with a never- ending web address...'

And just like that, they started talking about Steph.

CHAPTER ELEVEN

SEB WOKE TO the warmth of the sun against his skin.

It was an effort to open his eyes because his eyelids were heavy. His whole body was heavy, in fact.

It was early—early enough that the sun was still low and able to stretch its rays into the pool house. Beside him, on her side, lay Mila. She was still asleep, with yesterday's make-up slightly smudged beneath her eyes, one arm stretched out towards him. Her singlet top was twisted at her waist, revealing a strip of pale stomach above her jeans. Her feet were bare, her shoes kicked to the ground.

But she no longer touched him. At some point as they'd slept their hands had fallen apart.

Seb couldn't remember a decision to sleep in the pool house. All he remembered was the pair of them talking. Talking and talking—sharing memories of Steph. Memories of the three of them together. Memories of Steph and Seb and also of Steph and Mila.

The bottle of peach schnapps had been abandoned early on, to be replaced with a selection of other spirits from his parents' bar. The small stack of shot glasses lined up along the wooden back of the day bed perfectly explained his lethargy, as well as the fogginess of his brain.

'Morning,' said Mila, her lovely eyes blinking at Seb sleepily.

He smiled. 'Good morning,' he replied—and it was. A *really* good morning, he decided. Today, despite the after-effects of alcohol, he felt good. Really good.

'I guess all those people telling me I needed to talk about Steph were on to something.'

Mila laughed, the sound startling a small honeyeater perched on the glass pool fence. It flew away in a flurry of flapping wings. 'Talking *is* good,' she agreed. 'I did a lot of talking early on—to Ivy especially. She's a good listener.'

'I'm sorry I was so awful to you back then,' he said. 'You wanted to talk and I wouldn't let you.'

'Yeah…' Mila said, all matter-of-fact. 'Desperately. But maybe waiting wasn't so bad. I wasn't ready to talk about the good times straight after Steph died.'

And that was what they'd done. Once they'd laid all their guilt out on the table they'd simply reminisced together. Sharing everything and anything that included Steph, and nearly every story and anecdote had led to laughter.

That was what had changed in Seb last night. For the first time since Steph's death Seb had smiled as he'd remembered her. Together he and Mila had celebrated Steph, without allowing the shackles of grief and regret to weigh them down.

He *was* moving on. He believed that now.

Together they walked inside to the empty kitchen. His parents were nowhere to be seen, and a scribbled note on the counter indicated they'd headed out for breakfast.

The time on the microwave revealed it was really time to get to work, but they both seemed comfortable in their sluggishness. Without asking, Seb poured them both a long glass of water, and they stood, not so far apart, staring out at the garden as they drank.

Later they headed for their cars. They'd still barely spoken. Mila pressed the button on her key to unlock her car, and it did so with a definite *thunk*.

'Thank you,' Seb said, stepping closer to Mila.

She smiled. 'Thank *you*. I needed last night, too.'

She turned and opened the driver's side door, tossing her bag onto the passenger seat.

'So…' he said.

Mila twisted back to face him, her gaze direct. 'What happens now?' she asked.

Mila's note hung metaphorically between them: *We can't be friends any more.*

But surely that note could now be torn up and thrown away? Surely last night had shown Mila that their friendship was the furthest they could get from the *'waste of time'* she'd claimed it to be after that first kiss?

'I won't pretend to understand why you ran away on Wednesday morning.'

'I *didn't* run away...'A pause. 'Okay,' she conceded, 'maybe I did—but I thought it was the right thing to do. Because I knew what you'd say if I'd stayed.'

'That I wanted us to stay friends?'

He desperately wanted them to. He would say anything and everything to make that happen. Last night had only underlined how important Mila was to him. How irreplaceable she was. How irreplaceable their *friendship* was.

'I can't do that, Seb.'

'Pardon me?' Seb blinked, shocked to his core. 'So last night changed *nothing*?'

He couldn't believe this. How could last night mean so much to him, but nothing to her?

Mila shook her head. 'No. It changed everything.'

Seb went still.

Mila's gaze did not waver from his. 'I can't walk away from you. Not now. But I can't just be your friend. I can't pretend any more.'

This was not what he'd expected.

'I lied,' she continued. 'When you asked me whether I wanted you to kiss me at the beach. I *did* want you to kiss me. I just hadn't admitted it to myself yet. But I did. Maybe from the moment you stepped back into my life.' Half a smile. 'I don't want to lie to myself any more.'

Seb didn't know what to think. His brain, his heart, his pulse—everything—was ratcheting every which way.

'I wanted that kiss, too,' he said. Now was not the time for the subterfuge that Mila had once said she hated. 'I wanted *you*,' he clarified.

'Wanted?' she prompted.

'Want,' he said, running a hand through his hair, frustrated, because of course that was true. He wanted Mila. 'But I was hoping to manage that. For the sake of our friendship I thought I could withstand a bit of sexual tension—'

Mila laughed out loud.

He knew it sounded ridiculous. But he didn't know how else to deal with this. Of any other way to cope.

'I didn't expect this,' he said. 'I wanted our friendship back. Nothing more.'

Mila laughed again, this time high-pitched. 'And you think this is what *I* want?'

'What *do* you want?' Seb asked.

There was the slightest wobble to her gaze. Subtle, but there.

'I don't want to pretend around you,' she said. 'That's all I know.'

'I don't want to hurt you. And I don't want to lose you. And I have no idea how to stop both those things happening if we're anything more than friends.'

Abruptly, Mila climbed into her seat, calmly clicking her seat belt into place. 'We're *not* just friends, Seb,' she said, her words sharp. 'How can you say you want me in one breath and try to talk me into remaining your friend in the next?'

'We did it before—after that kiss,' he said, stubbornly refusing to concede. 'Why can't we do it again?'

Mila shook her head, breathing an angry, frustrated sigh. She reached for the door, to pull it shut. He could have held the door, forced her to keep it open, but what would that have achieved?

So instead he dropped to his haunches, laying his hand over hers. They'd spent most of the night holding hands. As friends, then, nothing more.

He'd hoped maybe by touching her now that he could prove his point. That they could put Tuesday night behind them. That he could show her how the electricity between them had abated.

As his fingers brushed her skin he realised how very wrong he was.

His gaze shot up, tangling with hers.

'No, we're not just friends,' he repeated.

He crouched between the partially open door and Mila. Her hand had fallen away from the door handle and he held it in both of his.

Outside of the sanctuary of the pool house—outside of that bubble they'd created for their memories—they were right back where they'd started. Right where they'd been since he'd walked into Mila's shop that very first evening.

Sensation shot between them where they touched. His body's reaction was visceral, needing her, wanting her.

No. He was too selfish. Too damaged. And Mila was too fragile. Ben, her dad…their appalling behaviour was still so fresh…

But all that made no difference. *Yes* was all his body could say.

Mila was looking away, out through the windscreen. 'I know you said you weren't ready for a relationship,' she said. 'And I don't think I'm ready either.'

Seb still held her hand. He ran his thumb along her palm, then loosely traced the shape of her fingers.

'So where does that leave us?' she continued, her words soft and breathy. 'Not friends. Not a relationship.'

'Does it matter?' Seb said. 'How about we just focus on not being friends for a while.'

'Not being friends?' She smiled. 'I like that.' Mila reached out again for the door handle. 'But I really have to get to work. My shop is supposed to open in—'

Seb silenced her with a kiss.

Ivy was working at the office today, so she arrived at the small café near April's place in her chauffeur-driven car.

Mila had arrived first, so she watched Ivy approach from her seat in the small booth she'd chosen at the rear of the café. Every person eating there watched her sister approach—people always did. Ivy had such an air of confidence and authority that she just drew people to her.

Today she wore one of her typically sharp work outfits—black cigarette pants with red-soled black pumps, cream sleeveless blouse tucked in neatly, and oversized Hollywood sunglasses. She looked exactly like the billion-odd dollars she was worth.

Ivy smiled as she spotted Mila, and whipped off her sunglasses. Her sister hurried over, completely unaware that she was the centre of attention. Mila smiled—her sister was definitely the most down-to-earth billionaire on the planet. Just one of the several hundred reasons Mila loved her.

She'd invited Ivy and April to lunch on a whim. The past week had been just...*so much*. Too much to process. Really, everything that had happened since she'd had that taxi drop her off at Seb's apartment building had been intense.

She needed her sisters.

Ivy slid into the booth beside Mila and together they perused the menu. April was always late, but she did manage to turn up only a few minutes past twelve. She glided into the café, the total antithesis of efficient, focused Ivy.

Today she was very much Boho, with her long blonde hair in loose curls that cascaded over the thin straps of her pale pink maxi-dress and the collection of fine gold necklaces that decorated the deep V of her bodice. But even dressed casually, April looked as if she'd walked off the pages of a magazine. Not that such a polished, perfect appearance came without effort, despite her sister's natural gorgeousness. Especially now that April traded so heavily on her appearance.

'Apologies!' April said, by way of a greeting. 'I have no perception of time. Hey—can I get the annoying selfie request out of the way? Mila, I'll tag your shop—it's sure to drive a few more sales. People went nuts for those concrete vase things the other week.'

'Molyneux Mining doesn't do social media,' pointed out Ivy. 'Or have any need to drum up business.'

'Nope,' April said cheerfully. 'But everyone loves a photo of Ivy Molyneux acting like a normal human being. I'm sure your marketing people have worked out how much your customer whatsit scores improved after you were papped with Nate at the supermarket.'

'You know,' Ivy said, 'reminding me of the time I was photographed without make-up and with baby spew on my shoulder is probably *not* the best way to convince me of anything.'

'Pfft!' said April. 'You always look beautiful. Plus you had a six-foot-four commando pushing your trolley. All anyone was thinking was, *Phwoar!'*

Ivy looked at Mila. 'I'm really not sure I'm following our sister's argument.'

'Just let her take the picture,' Mila advised. 'Then we'll get to eat.'

A few minutes of posing, and judicious application of filters, and April was happily hashtagging away while Mila went to order for them all at the counter.

She watched her sisters chatting as she waited in the queue. They were both so different—from each other and from Mila. Mila had always thought she was more like Ivy—more through process of elimination rather than any obvious similarities. Mila's view of life just seemed to have more of an acerbic edge than April's, and she guessed she identified with Ivy's more serious personality. But she was equally close to them both. April's sunniness and optimism were contagious, while Ivy could always be relied on for her wisdom—even if it was not always requested.

But Mila knew she wasn't going to tell them about Seb today.

It wasn't like her not to tell her sisters about men she was dating. It wasn't like her not to tell them about *anything*. It was just…she wasn't dating Seb.

What they had was too intangible. Heck, if she and Seb couldn't even give it a name what was there to tell anyone, anyway? That she and Seb *weren't* friends any more? But that they also weren't quite anything else?

No. It was definitely better to say nothing.

At the front of the queue, Mila ordered efficiently, then collected a frosty bottle of water and three small tumblers. Back at the table she poured them all a glass of water, then fell into the deep red padded seat of the booth. All her muscles ached—her body was remembering exactly how much she'd drunk last night, and how late she'd been up talking.

Eventually she realised her sisters were talking about their dad.

'I couldn't believe it,' Ivy was saying, 'when my assistant told me. It's been *years*.'

'What did he want?'

Ivy shrugged. 'I have no idea. I didn't return his calls.'

'Me either,' April said. 'Do you know he's finally worked out social media? His accounts are following all mine now. I did consider blocking him, but it seemed pretty petty when I share my photos and ramblings with literally everyone else in the universe.'

'I blocked him,' Mila said quietly. 'And my business accounts don't even have enough followers that I can really afford to do that.'

Blaine had called her, too, but there'd been no chance of her answering.

'So that's it, then?' Ivy asked. 'You're done?'

Mila nodded. 'Yes. *So* done. No more chances.'

'You sure?' April asked, looking over the top of her water glass.

Mila raised her eyebrows. 'Really?' she said. 'I thought you'd be overjoyed.'

'I am,' Ivy said firmly.

April rolled her eyes. 'I just wanted to make sure this was *your* decision. Not ours. Because it's a big one.'

Mila nodded. 'I get it. But, no—this one was definitely *all* on Blaine. Although—just so it's noted—you were both absolutely right. I should've stopped answering his calls years ago.'

She'd given Ivy and April a condensed version of her night at the film premiere—with the beach scene with Seb completely removed.

'Of course,' Ivy said with a grin.

Their lunches arrived, and Mila sat back in the booth as the waiter organised their food on the table. She'd ordered gnocchi, with a chunky tomato sauce piled on top.

Her sisters were sharing anecdotes about their dad. Each demonstrated his uselessness perfectly, and each, with the benefit of time, had become humorous. All of Blaine's failures preceded with a dramatic, *'And then he—'*

She smiled along with them, but wasn't really paying attention. Instead, all she could think about was Seb.

Had she done the right thing?

She was so confused. She'd thought she'd already dealt with this. The morning she'd walked out of Seb's apartment she'd thought she'd walked out of his life.

Last night, in the pool house, had been important. She was glad she'd followed her instincts when he'd called—glad she'd been there with him. Both for Seb and for herself. For the first time since Stephanie's death she'd laughed as she'd thought about her. Smiled as she'd remembered the girl, and the woman, who had been such a significant part of her life.

So that had been good. Great. But after…? Outside Seb's parents' house…?

She'd followed her gut once again—followed an almost primeval need to be authentic, to refuse to accept Seb's faux friendship, but this time also to refuse to deny the pull she felt to Seb.

When he touched her she could think of nothing else but him—the sensation of his hands against her skin was electric, compelling, addictive.

With Seb, whenever she was with him, it had just always felt *right*. And that, in itself, made her uncomfortable.

Because even *rightness* seemed an unlikely concept—too similar to her habit of manufacturing pretty delusions, like her fanciful hopes with her dad, rather than facing reality. It certainly wasn't something she could trust or rely upon as a gauge of anything real or substantial.

Mila's fork scraped against the bottom of her plate. She'd eaten most of her lunch, and now simply pushed the remaining little balls of gnocchi around in circles.

'You okay, hon?' Ivy bumped her shoulder against Mila's. 'You've been very quiet.'

It was tempting. It would be so very easy to tell them all that had happened in the past few days. She trusted them both. Completely. But she couldn't.

They'd disapproved of her persistence with their dad. They'd worried for her, and been there for her, but they'd never approved. They'd never really understood why she kept putting herself through something where the final destination was always going to be hurt and tears.

Would they think she was on the same journey now, with Seb?

He'd told her he didn't want a relationship, which Mila knew really meant that he didn't want a relationship with *her*. His words that night at the beach had made that clear: *'This is wrong...'*

It didn't get much clearer than that, despite all the supposed *rightness* she thought she felt.

She'd told herself that she'd keep an emotional distance from Seb. That this was just about a physical attraction. This was about them both each needing each other—right now—and nothing more. She wasn't ready for a relationship. She didn't even want a relationship with Seb...

And most importantly she kept telling herself that she'd learnt from what had happened with Ben, from what had happened with her dad. She was still in control. She wasn't going to get hurt.

But would Ivy and April believe that? Did *she*?

She didn't think she could face it—her sisters' concern for the naïve little sister they had to look out for.

No. She was an adult. She'd made her choice. She had to live with it—without her big sisters holding her hand.

'I'm fine!' she said with a smile. 'Really. Okay—now, who wants to share a slice of carrot cake with me?'

CHAPTER TWELVE

Seb knocked on the back door of Mila's Nest after work. They hadn't organised for him to come over, but Mila had known he would.

Mila had been wiping down the tables in the workshop and collecting stray pieces of clay left over from her students' endeavours. Sheri had already gone home, and the *'Closed'* sign was hung on the shop's front door. She had the radio playing, and an enthusiastic voice was currently describing the peak hour traffic conditions in significant detail.

Mila took her time walking to the door. She might have known that Seb would come over, but now that he was here she wasn't entirely sure how she felt about it.

She was acutely aware of her own heartbeat, madly accelerating away within her chest. Her cheeks felt warm too, as if she could feel Seb's gaze already—irrespective of the solid wooden door separating them.

Seb knocked again just as Mila's hand grasped the door handle, making her jump.

It seemed impossible that this time yesterday she'd been convinced she'd never see Sebastian Fyfe again.

Finally she swung open the door, and then the security screen. Seb waited impatiently, his gaze distracting, exactly as intense as she'd imagined.

'Hey,' he said.

Mila stepped back, gesturing with her arm that he should come inside. As she closed the door behind them, her back to Seb as she deadbolted the door and slid the security chain into place, she wondered what to do now.

Did she invite him to stay for dinner? Did they go out somewhere for a drink? She had no idea what the protocols were for not being friends.

She pivoted to face him. 'So,' she said. 'How do you want to do this?'

'Well,' he said, reaching for her, then tugging her close. 'How about we start with a kiss?'

And just like that his mouth was on hers, and Mila was incapable of thinking about anything but how good that felt.

She kissed him back as she drew him closer, twining her hands around his neck and her fingers in his hair. His hands were firm against her: at the small of her back and at her waist. Her T-shirt had ridden up, just a little, and when his hand touched her skin her belly flooded with warmth. But it wasn't nearly enough—she needed more. She was greedy for it.

There was a thunking sound as Seb's back hit the closed door behind him, and he smiled against Mila's mouth. She smiled right back as he moved her, and then she was the one against the door. Seb's shoulders—his height—boxed her in, but it was a delicious sensation…the sense of Seb's power, his passion—he wanted her. And of course she was an equal in this. She wanted him just as desperately—with her own touch: her mouth, her hands, she was just as powerful.

There was a freedom to this kiss. This was a kiss where there would be another. This wasn't a one-time chance. This wasn't a spur-of-the-moment decision.

Because Mila didn't just have Seb for tonight. She had him until…

Until when?

Beyond tomorrow, yes—but how long after that? Days, weeks, months? Until she wanted to end it? Or until Seb did?

Seb went still, his lips against Mila's neck. 'You're thinking too much,' he said, his breath hot against her skin. 'Is something wrong?'

She shook her head, then slid her hands beneath his shirt. His stomach was firm, his belt a hard edge beneath her palm.

'No,' she said. Firmly. Because nothing was wrong—and

nothing *would* be wrong. Unwanted thoughts of the future just fed into her old habits and unreliable hopes and dreams.

All she needed to worry about was right now. Not tomorrow, next week or next month. And right now only one thing was important to her.

'Kiss me again,' she said.

And he did—many more times than once—then followed Mila up the stairs to her apartment, holding her hand.

On Tuesday, Seb brought Mila lunch. She was busy with customers and classes, and he had a meeting to get to—but still he brought her lunch. He'd said he would, and he did—and that made Mila smile as she watched him stride from her shop, her gaze admiring the broadness of his shoulders.

Later, they ate fish and chips on Cottesloe Beach. Stealthy seagulls hovered just beyond the unravelled butcher's paper packaging, and the sea breeze blew Mila's hair in every direction.

They ate in the next evening, out on the balcony at Seb's place. The views across to the river were spectacular as they cradled crusty bread rolls filled with chevups, barbecued onions and tomato sauce.

The next night was Mila's monthly dinner with her mum and her sisters. Again, she didn't mention Seb—but this time, she did so with confidence.

At lunch at that café, she'd second guessed her decision, unused to keeping secrets from her sisters. But now, it just made sense.

She'd told Seb weeks ago that she hadn't yet worked out how to protect herself from getting hurt, but keeping their not-a-relationship secret felt like part of it. It was all part of keeping an emotional distance—of not imagining more than there actually was.

As soon as they told people expectations would be created. By others. By herself.

And without expectations, Mila was simply enjoying herself.

Really—if she thought about it—wasn't it *better* that she didn't leap back into a relationship after what had happened with Ben? Wasn't just relaxing and having a bit of fun a *good* thing?

And this thing with Seb was definitely *good*. She couldn't remember feeling this way before—all fluttery and displaced whenever she was around him. Or even when she thought of him. It hadn't been like that with Ben. Mila didn't know what it was. Maybe the remnants of her heart-pounding, hormone-infused teenage crush?

It must be, she decided.

And so—once again—she didn't breathe a word about Seb.

On Sunday, Seb and Mila sat side by side at one of the benches in Mila's workshop.

It wasn't too early—they'd both slept in, waking up tangled in Mila's sheets.

Seb had headed out in search of coffee and croissants, and now he tore off pieces of pastry from within a brown paper bag as he listened to Mila's instructions.

He'd asked, last night, about her classes, curious to know how her business had evolved. It hadn't surprised him at all to learn it had begun with a challenge: Ivy had proclaimed herself lacking any artistic ability, and the challenge had been on.

'To be honest,' Mila had said, 'she made a pretty awful little pot. But we had fun, and the idea just went from there. Most of my students haven't done anything arty since high school.' Somehow she'd convinced him to have a go himself. 'Don't stress,' she'd assured him, 'you're exactly my demographic.'

So here they were: a pair of Lazy Susans sitting before them, a small circle of clay placed in the centre of each.

'Right,' Mila said. 'Now we've got the bases done, we've

got to start rolling out our coils.' She handed Seb a lump of clay. 'Roll away.'

Seb dutifully followed Mila's instructions as she explained the technique they were using. 'You probably remember this from school—and maybe pinch pots, as well?'

Seb nodded as Mila showed him how to score the top of the long sausage he'd rolled out with a pen-shaped wooden tool she called a needle.

'In my adult classes we always start with these hand-building techniques before we move on to the wheel. Anyone can master them, and it gives everyone a bit of confidence as they're getting started. The kids love it too, and I love the wonkiness of their coils, the gaps they often leave between layers.'

Seb watched as Mila quickly rolled out her own coil, and then scored both the sausage and the circle of clay on her Lazy Susan. She then handed the needle to Seb, so he could score his own base.

'Now, we need just a little bit of water,' she said, dipping her fingers in the small bowl between them. She rubbed her fingers over the scored surfaces, returning for more water as needed. 'Then we join the coil to the base, using our thumbs to blend the clay.'

Seb followed Mila's instructions and soon they were both busily building their own pots, quietly rolling, scoring and stacking.

'You're very patient,' Seb said.

Mila smiled. 'That's a learned skill. Particularly with the kids. It used to be so tempting to take over and fix their mistakes. Now I know just to sit back and let them form their own creations.'

She was smoothing the outside of her pot with a rubber paddle, merging each coil into its neighbour.

Seb had finished his pot, too. It had ended up squatter than Mila's, with a wide mouth and a lopsidedness that he hadn't intended.

Mila transported both their pots to the kiln, Seb's little odd pot in stark contrast to Mila's pot of sleek perfection.

'It seems a waste of clay,' Seb said, looking at them both on the kiln shelves. 'You could make a much nicer pot out of it.'

'No!' Mila said, appalled. 'Don't say that. It's perfect.'

It really wasn't. Impulsively, he kissed her. Hard.

'What was that for?'

He met her gaze as they broke apart. 'For teaching me pottery.'

Mila eyes sparkled. 'Coil pots were on your bucket list?'

"Not quite," he said, and shoved his hands into his pockets, trying to explain. 'It's just—I've never seen you work before, or teach. This all happened while I've been away.' It was weird, really. Rather than highlighting how far they'd drifted apart in the past six years, Mila's pottery lesson instead seemed to fill in gaps—and draw them closer. 'You're really good at this.'

Mila's smile was wide. 'Thank you. So—you'll be signing up for my 8 week adult beginner's class, then?'

'No,'Seb said. Firmly.

And Mila burst into laughter.

CHAPTER THIRTEEN

THEY'D FALLEN ASLEEP in front of the TV. Seb was stretched across Mila's sofa, with Mila sprawled over him. His arm beneath her was numb, and his neck ached from the odd angle it was resting in against the arm of the sofa.

The series they'd been watching had stopped streaming, and the screen was politely asking if they were still there. But Seb couldn't quite reach his phone or the TV remote, so the question remained unanswered. He considered waking Mila. Her head was nestled against his shoulder, her dark hair tickling his jaw.

Her bed would be much more comfortable.

But Mila slept so peacefully, her breathing slow and regular, her long eyelashes fanning her cheeks.

It had been more than two weeks now, since they'd been 'not just friends'. They'd spent nearly every night together, and all day at the weekends.

It should have felt intense. Overwhelming, even. But it didn't.

Instead it felt completely natural. The obvious thing to do.

It also felt like a lot more than their admittedly silly construct of 'not just friends'. It felt like a relationship.

During the day he didn't let his thoughts drift in that direction. During the day, the concept was unwelcome. During the day he knew all the reasons why he couldn't commit to something more with Mila.

But at times like this—in the silence, while he lay beside a sleeping Mila—he questioned why that was. Because in the silence their being together felt easy. It felt right. It didn't feel complicated, or rife with difficult emotions and unavoidable hurt and disappointment.

At these times Seb had to remind himself who he was,

and who Mila was. Remind himself that Mila deserved more than a man incapable of truly engaging in a relationship. Of being there for his partner. Of giving her the love that she deserved.

But lying here, in the silence, with Mila in his arms…

So, no, he didn't wake her.

Instead he ignored his aches and discomfort and held her closer—listening to the rhythm of her breathing, of her sleep, and of her dreams.

He must have carried her to bed, Mila realised.

She stretched luxuriously across the mattress, her outstretched fingertips brushing the vintage cast-iron bedhead. She was still dressed in the T-shirt she'd worn last night; her jeans were in a puddle on the carpet.

Or maybe she'd been so tired she didn't remember Seb waking her. She rolled onto her side, tugging the sheets with her. Seb slept soundly beside her, flat on his back, wearing only a pair of navy blue boxer shorts, just visible above the sheet. One arm rested by his head, the other by his side, his hand flat on his belly.

With her gaze she explored all the muscles she still wasn't quite used to. The hardness of his body—he was all angles and solid surfaces. No softness. He looked incredibly strong.

His eyes slid open. 'Hey,' he said, all sleepily. 'I could feel you looking at me.'

'I was,' Mila said, with a smile.

'And what were you thinking?'

'Whether you carried me to bed.'

Seb had turned onto his side now, to face her, the sheet falling way past his hips as he did so. 'It would be more romantic if I had, right?'

'Of course,' Mila said.

'Then,' he said, leaning closer, 'I did.'

He kissed her, and for long, long minutes Mila was lost in the miracle of his kiss.

When they finally broke apart he grinned. 'Just for full disclosure, you also did not drool on my shoulder during episode seven.'

Mila shoved him in the shoulder. 'I do *not* drool!'

'Who said you did?' said Seb, eyes twinkling, and then somehow Mila had rolled on top of him, and they were kissing each other hard, and soft, and thoroughly, until the remainder of their clothing also hit the floor.

Later, Mila rested her head on his chest, Seb's arm snug beneath her breasts.

'If you want,' Seb said very softly, his breath tickling her ear, 'I'll carry you to bed tonight. Every night, actually, if you like.'

And for some reason those words made Mila smile, and also made her eyes sting with tears.

Suddenly this all just felt *too* good. *Too* perfect.

She lifted his arm off her and wriggled away and out of bed. He looked at her, confused.

'Where you going?'

'Breakfast!' she said, with probably too much enthusiasm. 'What would you like?'

Usually on a Tuesday afternoon Mila worked alone in her workshop. Sheri manned the shop, and Mila sat at her pottery wheel and created.

Today she once again sat beside Seb at a workbench, their now fired coil pots before them, both currently the unadulterated off-white of the clay. Seb had called earlier—he'd had an afternoon meeting cancelled. She'd invited him over without hesitation, and had kissed him the moment she'd opened the workshop door, equally so.

She did wonder when this would wear off. The little rush of butterflies in her stomach whenever she saw Seb. Or when he texted her. Or when her phone rang and his name came up on the screen.

Part of her wanted it to. Because without these tingles

and this excitement—this would end. There would be no more unspoken questions about what they were really doing or how long it would last. She would no longer have to halt her traitorous imagination which was so irresponsibly extrapolating their current closeness into plans for the future. A future with many more nights and weekends with Seb.

And that was unwise. Because there were no expectations between them.

She knew that, and she had to remember that. She had to learn from her past mistakes.

Seb had picked up his slightly wonky pot, and was carefully sanding away any imperfections, exactly as Mila had instructed. She leant towards him, balancing her hand on his jeans-clad thigh, and kissed his cheek. Immediately Seb placed his pot back on the table—without much care—and kissed her back on the mouth, quite thoroughly.

'Now, *this*,' Seb said, his voice rough against her ear, 'is a very interesting lesson...'

'Oh, good!' Mila said, leaning back and away from him, hiding her smile. She turned back to the pots and materials in front of them. 'It's always so exciting when my students are enthusiastic about glazes. But first—let's learn all about using a wax resist.'

Seb raised his eyebrows.

Mila picked up a small bowl filled with pale blue liquid and a foam brush. She then explained to Seb how the wax resist would prevent the glaze from gluing their pots to her kiln, and then spent some time on more decorative uses of the product.

As she applied the liquid carefully to the base of her pot Seb dragged his stool closer to hers, the wooden legs noisy against the floor. She glanced up. Seb was now so close their shoulders bumped.

'I was too far away,' he explained, his expression deliberately innocent. 'I think it's important I see every detail of this process. For my pottery education.'

Mila bit her lip so she wouldn't smile. 'I really admire your diligence.'

'Oh,' he said, leaning even closer, 'I really admire your—'

A loud knock made Mila gasp. She pushed her stool backwards, away from Seb, hard enough that it fell to the floor with a clatter.

Seb didn't move at all. Instead he simply looked up towards the open workshop door and through the locked security screen.

'Hello, Ivy,' he said simply.

With a deep breath Mila made herself calmly retrieve her fallen chair, put it back where it belonged, then turn to face her sister.

'Hi!' she said, sounding respectably close to normal. 'What a nice surprise.'

'Is it?' Ivy asked, looking confused. 'Don't we do this every week?'

From his pram, Nate gave a happy baby shout, his hands full of Ivy's mail—colourful flyers and envelopes with plastic windows.

Mila shook her head, unable to believe she'd completely forgotten about Ivy and Nate's visit.

Stupid heart-fluttering distracting tingles.

She strode to the door with a smile, unlocking the door to let Ivy and Nate in. 'Of course,' she said. 'I'm sorry. I don't know what I was thinking.'

Ivy was smiling as she pushed Nate's pram over the small doorstep. 'I could probably make a reasonable guess.'

Mila's cheeks warmed, but she didn't say a thing. Surely through the fly screen Ivy couldn't have seen too much?

Seb didn't seem to care. He walked over to kiss Ivy's cheek, then dropped down to Nate's level to smile at him.

'So,' Ivy said, 'taking some private pottery classes, then, Seb?'

Seb glanced at Mila.

She glared at him. *Don't tell Ivy.*

His forehead crinkled in confusion. 'Yes,' he said, standing up. 'I am.'

Ivy blinked. 'Oh. Should I go, then? I don't want to intrude on your lesson time.'

'You're not,' Mila interjected quickly. 'We were just finishing up.'

'Really?' Ivy said, looking at the still neat table. She knew exactly what the workshop looked like at the end of one of Mila's classes.

'It would seem so,' Seb said.

That wasn't at all helpful, and Mila shot him a pointed look. Why couldn't he just go along with this?

Instead his gaze was flat, unreadable.

'Look,' Ivy said, glancing between Mila and Seb, 'I *am* going to go.'

'Don't—' Mila began, but Ivy cut her off.

'No,' her sister said. 'I should definitely go.'

Ivy backed the pram away from Seb, then pushed it towards the door. She retrieved Mila's mail from Nate and handed it to Mila with a long, concerned look. 'You okay?' she asked, very softly.

Mila just nodded, then opened the door.

'I'll call you later,' Ivy said over her shoulder as she pushed Nate out the door.

Nate wailed in protest as they walked through the small rear courtyard and out to the access lane.

Quite firmly, Mila locked the security door, then shut the wooden door with a heavy thud. She didn't think it would work, but she tried it anyway:

'So,' Mila said with a forced smile. 'Should we get back to the wonderful world of glazing techniques?'

'No,' Seb said. 'I don't think we should.'

Mila nodded. 'I'm sorry that was a bit weird,' she said, with a deliberately casual tone.

'It *was* weird,' Seb said. 'Why?'

Seb hadn't moved, so they stood a good distance apart—Seb near the workbench, Mila beside the door.

Her instinct was to move closer to him. She didn't like being so far away, especially when he was looking at her like that—not that she could really interpret it. Disillusioned, maybe? But why?

'It's no big deal,' Mila said, attempting a nonchalant shrug. 'I just didn't want Ivy to know about us.'

She marched back towards him, dropping her mail on the workbench. Now she was closer to Seb, but he was still a few, frustrating steps away, in the middle of the workshop. She picked up a bowl of glaze, stirring it unnecessarily.

'Why not?'

'What's there to tell?' Mila said. The glaze was a murky blue colour—a shade that would magically metamorphose into an incredible vibrant purple in the kiln.

Seb crossed his arms. 'I was unaware that I was your dirty little secret.'

Mila paused in her stirring to catch his gaze. 'Now, *that* is a little dramatic,' she said.

'I don't know,' Seb said. 'You weren't at all happy to be seen with me.'

'Well,' Mila said, 'I wasn't aware that you'd been telling everyone about us. What did your parents think when you told them you were sleeping with me?'

There was a long pause. 'I haven't told them,' he said eventually.

'Exactly!' Mila said. 'So why do you care that I haven't told my sisters?'

'Because if my parents walked into a room while you and I were talking, or flirting—or kissing, even—there is no way I would run away from you.'

It was on the tip of her tongue: *I didn't run away!* But of course she had.

'So in this hypothetical situation,' Mila said, even more

defensive now, 'with you and me standing together and your parents right in front of us, what exactly would you say?'

'I don't know,' Seb said. 'I'd work it out at the time.'

Mila shook her head. 'No. You can't be all offended and up on your high horse with me and get away with that. Tell me—I want to know what you would say. How you would describe *us*.'

'It's no one's business but ours what we do,' Seb said. 'We don't need to define ourselves to anybody.'

Mila rolled her eyes. 'I'm really struggling to see how our positions are all that different.'

Seb ran his hands through his hair, his frustration obvious in every tense line of his body. 'I am aware that I'm not making the most logical argument,' he said. Then he sighed. 'All I know is that I really didn't like it when you wanted to hide us from Ivy. I really didn't.'

She hadn't liked it either, but she hadn't felt she had a choice.

Unless...

'Define *us*,' Mila said. Softly.

'Pardon me?'

At some point Mila had placed the bowl of glaze back on the table. Now she stepped close to Seb. 'If you want me to tell Ivy, and April, and everybody else in my life, then let me know what to say.' She smiled, but carefully.

'I didn't think you wanted to tell anybody?' Seb said. 'Isn't that what we're arguing about?'

He was right, but somehow Mila had moved on from that. She didn't care about Ivy right now, or what anyone thought.

Seb had said he didn't want to hide what they had. Deep down, Mila didn't either.

What did that mean?

'Define *us*,' she repeated.

He looked uncomfortable, shifting his weight from foot to foot. But in typical Seb fashion his gaze didn't falter, even as she could practically see the cogs in his brain whirring at full speed.

'I thought you were happy with this—with our…' He paused. 'With us.'

Our relationship. That was what he couldn't say.

That bothered her. And it really bothered her that it did.

'I thought I was,' she said. 'I thought we were both on the same page. It appears we're not.'

Seb shoved his hands into the pockets of his jeans. 'Can we just forget the past twenty minutes ever happened?'

'No.'

'Didn't you want to forget it had ever happened just five minutes ago?'

She shrugged. 'I changed my mind.'

There was a long silence. Seb just looked at her—*really* looked at her—as if trying to work out what she was thinking.

Which would be difficult, as she didn't really know herself.

This was too contradictory. Too confusing.

'Mila?'

She'd been quiet too long. They both had. The silence was heavy with too much… Just too much. Too much thinking, too much everything.

'I *really* want to forget this ever happened, Mila,' Seb was saying. His lips quirked upwards. 'This is the most fun I've had in…as long as I can remember. Years.'

'Me too,' she said. She couldn't pretend otherwise.

She realised she was tangling her fingers together and pulled her hands apart, laying her palms flat against her hips.

'You know,' Mila said, 'we weren't supposed to see each other every day.'

'What do you mean?'

Mila glanced down at her scarlet-painted toes and her tan sandal straps. 'This isn't what I expected.'

'This isn't what I expected, either,' said Seb. But he didn't elaborate.

'I think I need a definition, Seb. I need to know what *this* is.'

Mila knew this was all wrong—that this went against everything she'd been telling herself—but she was completely unable to stop it.

All along she'd been telling Seb that she didn't want to lie to herself. That she didn't want to pretend. But wasn't that exactly what she was doing? In the guise of keeping her distance? Of protecting herself?

She lifted her gaze, meeting his. Waiting.

'What *are* we, Seb?' she prompted.

'We're good,' he said, his voice a little rough. 'We're right. Things feel right when I'm with you.'

'And?' she prompted. They were nice words, but they didn't actually mean anything.

He was looking at her so intensely, looking right inside her.

'That's it,' he said. 'That's all I can offer.'

Nothing had changed.

Two weeks of laughing and pottery lessons, dinner and romantic mornings in bed…all irrelevant. They were still exactly where they'd started. Where they'd always been going: nowhere.

She'd known that. But it hadn't mattered. Now, for all her personal pep talks, she wanted more.

Now, she had a choice.

She could walk away—as she'd been trying to do ever since Seb had walked back into her life. It was the obvious decision. The intelligent one. If she had any chance of retaining control over her heart—and the pain that might be inflicted upon it—that was exactly what she should do.

Or she could stay. Which was the wrong decision. The nonsensical one. The one that had her all tangled up and clinging to hopes and dreams that would never materialise.

That would lead, inevitably, to rejection. Because Seb would move on—just as Ben had. He would reject her—just as her father had.

But of course it was too late. Because the idea of not seeing Seb again—or even not seeing Seb *tomorrow*—made her heart ache.

She wasn't strong enough to walk away.

She hated that.

'Mila?'

Calmly, she picked up the bowl of glaze again and settled herself back on her stool. She looked up at Seb and smiled. And it was genuine—even after all that just looking at him made her heart sing. It was infuriating, but it was also reality.

'Should we get back to glazing your pot?'

She could see the disquiet in his gaze. Reality had intruded. Mila could no longer pretend that what they had was anything but temporary.

Seb had never wavered from thinking it was. That was obvious. And she'd made her choice. For however long this lasted.

But Seb had a choice, too. The perfect bubble surrounding their idyllic not-a-relationship had been destroyed with awkward questions and incomplete answers. Was this still what Seb wanted? Would he walk away? The way Mila couldn't?

The legs of Seb's stool scraped loudly on the floor as he dragged it beside Mila's.

'Teach me everything you know about glazes,' he said.

Mila laughed out loud. 'That could take a while.'

And so—for now, at least—it seemed Seb had made his choice, too.

CHAPTER FOURTEEN

MILA STOOD IN front of Seb's bathroom mirror. She'd stayed over last night. They'd made their own pizza and talked about their days. It had all seemed pretty normal—really no different from any other evening over the past few weeks.

Except Seb hadn't stayed over at *her* place the night before—the night of their disastrous discussion in her workshop. She hadn't invited him to stay, and he hadn't asked. At the time, some space had seemed like a good idea.

By the next morning she'd missed him. They'd organised to meet up after work—she'd told him she'd make up a batch of pizza dough and bring it over. When he'd called he'd sounded completely normal. She'd sounded normal too, she thought.

She hadn't really *felt* normal, though.

And there was a tension between them now. A tension she really didn't like.

Except when they touched. Or kissed. Or made love. Then—well, then there was still tension. But it was the delicious kind. The kind that made the preceding tension worth ignoring, or at the very least worth forgetting about.

But later—like now, as Mila got ready for work—there was nothing to distract her. To make her forget. Instead it was just obvious that everything had changed.

Seb stepped into the bathroom, his length reflected in the mirror. His gaze caught hers momentarily. He was working on site today, so was in his work clothes, his feet still bare.

His gaze didn't reveal much. Although there wasn't really anything to hide. It was crystal-clear what was going on.

No longer could they blithely carry on as they had before. Now they both knew they wanted different things.

Mila had reflected, of course, on how exactly she'd

wanted Seb to answer her question. How she'd wanted Seb to define them.

There was really only one possible answer: she'd wanted Seb to say that she was his girlfriend.

It wasn't something she'd consciously considered. Up until the point when she'd asked Seb she hadn't allowed herself to think like that. Even now the concept felt slightly strange…that she could—theoretically—be Seb's *girlfriend*. It was a foreign label after a lifetime of friendship. But it was also the logical label—because she'd known the moment Ivy had walked in and seen them together that she wanted something more. Even as she had attempted to hide their relationship from her sister, she'd also wanted to flaunt it. And it was that contradiction that had fuelled her frustration, fuelled her need to demand from Seb answers he'd been unprepared to give.

But she couldn't regret asking her questions. No matter how badly Seb's response had hurt her.

With those questions she'd gained knowledge, and with that knowledge, choices. She might not have taken the opportunity to walk away from Seb then, but the option remained.

When it came to the men in her life, in recent memory she hadn't had a heck of a lot of control. It had been *their* choices that had impacted on *her*—while she'd had no choices at all.

So she *would* walk away from Seb—when she was ready. The uncomfortable tension between them meant it would probably be sooner rather than later, and that realisation was a sharp blow to her heart.

Mila brushed her teeth, as did Seb.

He applied sunscreen with a tropical coconut scent to his face, neck and arms as she did her make-up. Their eyes met again in the mirror as Mila applied her mascara.

And just like that the tension shifted. No longer awkward, but luxurious. Warm. *Hot*.

Mila re-capped her mascara calmly, placing it on the marble vanity. Then she turned to face Seb.

His gaze travelled all over her—caressing her legs, hips, waist, breasts…lips.

Mila smiled, then stood on her bare tiptoes to press her mouth against his. And that was that. The kiss was as intense and sexy and amazing and emotional as every kiss they'd ever had.

And later—with reapplied make-up and slightly rumpled clothing—when Mila walked out of the apartment building to her car she knew why she hadn't walked away.

Because not everything had changed between them. The connection between them that pulled them together so intensely had not deviated. It hadn't since that first kiss on the beach.

And that connection was so strong, and so unique—at least to Mila—she wasn't quite prepared to let go of it just yet.

A heatwave hit Perth the next day.

Seb stood on the side of the pool, his toes curling over the stone edging.

The diving board was long gone, tossed out during one of his parents' renovations. He missed it right now. He missed the way it would bend beneath his weight. He missed the slightly rough surface beneath the soles of his feet. He missed the satisfying *boing* noise it had made as he'd jumped.

Always one, two, three…*splash!*

But now he remained on the edge of the pool, perfectly dry in his board shorts, enjoying the oppressive blanketing heat against his skin. Even enjoying the way his sweat beaded and dribbled down between his shoulder blades and along the slight trough of his spine.

He'd always liked this—this getting deliciously hot and uncomfortable, knowing that the relief of the water was within his reach. The anticipation was half the fun.

Mila, of course, had always jumped right in. She'd walk through the gate, dump her towel on any available surface and leap into the water straight away. Every time. Every *single* time.

Seb bent his knees and pushed off from the edge of the pool, diving sleekly into the water.

It was so ridiculously hot the water wasn't really even that cold. But it still felt glorious against his skin, washing away the sweat and the heat in an instant.

He surfaced at the far side, where it was shallow enough for him to stand. He turned, propping his back against the warm paving, and looked back across the pool. At the end was the pool house. Empty now, with his parents away on a cruise, the bi-fold doors all closed up.

It was the middle of the afternoon. All day he'd felt restless. The heat, he'd thought—although that had made no sense within his air-conditioned office.

In the end he'd rescheduled his afternoon meetings, deciding some physical exertion might be what he needed. But now he was here he acknowledged it wasn't as simple as finding an outlet for his unease.

If he was honest, the restlessness wasn't even new. It had been hovering for days.

Three days, actually.

Since that afternoon at the workshop.

Seb sank beneath the water, then pushed strongly off the wall with his feet, swimming an expansive breaststroke, under water, to the other side.

Nothing had changed between himself and Mila. At least, not on the surface.

They still saw each other daily. Still shared the same bed.

But things had changed.

Of course they had.

That afternoon had exposed the naiveté of their arrangement. It was all well and good to just go with the flow, and get caught up in the thrill of being 'not just friends'—but it couldn't last for ever. He'd always known that. But he'd been ignoring it.

What had he thought would happen? *Really?*

Had he hoped that after sleeping together for a few weeks he and Mila would magically morph back into 'just friends' again? As if they'd simply needed to get it out of their system?

How stupid. How impossible.

He'd told himself he'd been honest and up-front with Mila. She knew his position on relationships. He'd been crystal-clear.

And he'd been honest that afternoon in the workshop. He'd been unwilling to define their relationship, but he'd told her how he'd felt, how she made him feel.

So he could tell himself that he'd done the right thing. That he was still a good guy.

But he wasn't.

Because when Mila had asked him to define their relationship she'd been telling him that she wanted more. He'd known that—of course he had.

And that had been his cue. His cue to end this—to walk away before it became even more complicated. Before he hurt her even more. And he knew he'd already caused her pain. He'd seen it in her eyes that afternoon.

But he hadn't walked away. In the end he hadn't been able to.

That had been as selfish as his refusal to go along with Mila's silent plea to hide their relationship from Ivy.

He'd had no right to react the way he had. But react he had, driven by an unexpected ache—disappointment, maybe?—that Mila didn't want the people she cared about to know about them. About the relationship he'd later refused to define.

And here he was—right amidst the tangle of contradictions that was Mila and Seb.

He couldn't give Mila what she wanted. But he also couldn't walk away.

How much longer could this last? How much longer could

they continue to fall asleep on Mila's couch? Or to wake up in his bed together covered only in the morning sun? How long before what they had deteriorated? Before what they had became so complicated that walking away felt impossible? And staying together felt unbearable.

How long before their lives became about history and obligation and not...?

Love.

Seb ducked under the water again. He swam as close to the bottom as he could, so that his knees and chest grazed the textured surface. When he reached the end he pushed off again, swimming another underwater lap, and then another—until his body was screaming for oxygen.

When he broke the surface he was gasping for air. He hauled himself out at the side of the pool and rolled immediately onto his back, water streaming from his body to cool the red-hot paving.

He looked up at the sun, right in the middle of the sky, blinding him so that he blinked and squinted.

This wasn't about love.

This was about finally doing the right thing by the women in his life.

He'd let Stephanie down—so badly. He wasn't going to make that mistake again. He just couldn't. He *wouldn't*.

He needed to do the right thing by Mila.

He needed to end it.

As Mila twisted the red and white sign to *'Closed'* two familiar faces walked up to the glass shop door.

April and Ivy.

And Nate, in his pram—invisible beneath a canopy of muslins.

'This is an intervention,' Ivy said in her big sister voice, crystal-clear through the glass.

Mila didn't really want to, but she opened the door. She'd

been dodging Ivy's calls, so this was not unexpected. 'I suppose you'd better come in,' she said.

'We should,' April said, deliberately cheerful. 'And, look—I brought doughnuts. Let's go upstairs.'

A few minutes later they were settled with cups of tea at Mila's dining table. Nate sat on an old hand-made quilt that had once been Mila's, sucking happily on a cracker that Ivy had produced from her handbag.

April had carefully sliced each of the different types of glazed doughnut into thirds, so they could all try each flavour. Unexpectedly, that simple, typically April gesture of kindness made Mila's eyes sting and fill with tears.

She blinked them away, annoyed with herself. What was she even upset about? But she wasn't fast enough.

'Oh, honey,' Ivy said, scooting her chair closer so she could wrap her arm around Mila. 'Please tell us what's going on. You had to know you couldn't get away with avoiding us for ever.'

April must have located her box of tissues, because they appeared on the table before her. Mila grabbed a couple, balling them together in her hands.

'I don't know why I'm upset,' she said. 'I don't have anything to be upset about.'

April raised an eyebrow. 'You sure?'

'Yes,' she said. Then, 'No.'

Dammit. She was supposed to be in control. Of what was happening with Seb. Of her emotions.

'If it helps,' Ivy said, 'April and I are confident that Sebastian Fyfe has not suddenly taken an interest in traditional pottery techniques. We've made an educated guess as to what's going on.'

'I'd hoped I was more convincing the other day.'

Ivy laughed. 'Mila, I practically had to fan myself when I walked in the door. *Nate* knew that Seb wasn't there to play with clay.'

Mila raised an eyebrow. 'He actually *is* pretty interested in what I do.'

'I'm sure he is,' said April, with a smile. 'But he's more interested in *you*.'

Mila's cheeks were warm. 'Okay…' she conceded.

'So why the secrecy?' Ivy asked. 'This isn't like you.'

Mila took her time selecting a doughnut piece, and then a bit longer to eat it. Even now her sisters knew something was going on with her and Seb, it was still difficult for her to articulate *what*, exactly.

'Because we're not going out,' Mila said. 'We're just sleeping together. Neither of us saw the point of telling anyone about something so temporary.'

'*Is* it temporary?' asked April.

Mila nodded.

'Is that what you want?' asked Ivy.

She shook her head.

'Ah…' her sisters said, together.

Mila shrugged. 'So that's it. But it's okay. I know what I'm doing.'

After a few moments Ivy said carefully, 'And what's that?'

'Look,' Mila said firmly. 'You really don't have to worry about me. I'll be fine. I'm not being stupid.'

'You're never stupid, Mila!' April said, raising her eyebrows.

Mila rolled her eyes. 'Oh, come on—you both think I'm stupid every time I answer one of Dad's phone calls. And you both thought Ben was a massive loser, long before he cheated on me.'

'Not *stupid*,' April said. 'Impressively optimistic.'

Mila's lips quirked upwards. 'I'm not being optimistic this time. I know Seb isn't desperately in love with me.'

She'd meant it to sound light, like a joke. But it hadn't really come out that way. Instead it had sounded like a statement of fact.

Which she supposed it was.

Oh.

Why did that hurt? As if this was a stunning realisation?

'If he doesn't, then he's the stupid one, Mila,' April said. 'And—'

Ivy interrupted. 'Does he know how you feel about him?'

Mila shook her head. How could he? She didn't really know either. She just knew she wanted more than he was willing to give. 'It doesn't matter.'

'I think it does,' Ivy said, all authoritative.

'No,' Mila said, equally definitely. 'He's made it clear. He doesn't want a relationship with me. It doesn't matter what I say.'

She didn't really want to focus too much on what she felt. It would only make everything that much harder.

And what were the options, anyway? For how she felt? They weren't in high school any more. She couldn't *like* him, like him.

But could she love him?

No.

'It doesn't matter anyway,' Mila said firmly. To herself as much as to her sisters. 'I'm going to end it soon. Before it gets even more complicated.'

'Good idea,' said Ivy.

'What a shame,' April said at the same time. 'It would've been kind of nice to end up with your first love.'

'You *knew*?' Mila said, genuinely stunned. April and Ivy, to the thirteen-year-old Mila, had seemed so much older. It hadn't been until her late teens that she'd started to share her romantic dramas with them both.

'Of course—' began Ivy, but then she was distracted by a thud.

Nate had crawled over to the couch and tugged Ivy's bag to the ground. He happily sat with the strap in his mouth, the detritus from within the bag spread around him—lip balm, tissues, a nappy, Ivy's purse, crumpled receipts...

'Oh, whoops,' Ivy said, getting to her feet. 'I'd better give this to you before I forget. I found it shoved down the side of Nate's pram this morning.'

Ivy came back to the table, handing Mila a slightly chewed package delivery card that Nate had presumably pilfered.

'I'm sorry,' Ivy said. 'It's a few weeks old. Hopefully whatever it is will still be at the post office.'

It was most likely supplies, so Mila wasn't too worried. Instead she focused on the still mostly uneaten doughnuts—and changed the subject. 'So, April,' she said, 'I saw you were making all your followers insanely jealous about a new watch today. New sponsor?'

Mila's phone rang as she was setting up a new window display. The shop was closed, although the sun hadn't quite set—the days were long now, as Christmas approached.

She fished her phone out of the front pocket of her apron, expecting it to be a customer who'd planned to call her back about a commission.

Instead, the number on the screen was international, and Mila's heart sank. She knew it was her father. She recognised the number she'd allowed to go to voicemail only a few weeks earlier. She hadn't listened to his message—only enough to verify that it was Blaine before promptly deleting it.

It had been easy to ignore Blaine then, amongst the drama of that first night with Seb. And it should be equally easy now—but then, he'd never called her this regularly before. And it had been unusual for him to attempt to contact her sisters...

She answered the call. She needed to let him know not to contact her again.

'La-la!'

Of course this was the one time her father had called her

without the unnecessary help of his assistant. Regardless, she had no qualms about telling him to go away.

'I don't want to talk to you, Blaine.'

'Blaine?'

'Yes,' Mila said. 'I don't want to talk to you, and I don't want you to contact me again.'

Her voice sounded strong, but the words were still so hard to say. She had to force them out, focusing on each word, one after the other.

'But, Mila, I have some wonderful news!'

That didn't matter. She should hang up.

'What, Dad?' she said on a sigh, not quite able to be the ice queen he deserved.

She immediately realised her mistake. *Blaine*—not Dad. *Blaine*. She gritted her teeth, furious.

She was so busy being annoyed with herself, Blaine's words didn't sink in at first.

'Pardon me?' she said, certain she'd heard him wrong. *'Wife?'*

'Didn't you get my message, La-la?' Blaine said, with a self-satisfied chuckle. 'I got married! To the most amazing woman!'

So it would seem that since she'd last seen him he'd married a woman Mila had never heard of, let alone met. Mila rubbed her temple, just wanting this call to be over.

'But that isn't why I called, of course—because the news is now even better! I wanted *you* to be the first to know, La-la—after my lovely wife and myself. Ha-ha!'

'First to know what?' Mila asked slowly, as horrid realisation began to dawn.

'Can't you guess? I'm going to be a daddy again, La-la! Isn't that amazing? A new brother or sister for you and the girls!'

Oh, God.

'I'm just so excited. I can't—'

But Mila had hung up on him, unable to stomach another

word. She squeezed her eyes shut, trying to process the news somehow, to deal with it in a calm and rational manner. Because, really, why did she care what her deadbeat dad was doing on the other side of the world? Why should she care if he was having another child for whom he'd just shown more interest, excitement and affection than Mila had received in *twenty-five years*...?

She turned, needing a glass of water or something. But as she turned her hand clipped one of the tall, elegant vases she'd just put in the shop window. It tipped over, instantly creating a beautiful multi-coloured set of dominoes as each vase smashed its neighbour.

She could probably have saved most of them if she'd reached out and caught one of those subsequent vases. But she hadn't. Instead she'd just stood there, allowing weeks of her work to be destroyed, until she'd found herself sitting cross-legged on the floor, with the remnants of her vases surrounding her and tears streaming down her cheeks.

The shop was empty, new ceilings and fresh plaster now hiding the electrical and plumbing work of the past few weeks.

Seb stood upstairs, standing in the long rectangle of fading light thrown through the street side window. The floors were still raw wood, waiting to be polished. A new kitchen waited to be assembled in the corner, in a collection of beige cardboard boxes.

Seb really liked this part of the building process—when the wooden skeleton was dressed in plasterboard and the interior began to take shape. Although he wasn't really walking around his shop to admire the workmanship of his builders.

He was stalling.

Mila was expecting him in a few minutes. He hadn't seen her since his swim—and his decision—because she'd cancelled their plans for yesterday after being invited out for dinner with her sisters.

He hadn't minded. He didn't mind delaying the inevitable—and he certainly didn't mind delaying hurting Mila.

He still knew it was the right decision. Twenty four hours of over-thinking it hadn't changed a thing.

But still he stalled.

He ran his fingers along the wall. The surface was smooth, but—

A loud crash stopped Seb in his tracks.

The series of crashes that followed had him racing down the stairs, his boots a loud staccato on the bare boards.

Outside, it was now almost dark, but Seb could still make out Mila inside her shop, her pale apron a contrast to the dark wooden floor. He knocked on the shop window and her head jerked upwards, her eyes wide.

'Are you okay?' he asked.

She nodded her head, but Seb was less than convinced.

Behind him, the street light came on, and for a moment—just before Mila glanced away—it revealed a river of tears on her cheeks.

Immediately Seb went to the door—of course it was locked.

'Mila, please let me in.'

She didn't look at him through the glass as she unlocked the door, or as she opened it, or even as he stepped through the doorway. Nor as she turned her back to close the door, and to lock it in a series of clunks and clicks.

But she did when she turned around.

She looked right at him—and then threw herself into his arms.

Mila pressed herself tight against him, wrapping her hands behind his neck and burying her face in his chest. He hugged her tightly—as close as he could.

'Mila, please tell me what's wrong.'

'Would you believe,' she said against the fabric of his T-shirt, 'that this is all because I broke a few vases?'

'No,' Seb said.

'Didn't think so,' she said, her words muffled.

'Do you want to talk about it?'

She lifted her head to meet his gaze. Her tears had smudged her make-up, so she had dark patches beneath each eye.

'No.' A beat. 'Yes.' She half smiled, then sighed. 'My dad,' she said. 'He called. Let me down—spectacularly this time.'

She'd loosened her hold on Seb, but hadn't made any move to step away.

'What did he do?' Seb asked, his words hard-edged.

'Well!' she said, expansively. 'It's quite a story. But the condensed version is this: my dad called me tonight to tell me he's married a woman I've never heard of and they're having a baby. Isn't that *great*?'

Seb swore harshly.

He hadn't thought it was possible to hate Mila's father more than he already did—but, yes, it clearly was.

'I am *so* sorry, Mila.'

She nodded again—a short, sharp movement. 'Me too,' she said.

She looked at him for a while, exploring his face, as if she was going to say more. Her tears had stopped, but her cheeks were shiny with their remnants.

Eventually, she just smiled. 'I'm starving—should we order dinner?'

He hadn't planned to stay. He'd planned a different conversation entirely. But he couldn't have that conversation now—not after Blaine's phone call.

'Sure,' he said, and followed her up the stairs.

And—while he would do anything to prevent Mila's dad hurting her ever again—he couldn't pretend he was anything but grateful to have more time with Mila.

Mila had fallen asleep on the couch. Her head rested just beside his shoulder, pillowed against the cushions.

He'd barely watched the movie; his concentration had

been focused on Mila. Her tears had dried, and she'd laughed when she'd seen the mess of her make-up in her bathroom mirror. Her face was now scrubbed clean, and Seb could just see the tiniest of freckles across the bridge of her nose. He'd seen them before—he now knew every inch of Mila Molyneux's body—but tonight they seemed particularly beautiful. Particularly poignant. Mila always washed her face before bed. So those freckles spoke of early-morning kisses, of sleepy cuddles and of making love before work.

All things he would never get to experience with her again.

Mila blinked and her eyes fluttered open. She shifted, resting her weight on her hands and leaning, just slightly, towards him. She was exploring his face—her gaze like a touch against the length of his nose, his cheekbones, his jaw, his lips.

'Kiss me,' she said, so softly.

A better man would've refused. It wasn't right, given his decision. But in the end the words he needed to say escaped him.

Her name fell from his lips just before they touched hers, his voice rough and jagged. He didn't kiss her politely. No— he kissed her as if all the reasons he shouldn't no longer existed. As if all that mattered was the part of him that *needed* Mila—needed her mouth and her hands and her freckles. That needed her smile and her wit and her drive.

Her mouth was equally desperate against his, as were her hands—tangled in his hair, shoved beneath his shirt. Hot and needy and frantic.

Now she was on top of him, sitting up to drag her T-shirt off over her head. She was so beautiful. So perfect.

Her skin was heaven beneath his hands and mouth, his skin hot beneath her touch. They both still wore too many clothes, but the narrow couch was making it almost impossible for Seb to move without tipping them both onto the floor.

So instead, in one movement, he stood, scooping Mila

up into his arms. She laughed against his neck, then kissed his jaw as he strode towards her room.

'I told you I'd always carry you to bed,' he said.

And with that everything stopped.

Mila went completely still—for a split second. And then she was struggling, pushing against his chest.

'No,' she said.

Immediately he let her go, standing her gently on the floor.

She practically ran from him, searching the small room for her shirt. She kept her back to him as she pulled it over her head—and the contrast of that gesture with its counterpart only minutes ago was as pointed as a blade to Seb's chest.

He had no idea what he'd done wrong. 'What's going on, Mila?'

She shook her head. 'I can't do this any more. You need to go.'

She was right. But… 'I can't.'

'Really?' she said, crossing her arms.

He'd never seen Mila like this before—with such nothingness in her gaze.

'What does that mean? Because I don't have time for empty promises, or for romantic gestures without substance.' She glared at him. '*"I told you I'd always carry you to bed,"*' she mocked. 'Right.'

'I meant that,' he said.

And he had.

None of this was anywhere close to what he'd planned. But he couldn't lie to Mila.

Maybe he could no longer lie to himself.

Mila laughed. 'Save your smooth moves for a woman you actually want to have a relationship with, Seb.'

'But I *do* want to have a relationship with you,' he said, the realisation hitting him as forcefully as a semi-trailer. 'Very much.'

This silenced her. For a moment he thought that maybe it would be okay. That he'd seen a flicker in the flatness of her expression.

'*No,*' she said. 'Not today, Seb. You are *not* going to pretend that you want me—not today.'

'I'm not pretending anything.'

He was standing near the hallway and he stepped towards her, hating being so far away. But she held up her hand, stopping him in his tracks.

'It doesn't matter, anyway,' Mila said. 'I've changed my mind. I don't want to be "not just friends", or your girlfriend, or your *anything* any more.'

'I don't believe you,' he said.

She waved her hand dismissively. 'Don't be so arrogant.'

But he wasn't going to let her do this. Not now.

'I think I've worked it out,' Seb said. 'What happened down in the workshop the other day…why I hated it that you wanted to hide us from Ivy.'

Mila was doing her best to look bored. 'I don't care,' she said.

'When it was you hiding us from Ivy it was all about what *I* wanted—I wanted those close to us to know about us, so I was hurt. But then—when you made it clear that you wanted more than what we had, that you were invested in us…' Mila was determinedly not looking at him, but he couldn't stop. 'Well, then it wasn't just me who could get hurt. And that was the problem—suddenly I held the potential to hurt you in my hands, and I couldn't deal with it.'

His pain didn't matter—he was used to oceans of it—but Mila's? He'd do anything to protect her.

'So you didn't want a relationship with me for my own good?' she said, raising an eyebrow.

'It seemed more noble in my head,' he said.

'And not as condescending?'

'Yes, that too,' he agreed, attempting a small smile.

Mila just narrowed her eyes. But she did move—striding towards him. She stopped just out of reach, her body radiating emotion.

'So you've decided that you *can* deal with the concept of us going out? Of us telling the world we're together?'

He nodded.

She nodded too, with the slightest of smiles. 'Fine,' she said. 'That's all fine. And I probably would've been happy with that any other day than today. But today that's not enough for me.'

After what had happened with her dad.

'Mila—'

She wasn't listening.

'I shouldn't let him hurt me so much,' she said. 'But I keep on doing it. I've been allowing it for years. Decades. I just keep leaving myself wide open.'

'Mila, it's not your fault—'

'It's taken me too long, but I've finally learned something from all Dad's years of crappy behaviour: I deserve better than that. I deserve to be prioritised and appreciated and *loved*. And I'm not going to accept anything else. From *anyone*.'

Finally Seb began to work out where Mila was headed with this. He met her determined gaze, painfully aware of the beat of his heart in his chest.

'Tell me if I'm going out on a limb, here, but my guess is that even though you say you want to be my boyfriend, you haven't thought all that far ahead. You're just thinking about the fun stuff: about messing about on the couch, nice dinners, barbecues with friends where you introduce me as your girlfriend. Right?'

Seb didn't move, but Mila knew.

'What about the other stuff? What about in three months' time? In twelve? Are we going to move in together?'

'Mila, I just thought we'd see how things go first—'

'And if we move in together, then what? Are we going to get engaged? Married? Get a dog? Have a kid?'

He shook his head. 'I don't know. You don't know either. We can't know—not yet.'

Seb felt as if he teetered on the edge of a watery abyss, helpless to step anywhere but over the edge.

'Of course not,' Mila said, almost kindly. 'But we *can* know if any of those things are on the agenda. Or even the vaguest possibility.' She paused. 'So—just to be perfectly clear—*are* they on your agenda? With me?'

'This isn't fair, Mila. I lost Steph less than two years ago. The last thing I'm thinking about is getting married again.'

He didn't understand why Mila was doing this.

'I get that—I do,' she said. 'Of course I do. And I'm not expecting a proposal any time soon. But how about the other bits? The house, the dog—you know. The stuff people do when things get serious. When they're committed to each other.'

He hadn't thought about this—about *any* of this. Fifteen minutes ago he'd been working out how he was going to walk away from Mila for ever.

'I don't know what you want me to say.' It was all he could manage, and he knew exactly how pathetic those words were.

'I just need a yes or a no, Seb. It's not difficult.'

But it was. For him and for her. He could see it in her face—could see that slight wobble to her gaze.

There was nowhere else to go—the abyss beckoned. Mila deserved the truth.

'No,' he said. 'No. None of that is on my agenda.'

He just couldn't do it. Ever again. To Mila or to himself.

'With me,' Mila clarified.

'With anyone.'

She shook her head. 'No. With *me*. I'm the only one asking you.'

She wasn't meeting his gaze now. Instead she studied the wall over his shoulder, and the light fittings. The floor.

'You don't understand, Mila, it's not about you—'

'Oh, *God*, Seb—do you hear yourself? Of *course* it's about me. It's *always* about me.'

Her voice cracked, and that just about killed him. But she didn't want to hear anything he said. And he didn't think he could even explain. How could she possibly know the emptiness he was trying to shield her from? Why couldn't she see how great what they already had was? Why ruin it with complications? With plans for the future?

'Why are you doing this, Mila? We've been together for no time at all. How can you possibly know that all those things are what *you* want? After just a few weeks?'

Now she finally came closer. She stood right in front of him, tilting her chin upwards to meet his gaze, her lovely eyes framed with her long naked eyelashes.

'It's not been weeks, Seb. It's been years.'

'Years?'

'Since before you kissed me behind the surf club.'

She closed her eyes and he watched her take a long, deep, breath.

'I've loved you since I was thirteen.' She laughed. 'Just to clarify—then it was hormonal, teenage infatuation. Then later it was platonic—with some effort. But now...'

'Love?' he repeated, shocked to his core.

'Yes,' Mila said. 'Love. It's taken me a while to work it out, but I knew the moment I looked out through my shop window tonight to see you standing outside... I *knew*. I wanted you with me in that moment more than anyone else in the world. I want you with me in most of my moments, actually. And I guess that's love, isn't it?'

Seb had absolutely nothing to say. His brain was desperately attempting to compute what she'd just told him.

'And if I love you then I'm not going to go through the charade of having fun and saying meaningless things about *not being good at relationships*. All that armour is ineffective, anyway—no matter how hard I try. I'm not going to be with you if the only possible outcome is you hurting me.

I've had enough of that. I've had enough of allowing that. My dad, Ben. You. I'm done.'

Seb supposed this was the point when he could deny everything that Mila had said. When he could reach across the small distance between them and drag her into his arms—when he could tell her that she was being ridiculous and that he loved her too, that he'd never, ever hurt her...

But none of that would be true.

He loved Mila. He'd loved her for ever. But had it changed from the love of childhood friends? Was he *in* love with her?

It didn't matter, anyway, did it?

Because he knew the second part wasn't true. He knew he couldn't tell her he wouldn't hurt her. He couldn't even tell her that he'd do his best to try not to... Because even that would be a lie.

He *would* hurt her. It was inevitable.

Once he'd loved Steph with all his heart, but he'd still driven her away. To drugs. To her death.

When it came to relationships he was unfixable. And Mila deserved so much more.

'I'm so sorry, Mila,' he said.

Then he left—because he had to.

And deep in his abyss Seb was drowning.

CHAPTER FIFTEEN

STEPH'S BIRTHDAY WAS only a couple of weeks before Christmas.

Mila's pottery classes had finished up a week earlier, but the shop was still incredibly busy, with Sheri and Mila often both needed to manage the constant stream of customers.

With so much demand, and no time to escape to her workshop during the day, Mila had started working late into the night. She'd managed to replace her window display of vases, but she still needed more to maintain a reasonable amount of stock. It was a really good problem to have—although that didn't make Mila any less exhausted.

If she was honest, though, Mila wasn't sure how much sleeping she would've been doing, anyway. Because—unless she was so tired she collapsed into her bed and into oblivion—it was in the darkness that her thoughts would drift to Sebastian.

It made her angry that they did that. It had been a week now, and she was still wasting her precious time on Seb. Which was pointless.

She'd done the right thing—she knew that. She'd already known she'd needed to walk away, but now she knew exactly why.

It wasn't about avoiding hurt, or rejection.

It was about love.

She deserved love. Nothing less was acceptable.

'Mila?'

Mila had been staring out of the window, her gaze unfocused on the passing traffic.

Sheri grinned. 'You look off with the fairies.'

Mila shook her head, trying to refocus. She'd been leaning against the counter, and now took a step back, running her hands through her curls. 'No, I'm fine.'

'Take the rest of the afternoon off,' Sheri said. *'I'll* be fine.'

The shop was currently empty, but Mila knew it wouldn't last. 'No, I can't do that. It's not fair on you.'

'Staying here isn't fair on *you*,' Sheri said, more softly. 'I know what day it is,' she added. 'I haven't forgotten.'

Mila chewed on her bottom lip, willing the sudden tightness in her throat away.

'If you need an excuse,' Sheri prompted, 'go and pick up that mystery package. A new delivery card arrived today. It's under the counter.'

By the time Mila had made it to the post office a few days ago, Nate's chewed delivery card in hand, her package had been sent back to the depot to be returned to the sender. Fortunately that hadn't yet happened, and the package had been directed back to Mila.

So she did have a reason to head out.

And, more importantly, Sheri was right. The shop wasn't where she needed to be.

Mila drove to the post office, only a few blocks away. The queue was short inside, and she was handed her package within a few minutes of arriving.

She flipped the large flat box over, curious to note the sender. She and Sheri hadn't been able to work it out—all their outstanding orders had already arrived.

But the handwritten name on the back made Mila go completely still.

'Can I help you with anything else today, miss?' the young man behind the counter prompted politely.

Mila just shook her head furiously and walked briskly to her car. And then she drove to the park. To the park near the street where she'd grown up, with that giant ancient fig.

Car parked, and the package carefully cradled in her arms, Mila walked towards the towering tree.

The fig's canopy was incredibly dense, stretching out so far that the grass ended some distance from its trunk, unable to grow in the heavy shade. The trunk was huge, with ropey root tentacles that stretched from its centre, large enough to sit upon and stare out across the park.

She chose a spot where she could lean against the base of the fig, and kicked off her flip flops so she could drag her toes in the dirt. She traced the sharp cardboard edges of her package, but didn't move to open it.

She hadn't recognised the sender's writing, but she'd certainly recognised the name. Steph's mum. With a new address from the most southern point of Western Australia, a day's drive from Perth.

Still, she didn't open it.

She'd come here so often with Steph. Exactly here, beneath this tree. This had been *their* place—a place where they'd met without Seb. They'd dreamed up elaborate stories for the fairies they'd imagined lived in the tree, they'd swapped homework answers, and they'd giggled about boys. They'd made plans for the future: envisaging horse-drawn carriages at their weddings to British princes—one each—the dresses they'd wear to their Year Twelve ball, and which boy they'd like to be the first to kiss them.

They'd been so close. Picture-book best friends.

And then Seb had kissed her.

She'd been thirteen, and the three of them had headed to the beach during the summer holidays. Mila didn't remember many of the details of the day—but she did remember her surprise when she'd realised *Seb was actually going to kiss her*. She'd had a crush on him for ever, but had never done anything about it. She hadn't known what to read into those times when Seb's gaze had tangled with hers, or what to do with the way she'd felt if they as much as bumped shoulders.

She also hadn't really known what to do when his lips had touched hers that first time. Maybe he hadn't either. Either way, it had been a little awkward—and she'd been so embarrassed that she wasn't better at this whole kissing thing. As soon as she'd been able to she'd scampered away—desperate to tell Steph and for her advice. After all, Steph had kissed *two* boys. She had experience.

Steph had been excited for Mila, and even a little jealous—she'd had a bit of a crush on Seb, too. They'd giggled, and planned Mila's next move—but in the end there hadn't been one. Seb had seemed to lose his nerve, and Mila had been so busy trying to play it cool that she'd ended up being snarky and stand-offish.

Mila remembered the day Steph had told her that Seb had kissed *her*. Steph had felt terrible, promising that it would never, ever happen again. Mila had been shattered. But she'd given her blessing. Maybe she'd always thought that Seb falling for her more flirtatious, more vivacious friend was inevitable. Maybe she'd never really believed that Seb could actually want to be with Mila.

And there it was—perfectly encapsulated. The impact she'd allowed her father to have on her self-worth. At thirteen, at almost thirty, and a million times in between.

How could she not have seen it before now?

Mila looked at her toes, her fire-engine-red toenails now dusted with dirt. A short distance away two small boys had appeared, tossing a Frisbee between them. A breeze ruffled the old fig's many leaves.

Mila *knew*. She knew why nothing had been clear until that night when her dad had called her with news of her future half-sibling. Up until that night Mila had held on to a skerrick of faith that somewhere deep down her father *did* love her. But he didn't. He didn't love her. He didn't care about her. He didn't even know her.

And in amongst the devastation of that realisation, there was freedom. No longer would she waste her love on those who didn't deserve it. And no longer would she wait so patiently for love that would never come her way.

She loved Seb. She knew that now. She'd loved him for

ever. In different ways, but unwaveringly. She couldn't just switch that off, and—unlike her thirteen-year-old self—she couldn't pretend it wasn't happening.

But at least this time she'd told him about it.

How might her life have been different if she hadn't run away when Seb had kissed her? Although to suggest it would've been different was a disservice to Steph, and to Seb.

For all the problems that Seb had said they'd had towards the end of their marriage, Mila couldn't wish away Steph and Seb's relationship. For a long time they had been incredibly happy together. Mila knew that—she'd been best friend to them *both*.

Steph and Seb had fitted together perfectly—for a long time. They'd had silly inside jokes, and Seb had used to have a really sweet way of tucking Steph's long, wild hair behind her ears. It had been almost reverent, as if he couldn't quite believe he was allowed to touch such beauty.

As a threesome, they'd just *worked*, too. They'd laughed and partied and travelled—it had been fantastic. Maybe she'd been envious of their happiness, but she'd never coveted Seb. Seb and Steph had just gone together. They'd been *meant* to be together.

Mila wondered—just a little—what would've happened if that night in her flat had ended differently. If Seb had said he loved her too. Would she still have wondered, somewhere deep inside, if she was some sort of consolation prize? If she could ever match up to Steph's memory?

A clattering noise grabbed Mila's attention. A bright yellow Frisbee lay only a few metres from Mila's feet, on top of one of the fig's huge roots. One of the small boys had run up to retrieve it, but had stopped dead on seeing Mila in the shadows, suddenly shy.

'It's okay,' Mila said, getting to her feet, placing her package carefully on a wide, shelf-like root 'I'll get it.'

She picked up the Frisbee and tossed it, reasonably impressed with her rusty Frisbee-throwing technique. The boy ran off to his friend and Mila walked the few steps back to her preferred location at the base of the tree trunk.

The sun had lowered further in the sky, illuminating different parts of the tree and its roots as light dodged through the branches. The package—with its plain brown cardboard wrapping and its small stash of colourful stamps—lay in a narrow strip of sunlight, waiting for her.

Mila felt somewhat as she did at the end of a fabulous book—desperate to know the ending, but also hating how few pages remained. Because this package, she knew, had no sequel.

It was from Steph.

How many times had she wished to see Steph just one more time? To talk to her? To hug her? This package—whatever it might be—was as close to granting her wish as she was ever going to get.

Finally she picked the package up and settled back into her seat against the tree. Then quickly—as fast as she could in the end—she tore off the packing tape and prised the box open with trembling fingers.

Inside lay a letter, on top of some fabric wrapped in purple tissue paper.

Dear Mila,

I'm not sure if you knew, but Steph was working on a new collection before she died. With the help of some of her old colleagues we're releasing one final Violet collection, with all profits to go to charity.

Most of her designs were still at an early design stage—including this dress. But this was the only piece she'd named, so I thought it was important I sent it to you. After all, it's named after you.

I've enclosed the sketches, as I thought you might like to read Steph's notes...

Mila barely read the rest of the letter, her vision blurry with unshed tears. Instead she carefully unwrapped the dress and held it up before her. It was simple—made of a structured, slightly heavy fabric that would reach to mid-knee. It had a boat neck and a flared skirt that would move and swish as she walked. And it was red—lipstick-red, fire-engine-red. Her favourite colour.

It was beautiful.

Carefully, she laid it back in the box and retrieved the small, thin pile of fashion sketches. Drawn in skinny black ink, the willowy model in the sketches bore no resemblance to Mila. But beside the posing, pouting figure were Steph's notes under a simple heading: *Mila*.

And there Steph had listed all manner of words.

Funny.
Determined.
Talented.
Wise.

Mila blinked.

Good listener.
Reliable.
Creative.
Gorgeous.
Loyal.
My best friend.

Underneath, in capital letters, Steph had written: *HOW DO I PUT ALL THAT IN A DRESS?*

Mila squeezed her eyes shut, but it didn't make any difference. Tears fell down her cheeks, splashing onto her jeans.

She'd spent a lot of time over the past eighteen months berating and hating herself for the way her friendship with

Steph had changed. For the first time she wondered if she'd been wrong.

Steph van Berlo and Mila Molyneux had been best friends from the age of four—through playgroup, school, university and beyond. Almost all their lives they'd been there for each other. Side by side.

So maybe—*maybe*—it was unavoidable that their lives had diverged. Maybe they'd needed space to grow up without each other—to stand on their own two feet. To be their own people, to be their own women.

And that had been okay, because Mila had known that one day they would come back together. In Perth, or London, or Paris, or San Francisco. Who cared? It hadn't mattered.

But that day had been supposed to come. The day when they would be Mila and Steph again. Just like the inscriptions on those cheap gold-plated pendants they'd bought each other in Year Five: *Friends For Ever*.

It wasn't fair.

Steph's whole life had been ahead of her.

As had a lifetime of friendship.

Mila missed her.

So much.

She stood up, turning her back to the tree, the sketches hugged carefully against her heart.

Mila still harboured a small mountain of regret. She wished she'd never fallen out of the habit of telling Steph about every vaguely exciting event in her life. She wished, desperately, that she'd sent those emails she'd kept forgetting to write. Made those phone calls planned with the best of intentions.

But now—thanks to a beautiful dress and some scribbly sketches—Mila realised that all of that had done nothing to minimise their friendship.

Their friendship *had* changed. It had been reshaped, repositioned. But it had endured—and, given time, it would have been reinvented.

And now Mila knew for sure that Steph had known that too.

The two kids and their Frisbee had left, and the park was now empty again.

'I love you, Steph,' Mila said to the park, to the tree and to the sky.

And Mila knew, more certainly than anything else in her life, that Steph had loved her too.

Seb had taken the afternoon off work to head to Cottesloe Beach.

Steph had loved this beach. Most people in Perth loved this beach. And today that was evident in the sheer number of people absolutely everywhere: inside the bars and restaurants along Marine Parade, walking along the street, scattered across the pure white sand and within the crashing waves.

This was where Seb—along with Steph's parents—had released Steph's ashes. So it was the obvious place to come if he wanted to feel close to Steph. And today he did—on her birthday. Twenty-nine today.

Happy Birthday, Stephanie.

Seb navigated the patchwork of towels and bodies on the sand to find a space for himself. He laid out his towel, then sat, his forearms resting on his bent knees, gazing out to the ocean.

I've mucked things up, haven't I, Steph?

With Steph, and now with Mila.

They'd had so much fun out here, the three of them. They'd used to catch the bus, sharing one big beach bag, stuffed with towels and sunscreen. Seb had always been lumped with carrying it—not that he'd really minded.

It had never quite seemed right that a rather nerdy, weedy, computer-obsessed guy got to spend so much time with such beautiful girls. But as soon as they'd all got old enough to start noticing each other beyond who was hogging all the Play Dough it had always been Mila Seb had been drawn to...

'You are so full of it, Seb!' Mila said, turning on her heel. 'You didn't hear the ice cream van. What a waste of time.'

Seb stepped in front of her, delaying her stalk from the surf club and back to the beach. 'Just wait a sec.'

'Why?' She crossed her arms in front of herself. She was wearing the two-piece bathers she'd got for Christmas— red with lime green polka dots. Her skin was a lovely olive tan, her hair wet and slicked back after a morning of body-boarding in the ocean.

'I want to talk to you,' he said.

Mila's eyes narrowed. Her gaze flicked over him—his bare chest, board shorts and bare feet—as if searching for whatever she thought he was hiding.

'Okay,' she said. 'Talk to me.'

But he hadn't really planned what to say. 'It's a nice day, isn't it?'

Really? Surely he could do better than that.

Mila rolled her eyes. 'Steph is going to be annoyed we didn't get any ice-cream.' She went to walk away.

'I like your bikini,' he blurted out. 'It matches your eyes.'

She went still, her gaze dropping to her feet. 'My eyes aren't red,' she said. 'Or green.'

'I meant...' he said, scrambling. 'I meant they complement them. Or something.'

Mila looked up, squinting a little in the bright sun. 'Thank you,' she said.

For a long moment she met Seb's gaze.

What did he do now?

He took too long.

'Well—' Mila began.

But in a rush of panic—or adrenalin, or hormones—he seized the moment.

Seized Mila, really.

He gripped her arms, just lightly, and bent his head towards her.

She blinked and looked stunned. But then she smiled—just a little—and that was all the encouragement he needed.

Her lips were soft and tasted of the ocean. He'd never kissed a girl before, so he didn't really do anything else but press his lips to hers, while his mind madly ran in circles, wondering if he should do something with his tongue.

Worried he was doing it wrong, he ended the kiss. He stepped back, releasing Mila from his grasp.

She lifted her hand and touched her lips.

Seb couldn't work out her expression. Had she liked the kiss? Had he done it right?

'I need to go,' she said, very suddenly.

Then she skirted around him and ran away—back to Steph and their towels...

He hadn't thought about that day in sixteen years. He'd been so embarrassed, and her rejection had stung. He'd read it all wrong.

He'd been so sure—until that kiss—that Mila had liked him. And, from what Mila had said a few nights ago, she *had*. But he'd been oblivious.

What would've happened if he'd known? Would he have ended up with Mila instead?

And did that mean that Steph wouldn't have moved to London with him, fallen in with the wrong crowd, and died?

He'd been staring out at the waves but now he lowered his head, burying it against his knees.

He been through this in the months after Steph's death. He'd blamed himself a million ways—and now he'd found yet another. If he hadn't been so stupid to not realise Mila loved him…

No.

He couldn't do this. He'd dealt with this.

I'm sorry, Steph. For being a crappy husband. For not

being there for you. But not for loving you. Not for marrying you.

He hadn't bought the drugs.

Steph had done that. Steph had chosen to take them.

'Steph's choices are not your responsibility.'

He hadn't believed Mila when she'd said that. He hadn't been ready to believe it. But these past few weeks something had shifted...

When he was with Mila there was a lightness to his life. A rightness. There was laughter, and silliness, and rambling conversations and *connection*. A connection to the present—to living every day to the best of his ability. A connection to Mila—intimacy, trust, passion. And a connection to his future...

And that was what had scared him.

The future was what had made him walk away. Because in the future things could go wrong. *Very* wrong. He could make mistakes. He could ruin everything. He could hurt Mila.

'Steph's choices are not your responsibility.'

He believed that now.

He did.

Her death hadn't been his fault.

As if you could make *me do anything!*

He could almost hear Steph's voice, and her laughter, caught up in the ocean breeze.

It wasn't his fault.

He'd told himself this a hundred times, and for the first time it seemed to sink in. For the first time he realised he believed it.

It wasn't his fault.

'Steph's choices are not your responsibility.'

They were hers.

And he sat there alone, on a beach full of memories, without the two women most important to him.

Because of Steph's choices.

And because of his.

The only reason Mila was not sitting beside him, right this second, was because of his own choices. His own decisions.

He was responsible for that.

Seb lifted his head from his knees as a seagull landed at his feet, pecking hopefully at his towel for food. Around him the beach practically heaved with activity and colour—with *life*.

Why wasn't Mila here with him? Sharing this with him?

Because he didn't want to hurt her. He didn't want their relationship to deteriorate as his relationship with Steph had.

But…

He didn't shirk from the role he'd played in his marriage falling apart. In fact he embraced it. He knew he was responsible for the mistakes he'd made. For the choices he'd made…

And of course that was it. *He* was responsible for his choices. Just as Steph had been for hers. Just as Mila was.

And Mila—unbelievably, amazingly—had chosen *him*. She'd chosen Sebastian Fyfe, with all his flaws and messy emotions.

And Seb—*he'd* chosen to run away from a Technicolor future with Mila. Out of fear.

Fear that when it came to relationships he was broken. Unfixable. That a relationship with Mila would inevitably lead to hurt and to pain. That he'd make the same mistakes as before.

As if he was just some helpless pawn in his own life, pre-destined to follow exactly the same path.

His ridiculous. How stupid.

He was responsible for his future. *He* was responsible for his choices—in life and in his relationship with Mila. He was responsible for learning from his mistakes.

So Mila had chosen Seb—despite the pain of her past, despite everything. Despite probably knowing that he was so caught up in his past that he'd reject her. She'd chosen courage.

While Seb had chosen fear.

That ended now.

CHAPTER SIXTEEN

THE NEXT DAY was Saturday. It had been *crazy* busy at Mila's Nest—the busiest day Mila had ever had. She'd even sat down and worked that out on her laptop. Online sales were through the roof, too—in fact she'd needed to close for new orders as she just couldn't keep up with demand.

Next year she'd need to work something out—maybe make some slip cast moulds, or even look into getting some of her designs commercially produced. The prospect was both exciting and a little sad—it felt like the end of an era. No longer would everything she sold be made with her own hands.

But tonight she was definitely using her own hands. She sat at her potter's wheel, the radio humming in the background, wet clay beneath her fingertips.

She was completely absorbed in her creation—gently manipulating the clay from featureless lump into an elegant, elongated vase—when there was a knock at the workshop door.

It was a warm December evening, so she'd left the door open. Only the security screen separated Mila from her visitor, and it rattled under the definite tap of Seb's knuckles.

'Hey,' he said.

Not sure what to do with Seb's unexpected appearance, Mila momentarily lost her focus—and under her wayward fingers the vase collapsed.

'Dammit!' She brought the wheel to a stop.

Seb swore. 'Sorry—I didn't mean—'

'I'm a bit busy at the moment,' Mila interrupted, as she patted the ruined vase back into a lump. 'Please leave.'

That had been incredibly hard to say—which Mila didn't like. She kept her gaze downwards as she slapped a new mound of clay onto the wheel head, then dipped her fingers into the adjacent bowl of water so she could dampen the clay.

'I'm not going anywhere,' he said.

Mila closed her eyes. 'It's a lovely night,' she said. 'There are thousands of better things you could be doing than watching me work.'

'I can't think of any.'

Mila shook her head. No, he didn't get to be charming.

She stood up and went to the sink to wash her hands, her back to Seb. She dried her hands on her apron, twisting her fingers in the fabric.

Why didn't this get easier? It had been a week. Shouldn't it not hurt so much by now? But instead Mila felt as raw as when he'd told her no.

He didn't want her. Why was he here?

She took a deep breath before turning and walking to the door. He looked as handsome as always—in a dark grey T-shirt and black board shorts—his shoulders broad, his calves muscular.

Maybe Seb had thought she was going to let him in—but he rapidly realised his mistake as she reached for the heavy workshop door.

'Wait, Mila,' he said. 'Please let me in.'

She shook her head again.

No, no, no.

'You know,' she said, quite conversationally from her side of the fly screen, 'I was thinking about Steph yesterday.'

She didn't need to clarify why.

He nodded. Of course he had been, too.

'I was thinking about how much I miss her. How I'd love to hear her laugh just one more time.' She took a deep breath. 'And then I started wondering what would have happened if you and I *had* started going out. If the other night you'd said yes instead of no.'

'Mila—'

'And I thought… I wonder if he would've compared me

to Steph? And if he did how would I have stacked up? Would I have been just the substitute, or the consolation prize, or simply his second choice?'

Seb was furious. 'Let me in, Mila. You are—'

'But then,' Mila said, 'I realised I was being an idiot.'

Seb went still.

'Because when I'm with you…' A pause. 'When I *was* with you, you never made me feel like that. You never made me feel like anything but the focus of your attention. When I was with you, you made me feel like the centre of your universe. You made me feel special, and treasured, and *valued*. Just for being me, nothing more.' She swallowed. 'I haven't felt like that before. I've never felt like someone's most important person. I liked it. I loved it, really.'

He was letting her talk now.

'I'm sorry it's over, but that's okay. I'm okay—really. You didn't need to check up on me, or whatever it is you're doing. Thank you for making me feel like that, and for helping me realise that I want that feeling again. That I deserve to feel like that.' Another long pause. 'But I don't want to see you again, Seb. It's too hard.'

She reached for the door, needing to close it quickly, so she no longer had to look at Sebastian.

'Let me in, Mila—please.'

She shook her head silently and gripped the door handle.

'Dammit, Mila, I don't want to say this through a fly screen. Let me in.'

There was nothing he could possibly say. She swung the door shut.

Seb spoke again, a split second before the door clicked shut.

'I love you, Mila!'

But the door was closed.

'I love you!'

He was shouting. She could hear him clearly through the door. She should walk away—he'd only clarify those words if she let him in: he loved her *as a friend*.

But when it came to Sebastian Fyfe, as always, she was weak. She opened the door, but not the security screen.

'I love you,' he said again. 'You *are* my most important person.'

'And you don't want to lose our friendship—blah-blah-blah. Haven't we been through this before? It's kind of old.'

'No,' he said. 'I've been an idiot. Please hear me out.'

She nodded, but sharply. 'Be quick. I have a vase to make.'

Mila crossed her arms, refusing to be anything but sceptical.

'I loved Steph,' he said. 'You know that. We loved each other like people do in books and movies, I thought it was perfect. I thought our relationship was perfect. But then we got married, we moved overseas, our businesses took off… and everything changed. I don't really know if it changed fast or slow—but one day our relationship had broken and it never stopped breaking. Our marriage was over in every way but officially. We were done.'

He stood there, on the other side of the security screen, watching Mila with a measured intensity.

'And that was the thing. Steph and I started with so much and ended up with nothing. *Worse* than nothing, actually. It was like we'd created a vacuum between us, which swallowed up all our hopes and plans for a future together and left us each alone in the darkness. It was miserable.' He swallowed. 'I made a lot of mistakes in my marriage. I prioritised my work over Steph. I prioritised my work over everything. And I shoved my head in the sand when it came to Steph and I. I hurt her—a lot. I hate that I did that. And I was terrified that I'd do that to you.'

Mila had uncrossed her arms, and her fingers were now tangling again in her apron.

'So when you started talking about love the other night I did panic. It's hard for me to believe in love, given what happened in my marriage. It isn't really an emotion that I trust. But mostly I was worried about you. I don't ever want to hurt anyone the way I hurt Steph. I believed I was beyond repair. That loving me meant that hurt was guaranteed. I couldn't do that to you.'

'What's changed?' Mila asked.

Seb nodded. 'You,' he said. 'You've changed me, Mila. You've shown me that I need to leave the past behind. That, while I need to learn from my mistakes, I need to move forward. You told me once about your plans to protect yourself from hurt in relationships—and I know how much you've been hurt in the past. And yet you threw all that away. For *me*. You risked hurt—hurt that you're all too familiar with— for a man you knew was all kinds of messed up and likely to throw it in your face.'

Because I love you—Mila thought. But she was wasn't ready to say it aloud. Not yet.

'Life is all about choices, Mila. I finally get that. And I promise you right now I choose *not* to be a selfish, distant workaholic ever again.'

Mila's lips quirked upwards, despite the swirling and still uncertain emotion between them.

'But I know that I'm not the only one with choices in a relationship. You have them too. And I think maybe it was those choices that I was most fearful of. What if you choose to hurt me? To walk away from me? To stop loving me?'

Seb's voice was strong, but raw. Mila's heart beat like a drum against her chest...her fingers twisted in knots inside her apron.

'But you know what? I can't control your choices. I can't control anything but my own. And, as scary as that is for me to realise, I've decided to run with it. To be—for the first time in way too long—truly, properly brave.'

He swallowed, his gaze exploring her face.

'So, Mila—I choose *you*. I choose to love you. I love you, Mila Molyneux, and that won't change—whatever you decide. Whatever you choose. I came here tonight because I thought you deserved to hear that—but also because I needed to say it.' A long, long pause. 'I came here with no expectations. I *will* leave, with no regrets and no bad feelings—I promise—if you don't want me. If you don't love me. If you don't choose—'

'Oh, *God*, Seb, shut up!' Mila said with laughter—and with love. 'Of *course* I choose you!'

With rapid, desperate movements, Mila opened the security screen. Instantly she was in Seb's arms and his lips were at her neck, her jaw, her mouth.

Her hands threaded through his hair. 'I love you,' Mila said softly against his lips.

'I love you, too, Mila,' he said, his lips against her ear, his breath hot against her skin. 'I've loved you since I was fourteen—in a million different ways. But the way I love you *now* is my favourite.'

'This *is* pretty good,' she teased, and then squealed as he lifted her into his arms.

'Can that vase wait?' Seb asked, nodding in the direction of the forgotten pottery wheel.

'That had better not be a serious question,' Mila replied, her mouth against his neck, her laughter only slightly muffled against his skin.

'Of course not,' Seb said, and he practically leapt up the stairs, putting his months of physical labour—Mila thought—to very good use.

At the top of the stairs, he paused. It was dark in Mila's apartment, lit only by the glow of the streetlight and a hint of the moon. But still, in the almost darkness, their gazes met and locked.

Seb was waiting, Mila realised.

Then she smiled.

'Carry me to bed,' she said, so softly.

'Every night?' he asked.

She nodded. 'For ever, please.'

* * * * *

"It'd be a shame. You coming out all this way just to go home so soon."

"I know," Casey replied. "But I can't impose on my sister for the summer—not now."

"That's right," he agreed. Then added, "I have a loft apartment above the barn. It's a little rough, but it's livable."

Casey looked at Brock and listened while he continued.

"The way you are with Hannah—it's pretty impressive. And it got me thinking that we could help each other out. Hannah does fine with academics—she's even strong in math and science. But it's her…"

"Pragmatics," she filled in for him.

He glanced at her again. "Exactly. How 'bout I let you use the loft for the summer in exchange for some private social-language support. How does that set with you?"

Casey stared at Brock's profile. "Are you serious?"

"Yeah. Why? Do you think it's a bad idea?"

"Heck no, I don't think it's a bad idea. I think it's a pretty genius idea."

* * *

The Brands of Montana:
Wrangling their own happily-ever-afters

MEET ME AT THE CHAPEL

BY
JOANNA SIMS

First Published in Great Britain 2016
By Mills & Boon, an imprint of HarperCollins*Publishers*
1 London Bridge Street, London, SE1 9GF

© 2016 Joanna Sims

ISBN: 978-0-263-92018-5

23-0916

Our policy is to use papers that are natural, renewable and recyclable products and made from wood grown in sustainable forests. The logging and manufacturing processes conform to the legal environmental regulations of the country of origin.

Printed and bound in Spain
by CPI, Barcelona

Joanna Sims is proud to pen contemporary romance for Mills & Boon Cherish. Joanna's series, The Brands of Montana, features hardworking characters with hometown values. You are cordially invited to join the Brands of Montana as they wrangle their own happily-everafters. And, as always, Joanna welcomes you to visit her at her website: www.joannasimsromance.com.

Dedicated to Aa and MM

Thank you for allowing me to use your proposal as inspiration. Congratulations on your engagement!

Chapter One

"Recalculating."

Casey Brand had been lost in thought until the portable GPS interrupted her daydream. She tightened her grip on the steering wheel of the moving truck, hands placed firmly at ten and two, before she glanced at the GPS screen.

"Recalculating."

"No!" Casey argued with the machine. "We are *not* recalculating!"

"Recalculating."

The map on the screen of the GPS had disappeared, replaced by a single word: *searching*. She hadn't been to her uncle and aunt's ranch since she was a teenager, so finding it by memory wasn't a viable option. She needed the GPS to do its job. Casey took her eyes off the road for a second to tap the screen of the GPS.

"*Darn* it!" She was going to have to pull over.

Her trip from Chicago to Montana had been fraught with setbacks: violent thunderstorms, road construction, bad food, horrible menstrual cramps and a rental truck that struggled to maintain speed on every single hill. Not wanting to risk stopping on an incline, Casey punched the gas pedal several times to help the truck make the climb to the top of the hill.

"Come on, you stupid truck!" Casey rocked back and forth in her seat. "You can do it!"

Halfway to the top of the hill, the check-engine light flashed and then disappeared.

"Don't you *dare*!" Casey ordered.

Three quarters of the way up the hill, the orange check-engine light appeared and, this time, it stayed.

Casey groaned in frustration. With every tedious mile, it felt like the universe was telling her that her trip was ill-fated. At the top of the hill, she turned on her blinker, carefully eased the truck onto the gravelly berm and shifted into Park.

"Recalculating."

"Oh, just shut up," Casey grumbled as she shut off the engine.

"You wait here," she said to the teacup poodle watching her curiously from inside a dog carrier that was secured with a seat belt. "I'll be right back."

She pulled on the lever to pop the hood and jumped out of the cab. At the front of the truck, she was immediately hit with a strong, acrid smell coming from the engine. The hood of the truck was hot to the touch; Casey yanked her baseball cap off her head and used it to protect her fingers while she lifted up the hood.

"Holy cannoli!" Casey covered her face with the

cap and backed away from the truck. A moment later, she ran back to the cab of the truck and grabbed the dog carrier, before she put distance between herself and the rental.

A small electrical fire had melted several wires in the engine; it looked as if the fire had already put itself out, but she couldn't risk driving the truck now. For the time being, she was stuck on a desolate road, with her sister's worldly possessions in the back of the broken-down rental, a teacup poodle and angry black storm clouds forming overhead.

Casey pulled her phone out of the back pocket of her jeans to call her sister.

"Come on, Taylor...pick up the phone."

When Taylor didn't answer, she called again. She was on her third attempt when a fat raindrop landed on the bridge of her nose. She looked up at the black cloud that was now directly above her.

"Really?" she asked the cloud.

Her sister wasn't answering, for whatever reason, so she needed to move on to plan B. She was about to dial her aunt Barbara's cell number when she noticed a horse and rider galloping across a field on the opposite side of the road. She didn't think, she reacted.

"Hey!" Casey ran across the road, waving her free arm wildly. "Hey!"

The rider didn't seem to hear her or see her. At the edge of the road, Casey looked down at her beloved Jimmy Choo crushed leather Burke boots and then at the rider. There was mud and grass and rock between her and the rustic wooden fence that surrounded the wide, flat field. Her boots had only known city sidewalks and shopping malls. She didn't want her beautiful boots to get dirty, but there wasn't a choice—she had to get the rider's attention. She ran, as softly as she could manage, through the mud and wet grass to the fence. She put the dog carrier on the ground so she could climb up onto the fence.

"Hey!" Casey yelled again and waved her hat in the air. *"Help!"*

This time, the rider, a cowboy by the look of him, saw her. He slowed his muscular black horse, assessed the situation and then changed direction.

"He sees us!" Casey told her canine companion. The closer the cowboy came, the more familiar he seemed. Casey stared harder at the man galloping toward her, sitting so confident and erect in the saddle.

"Wait a minute. I *know* you!"

Brock McAllister was galloping toward home, racing the rain clouds gathering to the west, when he spotted a woman perched on his fence, waving her arm to get his attention. Brock slowed his stallion and assessed the situation before he decided to change direction. As he came closer, he could see that the woman wasn't as young as he had thought. She had a slight build, borderline thin, and appeared to be in her midthirties.

"Brock! It's me—Casey," the woman called out to him with another wave. "Casey Brand."

The moment Casey added the last name "Brand" to the equation, Brock made the connection. He had worked on the Brand family's ranch, Bent Tree, since he was a teenager, and had worked his way up to ranch foreman. Taylor, Casey's older sister, was married to his stepbrother, Clint, and had just given him a niece. So he'd heard through the grapevine that Casey was coming to Montana to help her sister with the new baby, but he hadn't given her much thought one way or the other until he found her climbing on his fence.

Lightning lit up the gray clouds hanging over the mountains in the distance and the once-sporadic raindrops were coming with more frequency. He only had a few short minutes to stay ahead of the storm. If Casey needed rescuing, it was going to have to be quick.

"You have perfect timing!" Casey gave him a relieved smile when he halted his horse next to the fence. "Would you believe it? The engine caught on fire!"

Given that information, Brock made a split-second decision that he couldn't leave Casey behind in the rental while he went back to the farm to get his truck.

"We need to get out of the way of this storm." Brock walked his horse in a small circle so he could get closer to the fence.

"Is there someone you can call to come get me? I tried my sister, but she didn't answer."

"You can't stay here. We're under a tornado watch." Brock halted his horse and held out his gloved hand to Casey. "You need to come with me. *Now!*"

It seemed to him that his words hadn't registered. She stared at him with a stunned expression, but didn't budge.

"Come on!" Brock yelled at her, his large stallion prancing anxiously in place. "Give me your hand!"

The urgency in his voice, along with a clap of thunder, finally got her moving. But instead of giving him her hand, she gave him her dog carrier.

"Hold Hercules! I've got to get my wallet!"

Surprised, Brock reached out his hand to take the carrier before his brain had a chance to register that there was a miniature dog, the smallest dog he'd ever seen, inside of the designer bag.

"What the hell…?" Brock's low baritone voice was caught on a gust of wind. While he waited for Casey's return, Brock raised the carrier to eye level so he could get a better look at his new passenger. "What in the heck are you supposed to be?"

Casey ran on the treadmill regularly, so running the short distance to the truck and back was easy for her. She grabbed her wallet then locked the door. Brock's stallion was chomping at the bit, refusing to stand still by the fence.

"Easy, Taj…" She heard Brock trying to calm the horse while he circled back to the fence. On her way to the truck, the first raindrops had landed on the top of her head and on the tip of her nose. By the time she'd climbed back to the top of the fence, it had begun to rain in earnest. Casey straddled the fence while Brock steadied the prancing, overly excited stallion that was tossing his head and biting at the bit.

"Come on!" Brock ordered. "Use the stirrup!"

Casey grabbed ahold of the damp material of the cowboy's chambray shirt, slipped her left foot into the stirrup and swung her right leg over the horse's rump. Casey tucked Hercules under one arm and held on tight to Brock with the other. The heavy sheets of rain were being pushed at an angle by the wind, strong enough and hard enough that the right side of her face felt as if it were being pelted by rock salt. She tried to shield Hercules as much as she could from the rain while she tried to protect her own face by tucking her head into Brock's back.

Casey pressed her head into the cowboy's back, and tightened her arms around his waist. In her youth, she had been an excellent rider; she knew how to sit and she knew how to balance her weight on the back of a horse. So, even though his stallion had an extra burden to carry, the impact on the horse would be minimal. Loud claps of thunder followed the lightning strikes by only a few seconds, signaling to Casey that the lightning was too close for comfort. Riding on horseback in a lightning storm was an invitation to be struck.

"Yah, Taj!" she heard Brock yell as he leaned forward and prodded the sure-footed stallion. The stallion leapt forward and kicked his speed into an even higher gear.

Casey squeezed her eyes shut and concentrated on following the movement of Brock's body. All of her senses were being bombarded at once: the masculine scent of leather and sweat on Brock's shirt mingled with the earthy, sweet scent of the rain, the feel of Brock's thick thigh muscles pressed so tightly against her own, and the sound of the stallion's hooves pounding the ground as it carried them across the flat, grassy plain. When she heard what sounded like hooves hitting gravel, she opened her eyes. From beneath the brim of her baseball cap, she saw part of a denim-blue house with a flat roof and a white trim through a canopy of trees.

On their way up the narrow gravel driveway, they passed a faded brown barn and older-model blue-and-yellow Ford tractor. Now in full view, Brock's two-story house was square with two bay windows and kitty-corner steps leading up to covered porches on either side. Brock halted the stallion directly in front of the stairs, a maneuver Casey suspected he'd done many times before.

"Get inside. The door's unlocked!" Brock ordered. "I'll be back in a minute."

Brock held the carrier while she dismounted; once she was safely on the ground, he handed Hercules to her. She ran up the steps, and kept on running until she reached the shelter of the covered porch by the front door. She wiped the water off her face as best she could, but her clothing and hair and boots were sopping wet and her skin was wet beneath the material of her jeans and shirt. She hesitated by the door, not wanting to drip water all over his floor. But she heard Brock yelling at her as he dismounted, telling her to get inside. Casey took one last look at the blackened sky filled with swirling gray clouds pouring rain before she followed his direction and opened the front door to the farmhouse.

The heavy door swung open and Casey crossed the threshold into Brock's dark world. The house was old—she estimated by the look of the lead-stained glass windows abutting the front door that it had already celebrated its centennial birthday. But it had not celebrated in grand fashion. The curtains were made of a dark cherry brocade and were drawn shut to block out any light. Cornflower blue wallpaper dotted with small white flowers contrasted oddly with the forest green shag carpet. Casey knew from her sister that Brock was separated from his wife, Shannon. Brock and Shannon had been "an item" all through middle school and high school. Shannon had been a Miss Montana first runner-up and Casey could remember looking at her when she was a preteen and thinking that Shannon was the prettiest person she'd ever seen. They had married right after high school and the marriage had produced a daughter. But, according to Taylor, they were going through a messy divorce and custody battle and Shannon had been living in California with her new boyfriend.

Yes, Shannon was probably still a very beautiful woman—but she wasn't a housekeeper. Everything in the house seemed dingy and tired—in need of a good scrubbing to get rid of the wet-dog smell and a serious cleaning in general. Yet Casey could look past the clutter and floral decor to see the potential in the house. The dark, carved woodwork used for the crown molding, the built-in bookshelves and the stairwell, which appeared to be original to the house and beautifully made. The bay windows with those antique stained-glass windows were stunning. Even though the house seemed to be sagging beneath the weight of disrepair, with a lot of TLC, it could be something truly special.

"It's going to be okay." Casey put the carrier down on the ground so she could kneel down and take off her boots. No sense just standing there making a puddle in Brock's foyer. Casey took inventory of her options and then took Hercules, carrier and all, through the living room until she had reached what appeared to be the middle of the house.

"You wait here," she told Hercules; her pocket poodle had shocked her by not making a sound, even during his first jarring ride on a horse.

Casey went to a small bathroom just off the living room.

"Jackpot." Casey found a stack of clean, mismatched towels jammed under the sink.

She quickly dried her thick, waist-length hair before twisting it into the towel like a turban. With a second towel, she got the excess water off her shirt and jeans before ripping off her socks so she could stand on the damp towel in her bare feet.

Outside, the wind was howling around the house, sending loose leaves swirling past the window. The trees were starting to bend from the force of the wind and rain, which hadn't let up since they arrived at the ranch.

What was keeping Brock?

As if on cue, Brock burst through the front door and slammed it shut behind him. Not bothering to take off his wet boots, he strode into the living room and turned on the television. The severe-weather bulletin that had trumped regular programing was running images of a funnel cloud that seemed to be too close for comfort.

"Stay here," he said as he turned off the television.

Brock took the narrow stairs up to the second floor two at a time. He went to the master bedroom, tugged one of the plaid shirts down off the bedpost, then grabbed a pair of his soon-to-be ex-wife's jeans and socks out of a dresser drawer. He needed to get his unexpected guest taken care of before he went to go get his daughter, Hannah, who was at a friend's house roughly fifteen minutes away. He had to get to Hannah.

"They're clean." He pushed the clothes into her arms.

Casey was still trying to process the fact that she was caught up in a tornado situation, when Brock swung open a door that led to a cellar. A blast of stale air hit her in the face.

Brock switched on a battery-powered light. "Change and then you and your dog need to go down to the cellar. There's a weather radio down there, along with other supplies. Switch it on so you know what's happening. Wait there until I get back."

"You're leaving?" There was the tiniest crack in her voice. She was accustomed to blizzards, but tornadoes were an entirely different kind of natural menace.

"I'm going to get my daughter!" he hastened to say. And then he was gone.

She followed his directions—they were sensible and were meant to keep her safe. She stripped out of her wet clothes, wrung them out and hung them over the tub. The plaid shirt was huge on her—she rolled the sleeves up several times so her hands were free. Likewise, the jeans were loose around the waist and hips, and way too long. Casey folded the waistband down to make the jeans fit more securely, and then cuffed the bottom of the jeans so she could walk without stepping on them.

Once she was in dry clothes, she pulled the towel off her head and twisted her tangled hair into a topknot.

"Here goes nothing." Casey opted to breathe through her mouth to avoid inhaling the musty odor of the cellar. After some time down there, she hoped she wouldn't even notice it.

At the bottom of the rickety steps, Casey found a spot on the ground where she could unfold a blanket and hunker down until the coast was clear. The wind was so strong that it felt as if the house was swaying and groaning overhead.

"Come on out, little one." Casey opened the carrier and coaxed the rust-colored micro-poodle out onto the blanket.

She was glad that Hercules was content to curl up

in her lap, because she needed his company. He made her feel calmer. With a frustrated, self-pitying sigh, Casey turned on the weather radio and knew that the only thing she could do now was wait and pray.

"I'm so sorry, Brock." Kay Lynn opened the door to the trailer. "I had to call. I haven't seen her like this in a while. She was hitting herself and biting her hand again. She's been in a nosedive for the last hour or so."

"Is she in her normal spot?"

Kay Lynn nodded toward the hallway of the single-wide trailer. Brock walked quickly, but calmly, down the narrow hallway to the spare bedroom. Squeezed between a full-size bed and the wall, his twelve-year-old daughter was curled into a tight ball, rocking back and forth. In front of her, lying on top of Hannah's feet, was a golden Lab.

"Good girl, Ladybug." Brock knelt down, put his hand on the dog's head for a moment, before he reached out for his daughter's hand.

"Hannah," he said softly. "It's time to go home."

Hannah had been officially diagnosed with Asperger syndrome when she was eight. Her IQ was very high, but there were quirks to her personality that set her apart from other children her age. And, when a storm was coming, Brock always anticipated that she was going to have an off day. If he'd had any idea that she was going to spiral like this, he would have stayed home with her.

"Come on, baby girl." He directed the protective dog to move out of the way so he could help Hannah make the transition from the trailer to his truck. "We're going home."

Hannah lifted her head up. Her face, so much like his, was still damp from shed tears. His heart tightened every time his daughter cried. Brock wiped her tears from her cheeks before he lifted her up into his arms and hugged her tightly. The squeezing always calmed her.

"Why didn't you come sooner?" Hannah asked when he put her down.

"I got here as fast as I could." Brock took her hand in his. "Now, I need you to use your 'stay calm' plan on the way home. Okay?"

Hannah nodded. "Come on, Lady."

Now that he had his daughter with him, Brock felt complete. He could handle anything, as long as he had his daughter by his side. He could even handle a messy divorce from Shannon, Hannah's mother. They were in a custody battle for Hannah and had been for nearly a year. Shannon wanted to move Hannah out to California with her, and it was going to happen over his dead carcass. Hannah was going to stay in Montana, with him, in the only home she'd ever known. Period.

"You'd better hunker down, Kay Lynn. You're a sitting duck out here. You could come with us, but you've got to come now."

Kay Lynn's silver-streaked hair blew around the sunken cheeks of her face. She waved her hand as if she could bat away the tornado with her rough-skinned fingers. "That tornado don't want none of me, Brock. You go on and get Hannah home. I'll be right as rain."

There was no sense wasting time trying to convince Kay Lynn to leave her home—she was as much a part of the prairie surrounding the old trailer as was the willowy Junegrass. He'd offered, but knew she wouldn't take him up on it.

With a quick wave to Hannah's sometimes babysitter, Brock bundled Hannah into the truck and headed back to his little Montana spread. They didn't see much more than a few drops of rain on their short drive back. Brock pulled into the gravelly driveway that led to their farmhouse knowing that they were in a lull. The clouds above were still churning and angry, and it was only a matter of time before the wind would start howling again. They were in the most dangerous time of a tornado, the time when many folks get fooled into thinking that the threat was over, when in actuality it was just about to begin.

Chapter Two

"It's time for our storm plan, Hannah. Tell me what we need to do." Brock pulled the screen door open to their house. The rain was still misty, but he knew from experience that that could change on a dime.

Hannah was faithfully rattling off the steps of their storm plan when they reached the foyer safely. They had created the storm plan years ago, not only to keep safe, but to keep Hannah feeling calm and in charge during an emergency.

"Good job, baby girl." Brock shut the door firmly behind them. Now that they were inside the house, he could take his anxiety level down a notch.

Hannah was on the ground yanking off her wet boots and he was knocking the excess water off his cowboy hat when he heard a noise coming from the kitchen. Brock hung his hat on a hook by the door before he walked around the corner toward the sound of the noise.

"Oh!" Casey exclaimed, balancing a full glass of water in one hand and Hercules in the other. "Hey! You're back!"

"Why aren't you in the cellar?"

"The rain and the wind stopped, so I figured we were in the clear," she explained to him offhandedly on her way to greet his daughter. "You must be Hannah. I'm Casey. I've heard so much about you from my sister, Taylor." Casey smiled at the preteen who was nearly as tall as she was. "And this is the awesome Hercules."

Casey knew from her sister that Hannah was on the spectrum, so she understood when Brock's daughter didn't look her in the eye. She also knew that Hannah loved animals and it showed by the way Hannah reached over to gently pet Hercules.

"You can get acquainted in the cellar." Brock moved behind his daughter and put his hands on her shoulders. "It may look like it now, but we're not in the clear."

"No?" Casey asked him.

"No," he reiterated. "We all need to get down in the cellar. *Now.*"

For two hours, the three of them hunkered down in the cellar while the worst of the storm stalled in their region of the state. The wooden house creaked and groaned as the storm reenergized. She couldn't see it, but she had been able to hear that the force of the wind was blowing debris against the sides of the house. Casey was grateful that fate had landed her in Brock's cellar instead of being stranded out on a desolate road in a rented moving van. But her gratitude was beginning to give way to discomfort and claustrophobia. It was cool and damp down in the cellar—her skin felt clammy and she still felt chilled even after Brock gave her a blanket to wrap around her shoulders. Worse yet, the air was stuffy, and even though she had hoped she would be able to eventually ignore it, she hadn't grown accustomed to the smell at all. It was reminiscent of her middle school locker room—body odor and dirty socks.

"Do you think it's safe to go up yet?" Casey asked her host expectantly.

It had been at least fifteen minutes since the wind had knocked anything into the exterior of the house. The pounding sound that the driving rain had made as it pummeled Brock's antiquated farmhouse had died down.

"Give it a few more minutes. The last funnel touched down mighty close to here."

With a heavy sigh, Casey shifted her body to take pressure off her aching tailbone. Sitting on the floor had stopped being a fun option when she reached her thirties. She preferred a comfy couch or squishy chair. Sitting on the floor was for the birds.

"God—my poor sister. She has to be scared to death wondering where I am." Casey readjusted the blanket on her shoulders. "You know—my horoscope *did say* that this was a bad time to travel."

"You don't really believe in that, do you?" he asked her.

"Only when they're right," she said with the faintest of laughs. "I'd say a broken-down truck, a tornado and getting stuck in your smelly cellar are three very strong indicators that it was a bad time for me to travel."

She heard Brock laugh a little after she spoke, and then she realized what she had said. "That sounded really ungrateful."

"It's okay."

"I *am* grateful," she added. "I could still be out there, stuck."

"I knew what you meant," Brock reassured her.

"And now I'm babbling. If you want me to zip it, just tell me. I won't be the least bit offended. My mom has told me that I was a precocious talker and I've had the gift of gab ever since I was a toddler. Of course, Mom doesn't really mean that in the most positive of ways."

"Talking makes the time go faster," Brock reminded her.

"Well, now you're probably just being nice, but that's okay."

"I haven't been accused of that trait too often," he replied humorously.

Hannah made a content noise as she snuggled closer to her father. Ladybug, the golden Lab that Brock and Hannah called Lady for short, lifted up her head to check on Hannah before putting her head back down on her front paws. It was endearing to see the closeness between Brock and his daughter. They were so bonded that it was hard to imagine a third person in that dynamic.

Casey was sure that there were many sides of Brock that she hadn't seen—wasn't that the case with all people? But he'd been nothing but nice to her, and he was so gentle with Hannah.

"I've never seen anyone connect with Hannah as quickly as you did," Brock told her quietly.

Casey heard the admiration in his voice and it made

her feel good. "I work with kids with all sorts of disabilities for a living—I guess it's just second nature to me now."

"What do you do again? I think your sister told me once, but I apologize—I forgot."

"I wouldn't expect you to remember something like that, anyway." Casey uncrossed her legs to relieve the ache that had shifted from her tailbone to her knees. "I'm a special education teacher for Chicago public schools. I provide services for students who have individual education plans and need extra support to access the curriculum."

"Is that right?" Brock asked. "Chicago has a reputation for having some pretty rough neighborhoods, doesn't it?"

She nodded. Those rough areas were one of the main objections her father, a prominent judge in Chicago, had to her desire to become a teacher. For her mother, it was all about the prestige of the job and the money. Or lack thereof.

"I do work in a high-poverty school. It's not easy, and, yes, there are too many problems to count, but my kids make the challenges worthwhile. Most of the kids I work with—they're good kids. *Great* kids. They just need someone to care enough about them to help them succeed—to help them *supersede* their backgrounds." Casey's voice became more passionate as she continued. "Do you know that so many of the kids I serve wouldn't have needed the services of a special education teacher if they hadn't been born into poverty? They would have had the exposure to print and early literacy development, and different experiences to build background knowledge. And it's not that the parents don't *want to* provide their kids with the best start possible, but living hand-to-mouth..." Casey counted things on her fingers. "Food insecurity, illiteracy, lack of education and job opportunities, so many factors, that parents don't have the time, or the energy, or the resources to read to their children, or provide them with those vital foundational skills. By the time these kids get to kindergarten, they're already behind in all of those fundamental skills, like vocabulary and phonemic awareness... It's really sad. Shameful, really."

When Casey spoke about the kids she worked with in Chicago, her face lit up with excitement. It turned a rather ordinary face into one that was really quite extraordinary.

"You love your job."

Casey gave him a little smile that was self-effacingly saying, *What tipped you off?*

"I really appreciate your passion for your work." Brock seemed like he wanted to reassure her. To validate her. "Kids like my Hannah need teachers who are dedicated, who genuinely care about her success. You're a hero to parents like me. I mean, the way you redirected Hannah and kept her calm... It was impressive."

In the low light cast off from the lantern between them, their eyes met and held for the briefest of moments before Brock looked away. His dark hair, threaded with silver near the temple, was slicked back from his long face. His jawline was square, his brows heavy above deeply set blue eyes. When she was a scrawny teenager, and Brock was eighteen, she had thought he was *so* handsome—and she still did. But all signs of youthfulness had been worn from his face. The wrinkles on his forehead, around his mouth and eyes, were evidence of frowning and stress. This was a man who was under a major amount of pressure—she recognized the signs. She also recognized the signs of a devoted father. Whatever marital problems he was having—and she had heard from her sister that there were many—he hadn't let them interfere with his dedication to Hannah.

"Well, thank you." Casey felt her cheeks get a little warm. "I'm glad I could help."

Hercules picked that moment to sit up, stretch, yawn and then take a large leap off her thigh and onto the blanket.

"Is that a real dog? Or do you have to wind it every morning?" Brock had turned his attention to her teacup-sized poodle that had just made the large leap off her leg onto the blanket.

"*Hey!* Don't pick on Hercules!" Hannah scooped Hercules up and kissed him several times. "Though he may be but little, he is fierce!"

"Now it's getting serious. You brought Shakespeare to the table?" Brock teased her.

Hercules gave a little yap and ran around in a circle.

"A little Shakespeare never hurt anyone."

"Speak for yourself," he retorted. "I took a class on Shakespeare in college. Worst semester of my life."

"It pains me to shift the subject away from Shakespeare, because I happen to be a fan, but I think—" she nodded her head toward her pocket poodle "—he needs a bathroom break. He does have a microscopic bladder, after all—poor baby."

"Okay." Brock shook Hannah's shoulder to wake her. "I think it's safe to go topside."

Ignoring the stiffness in her joints from sitting for too long in one position, Casey stood up quickly, shed the blanket, scooped up Hercules and tucked him into the crook of her arm.

She was the caboose, and followed Brock, his daughter and their dog up to the main floor.

"Oh, wow." Casey walked to the closest window.

The storm had torn through the ranch, littering the yard with large, broken tree branches, overturned equipment and missing shingles from the roof of the barn.

"What a mess," she said to Brock.

"I'm going to check on the horses." The ranch foreman shrugged into a rain slicker. "Will you watch Hannah?"

She agreed to watch his daughter, of course. And, once both dogs had the chance to take care of business, Casey and Hannah took their canine companions back inside. It was drizzling outside, and the gray sky was so dreary, but it seemed as if the worst of the storm had finally passed them by.

"Do you have a landline, Hannah?"

Hannah showed her the phone on the other side of the refrigerator. She had periodically tried to get reception with her cell phone while they were in the cellar, without any luck. Now that they were out of the cellar, she still wasn't having any luck with reception.

Relieved to hear a dial tone when she picked up the receiver, she dialed her sister's number and silently begged her sister to answer.

"Hello?"

"Taylor! Thank goodness I got you!"

"Casey! I saw Brock's number on caller ID. I wasn't expecting to hear your voice, but I'm so glad it's you! I've been trying to get you on your cell phone for hours!"

"I knew you had to be freaking out. I'm sorry—the truck broke down, then the tornado… It's been a crazy day. How did you fare through the storm?"

"We're fine—we'll have to clean up the loose branches in the yard, but it could have been much, much worse. I'm just glad that you're okay," her sister said. "I didn't want you to drive all of my stuff here by yourself, anyway. And you said the truck broke down?"

"Small fire in the engine, yes."

"Ca-sey! I *knew* it was a bad idea!"

Casey heard the sound of her niece crying in the background. Penelope had been born premature and was prone to ear infections. She didn't say anything to her sister, but Taylor sounded exhausted.

"Tay—I wanted to do it, so I did it. I'm fine. Brock happened to show up at an opportune time, so no harm done."

There was a pause on the end of the line.

Then Taylor said, "I was wondering how you wound up with Brock."

When her sister said her brother-in-law's name, there was an underlying dislike in her tone. Casey knew from many conversations with her sister that Brock and her new husband, Clint, had a long-standing fractured relationship. From what she understood, Clint didn't like Brock any more than Brock liked him. And the only glue that bound them together was Hannah.

"He kept me safe. And he's been really nice to me."

"Well." Her sister seemed reluctant to give Brock a compliment. "That's good at least."

Casey smiled at Hannah, who was sitting at the table with an iPad while Lady took her position at Hannah's feet.

"And I've had a chance to make friends with Hannah," she said. "I hear my niece. How's she doing?"

"She's sick again." This was said with the tired voice of a first-time mother. "She hasn't slept, so I haven't slept. Clint broke his collarbone down in Laredo…"

"Oh, no, Tay—I'm so sorry to hear that."

"It couldn't be worse timing—the only upside is that he's coming home early. His best friend, Dallas, is going to drive him back and then we'll buy her a plane ticket to get her to the next stop on the circuit."

Taylor's husband was a professional bull rider; Casey didn't know how her sister, who was once married to a metrosexual man, could have wound up marrying a cowboy. But they seemed to just fit.

"He'll be home all summer then." Casey said the thought as soon as she thought it.

"That collarbone is going to be a tough one to heal, so I think he'll be out of the running this season. Maybe this will be the one that makes him rethink his career."

Still thinking about Taylor's small bungalow on the outskirts of Helena, Casey didn't respond right away. It must have clicked in Taylor's mind what she was thinking, because her sister hastened to say, "There's plenty of room here, Casey. I still want you to stay with us for the summer."

"Let's not worry about it now." Casey rubbed her temples. "First thing I need to do is find out from

Brock if the roads are even passable now so I can check on the truck. I don't think he'll mind taking me all the way into Helena if it saves you a trip."

"Call me as soon as you know the plan. Promise?"

"Of course. I love you, sis. Give Penny a kiss from me. I'll see you soon."

Casey used the restroom and then joined Hannah at the table. Hannah was looking at a large diagram of a ladybug's anatomy. Like many children diagnosed with autism, Hannah had become fixated on a topic, and that topic was ladybugs. The bathroom was decorated with ladybugs—ladybug shower curtain, ladybug toothbrush holder, ladybug towels. There was a ladybug on Hannah's shirt and Casey had spotted a ladybug backpack hanging on one of the hooks in the foyer. Their dog was named Ladybug. One of the ways she had distracted Hannah from being scared in the cellar was to redirect to conversations about ladybugs. Once Hannah got started talking about the topic that interested her most, she forgot about the storm and talked at length about the insects. Although Brock was impressed with her ability to pinpoint Hannah's interest, it wasn't rocket science. All she had to do was pay attention to observable details, which was part of her job as a special education teacher.

"What else do you have on your iPad?" she asked, curious to see Hannah's reaction.

"Stuff," Hannah replied without looking up from the screen.

Brock's daughter wasn't interested in showing her any other apps on the iPad—not in the middle of looking at ladybugs.

The door to the house swung open. Brock peeled off his wet rain slicker and tossed it onto a rocking chair just outside the front door. He stepped into the foyer, stomped his feet on the rug and slapped the rain off his hat by hitting it across his thigh a couple of times.

"How's it looking out there?" Casey asked.

Brock shook his head as he closed the front door tightly behind him. "It's a mess."

He joined them in the kitchen—it wasn't a tiny kitchen, but with Brock in it, it seemed to shrink before her eyes. He had been a tall, lanky young man the last time she had seen him. Now he was a large man, taller than most and burly. He was active and strong, but he had developed a bit of a paunch around the middle. A lumberjack. That's what he reminded her of—a Paul Bunyan lumberjack. Not many of those running around Chicago.

"I got ahold of Taylor."

Brock had just downed a glass of water and he was filling it up again. "Good. She doing okay?"

"Penny's sick again and Clint broke his collarbone, so he's heading back from Texas. She said that she weathered the storm okay, though. Just a couple of small branches in the yard. Nothing major." She noticed that Brock's demeanor didn't change at all when she mentioned that his stepbrother had gotten hurt. "What's the chance of you getting me into Helena tonight?"

"Zip." He put the empty glass on the cluttered counter. "Downed trees are blocking the major roads into town."

"You're not serious?" Casey said with a frustrated sigh. "You are serious."

"I can take you to Bent Tree or you can bunk with us tonight," Brock said. "Hannah—it's time to feed Lady. Turn off the iPad."

Hannah didn't respond.

"Hannah."

"Just one more thing." Hannah didn't look up—her entire focus was on the screen.

Brock was tired and she could see that he was losing patience.

"Here—let's do this, Hannah. I'm going to set my timer to one minute and when the timer goes off, you can turn off the iPad."

The timer on her phone was set, the one minute ran out and Hannah, albeit reluctantly, turned off the iPad and tended to Lady's needs.

Brock didn't say it with words, but there was a definite thank-you in his eyes when he looked at her.

"I don't know if I have the energy to face my aunt and uncle right now. But are you sure it would be okay if I crashed here tonight?"

"It's no problem. You can take my bed upstairs and I'll sleep on the couch."

"No—I'll take the couch."

"No—you'll take my bed. I sleep on the couch most nights, anyway."

Sleeping in a bed instead of on a couch sounded like a much better scenario. If the bed were usually empty anyway, what would it hurt to take him up on his offer?

"All right—but only if you're sure."

He didn't respond to that comment, but instead moved the conversation forward. "We'll get a good night's sleep, have breakfast and then we can stop off and check on the truck on our way to Helena."

"Oh." Casey groaned the word. "Geez. The *truck*. I hope *the Beast* is okay."

Chapter Three

By nature, she was a light sleeper. Always had been. But the night she had spent in Brock's massive California king-size bed had been one of her deepest sleeps on record. Perhaps it was the fact that she had been flat-out exhausted, or maybe it was the silky-soft material of the sheets. Either way, she had awakened from her sound sleep in the dead center of the bed, surrounded by a pile of plump pillows that had to be Brock's soon-to-be ex-wife's doing, feeling happy and content. She didn't even scramble out of bed, as was her usual practice. Instead, she opted to linger a bit, staring up at the ceiling with the comforter pulled all the way up to her nose.

"Dad says get up!" Hannah burst into the room without knocking.

Shocked out of her random, drifting thoughts, Casey

popped upright, her long auburn hair a mass of tangles. Hercules was vaulted forward, but he landed on all four paws. He waggled his tail and yapped at Hannah.

"If you want to come into someone's room, what is the polite thing to do?" Casey asked.

"Knock."

Casey gave the preteen two thumbs-up. "Okay— try it again."

"What?"

"Knocking before you come in. You knock, wait for an answer and then you come in. But only if I say it's okay. Okay?"

"Okay."

Hannah slammed the door shut, causing Hercules to yap wildly. Casey heard a knock on the door, but she waited for a couple of seconds before she answered just to make certain Hannah wouldn't burst in without getting the green light.

"Come in!"

Hannah flung open the door again with a laugh. "Breakfast!"

"Thank you, Hannah. Nice waiting, too." Casey smiled at the girl. "Can you do something for me? Would you take Hercules out to use the bathroom while I get dressed?"

Brock's daughter's face beamed at the thought of being able to carry Hercules for the first time.

"I know you'll make sure he's okay." Casey was re-assuring herself as much as she was reassuring Hannah. It was hard to let Hercules out of her sight. He was so small and vulnerable. But she had heard about Hannah's affinity for animals from Taylor, and she had seen how kind she was with her own dog, Lady.

Casey yawned several times, wiped the sleep out of her eyes and stretched her arms high above her head, before she scooted to the edge of the bed with a dramatic sigh. Rest time was officially over for her. Today, she had to go see how the Beast had fared in the storm, figure out how to get it towed if need be and then figure out whether or not she was just going to stay for a short visit with her sister and then head back to Chicago. She wanted to stay in Montana for the summer—it was too late to put in a request to work summer school. And she had been looking forward to this trip for months. She'd hate for it to all fall apart, but she couldn't imagine staying with Taylor and Clint, in their small rental, for three months. Even though Taylor would try very hard to make her feel like she wasn't a bother, she knew that she would, in fact, be an intrusion on the newlyweds.

Casey went into the tiny attached bathroom to fix her hair, if possible, and wash her mouth out with mouthwash. When she got a load of herself in the mirror, she started to laugh. She looked like a redheaded Medusa. She had tried to tame her hair before bed, but it hadn't worked. Now, it was even worse after a night of sleep.

"Whatever." Casey made a face.

She took off the white undershirt Brock had let her borrow. After getting dressed, she made the bed, and then left the folded undershirt on the comforter, along with the pajama bottoms she hadn't used. Brock's pajama bottoms had just slipped right down her hips.

Finally, she retrieved her beloved Jimmy Choo boots from beneath a nearby chair and stared at them sadly. They were ruined. Her beautiful, *expensive*, Jimmy

Choo boots that she had vision-boarded for months, that she had saved a little every month to buy, were caked with red clay and still wet from the day before.

"You poor, poor boots. You didn't deserve this. *I* didn't deserve this." Today, she wasn't even going to try to be careful with them. There was no use shutting the gate *after* the cow got out. Resigned to their untimely demise, Casey shoved her feet into the boots and headed downstairs.

"Good morning." Casey was met with a cornucopia of breakfast food smells when she entered the kitchen.

"Mornin'," her host greeted her. "Coffee's hot, mugs in the drying rack are a safe bet."

"Bless you." Casey poured herself a cup of coffee.

"If you need milk or sugar, they're somewhere in the fridge. Just fish around."

"I take it black." She took her coffee to the table.

Brock was manning the stove in a "Kiss the Chef" apron, while Hannah, who had already had her breakfast, was on the floor formally introducing Lady and Hercules in the light of day. They had met informally in the cellar, but this was the first time that they were nose to nose, so to speak. Lady was lying down on the floor, her head between her two outstretched front legs, obviously trying to do her best to make friends, while Hercules was yapping as loudly and as ferociously as he could manage in order to assert his dominance in the relationship.

"Hercules—that's not nice."

"How do you take your eggs?" Brock asked her.

"Are they eggs from free-range chickens?"

"The chickens live out back. Is that free enough for you?"

"Lucy and Ethel!" Hannah supplied the names of the chickens.

"*I Love Lucy* and ladybugs. That's what she loves." Brock looked over at his daughter.

"And animals," Casey added.

Brock turned his body away from the stove and toward Casey. This wasn't the first time he'd wanted to get a better look at her in his favorite shirt. It engulfed her, but it looked good on her. Her hair, seemingly more red than auburn in the daylight, was mussed and wild, and he could swear that she had the brightest green eyes he'd ever seen on a woman.

"And animals," he echoed her sentiment. Then, so he wouldn't be standing in his kitchen ogling her like a teenage boy, he asked again, "How do you take your eggs?"

"Scrambled works."

"How about some bacon made from free-range pigs?" Brock teased her.

"No. Thank you. I'm a pescatarian."

Brock wasn't exactly sure he'd heard her right, so after he got the eggs cooking, he turned back around.

"Did you say you were a Presbyterian?"

"No!" Casey laughed so easily. It had been a long time since he'd heard a woman laughing in his house. "Pescatarian. I don't eat meat, except for fish. But I'm trying to give up fish, too."

"What for?"

She smiled at him; she had deep dimples in each of her pale cheeks. Sweet.

"Health mainly—bacon is full of fat and salt. High in cholesterol." Casey wrinkled her nose at the thought of eating bacon.

"Dad has high cholesterol and high blood pressure," Hannah shouted from the living room.

"Hannah—remember what we said about private information?"

"But Dr. Patel says that he has the heart of a much younger man."

It was too late to cork that bottle—instead, Brock decided to ignore the fact that his daughter had just provided a near stranger with all of the recent results of his physical and finish scrambling the eggs. The only thing that she hadn't shared, because she hadn't been in the room to hear it, was the fact that he had a mildly enlarged prostate and needed to drop twenty pounds.

Brock put a healthy portion of scrambled eggs on the plate, along with cheese grits and a couple of biscuits.

"Eat it while it's hot." He put the plate down in front of her and then sat down on the opposite side of the kitchen table.

"Mmm. Thank you. I'm so hungry." Casey stabbed a couple of eggs with her fork. "What about you?"

"I ate hours ago. We've been waiting on you."

Casey chewed her eggs quickly so she could ask, "Why didn't you wake me up when you got up?"

"I got up while it was still dark."

"Oh." That was different. "Well, why didn't you get me up sooner, then?"

"No harm done. It's my day off and I'm not looking forward to getting up on the roof to see how many shingles need to be replaced. You need salt or pepper for the eggs?"

"No. I'm good. These eggs are delicious, FYI."

"That's good."

She finished her breakfast, offered to clean the dishes, which he refused, and then all five of them, two dogs and three humans, piled into Brock's truck. First stop was the moving truck and the second stop was Taylor's house.

"I feel really bad about Clint breaking his collarbone."

She watched Brock's face for a reaction. There wasn't one.

"He was supposed to be gone all summer," she added.

Brock glanced over at his passenger. She had been biting her lip nervously since they had gotten into the truck. Now he understood some of her nerves at least—she was worried about living in a house with a newly married couple and a newborn. Even if they told her that she wasn't going to be a bother, Brock had a feeling that Casey wouldn't even take the chance of being an inconvenience to anybody. During the short time they had spent together, she was always worried about his comfort and his feelings, as well as the comfort and feelings of his daughter. He found her politeness refreshing.

"Might be mighty tight over at their place," Brock said, broaching the topic.

Casey turned her head his way, met him eye to eye. She said, "I was thinking the exact same thing."

"You thinking about cutting your trip short?"

The woman beside him breathed in very deeply and then let it out on a long, extended sigh. "I'd hate to do that. But I just might have to…"

"It'd be a shame. Coming all this way just to go home."

Out of the corner of his eye, he noticed Casey making little circles on the top of Hercules's head. "I know.

But I can't impose on Taylor for the summer—not now. Newlyweds need their private time. Besides, Clint is hurt. He's not going to be in any mood to have a house-guest."

"That's right," he agreed, then added, "I have a loft apartment above the barn. It's a little rough, but it's livable."

Casey looked at Brock, interested.

"The way you are with Hannah—like I said last night—it's impressive. And it got me thinking that we could help each other out. Hannah does fine with academics—she's even strong in math and science. But it's her…"

"Pragmatics," she filled in for him.

He glanced at her again. "Exactly. As you can tell from our breakfast conversation, there's still a bit of a ways to go with that."

Casey nodded her agreement—a deficit with social use of language was a universal symptom of individuals with autism across the spectrum.

"How 'bout I let you use the loft for the summer in exchange for some private social language support. How does that set with you?"

Casey stared at Brock's profile. "Are you serious?"

"Yeah. Why? Do you think it's a bad idea?"

"Heck, no, I don't think it's a bad idea. I think it's a pretty genius idea," she said with a smile. "Can I let you know?"

"Sure. Offer stands."

Casey's smile was short-lived.

"Oh! No, no, no, no, no, no, no, no, *no*!" She put her hands on top of her head in disbelief.

The rental truck was knocked on its side.

"What's wrong?" Hannah looked up from her iPad.

Brock pulled onto the berm on the opposite side of the road from the rental truck.

"Damn."

"Swear jar!" Hannah yelled.

"Hannah," Casey said in a stunned, monotone voice. "Would you hold Hercules for me?"

"Stay in the truck and wait for us, okay, baby girl?" Brock pulled his hat off the dash and pushed it onto his head.

Together, they crossed the road. In silence, they both walked around the perimeter of the truck. The back was still locked, but the truck was facing the wrong direction.

"The only thing I can figure is that a twister caught it and spun it ninety degrees. Then for kicks, knocked it on its side."

Casey stood, shaking her head back and forth, and back and forth. She couldn't find words. Everything her sister owned, everything her sister cherished, was in that truck. There was a collection of Royal Doulton statues worth thousands, as well as a collection of Lladró figurines, also worth thousands. Taylor had been collecting them since she was a teenager.

"I want to cry," Casey said quietly. "I really do."

Brock looked down at her, she saw him in her periphery, and then he took his cell phone out of his pocket and made a phone call. She heard him make arrangements with a friend who had a tow truck made to haul big rigs to come and set the Beast upright and tow it to Helena.

"Thank goodness I took the insurance." Casey couldn't stop staring at the rental truck. She'd never seen one from this angle before. It was a bit like looking at a surrealist painting, trying to figure out why people were walking on the ceiling.

"Right?" Brock crossed his arms in front of his body. "My friend Billy will be able to get this right-side up sometime around noon."

"Thank you."

They stood together, both looking at the truck without anything else to say about it.

"Are you done looking at it?" the ranch foreman asked her.

Casey sighed. "Yeah. I guess. The damage is done."

"That's right."

The rest of the way into Helena, Casey felt sick to her stomach. Taylor was going to be heartbroken and it was her fault. She was the one who'd had the idea of saving her sister some cash by renting a truck and driving it herself. Taylor had said, repeatedly, that she thought it was best if professional movers brought her things to Montana. But, as she always did, she persisted until she wore Taylor down. And now, all of her belongings were trapped in a toppled rental truck on the side of a desolate Montana highway. Brilliant.

"This is it." Brock stopped at the end of the driveway of a little Craftsman bungalow.

With a heavy sigh, Casey nodded her head. "Yep."

"Can I go in and see Penny?" Hannah asked excitedly.

Casey met Brock's eye before she said, "Not this time, Hannah. Penny has an ear infection."

"Next time," Brock added. "I'll call you as soon as I hear something from Billy."

"Text me if I don't answer."

"Consider it done."

She stood with the truck door open and mustered a small smile for him. "Thank you for everything, Brock. Seriously. Above and beyond the call of duty."

He tipped his hat to her, and she interpreted that gesture as a *you're welcome* and a *thank you, too*. She got out of the truck and said goodbye to Hannah and her father.

Her sister was opening the door at the same time Brock was pulling away.

"Casey!" Taylor was holding her baby daughter in her arms.

They embraced tightly, as they always did. They were more than sisters—they were, and always had been, best friends.

"Oh, Tay—she's even prettier in person." Casey touched Penelope's creamy, chubby cheek. "Hi, Penny, you sweet, sweet thing. Your aunt Casey is going to spoil you *absolutely* rotten! Yes, I am!"

"She's so fussy right now because she doesn't feel well." Taylor kissed her daughter's warm forehead.

"Poor Penny." Casey looked at her little niece compassionately.

"I'm so happy to see you, Casey." Taylor hugged her again. "I've missed you like crazy."

Together they walked up the driveway to the front door of the bungalow. "I've missed you. I hate that we don't live in the same town anymore."

"Me, too." Taylor shut the front door behind them. "Let me see if she'll lie down for her nap. It'll give us a chance to catch up. She hasn't slept well for a couple of days, so cross your fingers."

Casey held up her crossed fingers for her sister to see.

Taylor didn't reappear for a while. When her sister returned to the living room, she was talking in a quieter voice.

"Okay—she's down. For how long is debatable! Is it too early for wine?"

"No. Bring it on, sis." She could use a large glass or two.

Taylor had been diagnosed with the inability to lactate after the birth of her daughter, and the only upside her sister could find was the fact that she had been cleared to drink wine.

Casey sat down at the breakfast bar while her sister got the wineglasses.

"Red or white?" Taylor asked her from the open refrigerator.

"Either—as long as it's not too dry."

Taylor held up a bottle for her to see. "How about this?"

Casey gave her the "okay" sign; generous portions of wine were poured and the two of them moved to the cozy family room next to the kitchen. Taylor immediately coaxed Hercules onto her lap, and the micropoodle didn't hesitate to abandon her owner for a novel lap.

"Traitor," Casey said to her canine companion.

"Here's to a great summer." Taylor touched her glass to hers.

"To a great summer." She took several large gulps of the wine. Taylor hadn't even asked her about the rental truck.

Her sister curled her legs to the side, leaned into the couch cushion and smiled happily at her. "I am so happy to see you."

"You may not feel that way in a minute."

Taylor's eyebrows dropped and her pretty blue eyes registered confusion. "What are you talking about?"

Casey downed the rest of her wine. One of her most intense childhood memories was the time that she decapitated Taylor's favorite Barbie doll and then flushed the head just to see if it would indeed flush. It had. And Taylor had gone absolutely crazy-town ballistic on her and then stopped speaking to her for a month. Granted, they were kids when that happened. But then again, this was much worse than decapitating Barbie. *Much* worse.

Chapter Four

Her sister's reaction to the news that her belongings were trapped in a tipped-over truck on the side of the road was not at all what she had anticipated. Taylor wasn't angry. Taylor wasn't looking to blame her. Instead, her sister was simply grateful that Casey and Hercules were okay. Taylor had always had a flair for the dramatic, and this change in her was unexpected, but it was a change for the better. Perhaps it was the fact that she was a mother now; or perhaps it was because she had already lost one of the most valuable gifts she had ever been given—Penelope's twin brother, Michael, had died soon after he was born. Casey hadn't experienced it, but she didn't have to experience something to understand that losing a child, an infant, could change a person forever.

"Are you sure you don't want to stay with us? Clint

and I both *want* you to stay," Taylor asked her as they walked together along the brick walkway that led to the driveway.

She'd been in Montana for a week already, and so much had happened: the Beast had been towed into town, her travel trunk and Taylor's boxes had been recovered and Clint had arrived home with his arm in a sling and loaded up on pain medication. According to the doctors in Texas, Clint's healing time would be roughly a month or two, but he wouldn't be fit to get back on a bull. He was grounded for the entire summer, at least.

Casey, who was holding her niece in her arms, was too busy nuzzling Penny's sweet-smelling neck to pay full attention to her sister. "Mmm, you have that new baby smell, Penny." She hugged her niece, not wanting to let her go. Casey smiled at her sister. "Babies! They always smell so *good*. I wish I could bottle this smell and take it with me."

"Casey! Please, stop ignoring me. You came all the way to Montana to be with Penny and me, and I feel like *deep down inside* you think that we don't want you here because Clint is home. And that's not the case at all."

Casey smooched her niece all over her face one last time before she said, "Trade."

Taylor frowned at her as they traded babies—her sister handed over Hercules and she handed over Penny.

"I don't think you're kicking me out, Tay. I know you want me to stay. I know Clint is sincere when he says that he'll be happy to have me staying on his couch for three months, but I'm telling you, it's gonna wear real thin by the end of four weeks. Trust me. He's an active guy and now he's stuck with his arm in a sling when he should be out earning points. Your husband is going to want to sit on his couch and watch TV, in his tighty-whities, whenever the mood strikes."

Her sister didn't respond for a second or two, because Taylor knew she was right.

"I'll come and visit all the time. I'll be here on a moment's notice if you need me. Nothing's changed."

For the last week, her sister had been debating her choice to stay in Brock's loft apartment with her. Taylor had her own agenda: she either wanted her to stay with her *or* stay with their aunt Barb and uncle Hank at Bent Tree Ranch. Basically, anywhere besides Brock's ranch.

Taylor's eyes had a watery sheen and Casey knew that her sister was upset to see her go. "Look—I know you don't like the idea that I took Brock up on his offer, but it really is for the best. His place is closer to Helena than Bent Tree. And I love the idea of being able to ride anytime I want. Brock says he has a palomino mare who's getting barn sour. I'm actually going to be doing *him* a favor by riding her this summer."

Her sister wiped under her left eye with her pinky. "I know how much you want to ride again."

This was Taylor's way of giving in to the inevitable.

"Come here and give me another hug." Casey hugged her sister again, and then kissed baby Penelope's chubby hand.

"I want one," she told her sister of her niece.

"It's the best hard work I've ever done," said Taylor.

Casey opened the door to the light blue vintage VW Bug sitting in the driveway. She paused before getting in the driver's seat.

"And Taylor...I'm perfectly ready to like your husband very much."

Taylor beamed at her with pleasure. "He's a good one, right?"

Casey nodded as she got into the blue Bug and then put Hercules in his new, less fancy dog carrier for safe traveling. She put the key in the ignition, cranked the engine, then rolled down the window.

"Thanks for loaning me your car, Tay."

After her divorce, Taylor had sold her BMW, left her executive job at the bank, put her stuff in storage and then drove this very Bug from Chicago to Montana. It was on that trip, a trip where she had ridden a portion of the Continental Divide Trail on horseback, that she met her husband, Clint.

"Now you won't be stuck," Taylor said to her. "That car brought me a lot of luck. Maybe it will be lucky for you, too."

Casey backed out of the driveway with a sense of anticipation and excitement that was making her stomach feel a bit queasy. It felt as if she were heading off to her own adventure, much like her sister had last year. She waved her hand, tooted the horn and shouted one last "I love you" to her sister and niece before Casey set her course for Brock McAllister's ranch. She had the distinct feeling that this summer was going to be one of the best summers of her life. And she couldn't wait for it to start!

Casey slowed her speed in order to take the bumps in the dirt and gravel drive to Brock's ranch. The heavy rain from the storm had deepened the potholes, which made it difficult to navigate in the VW bug. Brock, she noticed, had already gone a long way toward clearing the debris; stacks of large branches dotted the side of the road every hundred feet or so. As the house came into view, Casey had the strangest feeling in her gut. She felt like she *belonged* there. Whatever lingering doubt she had in her mind about her choice to stay in Brock's barn loft studio apartment vanished. She was in the right place, at the right time, and doing exactly what she was meant to do.

Brock was on the roof repairing shingles when he heard the distinctive sound of an old school VW coming up the drive.

Casey.

He stood upright, wiped the sweat off his neck with the bandana from his back pocket and then stared at the end of the driveway, waiting to catch the first glimpse of Casey as she arrived. He had seen her once over the last week, briefly, when he had picked up her trunk from her sister's house and brought it back to the ranch. He didn't understand it, really, but he had actually missed her. He had *missed* her. And, perhaps even more important, Hannah had missed her, too.

He waved his hand in the air so she would see him. At the same time Casey was waving her hand out the driver's window, Brock heard the slam of the screen door and the pounding of his daughter's feet on the wood planks of the porch. Hannah had been hyped up all day in anticipation of Casey's arrival. Right behind Hannah was Lady, barking and wagging her tail.

Normally, he didn't like to have a job interrupted once he started, but now seemed like a good time to take a break. He climbed down the ladder and followed his daughter and dog to where Casey had parked her car.

"Don't strangle her, Hannah." Brock laughed at how tightly Hannah was hugging Casey around the neck.

Brock watched as Casey made a fuss over his daughter, and then squatted down to hug Lady. A flush of excitement and happiness had turned her pale skin a pretty shade of light pink. In the sunlight, the reddish freckles on her face and the red of her thick hair pulled back into a ponytail were so striking. And then there were her eyes. So wide and so green—he always had to remind himself not to stare.

"You've really put a dent in it!" Casey said about the progress he had made with the cleanup.

"I've been hammering away at it. Little by little." Brock was glad that it was his turn to greet Casey.

She smiled at him with that open, friendly smile of hers. It had been an awfully long time since a woman had smiled at him like that—no reservation, no pretense or judgment, just open and friendly. That smile was a magnet for him and he realized that now—by the simple fact that he was standing down here instead of still working up on the roof.

"Do you want to start getting settled in?"

"Absolutely." Casey walked around to the passenger side and got Hercules.

Hannah was running like a wild child around in circles, her long, tangled curls flying behind her.

"She's been like this all morning," Brock explained. "Usually the medications keep the hyperactivity in check enough for her to function, but not on days like today, when she's excited about something."

"I understand," Casey reassured him.

That's when it really sunk in—he didn't have to explain or justify or apologize for his daughter's behavior. Casey worked with children with disabilities for a living—she, more than anyone else in his life, would truly understand Hannah. It was a relief to spend time with someone who could understand, and accept, his daughter for who she was, regardless of her behavior—good, bad or indifferent.

"I did warn you that it's humble," Brock said as they reached the top of the stairs that lead to the loft apartment above the barn.

"I'll spruce it up." Casey didn't mind humble. And, if it was dirty, there usually wasn't much that couldn't be fixed with elbow grease. She'd never been afraid of hard work or of getting dirty.

Brock opened the door and let her go in first. He was right—the loft apartment with its pitched roof and rough-hewn, wide-planked wooden floor was indeed humble. But the inside of the roof was lined with sweet-smelling cedar, and there was a single bed in one corner of the room, and a small love seat on the other side. The bathroom was tiny and the kitchen only accommodated a hot plate, microwave and little refrigerator. Her large black trunk, a trunk her mother had used when she went to boarding school, was waiting for her at the end of the bed.

Brock had to duck his head as to not bump on the low part of the ceiling—he could only stand completely upright when he was standing directly beneath the pitched ceiling.

"I tried to straighten up the place a bit." To her ears, he sounded a little self-conscious.

"This is great." Casey wanted to reassure him. "It's perfect for us."

She saw a faint smile move across his face. He was pleased that she was pleased.

"Well, I'll let you settle into the place. I've got more work to get done before supper," Brock said, his head bent down so he didn't bang it on the top of the door frame. "You can use the kitchen for cooking—the hot plate is only good for so much. And you're always welcome to join us for meals."

"Thank you—let's just play it by ear, see how it goes."

Brock nodded his agreement before he ducked his head completely free of the door frame, put his hat back on his head and then left her to her own devices.

The first thing she did in her new home was let Hercules out of his carrier so he could get used to the smells and layout of the loft. Next she checked the bathroom accommodations and the feel of the mattress, before she unlocked the trunk and began to unpack. Every now and again, she would look out the window and watch Brock at his work. He was focused and relentless in the way he attacked his work—that kind of work ethic was attractive to her. It reminded her of the work ethic that her own father and grandfather had both had.

It didn't take long for her to get settled into her summer loft apartment. Hercules had his toys strewn across the floor, which made her feel right at home. She scooped up her poodle and sat on the bed to contemplate her next move: to take a nap, or not to take a nap—that was the dilemma. In the end, the "take a nap" side won out. She kicked off her boots and curled up on her side. The bed was just big enough for her and Hercules.

"Mmm." Casey closed her eyes with a contented sigh.

She had managed to find the perfect spot to spend a stress-free, worry-free summer. She usually worked during the summer session—this was her first real summer off since she had graduated with her master's degree in special education and took a job with the public school system.

She was in a comfortable bed, the cedar on the roof smelled sweet and there was a gentle breeze coming in through the open window. Life was, indeed, pretty darn good.

Casey had dozed off quickly and was awakened abruptly. Hannah burst through the door; the door swung open and hit the wall with a loud thud. Casey sprung upright, catapulting poor Hercules forward.

"My stars, Hannah!" She clutched the material above her rapidly beating heart. "You scared me! Remind me again about what you should do before you come into a room?"

Hannah spun around in the center of her bedroom/living room combo space, her head tilted back and her arms spread out wide like airplane wings.

"I was supposed to knock." The girl kept on spinning. "Dad wants to know if you want to have some gluten-free mac and cheese with us."

Casey felt a little foggy brained; she rubbed the sleep out of her eyes, then blinked several times to get a clearer view of the preteen spinning like a top.

"Tell your dad I'll be down in a minute."

Hannah left as quickly as she came, without a greeting or a salutation. There was a lot of work to be done to improve Hannah's social language skills. It would just take time and patience. But the reality was, and she hoped Brock was realistic about it, Hannah was never going to have completely "normal" pragmatic skills; it was possible, however, for Hannah to have friends, a job and a fulfilling social life. With supportive people in her life, Hannah's quirks and slightly askew social skills would be expected, understood and accepted.

Casey freshened up a bit and then headed down to the farmhouse. As expected, Brock was at the stove with his standard "Kiss the Chef" apron on, which may have been feminizing on some men, but not on the ranch foreman. Hannah was at the table eating macaroni and cheese out of her plastic ladybug bowl, with her ladybug silverware. Casey had a feeling that Hannah insisted on eating out of that particular bowl, using those particular utensils—and if she didn't get her way, she would either begin to have a tantrum or flat-out refuse to eat.

"Thanks for the invite." Casey sat down at the table.

"It's gluten free." Brock handed her a bowl. "Hannah's allergic."

"I figured." Casey nodded. "I actually dated someone who had celiac disease, so I have a lot of gluten-free recipes stored on my phone if you want to see if I have any that you don't have."

"That would help," Brock told her. "I have a heck of a time getting her to eat much of anything other than mac and cheese. That's all she wants. Mac and cheese."

"I have some tricks up my sleeve," Casey reassured him.

Hannah finished her meal quickly, left the table

without taking her bowl to the sink and ended up on the floor in the living room playing with Hercules.

"I'd like to take a couple of days to get settled in here, let Hannah get used to the change, and in the meantime, we can sit down and talk about some practical goals," Casey said quietly.

Brock agreed with her timeline. Any change, even if it were a positive change like Casey coming to stay on the ranch for the summer, would be difficult for Hannah to process.

"I'd like to hear your thoughts." Brock stabbed a chunk of hot dog he had mixed into his mac and cheese with his fork. Before he took that bite he added, "I'm sure you have some."

He was right—she did. Her brain just naturally observed children with special needs, catalogued the behaviors to try to fit the pieces into a puzzle and then, always, there were a list of goals that emerged from her informal, naturalistic evaluation. She had been a special education teacher for a decade and it was like breathing now—it happened without thinking about it. And, in the short time she had observed Hannah, she had made a laundry list of pragmatic goals—but it was always up to the parent and child, if possible, to help prioritize those goals.

"This arrangement is going to work out real well for all of us," Brock interrupted her thoughts.

She looked up from her bowl—she had been staring at it, but her thoughts were on Hannah. "I think so, too."

After they were done with their food, they lingered at the table for a little while longer, making small talk mainly, before clearing the table. Casey offered to wash the dishes, but Brock told her to just pile them in the sink and he'd get around to them later. The outside of the house was where Brock liked to spend his time and energy—that was obvious by how far along in the cleanup outside he was. On the other hand, the inside of the house was as messy or even more messy than it had been a week ago. For Hannah's sake especially, some semblance of order and cleanliness needed to be established in the house. She wasn't going to lead with that thought—Brock might not appreciate her butting in that far to his personal space. Yet if she was going to earn her keep, she had to be honest with him. Part of her job had always been to have courageous conversations with parents.

"Good morning!" Casey greeted him with that bright smile that lit up her impish face.

"Howdy." He was surprised to see her up so early and said as much.

Casey fell in beside him and walked to the barn with him.

"I'm an early riser," she explained. "The other day was an anomaly. Can I help?"

He had gotten Hannah started with her morning routine and now he was going to move rapidly through his morning barn routine before heading over to Bent Tree Ranch for the day. He had been working at Bent Tree since he was a teen, and had managed to work his way to ranch foreman. It was a big job for a big ranch and he took his role seriously. And even though Hank Brand, Casey's uncle, gave him a lot of latitude and a flexible schedule, he didn't want to ever have it appear that he was taking advantage of his goodwill.

"I wouldn't mind a hand," he told her.

His new tenant was dressed for the barn in slim-fitting faded jeans, ankle-high paddock boots and an untucked Kelly green T-shirt.

"You mind mucking?" Brock led the way into the feed room.

"Don't think I'm weird—but I actually enjoy mucking out stalls." She took the pitchfork from him. "I always say that I have to be from good peasant stock because I'd much rather be mucking out stalls than sitting in an office somewhere. When I sweat, I actually feel like I accomplished something."

Brock easily hoisted a bale of hay onto his left shoulder. "I already think you're a little weird."

Caught off guard by Brock's rare show of humor, Casey had a delayed response. "I'll take that as a compliment."

Brock didn't turn around—he kept on walking down the concrete breezeway of the barn. But he did say, "It was meant as one."

Casey happily mucked out the six stalls in the barn and made the acquaintance of all the horses stabled there, as well as Lucy and Ethel, the free-range chickens. When she finished with the chore, she was winded and her shoulders were aching, but she felt proud of herself. She had ridden since she was a kid and she had competed in dressage nationally; when she went to college, her horses were sold and she hadn't had much of an opportunity to ride since. This was her chance to get back into a sport she loved. It felt so good to be back in a barn.

Chapter Five

"How'd we fare?" Brock had hay all over the front of his shirt and stuck to the side of his thick, ruddy neck. The man was truly built like a brick house—his muscles were thick, heavy and rounded—defined like a body builder or someone who worked out in the gym. She leaned the pitchfork against one of the walls and gave him a thumbs-up.

"He's amazing." Casey walked over to where Brock was standing.

A plate on the stall read "The Mighty Taj." The way Brock was petting and talking to Taj, she could tell how much he loved this big beauty of a horse.

"Is he a Friesian?" She reached out to pet the silkiest part of his nose—right between the two flaring nostrils.

"That he is," Brock said with pride in his voice.

"I've never seen one in person. Only in the movies—almost every black horse I see in a movie is a Friesian."

Brock rubbed Taj on the neck and then gave him a hard couple of pats with words of affection. And then he asked her, "What did you think of the palomino?"

"She's a sweetheart—and so pretty," she said happily.

Good as Gold, Gigi for short, was a stocky, twelve-year-old quarter horse mare that was to be her horse for the summer.

"I can tell that she's developed some bad habits, but nothing that can't be remediated with time. Thank you for letting me work with her this summer. It's really a dream come true for me."

"It's good for both of us. I don't have time to work with her. If you weren't here to work with her, I'd have to think about finding her a new home. It's not fair not to work her out regularly."

"Well, it means a lot to me. I've wanted to get back into horses for years, but it's expensive. And even though I love my job—and I do—it's just good that I'm not in it for the money."

"I remember you were a good rider," Brock said to her, their eyes meeting and holding for a minute or two. "I remember that about you."

She remembered so much about Brock—a young man who seemed to have disappeared completely. What a crush she had had on *that* Brock! She'd pined for him as only a teenage girl can pine—and the fact that he'd been engaged to Shannon, a beauty pageant winner, had been a knife in her tender teenage heart.

He was different now. It made her wonder—where had the old Brock McAllister gone?

"I'm going to get Hannah ready to go. I'll be at Bent Tree all day. Are you going to be visiting your aunt and uncle today?"

Good question. She had been in stealth mode, avoiding her extended family. Not because she *didn't* want to see them—she did—she had just wanted to do it on her own terms, when she was a little bit more rested.

She frowned in thought. Her preference was to start working with Gigi. But she had been in Montana for a little over a week without visiting her aunt and uncle— if she waited any longer she was heading into "hurt feelings" territory.

"I probably should." It was a statement that sounded a bit like a question.

"You probably should," he agreed with her without hesitation.

Oh, all right. Fine!

"I'll call Aunt Barb now," she told him.

"She'll be glad to hear from you." Brock started to head back to the house. "I saved some pancakes for you. Just nuke 'em if you want 'em."

Casey thanked him while she waited for her aunt to pick up the phone.

"Hello?"

"Aunt Barb? It's your wayward niece, Casey."

"Casey-face? I've been waiting all week for a phone call from you! What in the world took you so long?"

She wasn't too long into the conversation with her aunt before they made arrangements for her to have lunch at Bent Tree; it wasn't her first choice, but sometimes with family, you had to put off what you wanted to do in order to do the right thing.

Darn it!

* * *

"*Oh*, Casey! Give me a hug!" Aunt Barb greeted her as she always had, with a big smile on her face, warmth in her striking blue eyes and a genuine hug filled with love and welcome.

"Hi, Aunt Barb." Casey hugged her aunt tightly. "I'm sorry I didn't call right away."

Aunt Barb nodded her head. "I was very upset with you. I couldn't understand why you didn't call us when you ran into trouble with the truck—when you needed a place to stay. Do you want some coffee? I just put a fresh pot on."

Casey declined the coffee—she had already had two cups of Brock's personal high-octane morning blend. She followed her aunt into what had always been one of her favorite rooms in Bent Tree's main farmhouse—the study. The walls of the study were lined floor to ceiling with bookshelves jam-packed full of books. There was also a large hearth where her aunt hung stockings during Christmastime. Coming to Montana, to the ranch where her father had been raised, had always been magical for her. So many wonderful family memories were tied to this home, to this land—to the people of Bent Tree. And then, after her grandfather Brand's last will and testament was read, the family imploded and nothing was ever the same. Her father stopped speaking to his brother, her uncle Hank. Family vacations to the ranch ended. She still felt a little awkward being at Bent Tree now. Perhaps that's why she had put off coming. This was her first time back to the ranch since she was a teen. And somehow, even though her father knew she would be visiting the ranch, it felt like a betrayal.

"Is it okay if I let Hercules out?"

"Who?" Her aunt tossed some pillows out of her way so she could sit in her usual spot.

Casey held up the carrier that resembled an over-size purse. "Hercules, the greatest dog that ever was or will be."

Aunt Barb was an avid animal lover. The minute she realized that Casey had a friend she immediately changed course and, instead of sitting down, came over to say hello.

Hercules was let out of the carrier and into Aunt Barb's hands. "You are too cute. Is he a toy or a teacup?"

"He's a teacup—a micro-teacup, actually. I adopted him from the poodle rescue. My tiny apartment could only really handle a tiny dog."

"Well, you want to stay with your auntie for a while, don't you, Hercules? We had to put Ilsa down last month—it's been so strange without her in the house."

"Oh. I'm so sorry to hear that." She remembered playing with Ilsa, the family's German shepherd, when Ilsa was just a puppy.

"Thank you. Your uncle's been having the toughest time with it. They get in your heart, don't they?"

With Hercules in her lap, her aunt sat down, then Casey sat down across from her on the couch so they could talk easily.

"It's been such a long time, Casey." Her aunt looked at her with sorrow in her eyes. "So much time has passed. I don't want to dwell on what we can't change—what would be the sense in that?—but I have to say this. You do know that we always wanted to see you—you and your sister were always welcome."

This was the topic that made Casey squirm inside.

This "feud" had started between brothers, but it had impacted everyone. Taylor and she hadn't had a vote—their aunt, uncle and cousins were taken away from them without warning or discussion. When Taylor made the decision to return to the ranch last year, she blazed a trail for Casey's return. But she still didn't feel comfortable talking about it.

"I know, Aunt Barb."

"Well." Her aunt's hands were busy petting Hercules. "You're here now. That's what matters."

She *was* here now. The smells of the house, the sounds of the house, seemed to be a part of the very core of who she was now. Everything—*everything*—unlocked memories and brought them to the forefront of her mind. Things that she hadn't thought about in years—like the way the library always smelled a little soapy and clean because of the leather cleaner her aunt used to care for the furniture. And the way the wide wooden planks in the hallway creaked across from a grandmother clock that always ran fifteen minutes fast. It was…overwhelming.

They caught up for a while and then they moved to the kitchen for lunch. Uncle Hank made it a point to stop his work and drive back to the main house to join them. It was so strange seeing her aunt and uncle in person. Their images had stayed frozen in her mind—and even though she had seen pictures of them on social media, it was different seeing them in person. Uncle Hank, a tall, slender man with deeply tanned skin, deep-set blue eyes and white hair that he always parted on the left and combed neatly back from his narrow face, was still a handsome man—but he looked so old to her. And Aunt Barb, who was from Chicago and had worked hard to maintain her city chic in spite of the fact that she had lived on a cattle ranch for over forty years, had aged gracefully. But even though she still wore her hair pulled back in a neat-as-a-pin chignon, it wasn't blond any longer—it was silver. Time had moved on, had changed them all, and it made her acutely aware of everything she had missed.

"How's Brock been treatin' you over there at his place?" Uncle Hank asked her between bites of his baked chicken breast that he had smothered with homemade barbeque sauce.

"I already told her that she should be staying with us. We've got plenty of room upstairs." Aunt Barb sent her a disapproving glance.

"He's been so good to me," she told her uncle.

"He's a good man," Uncle Hank said simply, but Casey knew how much weight that simple compliment carried. Her uncle wasn't an easy man to impress.

Hank turned in his chair to look at his wife, who was opening the oven. "Are you joining us, Barb? We're almost done here."

"I'm coming, I'm coming." Aunt Barb brought a plate of corn bread hot out of the oven and then took her place at the table.

"I appreciate the offer to stay here, Aunt Barb." Casey took a piece of corn bread and slathered it with butter. "But I really wanted to be closer to town. And I like that the loft is my own little private retreat from the world." Casey poured honey all over her corn bread. "Besides, Brock's place is halfway between Bent Tree and Helena—I'm close to everyone there."

"Well." Aunt Barb's tone reflected her continued

dissatisfaction with the arrangement. "Now that you know the way, I'm sure you'll want to come to Bent Tree for regular visits."

Aunt Barb was happy to dog-sit Hercules while Casey visited the horses in the main barn on her way to see the chapel. The chapel, a one-hundred-year-old structure, had been built by her great-great-grandfather and had been moved down the mountain so that it could be restored and enjoyed by new generations of Brands for decades to come. Her memories of the chapel were seared into her mind. She couldn't wait to see the restored structure in person—she imagined that the pictures she had seen couldn't truly do it justice.

Casey took her time in the barn, personally greeting each horse and putting little pieces of apple and carrot in their food buckets as treats. So far, it had been a successful trip back to Bent Tree. She couldn't believe that she had been worried about opening her life to this part of her family. Yes, her father still refused to speak to Hank, but she was a grown woman. Ultimately, she had to decide who she let into her life.

"Heads up!"

Casey had been in her own world, deep in thought, when the loudly shouted warning shocked her back to the present. An early model pickup truck had been backed into an open part of the barn and there was a young man in his twenties preparing to throw a bale of hay in her direction.

"Did I scare ya?" The young man stood upright with a teasing grin on his face.

"That would be a *yes*!" she snapped.

He jumped off the back of the truck and sauntered over to her.

"Well, I'm mighty sorry about that." The cowboy pulled off his leather glove with his teeth so he could stick out his hand. "I'm Wyatt."

"Casey."

"I do apologize for scarin' you. I hope you can find it in your heart to forgive me."

She took in his dimples, the strong jawline, the masculine chin and the nice teeth to top off his lopsided, flirtatious grin.

Brushing off the flirtation, she said sardonically, "Consider yourself forgiven."

Something akin to surprise mixed with respect flashed in his light blue eyes. "Where did you come from?"

"Chicago." Casey shifted her body away from him, silently signaling that she was planning to end their small talk.

She took a small step back and Wyatt, she noticed, took a small step forward.

"Well, nice to meet you, Wyatt." She gave him a quick wave of the hand.

"It's always a pleasure to make the acquaintance of such a pretty lady." He tipped his hat to her.

His blatant attempt to flatter her, which was obviously a strategy that had worked extremely well for him in the past, made her laugh. It made her glance over her shoulder at him.

What a flirt!

Wyatt was still standing where she left him, grinning at her with both dimples showing. "Hey! Are you kin to the Brands?"

"Niece." She threw this response over her shoulder without looking back this time.

That cowboy didn't need a bit of encouragement. He was way too cute and way too aware that he was cute *not* to be playing the field. A cowboy like Wyatt could probably pick women up just as easily as picking up a gallon of milk at a convenience store.

"Hope to see you around!"

"Goodbye, Wyatt!" She gave another wave of her hand, but resisted the urge to turn around. He was a nice piece of eye candy—that was an undeniable fact. But she had been around the block enough times to know that eye candy like Wyatt was best left on the shelf.

She was, however, still smiling at his flirtation as she hiked up the hill where the chapel had been relocated. At the top of the hill, she paused to catch her breath. The change in altitude made the air thinner; it would take some acclimating before she could hike in the mountains, which was something she genuinely looked forward to doing.

Standing upright, hands on her hips, her cheeks feeling flushed from the exertion and fresh air, Casey stopped to admire the century-old chapel. It had a fresh coat of bright white paint and the curved, wooden door, hand-carved by her ancestor, had been restored.

"Beautiful," Casey said aloud.

After she had caught her breath, she kept on walking. Just over the crest of the hill, Casey spotted the tree that had been planted in memory of Penelope's twin brother, Michael, who had died at birth. She stopped by the oak tree to read the bronze plaque placed in front of the sapling.

Bowing her head, Casey said a silent prayer to her nephew. Tears of sorrow for her sister's loss, and for the loss of the entire family, started to flow without warning. She had thought that she had already cried all of her tears for Michael.

Casey wiped her tears away. Taylor, who had really been more of a mother than an older sister to her, had always taught her to keep moving forward. So, that's what she did. She said a final prayer for her nephew's soul and then walked the short distance to the chapel.

Of course, she wanted to see the inside. But she was saving it for last. She walked all around the perimeter of the chapel, touching the stained-glass windows original to the structure. The chapel, no bigger than a modern one-car garage, was so romantic, set high up on a hill overlooking Bent Tree Ranch, with regal mountains off in the distance. It was the perfect spot for a small, intimate wedding.

"I didn't know anybody else was up here."

For the second time in a relatively short window of time, she had been startled. She had a terrible startle reflex, so even the slightest surprise set her heart racing, made her jump and, when she realized that there wasn't any danger, it made her ticked off.

"Don't sneak up on me like that, Brock! Geez!"

The front of Brock's shirt was sweaty from working, and there was a ring of dirt in the creases of his neck. He was carrying a small cooler in his hand that she had seen him pack with snacks and food for lunch.

"I wasn't really sneaking…" he said. "But I am sorry I caught you off guard."

Her heart was *still* racing. It was a terrible feeling

to have her body overreact over the slightest thing. Having anxiety stunk.

"It's not you—it's me." Casey sighed with irritation. "Lunchtime?"

"I come up here sometimes. I like the quiet."

They both starting walking toward the front of the chapel—Brock had to deliberately shorten his stride to keep pace with her. It seemed to her that if he were walking normally, she would have to take nearly two steps to match his one.

"Have you seen the inside yet?" Brock asked her.

"I was just about to."

At the base of the steps leading to the front door, they paused together. Brock pointed to Michael's tree.

"I like to sit right over there." He pointed to Michael's sapling. "I wouldn't mind the company."

She went up the two small steps to the thick, curved door and Brock headed over to his favorite lunchtime getaway spot. Casey was glad that he didn't join her in the chapel—for a reason she couldn't exactly pinpoint, she had wanted to be alone when she saw it as an adult for the first time.

Walking into the chapel again was like taking a step back in time. She was eight or nine, and this was an enchanted cottage in the woods. Her imagination had taken her so many places when she had played in the chapel as a child—she had been a princess in a hobbit house or a forest fairy with magical gnomes and wild animals as friends. She'd never played "wedding"—it was never that for her.

The renovation had transformed the space from a dilapidated building decades past its glory days to a beautifully preserved representation of turn-of-the-century construction. She had watched the renovation unfold via social media, and she knew that her aunt and uncle had taken every measure to save as much of the original structure as possible. This wasn't the chapel of her memories. This was the chapel returned to its former glory.

"Holy cannoli…" Casey walked along the middle aisle, her eyes flitting from one spot to the next. She wanted to take it in all at once—she wanted to take it in one small piece at a time.

The prayer altar had been preserved and it was there that she found her name carved, by her own hand, into the age-darkened wood. She ran her finger along the groove of each letter and wished she could remember the details of the day when this was carved. She knew that she had been the one to carve it, and it had been carved with her cousin Tyler's pocketknife, but she couldn't recall much more than that. This beautiful, special place was part of her and she was part of it. No matter where she was living in the world, there would always be a piece of Casey Brand carved into the history of Bent Tree Ranch.

Chapter Six

Once she had taken in her fill of the interior of the little building, Casey walked back out into the sunlight. This wouldn't be the last time she visited this place. There was something very special about it—it was intangible, yet palpable.

Brock was propped up on one arm, lying in the grass with his long legs stretched out and his ankles crossed. He had earbuds in his ears and his hat off. When he spotted her, he stood up and waved her over.

"It's unreal in there," Casey said to the ranch foreman. "I could imagine what it must have been like to attend service there a hundred years ago."

"I saved you a spot." Brock gestured to a shady spot next to him.

She hadn't really thought of sticking around. In fact, she wanted to get back to the barn and start working with Gigi.

"I've got water and plenty of food to share." Brock opened the top of his cooler. "Are you hungry?"

Actually, she was a bit hungry. Her aunt didn't know she was a vegetarian, so she had only had salad and corn bread. The hike up the hill in the fresh air and sun had made her stomach start growling.

He must have anticipated that she was being persuaded to stay, because Brock seemed to her like he was trying to close a deal.

"I have egg salad made from eggs produced by free-range chickens."

Casey laughed. "Okay—you know you had me at free-range…"

She sat down in the shady spot, cross-legged. Brock tilted his hat back on his head and sat down next to her. He handed her a bottle of water after he had wiped the condensation off.

"Thank you."

He dug around in the cooler and pulled out a piece of fruit. "Peach?"

She loved peaches. "Thank you again."

Brock also offered her one of his two sandwiches, but she was happy with her peach. She bit into it and juices from the peach dripped down her chin.

"Mmm. This peach is incredible!"

He glanced at her while he was taking a large bite of his sandwich. "Here…" He reached into his cooler and pulled out a couple of paper towels.

She smiled at him and wiped off her chin. Casey didn't try to make conversation until she had eaten the peach all the way down to the center seed.

"That was a delicious peach."

"Good."

That was all that was said between them for a while—they enjoyed the breeze and the sunshine and the quiet together.

"What were you listening to?"

Brock cleaned off his hands, tossed his trash into the cooler, then held out one of his earbuds for her to put up to her ear. She listened, her brain sorting through her memories to put a name with the sound.

After a second or two, she looked up at him, surprised. "Beethoven?"

"Bach."

In the short time she had spent with him, this man had already surprised her a couple of times. He was burly and masculine and the antithesis of a metrosexual, and yet, he seemed to have...*depth*.

"I'll show you the best way to enjoy it," he told her. "Lie on your back."

If it had been anyone *but* Brock, she would have thought this was a ploy to get her in a compromising position—but Brock was straightforward. If he wanted her in a compromising position, most likely he'd come right out and say it.

She lay flat on her back in the grass, both earbuds in her ears.

"Now, close your eyes and let the music take you on a ride," Brock said with an enthusiastic smile. She could tell that he felt as if he was sharing a very exciting secret with her.

"I'm not a big fan of classical music," she warned him.

"Don't focus on that," he instructed. "Just close your eyes, try to turn off your thoughts and listen."

Casey's eyebrows rose as she gave a little shrug and then closed her eyes. Eyes closed, cool breeze brushing

over her arms and face, and the music in her ears—
it was…

She opened her eyes and saw Brock watching her
expectantly.

"Well?"

She pulled the earbuds out of her ears and handed
them back to him. "I liked it."

Brock pulled the cord out of his phone. "There's no
reason why we can't both enjoy it."

It wasn't her nature to take afternoon naps and she
usually ate lunch on the go at work. But she needed to
force herself to slow down. She was on her first true
vacation in years, after all. So, side by side in the grass,
not close enough to touch, but close enough to enjoy
the lilting strains of music, Brock and Casey spent
the rest of the foreman's lunch break quietly together.

By the end of her first month in Montana, Casey
had settled into life on Brock's ranch as if she had
been born to it. She had put her own homey touches
on the loft and now it felt like her own cozy cocoon.
Of course, during the heat of the day, some of the less
pleasant smells from the barn did waft upward and it
could be rather pungent. But it wasn't anything that
an open window couldn't fix. Casey had struck a deal
with Brock to rotate the cooking and pay a fourth of the
food cost, in light of the fact that Brock ate enough to
be counted as two people. The loft didn't have Wi-Fi,
so whenever she needed to use the internet, she took
her computer to the main house. Brock always left the
front door open for her, which allowed her to come and
go as she pleased. The idea of an unlocked door, coming from Chicago, took some getting used to.

Hannah had slowly adjusted to her new routine—during the week she attended summer school and on the weekends she worked with Casey. Casey was able to spend a lot of time with her sister and her niece. She had been working with Gigi regularly, she visited Bent Tree at least once a week and she was still plugged into what she loved to do: work with students with disabilities. At night, after dinner, and after Hannah had gone to bed, Brock and Casey would sit outside on the front porch together. Some nights they talked; some nights they didn't say hardly anything beyond "good night." And on the days she went to Bent Tree, she found herself walking up to the chapel to sit with Brock and listen to the genius of Bach and Beethoven and Tchaikovsky beneath Michael's oak tree. Casey couldn't remember a time in her life when she had been more content or relaxed. As it turned out, Montana was her idea of paradise.

"You coming out to Bent Tree tomorrow?" Brock asked her.

The dishes were done and they were relaxing, as was their way, on the porch.

Casey made a small circle with her finger on the top of Hercules's head. "Uh-huh."

"Do you want to meet me at the chapel?" he asked her after a pause.

She looked over at Brock's profile. It was a strong, masculine profile—hawkish, prominent nose, squared-off jaw. He wasn't a classically handsome man, but he was a man's man with some pretty appealing twists—like his dedication to being a father and his love of animals, his protective nature and his work ethic. The fact that he preferred to listen to classical music instead of country made him interesting to Casey. There was a lot to like about Brock; there was a lot there to respect.

"Sure." She nodded with a smile. "I'll pack lunch for us."

"Even better." He gave her a small smile with a quick wink.

She was just about to ask what kind of sandwich he would fancy—he liked ham and Swiss cheese on wheat bread with extra mustard—but the ringing of his cell phone stopped her from asking him the question.

Brock tugged his cell phone out of his front pocket, looked at the name on the screen and his expression changed.

He stood up. "Excuse me."

She gave him a nod to let him know that she had heard him. The screen door slammed behind him as he went inside the house. The nights were cool enough to leave the windows and the front door open for a cross breeze, so even though Casey didn't really want to eavesdrop on Brock's end of the conversation, it was impossible not to do it.

"No. Absolutely not. We already covered this in mediation."

Brock's voice started out fairly calm, but got increasingly agitated and forceful as he verbally volleyed with his soon-to-be ex-wife.

"We already *covered this in mediation*!" he repeated loudly.

At night, on the porch, and when they were in a talkative mood, they covered a wide variety of subjects. But there were two subjects they never broached: Shannon and Clint. They were two very emotionally charged subjects that both felt very comfortable avoiding.

"Shannon," Brock said and waited. *"Shannon,"* he repeated. "Damnit, I'm sick to death of talkin' about this with you," he snapped at his estranged wife. "Listen...listen...*no*...you listen! We'll either work this out in mediation...we'll either work this out in mediation *or* we go to court. Your choice. But I'm not selling the house. This is Hannah's home and I won't let you take it away from her. You've already got her so twisted up in knots with all of this *BS* you pulled, the doctor's had to adjust her meds *twice*."

Brock stopped talking, so Casey assumed that he had ended the conversation without saying goodbye. A minute or two later, the screen door swung open wide and Brock strode out onto the porch. He walked straight ahead to the railing post and rested his hand against it, his head lowered. He shook his head a couple of times before he banged the post with his closed fist.

"You ever been married?" he asked her without turning his head.

"No," Casey answered him quietly. She hadn't meant to know this much of his business; they were becoming friends of a sort, but they weren't confidants.

"I'm surprised." Brock took the rocking chair next to her. "You seem like the settling kind."

She didn't respond. She had always wanted to get married—hoped that she would while she could still have several children. Women were still having children into their forties, with some assistance from modern medicine, so she still had time. But she had considered freezing her eggs, just in case Mr. Perfect didn't show up in the next couple of years.

"I'm the settling kind, too." Brock seemed like he needed to talk.

Casey didn't mind listening.

"I always wanted to be married—have a wife, kids, the white picket fence. My mom took off when I was young. Hell, I wouldn't recognize her if I saw her in a picture. Matilda. Pop used to say her name like he was talking about a saint—she broke his heart. Left him to take care of me. Then Clint's mom broke his heart a second time—he adopted her kid and then she takes off, too. But, this time, good ol' doormat Dave—he didn't recover. He smoked himself right into an early grave. And I got stuck raising Clint who never failed to do the wrong thing."

At least now she knew why Brock hated her sister's husband so much—he blamed Clint and his mother for his father's death.

"I wanted that family I never had growing up. I wanted it *so bad* that I think I pushed it on Shannon." He nodded his head at himself. "I did. I pushed it on her. She never really wanted this life. Truth be told, between you, me and that fence post…" His voice lowered so that his next words would only reach her ears. "She never wanted to have kids."

Casey had been staring straight ahead at the darkening horizon. When Brock confessed to her that Hannah's mom might not have wanted her, she couldn't stop herself from sucking in her breath and turning her head to look at the man beside her. She understood why many women didn't want to have children. That was what they wanted out of life and that was okay. But to know this about Shannon and Hannah, it made her feel sad for all of them.

"I'm sorry." It was trite and stupid—yet it was all she could muster.

Brock stopped rocking and leaned forward so his elbows were resting on his thighs and his head was in his hands.

"All of this—all of this fighting about custody and about selling the house—that's not really what all of this is about." He sat back up. "Months of mediation, and the plain truth is that she's not going to stop until she gets what she wants."

"What does she want?"

"Taj." Brock gave a small shake of his head. "She wants Taj."

"Hey! Can I interest you in a ham and Swiss on rye?"

Casey appeared at the top of the hill, her face flushed from the wind and the climb up the hill to the chapel. She was smiling that smile that he had grown very fond of over the last several weeks. That smile transformed her girlish, impish, unremarkable face into something quite lovely. It had not escaped his notice that he had been staring at the top of that hill for fifteen minutes waiting for his tenant. It also had not escaped his notice that he felt a sense of excitement and anticipation on the days he knew Casey was going to meet him at the chapel for lunch. He would think about her arrival all morning—and much to the amazement of his men, he would let everyone finish a couple of minutes early for lunch.

He was genuinely happy to see her. That's what he was feeling—happiness. Perhaps it felt odd because it had been a long time since he had actually *felt happy*.

"Do you want to spread this out for us?" Casey held out the blanket she had brought with her.

Brock shook out the blanket and then laid it down

in the spot that had become their favorite place to eat lunch together.

"What's on the menu for you?" Brock held out his hand to help her sit down.

Casey was a petite woman; her hand felt dainty and fragile in his oversize hand. But he knew Casey wasn't fragile—she was a tough cookie. And she was a lot tougher than she looked by a long shot.

"Avocado and Swiss on rye." She sat cross-legged on the blanket.

Casey reached into her basket, a basket she'd borrowed from her aunt, and pulled out two fat sandwiches for Brock and a bottle of water.

"Didn't Hercules make the trip?" He unwrapped a sandwich and took a giant bite. "Mmm. So good. Thank you."

"Hercules is with Aunt Barb—she's obsessed with him. And, of course, he's not going to say no to all of the attention."

They chatted easily while they both ate their lunch. Brock thought that Casey looked particularly nice today—she had opted to wear her superthick, waist-length red hair loose today. Usually she wore it in a ponytail or a single braid down her back—not today. Today it swirled around her shoulders, wispy strands dancing on the wind, as shiny as Christmas tinsel in the afternoon sunlight. He wanted to reach out and see how soft it was to the touch. It looked soft.

"I'm going to have to cut lunch short today, I'm afraid." Casey balled up her wrapper and tossed it into the basket. "My sister is having an 'I'm almost forty' crisis."

He was disappointed—he had a new concerto he

wanted to share with her. And there was something he wanted to talk to her about—something that he knew needed to be said.

"What kind of crisis?"

"She needs glasses." Casey laughed. "I told her I would go pick out glasses with her. She's all worried because she thinks glasses are going to make her look old, and here she is a cougar—married to a younger man."

The words came out of her mouth and she wished she could reel them right back in. It was hard to constantly avoid talking about Clint when he was such a huge part of Taylor's life. And, while she knew Brock had his reasons, however unreasonable, she genuinely liked Clint. He loved Taylor and he was a good father to her niece. Whoever Brock was remembering his stepbrother to be wasn't there anymore. Clint had changed. It surprised her that Brock, who was known to be a tough but fair man, hadn't been willing to forgive Clint for his past transgressions.

After an uncomfortable silence, Brock cleared his throat several times. She looked at him curiously.

"Are you okay? Do you need another water?"

He shook his head.

"No. I'm just trying to get some words unstuck." Brock looked over her shoulder before he brought his eyes back to hers.

"I shouldn't have said all that stuff about Shannon last night," he finally said to her. "I don't want you to think she's a bad person. Because she's not."

Her eyes widened a bit at the turn their conversation had just taken. She had hoped that it was a moment that would just slip away, forgotten by the both of them.

"I don't want you to think that she's a bad mother," he continued.

"I don't." She furrowed her brow.

"She loves Hannah."

"I'm sure she does." Casey leaned back from him a bit and crossed her arms in front of her body.

"She'll always be Hannah's mother," he added as if he was saying it to himself instead of saying it to her.

He stopped talking then, and it took her a couple of minutes to figure out what she should say to him.

"We all need to vent sometimes, Brock." She uncrossed her arms to briefly touch his hand. "All it means is that you're human. I was there to be a sounding board—and I promise you, I'm not a reflective material. What you said won't be repeated."

Chapter Seven

"What do you think of these?" Taylor was modeling a pair of Vogue eyeglass frames.

Casey was in charge of pushing Penny's stroller, carrying Hercules on her arm and providing honest feedback for eyeglass frames.

She wrinkled her nose a bit and shook her head. "Uh-uh."

"Really?" Taylor looked at her reflection in the little mirror on the eyeglass display. "I thought they made me look sophisticated."

"Uh-uh," Casey repeated.

Taylor took off the frames and put them back on the display. "I've tried on almost all of the ones I like. I have to find something—turns out I'm blind as a flippin' bat!"

"What about these?" Casey handed her sister a pair of rimless frames.

"And the doctor tells me that I'm right on schedule—that when most people hit forty, their lens hardens and becomes less flexible. As if that really helps! Any way you slice it, I'm getting old." Taylor tilted her head and studied her reflection. "These aren't so bad. What do you think?"

Casey took a nice long look at her sister before she nodded and said, "Those are the ones."

Taylor got fitted for her glasses and then they decided to stop for a bite to get a caffeine infusion before Casey headed back to Brock's ranch. Taylor moved her straw around in her iced coffee, took several sips and then said, "When I talked to Aunt Barb yesterday, she said that you borrowed one of her picnic baskets to have a picnic with Brock?"

Casey knew that information traveled quickly in the family, and she hadn't told Aunt Barb *not* to mention the picnic basket. Why would she? She wasn't doing anything wrong, after all.

Taylor continued, "I guess I was just surprised that you would be spending so much time with someone you know has been a really negative person in my life. It's one thing to stay on his ranch and work with his daughter—but a picnic?" Her sister shook her head with a frown. "I just don't know why you would do that."

Casey was holding her niece, making her smile and laugh by playing peekaboo. "Tay—I'm trying to stay out of the middle of the family feud. I know that Clint and Brock have a problem with each other, but why does that mean that I can't have him as a friend? He's been really good to me, actually. And, as my sister, I would think that that would mean something to you."

She could tell that her words had struck a chord with her sister, but not enough to swing her opinion about Brock. Taylor shook her head and looked away, her brow furrowed. "I don't even understand what you would have in common with him. He's so…stuffy."

"He's not stuffy," Casey blurted out too quickly not to be noticed by her sister's keen ears.

"Huh…" Her sister put her drink down on the table harder than necessary. "That sounded awfully defensive."

"I'm not being defensive," Casey said in a sing-songy voice while smiling at her sweet niece. "Am I, Penelope? No, I'm not…"

"Is there something going on between the two of you?"

Casey held up her niece and smelled her. "Wooo! Penny! You stink. Here, Momma. This little piggy needs to go home and get changed."

Taylor took her daughter. "Nice try. What gives?"

They both stood up and prepared to drive the short distance to Taylor's rental house. Taylor could be a bit of a germophobe and wasn't crazy about changing Penny in public bathrooms and usually avoided it if she could.

"Nothing," Casey said—and when her sister gave her a look that said *I don't believe you*, she added, "I'm serious. He's going through a divorce and you know I don't do drama."

"But you like him, Casey." Taylor seemed genuinely puzzled by this fact. "I can tell."

Casey got into the passenger seat of Taylor's green Avalanche. "Well, yeah—I do. He's fun to be around."

"Not possible."

"Everyone experiences people differently." Casey shrugged a shoulder, not really wanting to talk about Brock. Perhaps it was because Taylor's questions were hitting a bit too close to home. She did enjoy spending time with Brock. He was nice and kind and liked to eat good food and listen to classical music on his lunch break. He was interesting.

Yes. She did like Brock McAllister. A lot.

"People aren't always what they seem," Casey said thoughtfully. "He's…introspective. He loves classical music."

"You hate classical music," Taylor reminded her. "You used to throw a fit every time Mom and Dad took us to the symphony."

That was true. She did used to hate classical music. But the way Brock introduced it to her, explaining the intricacies of the arrangements and the reason each instrument mattered to the composition of the piece, made classical music interesting through his eyes. And something that used to irritate her and make her feel impatient actually made her want to lie back, close her eyes and let the melody take her on an adventure.

"All I know is that Brock treats my husband like a second-class citizen. And my loyalty is to Clint. If Brock doesn't like the father of my child, then it's going to be really hard for me to overlook that."

Taylor should be loyal to her husband. But did that mean that Casey had to be loyal to her sister and stop spending time with Brock? Was the fact that she liked Brock a betrayal to her sister?

"I feel like you're expecting me to dislike someone just because he doesn't get along with Clint. That's not right, Tay."

Her sister pulled into her driveway, shifted into Park and turned off the engine. Hands still on the steering wheel, Taylor turned her body toward her.

"Maybe it is wrong, Casey. But I don't want you to end up with someone who I wouldn't invite to my house for the holidays."

Casey laughed with a shake of her head, breaking the tension. "Lord have mercy, Taylor! You have me married off to Brock and all I've done is have a picnic with the man! Let's not get ahead of ourselves."

Taylor stared at her—her eyes very intent on her face. "You don't see it, but every time you talk about that man, you smile like it's Christmas morning."

Every day, weather permitting, Casey went for a ride. To be riding again, especially such a beautiful palomino mare like Gigi, was beyond any of her original hopes for her summer vacation in Montana. To be given a horse for the summer—well, it was the greatest gift Brock could have given her and he had done it without having the faintest clue how much it would mean to her.

It was the day after her visit with her sister and she couldn't seem to get the conversation out of her mind. She was hoping that a long ride on Gigi would clear her head.

It was obvious why this was still bothering her—Taylor had a front-row seat to her developing affection for Brock. Just what were her feelings for Brock and was she getting too close to the rancher? It would be one thing if he were single and emotionally stable—but he wasn't single and the impending divorce from Shannon, understandably, had him shaken.

And yet, she couldn't stop herself from liking him. He was a tall, burly man who liked to cook and was a good father. He wasn't her physical type necessarily, as she often gravitated to more metrosexual kinds of guys—and Brock was the polar opposite of that. But that was just the outside. On the inside, Brock was exactly her cup of tea.

Casey swung the saddle onto Gigi's back after she groomed the quarter horse and picked out her hooves. After Gigi was saddled and bridled, Casey led her through the gate and then closed it behind them. She mounted and walked Gigi toward the open field, leaving the reins long so the horse could stretch her neck down while her muscles warmed.

Once Gigi's muscles were nice and loose from the heat of the sun and the walking, Casey clucked her tongue a couple of times to signal to the mare that she wanted her to start into a nice, easy jog.

"Good girl, Gigi!" Casey sunk down into the saddle to stabilize her seat. "Nice jog!"

Casey took Gigi through her paces, working her out at each gait, until Gigi was allowed to do what the mare loved to do: gallop. Casey stood in her stirrups, taking weight off the saddle, gave the mare her head and pressed the mare's barrel belly with her calves. Gigi jerked forward into a gallop, her legs churning, her hooves pounding on the hard earth. They galloped across a wide-open field, kicking up clumps of dirt and sending birds, who had been grounded in the bush, flying into the seemingly endless blue of the cloudless sky.

Paradise. I'm in paradise.

At first, when she heard a pounding noise nearby,

she thought it was the sound of her heartbeat thumping in her ears. But the louder the pounding got, the more she realized that the pounding was coming from behind her. She looked back quickly and saw Brock galloping toward her on Taj. The powerful Taj was twice as fast as Gigi, so it wasn't hard for Brock to catch her.

"Hey!" She smiled at him when they were side by side. "What are you doing?"

"I thought I'd join you for a ride."

They both slowed their horses to an animated walk. Gigi threw her head and nipped at Taj when he got too close to her.

"Man—does she look good. She's lost weight. Her muscle tone is rock solid."

Casey patted the palomino's neck. "She's such a great horse. I can't thank you enough for letting me have her for the summer."

Brock smiled at her. "Like I said—you're doing me a favor."

"Some favor." Casey laughed.

They rode together until they reached the end of Brock's land. Her face felt windburned, her thighs hurt from riding every day and she had more freckles on her face than she had had since she was a kid. But she really couldn't care less. This was an exhilarating way to live—and even though she genuinely missed going downtown to Water Tower Place with her friends and shopping the eight-level mall of fabulousness, it wouldn't hurt her feelings to ride like this every day of her life. Even if she did divert some of her shopping budget to renting a horse or buying a horse and stabling it on the outskirts of the city, there was no way she'd ever have the freedom to gallop across a flat, open field until the horse was dripping with sweat. The best she would be able to do was ride in an arena—it just wasn't the same.

They headed back to the barn—Brock needed to cool Taj down, rinse him off and then get on the road to pick up Hannah from school. The easy silence between them carried them back to the gate. Brock leaned down, unlatched the gate and pushed it open for Casey to ride through first.

"You should take Gigi to one of the local shows—put her through her paces. The two of you have an unusual look that would grab the attention of the judges."

Casey halted the horse and swung out of the saddle. She loosened the girth before bringing the reins over Gigi's head.

"I don't think so."

"Why not?"

Why not?

Performance anxiety. Abject fear.

"It's not really my thing." She shrugged off the suggestion.

"Well, let me know if you change your mind—I could get a friend of mine to hook you up with some Western pleasure show clothes."

"Mmm. Nah." Casey wrinkled up her face at the thought. "Not even for new pretty clothes."

Brock pulled his saddle off the Friesian; Casey knew two things for sure about Brock—he loved Hannah and he loved Taj. Every morning before the sun came up, Brock was in the barn grooming Taj. Almost every night, Brock was riding Taj—keeping him limber and fit. After the night Brock had confided in her that Shannon wanted Taj, she had never questioned him further about it, but that didn't mean she hadn't thought about it. Of course, she could understand why Shannon would want the stallion. He was beyond magnificent. But he belonged to Brock—he belonged *with* Brock. Ever since he had told her about it, she had silently prayed that he won that battle with Shannon.

She took care of Gigi, went to go get Hercules from the loft and then, since it was her night to cook, she headed to the kitchen while Brock headed out to get Hannah. She was going to make gluten-free lasagna— one vegetarian pan and one with Italian sweet sausage because it was Brock's favorite—but it had a long prep time so she needed to get started right away. The kitchen as usual was a disorganized mess. The dishes were all washed, but were piled in the dish drain and on the counters—everywhere but where they should be. Her desire to have everything in its place made it very difficult to work in the kitchen. She had been sucking it up because she was a guest on Brock's ranch. But she'd been around long enough to begin to make some changes to the inside of the house. And she had the autism research on her side—this chaos was not helping Hannah's anxiety or behavior. Hannah needed order and structure and a clean, organized environment. She wasn't just trying to meddle for no good reason. She was meddling for a *very good* reason.

"I've got to get a handle on this." Casey stood with her hands on her hips, feeling overwhelmed by the stacks of dishes and pots and silverware scattered about.

In fact, when she looked beyond the kitchen to the living room, everything in the house felt congested. The flow was bad. The colors were bad.

"Brock and Hannah need feng shui in their lives," Casey decided aloud. "This whole house needs to be rearranged, reworked and decongested."

It was decided. Now all she had to do was get Brock on board and figure out how to completely unclutter and unclog the dilapidated farmhouse without sending Hannah into a tailspin.

Later on, over piping hot plates of gluten-free lasagna, Casey broached the subject of changing the interior of the house. It made sense that the work she had already been doing with Hannah would continue, but it would continue within the context of having the preteen take control of her own environment. Instead of her feeling that the changes were happening to her, she would be the one in charge of the change. Brock surprised her by being open to the idea.

"What do you think, Hannah? Are you up for a little renovation?"

Hannah was eating her second helping of the vegetarian lasagna. "I hate the carpet."

Casey couldn't disagree with her—the carpet was a hideous throwback from the seventies. It gave her the heebie-jeebies just thinking about what might be living in that gnarly shag.

"It's definitely got to go," Casey agreed.

"Well." Brock dropped his napkin on his plate. "Make a list and we'll get started."

That was all the encouragement Casey needed. At home, her apartment was basically the size of the kitchen. It was tiny and she had already feng shui'd it, rehabbed it and decorated it several times over.

Now she had an entire house with which to go crazy? Heaven.

Hannah and Casey spent the next hour writing a priority list for the house while Brock watched TV. They both agreed that the living room was the first room to be tackled. Even though Hannah wanted to be there for every inch of the demolition fun, they decided that it would be better if Casey got started first thing in the morning before Brock had a chance to think about it and change his mind.

So, first thing after breakfast, right after Brock and Hannah left for school, Casey did what she had wanted to do since the very first moment she had walked into the dreary living room—she began to pull down the awful brocade curtains that must have been hanging there since the house was first built. One by one, the curtains were yanked down, leaving plumes of dust hanging in the air and flying up Casey's nose.

"Achoo!" Casey started to sneeze. *"Achoo!"* She sneezed again and again until her eyes were watering and her nose was running.

She left the pile of curtains in a heap in the center of the living room and ran to the bathroom.

"Oh, lord." Casey looked at her reflection. Her eyes were swollen from the dust; the end of her nose was red from her itching it. She splashed water on her face, hoping to get the dust out of her eyes and her nose. It was in her hair, on her shirt, *inside* her shirt, on her pants—the fine dust that had accumulated for years had landed on her.

She came out of the bathroom only to hear the faint noise of a micro-poodle sneezing.

"Oh, not you, too, Hercules!"

The teacup poodle had been sleeping contentedly in his carrier—but he wasn't sleeping now. She had thought that she had put him out of range and out of danger from the dust, but she had miscalculated the sheer quantity that had been collected on Brock's curtains.

Hercules sneezed once, twice and then again and again, until she lost count.

"I'm so sorry, sweet boy!" Urgently, she got the poodle out of the house and up to the loft where she kept a bottle of liquid Benadryl to control Hercules's allergies.

She was just finishing tending to her micro-poodle and he had just stopped sneezing, thankfully, when she heard a truck pull up. Assuming it was Brock returning to the ranch because he had forgotten something, she hurriedly went downstairs to meet him. But when she reached the bottom of the stairs, she saw that the truck stopping in front of the house didn't belong to Brock at all.

"Howdy!" Wyatt, the flirtatious cowboy from Bent Tree, hopped out of his early model Ford truck.

"Hi."

Wyatt met her halfway. "I took a chance that you'd still be here."

Taken aback, Casey's eyebrows lifted and then drew together. "You're looking for me?"

Wyatt adjusted his brown cowboy hat on his head. "I'm looking for you."

"Why?"

The stark confusion in her single-word question made the young cowboy laugh. Man, oh, man was Wyatt easy on the eyes. So handsome—golden skin, dark gold hair, good nose, straight teeth, deadly dimples… Wyatt must have been leaving broken hearts and broken dreams all over the state of Montana. He wasn't of a settling age, but she had no doubt that female after pining female had given it their best shot to wrangle him.

"I've been trying to catch you at Bent Tree, but I keep missing you. I was starting to wonder if you were avoiding me." Wyatt smiled at her. "But then I thought—that's not possible."

Now it was Casey's turn to laugh. It was a foreign concept to Wyatt that a female wouldn't be swooning at the thought of his baby blues—she didn't have the heart to tell him that she had forgotten about their brief meeting in the barn.

Wyatt reached out and pulled some chunks of dust out of her hair. "You look like you've been rolling around in a dustbin."

"Close." Casey laughed. "I was trying to get rid of Brock's curtains. I'm afraid I lost that battle."

"Do you need a hand?"

She actually did need a hand. But it struck her as weird that the cowboy had stopped by to see her in the first place.

"No. I've got it." She put her hand up to shield the sun from her eyes. "Why'd you say you were looking for me again?"

Chapter Eight

Wyatt didn't get to answer that question, because Brock pulled up and parked his truck right next to the Ford.

Brock didn't look happy to see Wyatt. The ranch foreman's strides were long and determined, and he covered the distance between them quickly and with purpose.

"I wasn't expecting to see you here, Wyatt."

"I was just stopping by to see Casey." The young cowboy held his ground, which impressed Casey. Brock was a big man with a big presence, *and* he was this cowboy's boss.

Brock looked at his watch. "Last I checked, you're supposed to be saddled up and heading up to the north pasture to move the herd."

Wyatt grinned sheepishly—he winked at Casey. "Busted."

"You're late," Brock snapped.

The cowboy tipped his hat to Casey. "Have a nice day."

Wyatt gave one last wave of his hand before he disappeared down the driveway.

Brock stood watching him for a minute; he turned to her. "What was all that about?"

Casey shrugged. "Beats the heck out of me."

"Huh." Brock's jaw was tense—his lips thinned. "I expected to find you tearing apart my living room."

"I was!" Casey explained. "But I caused poor Hercules to have an allergy attack. I had to give him a shot of Benadryl and left him in the loft so he can get some rest."

"Let's go take a look."

Once inside, they both stared at the lumpy pile of heavy brocade curtains she had left in the middle of his living room. She looked between the curtains and Brock to see a reaction—she was pleased to discover that he wasn't upset.

"Well…" He took his hat off and hung it on one of the hooks in the entryway. "It is much brighter in here. I'll say that."

He rolled up his sleeves and started to haul the curtains outside. The minute he started to move the curtains, the plume of dust was back, and they both wound up coughing and sneezing out on the porch. Somewhere in the middle of coughing and sneezing, Casey started to laugh and so did Brock.

"I think I'm going to need a hazmat suit!"

Still coughing a little, Casey wiped the tears from her eyes. "I can't go back in there. I really can't. I'm allergic to dust."

"You stay out here," Brock said, and she was only too happy to oblige. An allergy attack, once started, could last for days.

Brock covered his nose by tying a bandana around the lower half of his face. He dragged the curtains outside, down the porch steps and away from the house. She let the dust settle a bit and then she braved the inside of the house.

"Seriously," Brock told her when he came back inside, "it's a lot better. What next?"

Casey looked up at him. "Don't you have to go to work today?"

"I can take a day off. I've got time on the books."

Casey looked around the room—the one place her eyes kept landing on was the carpet. "Carpet?"

"I'm game. I've actually been wanting to get rid of this for years—you've motivated me to do it now."

"Well, the question is then—what's going to take its place?"

Brock gave a small shake of his head. "I've always wanted to go with wood."

"You could consider something sustainable—like cork."

He smiled at her with an amused smile. "Let's not get crazy."

Several hours later, Casey was amazed by what they had accomplished. The carpet had been torn out of the living room, the hideous curtains were gone and there was now a nice rug on the living room floor to cover the cold concrete until new flooring could be purchased and installed.

"I'd really like to get rid of the wallpaper—paint the walls with a fresh coat of paint and, of course, paint all of this dark wood white so it's not such a downer in here."

"It'll all get done," he reassured her. "It's started now."

Brock took the rest of the week off from work, and because he never called off from work or took time for himself, Casey's uncle gave him the time without question. Hannah helped them pick out flooring and paint and much of the work got done while she was at school. Casey was relentless when it came to projects—she didn't like to slow down and she didn't like to take a lot of breaks. Brock matched her work ethic and, because of that, by the end of the week the living room had been transformed. Brock removed the wallpaper—a tedious job she was glad to hand over to him. She was in charge of following behind him with a fresh coat of paint. They had picked a pretty light green for the walls that looked soft and inviting, but not too feminine.

"I am beat." Brock slumped down onto the couch.

She had to give the man credit—he didn't give up and he didn't give in. He just kept on working until Humpty Dumpty had been put back together again. Casey joined him on the couch. She didn't have the heart to tell him that the furniture really needed to get taken to the dump with the curtains and the carpet. Baby steps.

"We rock."

Brock put his hands behind his head. "We do rock."

She felt too tired to smile or laugh. She just wanted to melt into the couch and never get up.

"You have paint splattered all over the top of your head," Brock informed her.

Eyes at half-mast, she rolled her head to the side so she could see his profile. "You have paint all over your beard."

"I should probably take a shower," he murmured. "Do I stink?"

"A little ripe—yes." She rubbed her eyes and yawned. "Oh, my stars. So tired."

Those were the last words she remembered mumbling. The two of them fell asleep on the couch, side by side, completely exhausted. And it wasn't until she heard Brock moving around that she realized she was curled up on her side, her face planted in the knotty fabric of the old couch, drool on the corner of her mouth.

Lovely.

"I've got to go pick Hannah up from school." Brock looked worried.

"Okay." Casey pushed herself upright.

"I think we went too far with this thing. She's going to freak out."

"If she does, we'll handle it. We've involved her in the decision-making process, so this isn't going to be a surprise. Why don't you take pictures of it so she can look at them on the way home?"

Brock took pictures of the new and improved, uncluttered and unclogged version of their living room. Even with all of the prepping and priming Hannah to handle the change, it still could be tough going for the first couple of nights. But it had to happen at some point. The house needed to change in order to provide Hannah with the most supportive, stable environment possible. Change was hard—yes—yet Hannah had to learn that it was also a part of life. If Hannah was going to live an independent adult life, Brock had to start developing her coping skills now.

As it turned out, Hannah had several meltdowns over the changes in the house. But when Brock realized that his daughter had to be able to process and cope with change while she still had the benefit of a strong support system, he focused all of his attention on rehabbing the living room. There was still a monumental amount of work to be done in the house beyond this one room, but the living room was the most used room in the house besides the kitchen and Hannah's bedroom, so it was the most important. Casey was impressed with Brock's determination and work ethic—once the man got going, there really wasn't any stopping him. Casey didn't like to take breaks, but Brock was even worse. She constantly had to remind him to hydrate and eat a snack or break for lunch. If the rancher got it in his head that what he was doing was for the betterment of his daughter, he was a man with a righteous purpose. In that way, Brock was very much like her own father.

After a physically taxing week of painting and renovating and cleaning, Casey decided to allow herself the rare luxury of sleeping in and lingering in bed. She had grown attached to her loft—early in the morning, before sunrise, she would hear the horses begin to move in their stalls, whickering as the time when Brock would feed them drew near. Sometimes she would awaken completely and listen to the sound of Brock's deep, distinctive bass voice as he went about his morning routine in the barn. There were some mornings she would meet him in the barn and share the chore of feeding and mucking out the stalls. Occasionally, like today, she would hear Brock's voice and the sound of the horses in a half-asleep, half-awake state. She remembered it happening later, but she had been too tired for the noise to awaken her fully.

"Oh…" Casey felt a cramp in her stomach, so intense that it yanked her out of a dream and slammed her into reality without any warning.

"Oh!" She curled her legs upward and pressed her hands into her stomach. Her body broke out into a cold sweat. She pushed her face into the pillow; tears of pain and confusion were absorbed into the pillowcase.

Hercules started to whine—he licked her cheeks and her forehead.

"It's okay, sweet boy." Casey bit the words out. "Momma's okay."

She pushed herself upright and then immediately buckled forward to rest her head on her knees. She swallowed several times, pushing down the feeling that she was going to be sick.

"Uh!" Casey forced herself to stand up. She pressed her hands tightly into her abdomen as she ran to the bathroom. Hercules was too short to make the jump off the bed—he stood at the edge of it barking in distress.

Casey grabbed the side of the pedestal sink to hold herself up. These couldn't be menstrual cramps, could they? She'd always been irregular and had terrible pain during her periods, but nothing like this. She was bleeding. Hard. As soon as she put a heavy-flow sanitary napkin in place, she fished around in her travel bag for ibuprofen. Still bent over, she fumbled with the top of the bottle until it popped off and fell into the sink. She shook out several pills, the maximum allowed in a day, and stuck her head under the faucet to fill her mouth with water.

She sat back down on the lid of the commode and rocked back and forth, pleading with God to stop the pain. The entire time she was waiting for the meds to kick in, she counted backward and realized that it was about the right time for her to have her period. The last period had been over a month ago on the trip from Chicago to Montana. The cramps had been so bad that time that she'd had to add another day to her travel plan so she could rest in the hotel. Her gynecologist, a woman she went to out of habit and a lack of enthusiasm for going through the hassle of finding a new doctor, diagnosed her with endometriosis and suggested that she get the Depo-Provera birth control shot to control it. When she told the doctor she wanted to think about it and the doctor responded by asking why—Casey knew that the patient-doctor relationship was over for her. She fully intended to find a new gynecologist after her summer in Montana—if her body would just *cooperate* until then!

If she didn't have Hercules to worry about, she would have stayed locked in the bathroom. But the tiny poodle hadn't stopped whining since she had left him abruptly. She would need to get dressed and get him downstairs to go to the bathroom, feed him breakfast and then get right back into bed. At the moment, that little to-do list seemed insurmountable.

Casey slowly pulled on her jeans and her favorite comfy Chicago Cubs sweatshirt. She had just sat down on the bed to push her bare feet into her boots when she heard a knock at the door.

"Casey?"

It was Hannah. Even feeling lousy like she did, she waited to see if the social stories and all of the practice had paid off—would Hannah wait after she knocked? She had been knocking consistently—now for the next step.

"Come in, Hannah."

Hannah bounded in. "I knocked."

"And what else?" Casey prompted in a slightly strained voice. She pasted a weak smile on her face, not wanting to alert the preteen to the fact that she wasn't feeling well.

"I waited."

Casey held up her hand to give Hannah a high five. "Nice work!"

"Do you want me to take Hercules out?"

Blessing from above!

"Yes—thank you." Casey pointed to his bowl and his bag of specialty food for a sensitive stomach. "Could you feed him, too, and then watch him for a bit?"

Hannah was enamored with Hercules and the feeling was absolutely mutual. Brock's daughter couldn't take her up on the offer fast enough.

"Are you coming for breakfast? Dad wants to know."

"Oh, no, honey. Tell him I'm not feeling hungry."

Hannah nodded and then slammed the door behind her. They had made a lot of progress on the entrance, but they were going to have to work on Hannah's exit strategy next.

Casey rolled into the bed with her knees tucked up to her chest, pulled the comforter over her shoulders and closed her eyes. The ibuprofen had begun to take the edge off, but not enough to feel remotely normal. Female problems. What a bum rap. She must have dozed off again because she hadn't heard Brock come up the stairs leading to the loft apartment.

"Casey? It's Brock. Can I come in?"

"Come in."

Brock opened the door to Casey's world. The loft had been transformed with some artfully placed rugs and throw pillows and vases with freshly cut flowers. Admittedly, he hadn't known her all that long, but the one thing he had picked up on was that she liked her breakfast. It didn't matter if it was a light breakfast, like a protein bar, or a heavy breakfast, like eggs made by free-range, vegetarian, happy chickens, Casey ate breakfast.

"I was concerned about you." Brock had his hands tucked into the front pockets of his jeans. "Are you okay?"

What should a woman say to a question like that? Skate around the issue or just be blunt?

"I'm not feeling my best today." She didn't lift her head off the pillow.

Brock pulled a hand-carved wooden chair closer to the bed and sat down. Casey had pale skin, but today it looked pasty and gray. Her cinnamon freckles stood out in stark contrast compared to the paleness of her cheeks.

"What's going on?"

The fact that he had pulled the chair up and sat down signaled to her that he wasn't going to go away without some sort of legitimate explanation.

"Female problems."

He processed the information for a moment, didn't seem fazed, and then leaned forward, his hands clasped.

"Is there something I can do to make you feel better? I think we have a heating pad. Would that help?"

"Thank you. But I think I just want to rest." She tried to smile at him so he was reassured. "I'll feel better by tomorrow."

"I've got to go to work today," he explained, as if he needed to.

"You've been out for a week already," she agreed.

He didn't get up right away. "Are you sure you don't need anything?"

"No—just remind Hannah to bring Hercules back before you leave. Okay?"

Brock stood up and moved the chair back a little. "Will do."

He paused at the door. "You feel better."

"Did Aunt Barb call you about our birthdays?" Taylor raised her voice because Penelope was banging on her brand-new xylophone.

"No." Casey was sitting in the long window seat in front of the large loft window. The cramps had, for the most part, subsided with the help of the ibuprofen. Her bleeding was still unusually heavy, which concerned her, but at least she felt well enough to be out of bed.

"She wants to throw us a birthday party out at the ranch."

Their birthdays were a week apart—she would be turning thirty-five and her sister would be turning forty.

"That would be fun." Casey leaned her head against the window—the cool glass felt nice against her skin.

"I think so, too. I'm just worried about how that would work out with Luke and Sophia…"

"What are you talking about?"

Luke was Aunt Barb and Uncle Hank's oldest boy; he was a retired marine captain and a veteran of the war in Afghanistan. From what she had gathered, Luke had been deployed to Afghanistan five times and had been injured once. Luke was married to Sophia and they had three young children together. Taylor had decided to rent her house in Sophia and Luke's neighborhood so she would have a built-in support system; Taylor and Sophia had become very close friends.

"Oh, I haven't told you. I just found out myself."

"Found out what?"

"Luke moved back to the ranch."

Casey didn't say anything—it took a minute for her sister's words to sink in. "Wait—are they separated? They're not getting a divorce, are they?"

Taylor sighed. "I don't know. Luke has really struggled since he retired—he's been diagnosed with PTSD and it's just taken a toll on their marriage."

"I'm so sorry to hear that." Now she understood what Taylor meant about the birthday party. How would Luke and Sophia feel about being at the party together? Was Aunt Barb, who had a very difficult time not meddling in her children's lives, hoping that the party would be a good reason for them to be back under the same roof together?

Taylor agreed with her. Luke and Sophia were the perfect couple—if they couldn't make it, who could?

"We've got a couple of weeks—let's just see how it pans out. Maybe they'll figure it out by then."

Her sister agreed again and then changed the subject. "You sound tired, sis—usually you've got energy to spare. You okay?"

"Um…" Casey's hand went to her abdomen. "Yeah…

I don't know. I got awakened out of a really sound sleep by horrible menstrual cramps."

"Out of a sound sleep?" Taylor asked, concerned. "That worries me. I mean, you've always had a rough time of it but never that bad. The shots didn't help?"

"Not really," Casey told her. "If anything, I think it's gotten a little worse. The bleeding is really heavy."

Casey recounted her experience with her ex-gynecologist and when she was finished, her sister said, "I think you need to see someone ASAP."

"I'll see." Casey did not want to add a pelvic exam to her list of fun things to do on her summer vacation schedule. No, thank you.

"Aunt Barb has the name of a really good gyno—it's kind of weird that this doctor basically has a monopoly on all of the Brand vaginas in the greater Helena area, but if you can get over that…"

"Say hi to Clint for me. And give that good-lookin' niece of mine a big smooch on the cheek. 'Kay?"

"You got it. Love you."

"Love you."

Chapter Nine

Brock came back to the ranch for lunch. He took Hercules out and then brought Casey some fruit, crackers and cheese to eat. It was a kind gesture—a caring gesture. The man truly had a good heart.

"Hercules wants up." Casey covered her mouth with her hand. She chewed a couple more times and swallowed. "He really likes you."

Brock stared down at the micro-dog at his feet. "I'm still convinced that he runs on batteries."

"Oh, be nice to my baby boy!" she chided the rancher. "He can't help it that he's tiny any more than you can help how big you are."

As if on cue, Hercules yipped and hopped in a small circle.

Brock scooped up the poodle that fit in the palm of his hand—and still had room to spare—with a shake of his head.

"Wait—hold that pose. I want to get a picture of the two of you together. It's like one of those pictures where they put a Great Dane and a Chihuahua together in a shot with a silly caption like 'opposites attract'…"

Casey held up her camera. "You're not smiling."

"I'm not going to…"

"Spoil sport." She took the picture, anyway.

Brock always had a comment about Hercules, but she knew that he secretly liked her canine companion. Instead of putting the poodle on the window seat next to her, or back on the ground, Brock put Hercules on his thigh and went back to drinking his water.

"This was nice of you. You didn't have to…but I appreciate it."

"I'm a nice guy." He gave her a little smile. "I'm glad to see that you look like you feel better."

She raised her eyebrows with a small nod in agreement. She was glad that she looked like she was feeling better, too.

"You know what?"

"Hmm?"

"I've been meaning to ask you about this furniture."

Brock seemed guarded. "What about it?"

"Where'd you get it? It's beautiful. All of the hand carving—the details—it's really well made. I'd love to have a set like this. Did you buy it local?"

Brock finished his water, twisted the top back on and put the bottle down on the floor next to his chair.

"Nope. I made it."

Now it was her turn to look surprised. Casey tilted her head questioningly. She pointed to the bed frame. "You made that?"

"All me."

"No, you didn't." She shook her head. "Really? You made all of this—the dressers, too?"

"Every bit of it." Brock picked at his thumbnail before he chewed on it a bit. "And the rocking chairs."

Casey's mouth dropped open. "Why didn't I know that?"

Brock looked down at the poodle that had made himself at home on his thigh. "I don't know. I suppose I never had a reason to bring it up."

"Well," Casey said, amazed, "you are talented as all get out. I'm telling you that right now. You could sell the heck out of this stuff in Chicago. Are you kidding me? You could sell the heck out of this stuff online— get a website built."

Brock scratched his beard—a beard that had gotten way too long and was pretty salty on the bottom part of his chin. "I don't really tinker with that too much anymore."

"That's nuts. Why not?"

"I don't know. Haven't really thought about it. We had Hannah and it seemed like she took up most of our spare time." Brock handed Hercules over to her.

"Do you want to see some of the stuff I made along the way? Maybe you'd see something you could salvage."

When she hesitated, he added, "It might do you good to get some sun on your face. You're looking a little green around the gills."

"Gee." She rolled her eyes at him. "Thanks a lot."

She grudgingly got up and reached for her shoes.

"Hold Hercules while I put on my shoes, will you? He doesn't want to be on the ground right now. Imagine that everything in your world was giant?"

"Everything in my world looks small." Brock directed his next comment to Hercules. "Especially you."

Brock held the poodle close to his face and the teacup rescue bit him gently on the nose.

"Did you just see that…?" Brock laughed. "He just bit me on the nose!"

Casey stomped her feet into her boots, stood up and flipped her hair over her shoulder. "See? I told you he liked you."

Brock, still carrying Hercules in his hand, took her to a shed set back a ways from the barn. He grabbed ahold of the handle and pulled hard on the sliding door. The door didn't budge, so Brock handed Hercules to her and used both hands to force the door open. Inside of the shed, piled high almost to the ceiling, handcarved furniture, made with quality wood like oak and maple, had been haphazardly packed. Forgotten treasure.

Casey didn't know what to say. Some of the furniture was showing signs of water damage—the wood was rotting and there was a layer of white powdery mold on the legs of the chairs and on the desktops. The shed was long and wide and filled with all of this incredible furniture that could have been appreciated by someone.

"I don't understand." She looked at him. "Why would you throw all of this incredible furniture in this shed and let it rot?"

He didn't answer her. There had to be more to this story than what he was willing to say. And that was okay.

"You're an artist, Brock," she told him, her eyes trying to distinguish shapes and patterns in the dim light at the back of the shed.

"I know how to use a saw and a hammer. That's all."

"No." She shook her head. "That's not all. You are an artist."

If she weren't starting to feel tired and light-headed, she would crawl on top of that pile and see what was in the back. She'd have to save that activity for another day.

"Were you serious about giving me some of this?"

"You can have it all." Brock waved his hand like the stuff in the shed didn't matter—like it was just a pile of junk. "I'll start pulling some of it out and you can point out what you want."

Casey was blown away by the offer and she had every intention of taking him up on it.

Brock continued after a minute or two of thinking. "I may as well pull all of it out. I can burn what you don't take."

She gasped—literally gasped—at the thought of Brock making a bonfire out of his incredible creations. In fact, that was a fantastic business name—Incredible Creations—handmade in the USA.

"That is not going to happen! I'll take every last chair and table and desk before I let you do that!"

Brock pulled the door to the shed shut with a hard slam.

"You take what you want. If you want it all, I'll be happy to load it on a truck and send it back to Chicago with you."

Her apartment wouldn't be able to accommodate but a couple of pieces, but there wasn't any way she was going to let him burn it like scrap wood. She

didn't know what she was going to do with it all—
maybe store it until she could find good homes for each
piece—but none of it was going to go up in flames.
Not on her watch.

They walked side by side in silence. Brock seemed
pensive now. This whole thing had to be related to his
marriage—and his impending divorce. Nothing else
made sense. Why would he give up something that he
had obviously loved? Why had he given up something
that he was so talented at doing?

"If I asked you to make me something custom,
would you consider doing it?"

Brock stopped in his tracks—looked at her.

"No. I'm sorry. I don't do that anymore." He stared
at her a minute longer, long enough for her to catch
the raw pain in his eyes. "Not for anyone."

The pain and discomfort lasted longer than usual
this time, but it did subside. Yet—she couldn't ignore
that what she was experiencing simply wasn't the
norm. And whatever was wrong—if it was, in fact,
endometriosis—it seemed to be getting worse. She
didn't like to think it, but she would probably have to
go to that doctor Taylor had mentioned. The next time
she was at Bent Tree, she'd have to ask Aunt Barb for
the name of her doctor and a contact number.

"What's on your agenda?" Brock picked up her plate
and took it to the sink for her.

"What?" She had drifted off in her mind. "Oh, gosh.
Sorry. I was somewhere else."

He was in the habit of asking her about her plans
for the day over breakfast, and then after dinner he
would ask her how the day had unfolded. She'd never

had any man show this much interest in the mundane details of her life.

"Actually…" she continued. "I was thinking about exploring the shed today. Is that okay?"

"You're feeling up to that?" He stopped rinsing off the plate to look at her.

"I feel much better today." That wasn't exactly true. She was better, but still not 100 percent. But sitting around waiting to feel better made her nuts.

She didn't tell the ranch foreman the entire truth because she had picked up on the fact that Brock, underneath his hard, brick-and-mortar exterior, worried about the people in his life. No sense adding to the burden he was already carrying because of the divorce. A divorce and custody arrangement that seemed to be dragging out and dragging out—it always came down to three things: joint custody of Hannah, selling the house and ownership of Taj. Brock didn't open up much about his ongoing mediation with Shannon—the little he did share with her, away from Hannah's ears, told her they had reached an impasse. Mediation had failed and they were going to court.

Hannah, who had been quietly scrolling through her iPad with her left hand and taking bites of food from her plate with her right hand, asked them, "Did you know that ladybugs are cannibals?"

Casey had been encouraging Brock to redirect some of Hannah's intensive interest in ladybugs to other subjects in order to increase her ability to function more appropriately and socially with her peers. But it was also true that those intense interests or passions that often came with a diagnosis of autism could lead to a career down the road.

"I had no idea," Casey said to her. "I thought lady-bugs were harmless."

"They are harmless." Hannah looked at her so seriously, as if she were defending the honor of a close friend. "They only eat their siblings if food is scarce."

Brock met her eyes and they smiled at each other.

"Well." Casey pushed back her chair. "That's certainly good to know."

The ranch foreman rested his hands on the back of one of the kitchen table chairs—Casey often found herself staring at his hands. They were massive. Not the kind of hands that you would suspect washed dishes or cooked stick-to-your-ribs, down-home country food.

"Come on, Hannah. Get your stuff together. It's time to get you to school."

It took Hannah a little bit longer than other children to shift her focus, but she had made progress.

"Check your schedule," Brock reminded her. "Make sure everything's checked off."

A visual schedule with a list of chores always worked in Casey's classroom, so she suggested that Brock create one for Hannah at home, and it seemed to be reducing the number of outbursts in the morning. Hannah knew what she was expected to do and she was in charge, in control, of getting the chores done and checking them off the list.

Hannah picked up her plate, rinsed it off and put it in the dish drain. Then she checked that chore off her list. Brock waited until he heard Hannah's heavy footsteps reach the top of the stairs before he said, "You've done so much with her in such a short time."

Casey was kneeling down beside the family dog, Lady, who had taken a liking to Hercules—and now the feeling was mutual. They were a very odd pair, but it appeared to be love. Whenever they were in the same room, Hercules would be glued to the yellow Lab, and if Lady was lying down, the poodle would lie down atop her outstretched paws.

Casey didn't want to take credit for Hannah's hard work. All she did was make some changes to the home environment and work on some essential social skills.

"She's a really hard worker." Casey scooped up Hercules. "There isn't any reason why Hannah can't go to college, have a career, get married."

Brock stared at her wordlessly for so long that she was prompted to ask, "What?"

"I'm just not used to hearing someone be so positive about Hannah." Brock's voice had an odd waver in it that made her look closely at his face. "I've heard a lot of negatives for most of her life—what she needs to work on, what her limitations are going to be, behavior plans. I don't hear about all of her strengths much.

"Thank you for that," he added.

Before Brock piled Hannah in the truck, he opened the shed door for Casey. She had promised to be careful; he had warned her to watch out for creepy-crawly inhabitants as well as slithering ones. It was a large shed, the size of a two-car garage but twice as deep. This was going to be a challenge, push her strength to the limit, but she thrived on seemingly insurmountable tasks. It was fun for her and she could happily lose herself in a job like this. She didn't really have a rhyme or reason to her method of how she was going to unload the furniture—she was just going to dig in.

One by one, she untangled loose chairs, easy to

lift and move out of the way. Then she crawled up on top of the pile to reach for the chairs at the peak. It was warming up quickly inside of the metal structure, and several hours into the chore, Casey had to take a break. She had begun to sort the pieces according to style or function. Her favorite pieces were the heavy rocking chairs—Brock could sell these like crazy on a website. She just couldn't understand his stubbornness on the subject.

Casey dusted off one of the rocking chairs, sat down and sighed the sigh of a woman who was feeling a rush of endorphins from exerting her body. She guzzled down a full canteen of water before she closed her eyes and rocked happily in the rocking chair. This chair, for sure, was going back to Chicago with her. She already had the perfect spot picked out for it.

"Howdy!"

Casey's eyes flew open—she shouldn't be hearing anyone else's voice. She was supposed to be alone on the ranch.

Wyatt, the cute cowboy.

"I was beginning to think that I wasn't going to find you." Wyatt walked over her way.

She couldn't help herself—he was young, but boy was he cute. The way his faded blue jeans fit his thighs, the way his hat rested on his head—that smile.

"How are you, Wyatt?" Casey stood up. She supposed her break was over. She'd find out what Wyatt wanted, then send him on his way so she could get back to work. She had it in her head that she was going to pull every stick of furniture out of the shed so she could sort it out. Some of the pieces were damaged beyond repair, but most of the pieces just needed a little love and elbow grease.

Wyatt tilted his hat to her in greeting. "Just another day in paradise."

Her eyes landed on the beautiful mountains in the background, the flat prairie perfect for galloping Gigi and the wide expanse of blue sky. It *was* paradise—or the closest thing to it for her. She had been wondering lately—if she could brave Chicago in the winter, could she survive Montana in the winter?

"Whatcha got going on here?" Wyatt looked at the furniture strewn about.

"I'm unloading this shed," she explained the obvious. "Brock said I'm free to take what I want. It's such beautiful stuff, I wish I could take it all."

"This is Brock's work?"

She nodded. "Speaking of work—aren't you supposed to be at Bent Tree?"

"Day off." He smiled at her.

"And you thought you would just stop by to say hi?"

"Yep." Wyatt took a look inside of the shed. "If you're gonna move all this stuff out of this place, you're gonna need some help."

She tried to decline his help, but he wouldn't hear of it. For some reason, the cute cowboy wanted to stick around. And yes, he was a flirt. But he was harmless. Her aunt and uncle both liked Wyatt—he was young and took wholehearted advantage of his natural good looks, but he wasn't there to hurt her.

"All right—all right." She finally gave in. "If you want to help me, help me. You can start by moving that desk right there."

Wyatt dove into the project and his muscles did

come in handy. Somewhere along the line, he shed his button-down shirt and was bare-chested. He reminded her of the Matthew McConaughey of the nineties, when he took every opportunity to take his shirt off because he knew that he looked that damn good. Well, Wyatt looked that damn good. Golden skin, golden hair, shredded abs, defined arms. He was the whole sexy package.

"Woooo!" Wyatt jumped down from the top of the smaller pile of furniture. "I'm sweating like a whore in church!"

She was trying to woman-handle a heavy desk to its section with only minimal success. She had pulled it, pushed it, cursed at it.

"Wyatt! Would you help me, please?"

The cute cowboy was wiping the beads of sweat from his chest and forehead and face. He tossed his shirt over the back of a nearby chair and then headed her way.

"Here—move on over." Wyatt winked at her. "This is a job for a man."

Oh, really?

"Is that so? Then I suppose I should wait until one arrives, huh?"

Wyatt tugged on the table that was caught on a root in the grass; he laughed at her comment, but kept on tugging until the table was free. The smile of triumph he gave her when he easily dragged the table to its "section" with one arm was so cocky that she couldn't even hold it against him. It was undeniable—Wyatt was flat-out likable.

"Thank you," she said.

The cowboy posed for her like he was in a body-building contest, showing off his biceps. "Count on the guns!"

Casey rolled her eyes. "Yes, yes. I see them." She grabbed his damp shirt and tossed it to him. "Now put them away before you hurt somebody."

Chapter Ten

They worked side by side, only taking breaks for hydration, until the shed was completely empty and every piece of furniture was categorized. The furniture that wasn't salvageable was put off to the side for Brock to handle in his own way.

"Holy cannoli." Casey couldn't believe what they'd accomplished. "That was a chore. Now I've got to figure out how to get it back in there so it's easy to get around."

She walked over to the area of the yard where she had put the several styles of bed frames. There was one in particular that she liked. She moved a couple of things out of her way to get to the bed frame she had in mind to put on the "take to Chicago" list when she spotted something move near her foot.

"Oh, crap! Oh, *crap*!" She scrambled up onto a

nearby desk, stood up and searched the ground for the snake that had just slithered between her legs.

She pointed. "Snake! Right there! Snake!"

Her heart was racing like crazy. She hated snakes. She *hated* snakes. And that one had the audacity to slither right between her boots like he was going under a bridge!

"You're fine." Wyatt brushed off her panic. "It's probably harmless. The only venomous snakes we have in Montana are rattlers. Did you see a rattle?"

She frowned at him. "No."

"Then quit your yelling, woman. He's more scared of you than you are of him."

"*That* is not true!" she snapped at him. "You quit lecturing me and make sure he's gone!"

Wyatt kicked some of the wood around where she had found safe ground. It took a minute, but then she heard him say, "There you are."

"What are you doing? What are you *doing*?"

Wyatt had dived forward, his hand outstretched. When he straightened upright, he had a snake in his hand.

"Look—see? It's just a gopher snake. He's not gonna hurt you." Wyatt started to walk toward her with the snake.

"Don't you dare bring that snake over here, Wyatt! Don't you dare do it!" she hollered. "Take him out to the field—far enough away so he won't come back!"

Wyatt grinned at her, but he didn't come any closer. "He's just a kid. Are you sure you don't want to see him up close so you know another gopher snake when you see one?"

Her heart was beating so hard that it sounded like

a drumbeat in her ears. Her legs were shaking and she felt completely freaked out.

She jabbed her finger toward the field. "Over *there*!"

The cowboy complied with her command—he was laughing good-naturedly on his way to setting the snake free. Wyatt strolled back to where she was still standing atop the desk.

"The coast is clear. Do you wanna come on back down?"

"Which direction did he head?" she asked cautiously.

"He's halfway to Canada by now." Wyatt held up his arms so he could lift her down. "Come on now. I think you owe me a cold drink and some conversation."

Casey let Wyatt swing her down from the desk. Up close, he smelled kind of sweaty and woody and musky, but it wasn't offensive.

"You're just a little thing, aren't you? How tall are you, Casey?" Wyatt asked her as they walked back to the farmhouse to get something cold to drink.

"That's a strange question." Casey lifted an eyebrow at him. "Five two and three quarters. My sister and I totally got gypped in the height department— we took after our mom's side of the family instead of the Brand side.

"Lemonade okay?" Casey asked when she reached the top step of the porch.

"That'd taste mighty good right now."

"Have a seat out here—I'll get it for us."

Casey wasn't sure how Brock would feel about Wyatt being in his house—but if she had to take a guess, it would be that he wouldn't be too fond of the idea.

She reappeared with a pitcher of lemonade and two

glasses full to the rim with ice. She pushed the screen door open with her shoulder and carried the tray carefully over to where Wyatt was kicked back, his boots propped up on the porch railing.

"Here!" He jumped up. "Let me help you with that."

"You're just full of help today, aren't you?"

Wyatt gave her one of his quick winks. "Yes, ma'am."

Did he just ma'am me? Maybe he isn't trying to hit on me.

She poured the lemonade for them, handed him his glass and then sat down. Her body thanked her for sitting down. She was worn-out. And the endorphin high that she had been riding for hours had disappeared, leaving her feeling a pain on the right side of her abdomen again.

"Thank you, Wyatt. Seriously. I was in over my head and didn't know it."

He gulped down the lemonade in one shot and then went back for more. He gulped down a second glass before he came up for air.

"That's darn good lemonade."

She nodded her agreement; when she looked over at the cowboy, she just couldn't stop herself from clearing up any confusion she was feeling.

"Wyatt…I need to clear something up in my own mind. You aren't…hitting on me, are you?"

Wyatt laughed an easy laugh. "I've been tryin'."

Baffled, Casey asked, "Do you even know how old I am?"

He gave her a sheepish look. "I carried your aunt's groceries in the other day. I might've accidentally seen your birthday candles. You're either gonna be thirty-five or fifty-three."

He was trying to make her laugh and it worked. To have such a good-looking cowboy paying attention to her, it was flattering. It really was.

"Just exactly how old are you, Wyatt?" She didn't think that she was all that much older than him in years, but she was light-years older than him in maturity.

"Twenty-four next month."

"I'm a decade older than you." Casey took another sip of her lemonade. "Why do you think you want to go out with me?"

Wyatt looked at her face appreciatively. "I'm a sucker for a redhead."

"And?" she prompted him when he didn't say anything more.

"Does there have to be anything more than that?" Wyatt asked, and for the first time, he actually sounded serious. "I think you're pretty and I want to take you out."

He filled in the empty space in the conversation by adding, "And I personally think you should go out with me. I guarantee that you'd have one of the best nights of your life."

"I'm flattered, Wyatt." She smiled at him. "I really am. But I just think we're the wrong age for each other."

"I'm not asking to get married," Wyatt bantered. "I just want to take you dancin'."

It struck her as out of character that part of her wanted to go out with the cowboy. Yes, he was younger than her, but like he said, he wasn't looking for marriage. He just wanted to take her out for the fun of it.

"I asked your aunt about you." Wyatt stood up and leaned against the railing opposite her chair.

"You asked my aunt about me? How'd that go?"

"She told me that you aren't fast." Wyatt rested his hands on either side of his body. "But I don't mind slow. As a matter of fact, I think I'd like to try out a new gear for a change."

Wyatt helped her repack the shed so that there was an aisle in the middle. All of the furniture was organized now and easy to access. When Brock returned home that evening, he was shocked to see what she had managed to accomplish.

"You did all of this by yourself?"

There was a moment, right before she told him that Wyatt had helped her, that she felt nervous to tell him. No, she hadn't been officially dating Brock, but they had been spending so much time together that it kind of *felt* like something might be building between them. But there was always the divorce hanging overhead like a nasty storm cloud.

"Wyatt was here again?" Brock's heavy dark brows drew together severely. "I need to have a talk with that boy."

"No." Casey wanted to reassure him. "He's not bothering me. Really. He's harmless. And actually, he was a really big help."

"So—did you find anything you wanted?" Brock asked her after he had cleaned his plate.

"Are you kidding?" She was in awe at the man's talent. "Everything!"

"If you've got a place to keep it, you can have it."

He was serious, too.

"No—I wouldn't do that. It's too much."

She waited for a moment before she added, "You

are going to get irritated with me for saying this, but you are so incredibly talented, Brock. I just wish you would do something with that gift—it's such a waste if you don't."

"Are you done?" He pointed to her plate; she didn't feel hungry. She would have thought she would be famished—but she wasn't.

He took her plate when she nodded yes in response to his question.

"Why don't you want to make furniture anymore?" She really wanted to know. God-given talent like that shouldn't be squandered for no good reason.

Brock sighed—he had his hands resting on the edge of the kitchen sink, his head bowed down, his back to her.

"I just lost the desire," he finally told her. "I didn't have the heart for it anymore."

His words struck a nerve in her, stirred up a painful memory of love lost from her college years. She used to write poetry—and she was pretty good at it, too—but after her first real boyfriend didn't want to be with her anymore, she lost the desire, the heart, to write poetry, and she hadn't written any poetry since. That was the last time she was going to pressure Brock about it. His heart was broken and she doubted he'd make another stick of furniture until that broken heart was mended.

The family was gathered in the large kitchen of Bent Tree where a long table carved from one of the fallen trees on the property allowed seating for the entire family and guests. It was the room in the house that was always warm, no matter the season, because the ovens were always on. Aunt Barb was an avid cook and loved to make homemade meals and desserts for her family. That was one of the many ways her aunt showed everyone in the family how much she loved them. So, when her aunt insisted on hosting a "semi-surprise" birthday party for her and Taylor, she couldn't refuse. It would hurt her Aunt Barb, and now that she was a regular visitor at Bent Tree, she was feeling less like a stranger and more like family.

Uncle Hank, who had a very nice singing voice, added after everyone else had stopped singing, "And many more!"

Aunt Barb clasped her hands together, her finely structured face lit up with joy because the family had gathered. She was such a family-focused woman—if she could, she would have all four of her living children living on the ranch so she could see them every day and spoil the living dickens out of her grandchildren.

"Make a wish!" everyone shouted at them. The cake had a three and a five on one side for her, and a four and a zero for Taylor on the other side.

"You go first," she said to her sister. Taylor closed her eyes tightly, thought for a moment and then blew out her two candles. Everyone cheered when the candle flames were blown out.

"Your turn," Taylor said. "Wish for something wonderful."

Casey held her long ponytail close to her body so wayward strands wouldn't get caught by the candle flames. She closed her eyes tightly and wished for what she had wished for the last several years: *a family.*

Casey opened her eyes and blew out the flames, first on the number 3 and then on the number 5. The family cheered for her; there was so much love in the room aimed at her, it made her wonder how she would ever go back to her fairly solitary life in Chicago. Yes, she had friends. But most of her friends were married now with children. She was one of the last single friends from college; she didn't blame her friends for not having much free time—if she had the family she wished for, she wouldn't have time to go shopping or go out to eat downtown. She would be at home, with her husband, enjoying her children.

"Thank you, everyone!" Casey blew kisses to her family on the other side of the table. "Let's eat cake!"

Aunt Barb, by her request, had baked a five-layer red velvet cake with thick, rich, buttery, cream cheese frosting. She had her first slice then immediately went back for a second slice.

"Am I too late for the party?" Wyatt came waltzing into the kitchen.

She had already said "no thank you" to the cowboy twice now, but he just kept on coming back for more rejection. At least he rebounded quickly.

Her uncle Hank and her cousin Luke greeted Wyatt without any reservations. They shook his hand and gave him a pat on the back.

"For the birthday girl." Wyatt pulled a single red rose out from behind his back.

Casey's eyes skirted around to her family to see their reaction. This was completely embarrassing. And yet, it was…nice.

She accepted the flower and smelled it right away. "Mmm. Thank you, Wyatt."

"Sit down and have a piece of cake, Wyatt," Barbara said to the new arrival. It was always the more the merrier for her.

Casey was glad to see Sophia and Luke sitting next to each other at the table, each holding one of their twin toddler girls, Annabelle and Abigail. Their son Danny had gone outside to play, and Casey thought that his parents would be glad that he was going to work off some of that rare sugar infusion before bedtime. But even though they were sitting next to each other, there was a weird tension between them. They didn't exchange but a handful of words, and they hadn't touched each other, not even when Sophia had first arrived with the children.

"Do you mind slidin' over a bit?" Wyatt asked Taylor. "I really had my heart set on sittin' next to the birthday girl."

"Woman," Casey corrected. "I'm the birthday *woman*."

Taylor did the unexpected, at least in Casey's opinion—she scooted over to make room for the cowboy.

"She thinks that I'm too young for her." Wyatt grinned at the table full of friendly faces. "How's the collarbone, Clint? I heard you banged it up but good down in Texas."

Clint was sitting next to Taylor, holding a sleeping Penelope in his arms. "It's knitting back together alright."

Taylor didn't say a word, but Casey knew from their conversations that her sister wished her husband's professional bull riding days would soon be behind them.

"You thinkin' about retiring?" Wyatt asked before he put a huge bite of cake in his mouth. He gave Casey a closed-mouth smile while he chewed with a wink.

Incorrigible.

Clint's conflict about his career showed on his face. "It's lookin' that'away."

"So…" Wyatt turned his attention on her. "You've turned me down twice. She's turned me down *twice*," he said louder to the whole table.

"That's a record right there," Luke, who was typically quiet in a crowd, said loudly with a sharp laugh.

"That's got to sting," Uncle Hank said before he took a sip of his coffee.

"That's okay—that's okay—there's more than one way to lasso a calf."

Casey peeked around Wyatt to her sister. "Did he just use a cow metaphor in relation to me?"

"I've decided to ask Ms. Barbara," Wyatt continued loudly, "for her permission to take her lovely niece out dancing to celebrate her birthday."

"That is playing dirty, my friend," Casey said to the cowboy.

"I think it's a wonderful idea, Casey." Aunt Barb beamed at her. "I think you should go."

Brock heard Casey come in from her night out on the town with Wyatt because he had been awake, on the couch, waiting for her to come home. It was inconceivable to him that he had let that smooth-talking cowboy get the better of him with Casey. Not that he had an agreement with the pretty redhead. He didn't. But the minute she'd come home from her birthday party, flushed in the cheeks and telling him in a rush that she had to find something to wear for a night out on the town with Wyatt, he knew that what he had been feeling, and concealing, was more than just a passing fancy. He had real feelings for Casey. He had deep, genuine, impossible-to-shake feelings that he had kept hidden because he was legally married. It didn't matter to him that they were separated; it didn't matter that he knew Shannon had already moved on. It mattered that in the eyes of the law and God, he was a married man.

Oblivious to the anguish he felt at the thought of her getting dolled up for anyone but him, Casey had burst through the screen door to ask him his opinion on her dress. Her beautiful hair had been washed and blow-dried; when she walked, the ends of her hair swished enticingly just above her derriere. He had thought about touching her hair—so many times. She had spun in a circle, in her pretty forest green dress.

"Please be honest…" She looked down at her dress self-consciously. "Does it look like I'm trying too hard?"

"No." He had to tell her the truth. She looked like a genuine cowgirl with that flouncy skirt that ended just above the knees and a new pair of boots. "That dress suits you."

She had hugged him then. It was a spontaneous hug that had nearly bowled him over—he could still feel her arms around his body. They hadn't been that close—not since the first day he had rescued her. He wanted to wrap his arms around her and not let her go. She shouldn't be getting gussied up to go out with any man, unless that man was him.

"You'll watch Hercules, won't you?" she had asked him. "I can't leave him alone up there. He'll be too scared."

Casey had asked him to watch her most beloved thing in the world—Hercules the micro-poodle. So he understood that it meant something that she had entrusted Hercules into his care. But, and this was a *huge* but—any scenario where he ended up on his couch holding a teacup poodle while Wyatt *damn* Williams got the girl—was a *bad* night.

So, no—he wasn't really asleep when Casey tiptoed into the house at 2:00 a.m., slightly tipsy and humming a popular country tune.

Of course Wyatt tried to kiss Casey. That was the whole point of the pursuit. But the question that had been running around in his mind, over and over, like a skipping record, was: *Did she let him?*

Did Casey let Wyatt kiss her? And, even more important—did she kiss him back?

Casey tried to be very quiet when Wyatt dropped her off, but she was a little wobbly from a couple of celebratory drinks, so she wasn't *as quiet* as she had planned.

In the foyer, she took two steps forward and then two steps back. She spun around, which made her lose her balance.

"Shhhh." She laughed at her near fall into the wall.

On her tiptoes, she went to the couch where Brock always slept, knowing that Hercules would have found a comfortable place to sleep somewhere on that giant expanse of the ranch foreman's body.

"Hi, puppy face!" Casey found Hercules tangled up in Brock's unruly beard.

"Shhhh," she chastised herself. "People are sleeping."

She scooped up her poodle and, after bumping into an end table, she opened the screen door very, very slowly in an attempt to keep the squeaking to a minimum. However, once through the door, she forgot to shut it gently and it slammed back into place, making a loud racket.

"Oh! Shoot!" Casey froze in her tracks. "Darn it! *That* was *not* quiet *at all.*"

Chapter Eleven

On the way back to the loft, Casey hummed and twirled and kissed her poodle on the head happily. What a night! What an incredible, fun, unexpected night! Wyatt hadn't lied—he had shown her one of the best times she'd ever had. He was full of life and he was popular and he was so much fun to hang out with. And the boy could dance. He really could. In fact, he showed her quite a few moves.

They had laughed and talked about nothing important or serious. Wyatt wasn't serious—he didn't follow politics or the economy. He wasn't the kind of guy a woman of her age should allow too far into her life— but for a whopping good time, no strings attached, no commitment required, he was a total blast!

She continued to hum as she opened the door to her loft. Casey put Hercules down and then twirled her way to the bed. She was just about to flop onto the bed when she noticed a present on her bed.

"Ah!" she exclaimed. "A present!"

It was wrapped haphazardly by hands unaccustomed to that sort of activity; there was a giant silver bow on the present and a note card that merely said "Happy Birthday, Casey" in scratchy handwriting.

"What could this be, puppy face?" Casey ripped the wrapping off the present, balled it up and threw it over her shoulder.

In the low light, and looking through wobbly beer-goggle eyes, Casey couldn't immediately tell what she had just unwrapped. But then it hit her—Brock had made something just for her. Something that he knew would touch her heart the most.

"Oh, Brock." Her hand went to her heart. "You dear, sweet, complicated man."

The morning after her birthday, Casey woke up with her first hangover in years. She hadn't "partied" in ages. She was a career woman—she was an educator. Her life didn't involve late nights or drinking more than a couple glasses of wine on the weekend. Last night, in the spirit of letting down her hair and kicking up her heels, she'd had several drinks past her limit. It had been a good time that didn't feel so good the next morning.

When she sat upright in bed, she immediately collapsed forward and dropped her head into her hands. The pounding in her head was so hard—*thump, thump, thump*. Why hadn't she remembered to drink water before she went to sleep?

"Why didn't you just say no to the last three drinks?" she grumbled.

She fell over on her side with a moan. "I'll never do that again."

Hercules barked and that got her attention. She inched over to the side of the bed, pushed her wild locks out of her face and looked down at her canine friend.

"Look at you, puppy paw!" She smiled weakly at the little poodle.

Hercules was the proud owner of a Brock McAllister custom creation. For her birthday, Brock had made Hercules his own miniature bed.

"You like your new bed, don't you?"

If she didn't have Hercules to tend to, perhaps she would have lingered in bed for an hour or two longer— let the headache subside. But Hercules had a thimble-sized bladder, so he couldn't be held accountable for any accidents that were caused by a human being gone longer than his bladder could manage.

"Okay." Casey inched even farther over to the edge. "You can do it."

She slid off the side of the bed and melted downward to the floor. The room started to spin in the most upsetting way. Her stomach started to churn and the next thing she knew, she was on the floor in the bathroom.

"Starting off thirty-five hungover." The cool ceramic of the tub felt nice on her forehead. "Awesome."

First, Hercules got to go out and then he was served breakfast. Then she showered, brushed her teeth for an extended amount of time and then braided her hair to get it out of the way. Her eyes were bloodshot and her coloring looked jaundiced.

"But, besides that—" Casey held up both her thumbs "—two thumbs-up."

She slowly made her way down the stairs and to the kitchen. Brock and Hannah were long gone—it was almost ten. Today was Wednesday—this was the day that she usually met Brock at the chapel. She had a feeling he wouldn't be expecting her, but she just couldn't wait to thank him for the beautiful gift. Her family had been generous this year, spoiling her with gift cards to her favorite shopping haunts and bottles of her favorite perfume. But for Brock to secretly make her a mini version of his incredible bed frames for Hercules? That was another level entirely.

She had a light, bland breakfast, afraid that anything she put in her stomach wouldn't stay there for long. She popped a couple of over-the-counter pain relievers for headaches so she could make the drive to Bent Tree without her head throbbing incessantly. Brock would already have his lunch, and she wasn't up to full speed yet—she opted to not bring anything to eat. She grabbed a couple bottles of water before heading to her loaner VW Bug.

"Come on, puppy face." Casey secured the poodle's carrier with the seat belt. "Let's go see Brock."

Casey dropped Hercules off with Aunt Barb, who was happy to dog-sit for her. She climbed up the hill, the same way and at the same pace as usual. This time, it felt like the hill kept on getting taller and taller and the top kept on getting farther and farther away. She was sweating through her T-shirt by the time she reached the top of the hill.

After making such a physically taxing climb, Casey was disappointed that Brock wasn't in his usual spot. She pulled her phone out of her back pocket and checked the time. It was the right time and the right place. But still no Brock.

"Oh, my head, my head, my head." Casey was flat on her back in the grass, legs stretched out, with her arm over her eyes.

Her cell phone, which Taylor had been blowing up all morning, started to tweet, which let her know that she had just gotten a new text.

With a frustrated noise, Casey texted her sister back:

Yes, I had a good time, no, I didn't let him kiss me, yes, he tried, no, he didn't try to cop a feel and no, neither did I!

Casey turned the volume off on her phone so she couldn't be annoyed by texts or emails, Snapchats or Instagram updates. Her head really needed it to be quiet.

"I was wondering if you were going to make it today."

She lifted her arm from her eyes and stared at an upside-down view of Brock. He looked even taller from this angle.

"I wanted to say thank-you for my birthday present."

Brock sat down in the grass beside her. "I'm glad you liked it. How does Hercules like it?"

"Are you kidding me? He thinks he's King Badass now. He didn't want to sleep with me last night. He slept in his new bed instead."

Casey sat upright; she grabbed her head with a groan. "Headache?"

"Totally my own fault." She tapped the camera icon on her phone to pull up pictures of Hercules in his bed. "Your first satisfied customer."

That got a smile out of him. Was she wrong, or was he extra pensive today?

"I didn't bring anything for you. I really didn't think you'd show."

Casey moved onto her side, resting her head in her hand. "It's fine. Believe me. My stomach isn't happy with me right now. You seem tired today." She noted the dark circles beneath Brock's eyes.

"I didn't sleep so well last night."

"That's because you always sleep on that couch," she said. "You need to sleep in your own bed. If you don't want to sleep on that mattress, then go buy a new one."

The conversation ground to a halt after Brock unpacked his lunch and began to eat. He didn't talk during meals—he focused on the food. But today, she couldn't hold up both ends of the conversation like she normally would. They sat together in comfortable silence; she enjoyed the feeling of the sun on her arms and her face. She closed her eyes and soaked in the vitamin D.

"You had a good time." It was a statement, not a question.

She opened her eyes when she answered, "I did. I can't remember the last time I had that much fun going out. Wyatt taught me the two-step!"

More silence. Brock was in a very strange mood

today. He looked drawn in the face and he had a distant look in his eyes.

"I wish you could have come to my birthday party." She picked at a blade of grass.

She had invited him but knew in advance that he wouldn't come.

"Hannah has never been able to handle parties like that. It's too much stimulation for her."

Casey understood that and she had told him as much. But she also knew that Brock wouldn't have wanted to attend because of Clint. The longer she was in Montana, the more difficult it was to work around that fractured relationship, and honestly, the more annoyed she became with the entire situation.

She had grown to genuinely care for Brock; he was a good man. But when it came to his stepbrother, he really needed to get it together for the sake of the entire family—including Hannah.

Brock stood up abruptly, brushed the loose grass from the seat of his jeans and held out his hand to her.

"I need to talk to you."

"And we need to stand up to do it?" She slipped her hand into his and let him help her stand up.

He nodded toward the chapel. "Let's go sit on the steps."

A shrug. "Okay."

Brock, ever a gentleman, waited for her to be seated comfortably before he sat down beside her. Looking at their bodies side by side, Brock's legs were almost twice as long as hers.

The ranch foreman looked straight ahead with his standard-issue Stetson sitting squarely on his head—

his elbows were resting on his knees and his fingertips were pressed together.

She had no idea what he wanted to discuss with her—maybe something happened with the divorce or he wanted to work on different skills when summer school ended for Hannah next week. This was Brock's conversation, his topic, so Casey waited quietly for him to begin talking.

"I didn't like you going out with Wyatt last night," Brock said quietly.

Of all the things Brock could have said, that wasn't what Casey was expecting. And, because she wasn't expecting it, she couldn't think of anything to say in return. So she stayed silent and listened.

"I'm still married." He glanced over at her for the briefest of moments.

She nodded her agreement.

"She's moved on with her life already," Brock said of Shannon.

That was new information he was sharing with her.

With a hollow laugh, he added, "She's already engaged. I didn't know someone could get engaged before they're divorced, but I guess it can happen."

Brock looked at her now. "Hannah doesn't know."

Casey swallowed hard a couple of times; her mouth had just gone completely dry. "I won't tell her."

"Thank you."

There was another break in the conversation before Brock went on to say, "I had been so focused on Shannon and the fact that *she* had moved on from our marriage that I didn't know that I had moved on, too."

Casey's eyes widened as they shifted to his profile.

Slowly, as the conversation progressed, her heartbeat was picking up pace, picking up pace…

"When I saw you go out the door last night with another man…" Brock kept his eyes locked onto the horizon. "I knew that I couldn't go another day without telling you how I feel…about you.

"You are such a good-hearted woman, Casey. You honestly are. Everyone loves you because you're just so kind to people."

He looked at her as he continued. "You always try to see the best in people or look on the bright side… Even when you aren't feeling well, you still try to find a silver lining."

"Some people find that to be super annoying," Casey said.

"Then I find them annoying." Brock was quick to jump to her defense. That was his first instinct—to protect those people he cared about the most. She was beginning to realize that *she* was now one of those people.

"You're so good with Hannah—she loves you."

"I love her, too."

Brock's daughter had become very important to her.

"You've become one of my best friends." The ranch foreman took her hand and held it gently in his. "But I want more."

Their eyes locked in a way that had never happened before. There was a trust there, a sense of security, and because of that foundation, they were able to be vulnerable with each other. Brock's eyes, the true windows to his soul, were open so she could see his heart—his intentions.

"Do you…want more…with me?" In that moment,

he was opening himself up to her—he was taking another shot at love after being badly hurt—and this spoke volumes about his character.

Casey squeezed his hand with her fingers to reassure him. "I do."

His shoulders dropped in what Casey could only describe in her mind as "relief" at her response. Her feelings for Brock had been growing steadily since the moment he had rescued her off that fence. But he had been understandably focused on his divorce from Shannon and raising his daughter, so she had pushed her feelings aside.

"But…" she added, "I think that we just need to take things real slow. You're still not through the divorce with Shannon—that's going to take a toll on you. And to layer a new relationship into the mix… I don't want to do anything that would hurt our friendship. Because your friendship has meant the world to me—it really has."

Brock gave her hand a quick kiss. "I agree."

His lunch break was over; it was time to let him get back to work so she could get back to her plan for the day—riding Gigi.

"Hey!" Casey climbed to the chapel step and waved her hand for Brock to come stand by her. "Now I'm as tall as you are."

Brock smiled at her affectionately.

"When's the last time you gave someone a piggyback ride?" She had her hands on her hips.

"I don't know—not since Hannah was young. Why?"

She made a circle with her finger. "Turn around, mountain man. I need a ride."

He looked at her like she had fallen off her rocker, but he did turn around.

Brock needed to lighten up and have a good time every now and again. And, if showing him a good time also included getting a piggyback ride down the hill? All the better for her.

It was easy to climb onto his back from her perch; she put her arms around his neck and he hooked his arms behind her knees.

"Where am I taking you?" he asked.

"Down the hill," she ordered him playfully. "Can you handle it?"

"Can I handle it?" he asked, feigning insult. "Just watch and learn."

Brock didn't walk to the hill; instead, he took off like a bull charging a red flag—head down and full steam ahead. She screamed in surprise and tightened her grip on his neck.

"Hold on! We're going for it now," he warned her.

She was amazed that a man his size could move that fast. He barely slowed down when they started down the hill. Casey, who had zero control in this situation, could only hold on and enjoy the ride. He wasn't going to drop her—she knew that. So she started to laugh—because it was fun. And because he had surprised her in a wonderful way.

At the bottom of the hill, Brock stopped and let Casey go. He was out of breath from a different type of exertion he was accustomed to doing from day to day. His eyes were shining and it was nice to see him smile the way he was smiling at her now—no reservations. Just pure happiness.

Casey, who didn't like anyone to have the upper

hand, decided to practice her self-defense training. Without any warning, she stepped on his instep and pushed on the spot on his body were his leg met his groin, and before the ranch foreman knew what was happening, he was sitting in the grass.

The reaction on his face was priceless. *Priceless!*

Casey held up her arms like Rocky Balboa and pranced around in a circle while she loudly hummed the Rocky theme song.

When she was done celebrating, she stood, hands on hips, triumphant. But it didn't last. Brock reached out with his long arms, grabbed her wrist and pulled her down beside him.

"Where'd you learn how to do that?" Brock asked her. "Not many people can say that they've gotten the better of me."

Casey made a karate chop in the air. "Taylor and I took a self-defense class."

They both started to laugh and it felt *right*. The sun was shining, the grass was soft, the sky was bright blue and she was having the time of her life with a man who was a great friend. And maybe…just maybe…*more*.

The next night, Casey and Brock sat together on the porch after Hannah had gone up to bed. Brock had Hercules in his lap—it was undeniable that the poodle had won the ranch foreman over. And it was a good sign to her that Hercules loved Brock in return.

"I talked to Shannon today."

Casey's heart gave the tiniest jump before resuming its regular rhythm.

"We've agreed on a settlement."

There had been this struggle between Brock and

Shannon, lurking beneath the surface, impacting Hannah and Brock and her in ways that were often indescribable. She could almost always tell when he had dealt with "California," as he put it, because his demeanor was so different afterward. As much as he tried to hide it and keep it separate from his life with Hannah, he wasn't a man who could easily paste a smile on his face and pretend like everything was peachy when it wasn't.

"Hannah will live with me during the school year. She'll live with Shannon during the summer. We'll rotate major holidays. Shannon gets Taj…"

Casey couldn't help it—she gasped at the thought of Brock losing his stallion.

"I will keep the house and give her a credit for half the value of the house, minus the value of Taj."

She reached out to hold on to his hand. "I'm so sorry about Taj, Brock. I know how much he means to you."

"I'll miss him," Brock acknowledged. "God knows I will. But I had to do what was best for Hannah. It took me a while to realize that I was holding on for all the wrong reasons. Letting go of Taj—I'm doing that for the right reason."

"Shannon will be here next week to take Hannah to California for the rest of the summer break. She'll pick up Taj and take him with them."

She squeezed his hand to comfort him. "I'll sign the mediation agreement, have it notarized—after that, we just wait for a court date so a judge can declare us officially divorced."

There was pure bitterness in Brock's voice when he said the words *officially divorced*. She knew that Brock *wanted* to be ready to move on, but his emotions were going to be all over the place for a while—that was normal. It was also perfectly normal for her to move with caution with this man and protect her heart.

proualliiig an over the place in a Goth romance
normal. It was the perfect vacation for her to hear
with a true with mareumernelial before him.

Chapter Twelve

A week after Brock announced that he was moving forward with his divorce, Shannon arrived with a shiny black Silverado truck and a shiny black horse trailer. When Brock's soon-to-be ex-wife showed up, Casey was sitting in one of the rocking chairs answering emails on her computer. It was a bit awkward because Brock hadn't returned from taking Hannah to a doctor's appointment in Helena.

Shannon stepped out of the truck looking like she had stepped right out of a *Vogue* magazine shoot. Her long, flowing, perfectly highlighted, brandy-colored hair framed her undeniably beautiful heart-shaped face. She was six feet tall, slender but with nice curves in the right places. Honestly, Shannon was the kind of woman you assume doesn't exist in real life. And yet, there she was—it was like spotting a unicorn.

Shannon slid her mirrored aviator sunglasses to the top of her head before she looked around the ranch. Casey could read her expression as easily as she could read a Dr. Seuss book—*what a dump*.

"Hi there!" Shannon walked over to the house. "You must be Casey."

Casey put her computer on the seat next to her so she could stand up to greet Hannah's mother.

"Guilty." Casey smiled a friendly smile and offered Shannon her hand.

They shook hands and then Shannon looked around again with the slightest disapproving shake of her head, and said, "I was so hoping to see Brock take initiative with this place. It's sad when people don't live up to their full potential."

Casey had to bite her tongue—literally bite her tongue. She had promised herself that she *was not* going to get in the middle of this divorce. Yes, she was a friend of Brock's, and they were considering exploring a deeper relationship, but to get sucked into the muck that was the end of a marriage? No, thank you.

On the other hand, it pissed her off that Shannon was putting Brock down. The man had an outstanding work ethic.

"Brock and Hannah should be back from Helena soon—do you want something to drink? I just made a fresh batch of sun tea."

Shannon stared down at her. "Well, isn't that *sweet* of you. I guess I'll just have to get used to a stranger inviting me into my own home."

After she threw out the barb, Shannon laughed to signal that she was "just kidding." But Casey had been in the company of catty women before, and this kitty cat had very sharp claws.

"And the surprises just keep coming," Shannon said when she walked into the house. She walked straight into the living room, looking at the new wood floors and the freshly painted walls and molding.

Hannah's mom turned around and smiled a stiff smile at her. "Well, you must be a little miracle worker, Casey. I could never get Brock to change a lightbulb in this place if it'd burned out."

Casey refused to let the woman bait her. "He did it for Hannah."

"Now, that's the Brock I know." Shannon accepted the glass of tea Casey offered to her. "Anything for Hannah."

Casey didn't like the way the ranch felt after Hannah and Taj left. There was a gaping hole left by them, a vacuum that couldn't be filled. Brock told her again and again that he was "fine," but the ranch foreman looked like part of his heart had been ripped out of his chest. There was sadness in him now, so much sadness that he refused to give a voice. Instead, he was stuffing it down and going on about his business as if nothing was wrong and everything was the same. As far Brock was concerned—he was fine—just fine.

Brooding had never been her MO and it was hard for her to handle it in other people. She was more of a "pick yourself up, dust yourself off and get the heck on with it" kind of gal. Wanting to escape the black mood that was currently occupying Brock's ranch, Casey went into town to spend the day with Taylor and Sophia and the four little ones.

The seven of them walked to the nearby park. Casey carried her niece, who had on a pretty sunflower dress and a matching yellow headband. As far as Casey was concerned, she was the cutest baby on the planet.

"I can't wait to have my own," Casey said as she put Penny in the baby swing.

"If you'd married Scott," Taylor reminded her, "you'd be living in the suburbs with a couple of kids."

"How long ago was Scott?" Sophia was kneeling by her son, Danny, tying his shoelace in a double knot.

"I don't know." Casey gave her niece a little push and loved to see her smile as she swung closer and then swung farther away. "Five years ago?"

"He was such a nice guy," Taylor reminisced. "He got along with Mom—*impossible*—and Dad recommended him as an intern at the firm."

Taylor said directly to Sophia, "And he was crazy about Casey. He wanted babies, she wanted babies… he gave her a ring, they set a date and then…"

Sophia kept a keen eye on her children, who were playing a few yards away. "Cold feet?"

"Frozen is more like it." Casey laughed. "I felt horrible about breaking off our engagement. I really did. But it didn't matter how sweet he was, or attentive he was, or how perfectly he fit into my plan…we just weren't *compatible* in the bedroom department."

"Oh, no." Sophia's face registered complete understanding. "That *has* to work. It's not everything, but it has to be *something*."

"Exactly." Casey made a face at her sister. "See—Sophia understands."

"I didn't say it didn't matter… I just don't think you should throw away a perfect guy over it. They have retreats—don't they, Sophia? You go out into the woods and hit drums and dance in circles naked…"

Sophia, who was a trained psychologist, smiled at the thought. "That's not really my area of expertise…"

"It was really hard to break up with him," Casey admitted. "I cried. He cried. It was a whole scene."

The breakup with Scott had really made her gunshy about getting into another relationship. She dated here and there, but the men she attracted just weren't *right*. But she could never pinpoint exactly what was missing.

"I tell you what, the ranch seems really strange without Hannah around. It's been really tough on Brock."

The minute she brought up Brock to her sister, Taylor's body language changed and the silent message she sent was: *I don't want to talk about him.*

But she *did* want to talk about Brock. She saw a future with the ranch foreman—she saw a future with the family she had been craving for so long. Somehow, this mess with Clint and Brock was going to have to be sorted out.

"How have you been feeling? Did you ever get in touch with that doctor?" Taylor was consistent and changed the subject right on schedule.

"No," Casey replied. "I've been feeling okay. I still have a twinge of pain here and there, but that's to be expected with endometriosis."

"Dr. Hall is the best gynecologist on the planet," Sophia chimed in. "I swear that woman knows her way around a vagina. I think she's flat-out amazing. She warms the speculum, too, so that's a bonus."

"For sure she gets kudos for the warm speculum. *But* if I don't need to go…then I'm not gonna volunteer to have a stranger poke around in my nether regions just for the fun of it," Casey said. "Thank you, but *no thank you*."

Back on the ranch, she was surprised to see Brock home so early. She stood by the VW for a moment—she had been giving Brock his space and he had been taking it. But something in her gut told her that, as his friend, enough was enough. She put Hercules on the ground so he could greet his girlfriend, Lady.

"Hi, Ladybug." Casey gave the Lab a scratch on her neck, which was her favorite spot.

Brock was at the kitchen table; on the table was an open bottle of some sort of alcohol and a single glass.

"What's the occasion?" Casey asked him.

Brock looked up at her as if he had just noticed that she was there. His shirt was unbuttoned and his hair was mussed. It seemed that he had already indulged quite a bit—his eyes were glassy.

"Here…" Brock reached behind him to grab a glass from the drain. He slammed the glass down on the table, pulled the cork out of the bottle and poured her a drink. "Join me."

He poured himself another drink—it was a sloppy pour and liquor sloshed over the rim and onto the table.

The ranch foreman held out his glass to toast her. "Congratulate me."

"For…?"

"I am—" Brock pointed at his chest "—a free man."

"Wait a minute…" Casey sat down and put her glass down. "You're divorced? How could it have possibly happened that fast?"

Brock tipped his head back to polish off every bit

of liquor in his glass. "Well, funny story. Shannon's fiancé, Carl… His father skis every winter in Montana with a law school buddy of his, who—you guessed it—is a judge in Helena. The father asks his friend for a favor, and since everything's already been settled through mediation, the judge fast-tracked our case. Shannon's decided to keep the name McAllister and hyphenate after she gets married. She's shooting for a June wedding next year so Hannah can attend."

Now *she* felt like she needed a drink. Brock being married had always been a reason to keep him safely in the friend zone—now that he was a free man, the dynamic between them would undoubtedly change.

"What is this?" Casey sniffed the alcohol.

"Cognac," Brock told her. "Good cognac. Sorry I don't have the proper glasses."

Casey held out her glass. "What does one toast to in a situation like this? Happy divorce?"

Brock poured himself another. "That'll do."

They touched glasses. Brock downed his and she took a healthy sip of hers. He slammed his glass down and then drummed his fingers on the table.

Casey looked up to find Brock staring at her.

"What?" she asked him when he just continued to stare at her as if he didn't recognize her.

"Are you my friend, Casey?"

"Yes," she told him. "Of course I am. Why?"

"Because I intend to get drunk tonight and I might show my ass, if you know what I mean. If you're my friend—you won't judge me."

"I'm not going to judge you," she reassured him. "I'll even pour the drinks for you. But you've got to make me a promise, Brock…"

"I'm not sure I'm in any condition to make a promise, but go ahead…"

"After tonight? You've got to snap out of it and start enjoying your life again. God knows Shannon isn't sitting around crying in her beer."

Brock raised a brow at her. "Now—that was cold."

Casey leaned forward. "I know—did I go too far? I was trying to motivate you."

"No." Brock surprised her by chuckling a little. "I like your style."

Casey sipped on her one glass of what turned out to be very expensive vintage Hennessey cognac that Brock had been saving for a special occasion. Brock polished off the entire bottle. She kept him company and she was there for him to lean on when he needed a guiding hand to get him safely from the table to the couch.

"Why are you so good to me?" he asked her when she helped him pull off his boots.

"Because—" Casey handed him a large glass of water and some aspirin "—you're my friend and I love you."

Brock popped the aspirin into his mouth before he guzzled the water. "I love you."

One minute she was standing upright and the next thing she realized, she was half sitting, half lying on top of a now reclining Brock. He had reached out, scooped her up like she didn't weigh an ounce, and he had her in a bear hug with his face buried in her hair.

"You smell good," he murmured drunkenly. "Lemony."

"That's the dishwashing soap."

"Mmmmm." This was the only response she got out of him.

"Brock? I need to get up now."

This wasn't sexual—it wasn't a come-on—he was cuddling her like she was a life-size teddy bear. Then she heard him snoring.

"Really?" Casey started to wiggle her body in earnest and managed to wriggle free of his heavy arms.

She got the blanket off the back of the couch to drape over him. Casey stared down at this man who had become so important to her. She'd told him she loved him and she'd meant it. She did. No matter if they went any further with each other—that was another subject entirely—but as a person, as a friend, as a man, she loved him.

"Lord have mercy, Brock." Casey breathed in deeply and then sighed it out heavily. "We have got to get you back in your own bed."

"Good morning!" Casey poked a snoring Brock with her finger.

The man must have really tied one on because she had been banging around in the kitchen for an hour and the only time he'd moved was to turn over with an annoyed grunt.

"Coffee." She tugged on his beard. *"Coffee!"*

"Blast it, Casey! I heard you! Coffee! I heard you!"

"If you heard me," she said sweetly with sarcasm laced in, "then get up! Day's a'wastin', my friend, and we have a full agenda."

"It's my day off." He covered his eyes with his arm.

"I know," she told him. "It's your day off and we have a lot to do. How's that hangover?"

"Not too bad. Considering."

"I made you drink water before you passed out." Casey put some scrambled eggs on a plate with toast. "Come eat some breakfast."

Brock ate a couple helpings of eggs, three pieces of buttered toast, a glass of orange juice and two cups of coffee. The man could really pack it away, even after a night of drinking.

While she washed the dishes, he went upstairs to take a much-needed shower and change into clean clothes. He looked refreshed and clean—his shirt was tucked in and his hair was combed back off his face. The man smelled good again.

"Now what do you have up your sleeve?" Brock had sat back down at the table and was watching her put away the dishes that had dried in the drying rack overnight.

Casey shut the cabinet door. "We're going into town so you can pick out a new mattress."

When he didn't say "yeah" or "nay" she stood in front of him and asked, "No objection?"

He shook his head. "You slapped some sense into me last night. I've got to get the heck on with it. A new mattress is a fine place to start."

"Huh…" She liked to see him taking the bull by the horns, so to speak. "If that's how you really feel, then you shouldn't object to one thing I want to do."

He raised his eyebrows questioningly.

"Brock—I say this with love, I really do, but you have to let me trim your beard."

Brock rubbed his hand over his scruffy beard. "You don't like the beard?"

"No. I didn't say that. I like it actually. And beards

are in now. But I think we need to take it down a couple of notches from Neanderthal."

His long legs were stretched out in front of him and she was standing in the space between his calves. He looked at her face with such admiration that it made her cheeks feel hot, like she was actually blushing.

"You are mighty pretty, Casey Brand."

"Don't change the subject."

He hooked his pointer finger in the loop of her jeans. "I'm not. If you want to trim my beard, you are welcome to have your way with me."

Brock tugged her forward so he could put his hands on either side of her hips. Now that he was a free man, he was very comfortable touching her. She wasn't sure she was as comfortable as he was, but on the other hand, she didn't have any desire to pull away from him. It would just take her a minute to get used to this sudden shift in their boundaries.

"You told me you loved me last night." He was staring into her eyes so intently.

She had to look away—it was like he was trying to read every word written on her soul. "And I meant it."

"Hey..." He wanted her to shift her eyes back to his. "I meant it, too."

"Could we just...slow down for a minute?" She pushed away from him.

Brock let her go. "I've wanted to be able to touch you for a long time now."

She crossed her arms in front of her body. "I know. And I respect the fact that you wanted to finish with one relationship before you started another. That's something I really respect about you. But it hasn't even been twenty-four hours yet."

"Okay." The one word was all he said.

"I just need time to process, I think."

He reached for her hand and gave it a reassuring squeeze. "So what do you want to do first? Mattress or beard?"

They were back in safe territory now, which suited her.

"I never say no to shopping. So, mattress first, beard later."

Shopping in Helena, Montana, was the polar opposite experience to shopping her favorite haunts in Chicago. Chicago was teeming with choices and price points—a shopper's paradise. Helena on the other hand? Not so much. However, there did seem to be quite a few places to shop for mattresses in Helena. Brock had Wi-Fi in his truck, so she researched stores while he drove them into town.

"Okay—I'm leaning toward Macy's because they're familiar. But I have to tell you, Mattress Madness is tickling my fancy. It's a stove and mattress combo store."

"Good deals there."

She raised her eyebrows at him. "You knew I was being facetious, right?"

Brock gave her a quick little wink. "Yes, dear."

When she had originally had the thought to take Brock to buy a new mattress, it never occurred to her that she would be helping him make a selection. At least not in the way he wanted her to help him.

Brock had been lying on one of the higher-end mattresses with his arms at his sides and his eyes closed.

"Well?" she asked him impatiently. "What do you think?"

"I've been waiting on you." His eyes still closed, he patted the empty spot beside him. "Give it a whirl."

"What I think doesn't matter. It's *your* mattress."

Brock opened his eyes. "Down the road a piece, you're going to be sleeping in it with me, so you've got to tell me if you like it or not."

Casey looked around to see if the salesman helping them was in earshot. "That's putting the cart *way* before the horse, don't you think?"

"No." He patted the empty spot again. "I've got a real strong feeling about me and you."

Chapter Thirteen

She didn't necessarily agree with him that she was picking out a mattress for *them* as opposed to *him*, but Brock refused to get up until she gave him her honest opinion. Soon, because she had a strong opinion about everything shopping, she was trying out all of the mattresses with him. Brock purchased a California king that would fit the bed frame in the master bedroom upstairs and then he shadowed Casey as she wove her way through the misses and junior clothing department, through accessories, around the perfume and makeup counters into the shoe department.

I'll just try on a few pairs turned into Casey happily surrounded by a wonderful fort of boot boxes. Brock sat across from her, his big frame stuffed into the standard-issue shoe-department chair. He couldn't be comfortable, but to his credit, the man just sat there scrolling through his phone while she tried on one style of boot after another after another. She lived on a teacher's salary, so she knew that once she did have a family the shoe obsession would have to be tamped down—but as she didn't have kids at the moment, shoes were part of her family.

She left Macy's with three new pairs of fabulous boots—one ankle boot to fill the empty void left by her ruined Jimmy Choo boots, may they rest in peace, and two pairs of knee-high boots, one black and one tan and brown ombre. Brock carried her bags for her while she chatted happily about stumbling upon such a great shoe sale. It wasn't right—she knew it wasn't right—but shopping always gave her a wonderful shot of endorphins.

Brock opened the truck door for her and she climbed up into the cab of his truck. She was still talking about their shopping excursion when he cranked the engine.

"Aren't you happy that we found a new mattress for you?"

The ranch foreman nodded.

"Yeah—me, too." She sighed, pleased with how the morning had worked out for the both of them. She was on a talkative streak, which could be attributed to the new boot cache in the backseat *and* the giant high-octane coffee she had power guzzled for energy prior to her search-and-rescue mission through the shoe department.

The most she was able to get out of Brock was a couple of grunts and nods.

"You aren't saying much," she finally complained.

He glanced over at her as they came to a red light. "I'm listening to you."

"A conversation usually includes two people." She held up two fingers. "I say something, then you say something... Where are we going?"

He wasn't taking the road back to the ranch.

"I made an appointment to get a haircut and a shave. You wanted me to get that taken care of, didn't you?"

Casey turned her body toward Brock—the man never stopped surprising her. He really didn't.

Bone's Barber Shop was the next stop on their "just divorced" victory lap. When the barber asked Brock what he wanted to have done, the ranch foreman had nodded to her and said, "Whatever she wants."

Casey had to admit that she was mesmerized by the slow transformation of Brock McAllister from a mild-mannered mountain man to a straight-up hunk. The barber started with the shaggy hair. Brock's hair had grown in unruly waves down to his shoulders, but when the barber was finished cutting, the rancher only had an inch of hair on top. The barber then cleaned up the line around Brock's ears, ears that Casey couldn't remember seeing before, and cleaned up the edge of his hair just at the nape of the neck.

The beard—a beard that could require its own zip code—was tackled next. The hot towel came off Brock's face and the straight razor came out. As per her request, the barber kept the beard, but trimmed it down considerably. Totally trusting the process, or maybe he just wasn't concerned all that much by his appearance in general, Brock had his eyes closed while the barber worked with a straight-edge razor and shaving lotion beneath his chin and neck.

Brock had almost dozed off when he felt the barber wipe down his face with a lukewarm towel; the barber applied aftershave and then sat him upright. He opened his eyes and stared at his reflection in the mirror—he didn't look like himself anymore. At least not the man he had been for the last several years. His eyes sought out, and found, Casey's eyes in the mirror. He was hoping she would look pleased, but her reaction was far more gratifying. It was as if she were seeing him, truly seeing him, for the first time. Perhaps she was.

"Do I meet with your approval, Ms. Brand?" he asked her.

She walked around to the front of his chair, surprise and, yes, *attraction*, there for him to easily see in her wide green eyes.

"You are handsome," she told him plainly. And he knew she meant it.

He paid the barber a generous tip then asked the redhead of his affection out to lunch. It felt like their first date…even though they had been meeting at the chapel every week this summer, this was the first time they were "going out" together. He felt proud, very proud, to have Casey walking beside him. And now, with his new image, he hoped she was proud to be walking beside him.

"I'm am *so* hungry!" Casey sat opposite Brock.

He had brought her to his favorite pizza spot—Bullman's Wood Fired Pizza. The pizza oven was right there for all the customers to see—and the name wasn't false advertisement, either—a wood-burning fire heated the pizza oven.

"It smells so good in here." Casey's stomach, which had been rumbling before, started to hurt from the hunger.

She scoured the menu and decided that she had to

be adventurous and try the Bitterroot. She'd never eaten a pizza with the interesting combination of pistachios, red onions, rosemary, mozzarella, olive oil and sea salt. Brock ordered the Bitterroot for her and the Crazy Mountain for himself and added two bottles of Montana-made cider.

"What should we toast to today?" Casey asked him. "To freedom?"

Brock stared at her so intently that it made her squirm in her chair.

"I don't want my freedom," he told her. "I want to be with you."

"Brock…" she said gently. "I think it's too soon. You've only been divorced for one day."

"That's true," he agreed with her. "But I've been separated for years."

She wanted to change the subject. She had always liked to keep things light and upbeat—and this conversation was heading into territory that made her uncomfortable. Some, like her sister, would call her commitment-phobic. She had diagnosed herself as chronically cautious with her heart.

He must have read the resistance on her face and in her body language, because his next words were designed specifically to make her laugh and smile. And they worked.

"How about this? Let's toast to the buy-one-get-one-half-off shoe sale at Macy's."

Casey laughed and willingly held out her cider bottle. "You're a very quick study, aren't you, cowboy? Cheers to that!"

She tried to pay her portion of the bill, but Brock wouldn't hear of it. Casey couldn't believe how much pizza she had stuffed into her face. And she said as much to Brock when he climbed into the driver's seat.

"Look at this..." Casey pulled up her shirt and showed him her belly. "I ate so much of that pizza that I actually have a food baby."

"Not too many women will put food away like you do."

She frowned at him. "I think you meant that as a compliment...?"

"Of course I did."

"I've always been hyper as all get out. I burn through my calories and need to fuel right back up again. I usually go up and down about ten pounds—so I have two different wardrobes in my closet—but it's not my weight that gives me trouble, it's the cellulite. It just shows up, unannounced, now that I'm in my thirties. It's very annoying."

Brock was smiling at her minidiatribe about the woes of cellulite.

"That was the cider talking." Casey laughed. "I have no idea how my cellulite entered the conversation."

"I like to listen to you talk," Brock told her. "Today is a good day."

That day, the first official day of Brock being a free and clear man, was the beginning of a new chapter in the evolution of her relationship with the ranch foreman. His resolve, his focus and his quiet persistence on the matter of their future eroded most of her resistance. His appeal to her now, an appeal that had always been about who he was as a man—who he was as a father and a protector—had shifted. His makeover allowed her to see him in an entirely new light. He had always been hypermasculine and burly in his appearance—which wasn't repellent by any means—but the short hair and the groomed beard had transformed his face. She could see his teeth when he smiled, including the bottom two teeth that crossed just a little, which she now found endearing. She could see his eyes—clear eyes that admired her and had nothing to hide.

Over breakfast, she found herself staring at him. On their frequent rides together, she found herself staring at him. At the dinner table, more staring. He was so handsome to her eyes. So handsome. Inside and out. The real Brock had been hidden behind all of that hair for years.

Every morning, after breakfast, Brock would always ask her, "Are you going to meet me at the chapel today?"

In the beginning, they would plan a picnic at the chapel one time a week—but that wasn't enough for Brock anymore. He wanted her to meet him at the chapel every day. At the start of this new routine, she felt as if she were doing it mostly for Brock. Over time, she began to realize how important those picnics at the chapel were to her.

"You've got your hands full! Do you need a hand?"

Casey had been so intent on getting the picnic basket, Ladybug the Labrador *and* Hercules the all-time greatest poodle from the vintage VW up to the chapel, that she hadn't noticed the young cowboy tending to one of the mares in the foaling barn. She had discovered the short cut through the barn only last week.

"Wyatt Williams!" Casey stopped in her tracks to give her startled, racing heart a chance to recover. "*Why* do you always *do* that to me?"

Wyatt was hanging his arms over the stall gate, grinning at her as he always did. "Do what?"

"Scare the living daylights out of me! That's what!"

Wyatt came out of the stall to stand next to her in the barn aisle. "I don't mean to."

"I know. I know." She let him off the hook. Wyatt didn't have a mean, or serious, bone in his body. He was like an overgrown playful puppy.

"Let me give you a hand." Wyatt reached for the basket.

Casey didn't know how Brock would react to seeing Wyatt walking her up to their picnic spot. On the other hand, her hands were too full and there was a pretty steep hill to climb up to the chapel.

"All right." She handed him the basket while she managed Lady's leash and Hercules's carrier.

"I haven't see you in a while," the cowboy said. "You settling into fifty-three okay?"

"Very funny." She smiled at him.

She hadn't seen Wyatt since he had taken her dancing on her birthday. They'd texted a couple of times, but she knew that he was having fun and playing the field, and would get bored pursuing her without results.

"I didn't know you were Brock's girl. I wouldn't have taken you dancin' if I'd known that."

"I wasn't Brock's girl then."

He looked down at her with that perfectly symmetrical, chiseled, golden face. "But you are Brock's girl now."

The sound of that made her smile again, but this time it was a shyer, more self-conscious smile.

"Yes." She nodded her head. "I am Brock's girl now."

* * *

Brock had been thinking about this day for weeks; today was the day that he was going to kiss her. And not the kiss on the cheek that she had been holding him to for far too long. He had been wooing Casey Brand slowly and gentlemanly so he wouldn't spook her. He'd spent enough time with her now to figure a few things out—Casey wanted to have a husband and a family, but she was scared to death of taking a chance and risking failure. They had held hands and snuggled on the couch. They had gone for long, romantic rides and picnics at the chapel. But whenever he got close to going in for that first kiss, he always ended up holding Hercules instead. Casey could *sense* that the all-important, barrier-breaking kiss was upon them and she would find a reason to exit stage left. He didn't know how he had been maneuvered into this corner—a teacup poodle was regularly blocking his romantic mojo. How could something so tiny cause him so much trouble?

"Hi!" Casey called out to him breathlessly as she reached the top of the hill. "Wyatt was kind enough to help me."

Brock covered the distance between them in a few long strides. "I've got it from here. Thank you, Wyatt."

Wyatt handed the basket to the ranch foreman, tipped his hat to both of them and then jogged down the hill and back to the foaling barn.

"Well, that was a lot more civil than I thought it would be," Casey said of the interaction between the two cowboys.

Brock took the blanket out of the basket and spread it out in their favorite spot. "I had a talk with him."

Casey was about to sit down but snapped upright instead. "You *talked* with him? Like you staked your claim?"

"We talked."

Her hands were on her hips. "Well, that was mighty 1890s of you."

"Quit your bellyachin', woman," Brock teased her, "and fix me my lunch."

They unpacked the picnic—she had brought a brand-new, giant-sized Milk-Bone for Lady and a miniature-sized Milk-Bone for Hercules. Once everything was unpacked and the four of them were settled in, Brock turned on one of her favorite classical pieces.

"What kind of wedding do you want to have?" Brock had finished his food and was lying on his side petting Lady. Hercules was sitting on the top of Brock's boot, so the ranch foreman was careful not to move his legs and launch the mini-poodle.

Casey wiped her mouth with a napkin. "Small. Intimate."

She hadn't always dreamed of her wedding like many of her friends had—but she had dreamed of the children who would follow the wedding.

"I think I'd like to marry you right here," Brock told her. "In this chapel."

In her mind, she saw herself, in a simple antique white lace dress, standing hand in hand with Brock, inside the chapel. And the thought didn't scare her.

"I think the chapel would be the perfect place to get married," she agreed.

He reached for her hand. "If we kept it small, Hannah would be able to attend."

Casey rubbed her finger over the nail of his thumb. "I miss her."

"So do I."

Their minds turned to Hannah and neither of them spoke for a couple of minutes. Then Brock brought up the subject that had been on his mind all morning.

"I'm going to kiss you today, Casey."

His comment had shifted the topic pretty dramatically and it made her laugh. He could never do anything in the conventional way.

"I'm giving you fair warning," he added.

"Why do you think that I need fair warning?"

He gave her a look. "You know why."

She did know why—every time Brock had even remotely acted like he was going to kiss her, she managed to find a reason to stop him. She had never been a fan of the first kiss—it was built up so much and what if she hated it? It was hard to imagine marrying someone you didn't like to kiss. That one kiss could ruin everything. And she hadn't been ready to risk it.

"Okay." Casey made a decision; she stood up and held out her hand to Brock. "Come on."

Brock smiled up at her. "Where are you taking me?"

"I'm going to kiss you." She shook her hand for him to take it. "Are you coming or not?"

"Sorry, buddy, but you need to stay here." Brock picked Hercules up off his boot and put him on the picnic blanket.

When the ranch foreman was standing, Casey took his hand in hers and led him decisively over to the chapel steps.

"You stay down there," she told him while she walked up the first couple of steps. She turned around, and now that she was standing on the chapel steps, they were almost the same height.

Without hesitation, Casey put her hands on either side of Brock's face and pressed her lips to his.

It wasn't a deep kiss, but it was the kind of kiss that left an impression. She liked the feel of his beard beneath her fingertips and the firmness of his lips as they were pressed against hers.

"There!" she said when the kiss was over. "Now that's done."

Brock seemed glad that they had broken that barrier. But she could see that he wasn't satisfied with just one short kiss.

"You're beautiful to me." Brock pulled her closer. "I love you, Casey."

And then he kissed her. His way. Slow. Deep. Sensual.

He held her so close that she could feel his heart beating against her breast. The first kiss confirmed that she loved him. The second kiss convinced her that she wanted to make love with him.

When they came up for a breath, Brock kissed her forehead and her cheeks and her neck.

"Tell me that you'll marry me here one day, Casey," he said into her neck.

She hugged him tightly, resting her head on his chest, so she could still feel his heart that was beating so strongly for her.

"I promise that I will marry you here one day."

She said it and she meant it.

Brock let out a whoop and tossed his hat in the air. He picked her up off the step and swung her in a circle until they were both a little dizzy.

They were laughing and out of breath when he stopped swinging her and let her slide down his body until her feet were safely on the ground.

Now that he could kiss her—now that she was willing to *let him* kiss her—that's all he wanted to do. There, in the sunlight, in front of the Bent Tree chapel and beneath the bright blue expanse of the Montana sky, the ranch foreman kissed the woman he knew would one day be his bride.

Chapter Fourteen

The decision to leave her bed that night and go to Brock wasn't difficult to make. The full moon was so crisp and clear in the starless sky and cast a glowing yellow light through the large loft window. She hadn't been able to sleep and she knew why. Brock was alone in the upstairs bedroom while she was alone in her bed—and it didn't need to be that way. They didn't need to be alone anymore. Not when they had each other.

Casey left the loft with poodle in hand—she quietly entered the house, dropped Hercules off with his girlfriend and then used the flashlight on her phone to light her footsteps up to the second floor. The same moonlight that had lit the loft was streaming into Brock's bedroom and dancing across the bed where her man was sleeping.

She stood by the empty side of the bed and pulled her braid over her shoulder to pull the hair tie from the bottom of the braid. She slowly unbraided her hair until it was swinging loose down her back to the top of her derriere. Brock was snoring softly, lying on his side, unaware that she was in the room with him. He wouldn't reject her. He had been patiently waiting for her. Casey pulled her nightie off and dropped it on the floor beside her bare feet. She hooked her thumbs on her silky bikini panties, slid them down over her hips, down to her ankles and then stepped free of them. Now she was completely naked in the moonlight. Vulnerable as she had never dared to allow herself to be before.

"Brock." Casey said her love's name.

Brock heard his name as if he were hearing it in the distance—in the fog—so soft that he thought he was dreaming it. When he opened his eyes to find an angel with pale, pale skin covered only by beautiful strands of red hair, he thought he had imagined her. That he had wanted Casey to come to him so badly that his mind had manufactured her likeness out of thin air.

"Brock."

She said his name again and this time he knew that this was not a dream—she was real. Casey had finally come to him as he had willed her to do in his mind so many nights.

"Are you sure you're ready for this?" His voice was husky from a mixture of sleep and need.

He saw her nod her head—he saw a small smile on her pretty pink lips. He pulled the covers back for her. As she walked the short distance to the bed, he soaked in the image of her ethereal body—so much softer and feminine in its nakedness. Her breasts were naturally

rounded, not large, but perfectly shaped. The nipples—
they had grown hard in his mouth. At the apex of her
thighs there was a triangle of red curls. He wanted to
bury his face there and taste her sweetness.

And then she was in his arms. Her skin was chilled
from the night air—he covered her with the blanket
and wrapped her tightly in his arms. She was shiver-
ing. He would have to go slow—it had been a long time
in between lovers for both of them.

"This is it for me, Casey." Brock curled his body
around hers and kissed the back of her neck. "I love
you."

Casey responded by kissing his hand. "I love you."

When her body was warmed, Brock let go of her
just long enough to discard his underwear. She turned
in his arms and they pressed their bodies together, for
the warmth and the comfort. Her skin, so smooth and
soft, was everything his skin wasn't. He was hairy and
rough—she felt like silk all over.

He kissed her, slowly so he could enjoy it and deeply
so she was reminded of things to come. She tasted
minty, like toothpaste, and she moved her hips into
his body as he deepened the kiss.

She gasped the sweetest, sexiest gasp when he
flicked his tongue across the hard tip of her nipple.
He held her breast firmly in his hand and sucked her
nipple until she dug her fingernails into his shoulder.

"I've wanted to touch you like this for so long."

Casey reached between them and wrapped her fingers around his erection.

Brock's body shuddered at the touch of her hand—
it had been years since a woman had touched him
like that.

His need had been so great, for such a long time, that he had been afraid he wouldn't be able to love her the way he wanted to on their first night. For weeks, he had been releasing himself so he could last long enough to bring her to climax. If he hadn't been preparing his body, that first touch of her hand may have been his rapid, untimely undoing. Especially since they had agreed that condoms weren't required—Casey had received a long-lasting birth control shot and neither of them had been sexually active in several years. Without a condom to reduce sensation, he could climax before they even got started.

"Are you okay?" he asked his love.

"I'm happy," she said so quietly. "I love you."

Brock worried that his hands were too big or too rough as he ran his fingers down her belly and along her muscular thighs. Her legs had grown so strong from a summer of riding—he could feel the power in them just as he felt the satin of her skin. He slipped his fingers between her thighs—so warm, so wet, so ready for him. He wanted to taste that warmth between her beautiful thighs, but he knew that he had to take his time with Casey. There would be time for more exploring and experimenting later. For now, he just wanted her to be comfortable in his arms, in his bed. He wanted her to adjust to his weight on top of her and the feel of having his body filling hers.

Casey started to tug on his arm, pulling him toward her. He lifted himself up and moved between her thighs. Brock held himself above her—he wanted to look down on her; what a pretty vision she created with her ivory skin against his dark sheets and her hair spread across his pillows.

She reached down between them to guide him. So tight. So tight and warm and slick. He slid his body into hers and they moaned in unison. Her body completely enveloped him; she felt like nothing he'd ever experienced before. Their bodies fit together so perfectly—it didn't make sense, but it didn't have to.

Brock lowered his body until his chest was pressed against her breasts. He slid his arms beneath their bodies so he could hold her even tighter against his chest. She mirrored him, wrapping her arms and legs around his body—drawing him in deeper and deeper.

"Am I too heavy for you?" he asked when he heard her gasp.

She gasped again and he lifted up his body just in time to see how the woman he loved looked when she climaxed. He stopped moving his body so she could set the rhythm, so she could use his body to prolong the orgasm. When she cried out again, and he felt the wetness of her release on his thighs, he couldn't hold himself back any longer.

"God, God, God…" Brock's body shuddered and his arms tightened around Casey.

After a minute of Brock laying his full weight on top of her, Casey pushed on his shoulder with a languid laugh.

"*Now* you're too heavy for me."

He carefully disconnected their bodies then rolled onto his back. "Come over here with me."

Casey curled up next to her bear of a man—she rested her arm on his shoulder, her hand on his furry chest, and put her leg over his thick thigh.

"Mmm." She closed her eyes with a contented sigh. "We're really good at that."

Brock laughed and kissed her on her damp forehead. "We are good at that."

"I'm going to sleep now, okay?" Casey turned over onto her other side.

"Me, too." He turned with her.

Brock shaped his body to hers, his arm beneath her body and holding her across her chest. "I love you."

Casey tilted her head back so she could kiss him one last time. "I love you, sweet man."

That first night of loving sparked a wild week of lovemaking. The more comfortable Casey became with him, the more risks she wanted to take. In fact, he wasn't usually the aggressor in the sexual arena— she was. She would come up behind him when he was cooking, unzip his pants and stimulate him with her hands. He could count several ruined meals because he wasn't about to pass up an invitation like that from Casey. She also enjoyed making love in the morning. He'd wake up with her mouth getting him hard and ready. Those were his favorite mornings—groggy with a raging hard-on and the love of his life climbing on top of him. That lovemaking was always sensual and slow, with Casey covering his body with hers, both of them beneath the covers. He'd wake up every morning that way if he could.

They loved each other so much that their body parts were sore—but it didn't matter. They couldn't keep their hands off each other and they didn't *want* to keep their hands off each other. And that included when they were supposed be showering to go out.

Instead of waiting for her turn in the shower, Casey opened the shower door and stepped inside. Brock was standing with his back to her, rinsing the soap off the front part of his body. She ran her hands across his back and started to lick little droplets of water from his skin.

"Mmm. That feels nice, baby."

Brock turned around so they could hug each other while the hot water ran over their bodies. It didn't take long for her to feel his body start to respond. She leaned back and smiled up at him.

"Look at what you do to me—all you have to do is touch me."

Casey lowered her body down, running her hands over his stomach.

"I need to lose a couple of pounds," he said about his less-than-flat stomach.

Casey put her finger to her lips. "Shhh."

When she took him in her mouth, he reached out to steady himself by putting his hands flat on either side of the shower. The hotness of the shower, the hotness of her mouth—he knew what she wanted from him— she wanted him hard and ready to love her. And that's exactly what she got.

Brock lifted Casey up into his arms, walked her to the edge of the shower so her back was pressed against the cool tile and while he was kissing her, he was sliding her down onto his shaft.

"Ah…" Casey dropped her head back as he kissed the water from her neck.

"It's too damn slippery in here." Brock laughed. "I need to put something on the floor to keep my feet from sliding."

Casey wiped the water off his face and kissed his lips. "Take me to the bed."

Their bodies dripping puddles of water on the floor, Brock carried her to the bed and laid her back with her legs hanging off the side. Still standing, he guided himself back into her body and pushed her knees to her chest. They had loved each other enough that they could look into each other's eyes as they made love—and this was an entirely new position to enjoy.

Casey arched her back to take him deeper and then he hit something that hurt. She pulled away and held out her hand.

"Are you okay?"

She frowned with her hand on her abdomen. "That hurt."

"You get on top so you're in control," Brock told her.

That seemed to work. There wasn't any more pain. She rode him exactly the way she wanted to while he watched. She knew that he loved the feel of her hair brushing against his thighs when she was on top of him, so she tilted her head back and let her long hair slip across the tops of his legs.

Harder, faster, deeper, stronger—he let her choose the pace and the rhythm. So close, so close... Casey opened her eyes to find Brock staring at her.

"Come with me." Casey put her hands on his chest and bore down on him.

Brock grabbed her hips and pushed her down onto his erection—faster and faster, harder and harder.

Casey dug her fingernails into his chest and tossed her head back at the same time he thrust all the way up inside her. Together, they climaxed, and Casey heard herself scream so loudly that it was fortunate that they didn't have close neighbors to hear her.

She collapsed on top of her lover, completely satisfied and happy.

"God I love you, Casey." Brock held her closely, his fingers in her wet hair.

She loved how this man felt, how he smelled, the sound of his voice, the way he loved her with his words and with his body.

"I love you."

Simple. To the point. True.

Later that night, after they had made love again, Brock was propped up on pillows and holding her in his arms. He was rubbing her back with his strong hands, kneading her shoulder muscles and making her moan in an entirely different way.

"Do you want babies, Casey?"

"Yes," she murmured, not wanting him to stop the massage.

"Soon?"

"Yes." She turned her head so it was flat on his fuzzy chest.

"I'll give you as many babies as you want," Brock promised her. "Motherhood is going to look so good on you."

"Fatherhood already looks good on you."

They talked about the future and how the logistics could work. Casey had her condo in Chicago that needed to be leased or sold and then there was her job she had to consider. She loved her school. She loved her fellow educators. She loved her students. It would be hard to give up everything she had built there and start anew in Helena. But at least she had the type of career that could be translated to even a small community like Helena, Montana. She had to work. Even after they started a family—work would always be an important part of her life. Casey broached the topic of Clint and the tension it was causing with her sister, and to Brock's credit, he promised that he would try, for her sake, to forge a different path, a better path, with his stepbrother.

And, most important on his end of things, there was Hannah. She needed time to adjust to the reality of the divorce. Yes, her mother had been living in California for a while, but the divorce had officially ended that chapter. It wouldn't be right for her—for any of them—for Brock to jump right back into a marriage with Casey. And Casey had always believed that Brock needed time to process the end of his first marriage. Of course, she was concerned about her fertility window. Yes, she was still young enough to bear a child, but the clock was ticking. But, at least for now, she just wanted to enjoy the time she had left of her summer vacation, having fun and making love with Brock.

Casey had been in a deep sleep, curled onto her side with Brock's warm body pressed against her. A sharp, stabbing pain, like an ice pick being shoved into her stomach, made her jerk away from Brock. She lurched forward, eyes open, hands pressed into her abdomen.

"Oh!" she cried out. Her loud cry awakened Brock.

"What's wrong?" He knocked items off the bedside table on his way to switching on the light.

Casey pushed herself to the edge of the bed. "I don't know! I don't *know*!"

She got herself out of bed and ran to the bathroom. She slammed the door shut behind her and locked it.

Brock had followed her and was outside the door

calling her name. "Casey." He knocked on the door. "Casey!"

Casey crumpled onto the floor holding her stomach—the pain was so strong that she felt like she was going to pass out or be sick.

"I'll be out in a minute!" she tried to reassure Brock.

Through her tears, Casey noticed a large spot of blood on the nightshirt she had put on right before she'd gone to sleep.

"Casey! Did you get your period? There's blood on the sheets."

"I don't think so…" She forced herself to stand up so she could get herself cleaned up. "It's not time."

Putting off going to the gynecologist was no longer an option. Taylor talked the receptionist into squeezing Casey in for an appointment the day after she had started the irregular bleeding. She had experienced spotting and pain before, but had always chalked it up to her diagnosis of endometriosis and nothing more. Even the times when the sex with Brock was a little painful, she had always attributed it to her previous diagnosis. But this pain and this bleeding were *not normal*.

The doctor took her history, conducted a pelvic exam, made contact with her recently fired, but not yet replaced, gynecologist and collected urine and blood. Brock and Taylor didn't hesitate to put aside their differences and focus on Casey. Brock waited in the waiting room while Taylor held her sister's hand through the transvaginal ultrasound and an endometrial biopsy.

Several days later, the tests results were back and she was back in Dr. Hall's office with Taylor by her side and Brock in the waiting room. But even after the doctor gave her a diagnosis, explained her treatment options and then gave her some time to process the information with her sister, Casey's mind had gone completely blank. There was a noise in her head like a TV station that had just gone off the air—and she could hear her sister talking to her, but it sounded like she was talking to her with a tin can on a string.

"I have to go talk to Brock," Casey finally said after a minute of staring at a jar of tongue depressors on the table across the room.

"Okay." Taylor stood up and put her arm around Casey's shoulders. "Let's go talk to Brock."

Brock wasn't sitting down where they had left him. He was standing just outside the door, pacing on the sidewalk in front of the doctor's office. Casey finished her business with the receptionist before she went outside to see Brock.

"Hey!" Brock spotted her and came immediately to her side. "What did the doctor say?"

"Um…" Casey slipped her hand into his. "I'd rather tell you after we get in the truck, okay?"

Casey saw Brock and Taylor exchange a look. Taylor hugged her sister and said, "I'm going to let the two of you be alone. Call me the minute you get back to the ranch, Casey. We have to figure out our next steps."

Casey hugged her sister tightly, so grateful for her. "I will."

It was nice to see Taylor and Brock rally during a crisis—it made her feel like there was hope for them to all be able to get along. Taylor surprised both of them by hugging Brock before she got into her truck and drove away.

Once they were inside the truck, Brock turned toward her and stared at her face intently.

"Tell me—what's going on?"

Casey held his hand—glad for the comfort she received from the warm strength of his fingers and hoping to give him some comfort in return.

"I have cancer," she told him simply. "Endometrial cancer."

Chapter Fifteen

Brock didn't waver in his resolve to accompany her back to Chicago. They were both so stunned by her diagnosis that most of the movement was muscle memory—making plane reservations, making arrangements for the animals to be cared for on the farm and making sure she was packed and ready to go back to Chicago. Brock picked up the tab for the rush-order tickets to get them from the Helena airport into O'Hare. Casey insisted that she pay him back for the expense of the tickets, but Brock refused to argue with her about it.

"Let's just get you home," he had told her. "The rest can wait."

The day that she was scheduled to leave Montana, Casey sat down one last time in the window seat. This had been a favorite spot—a little cubby tucked away that had an amazing view of the world below. She had watched Brock work from that window—and she had began to admire the man from this window seat.

"I'm going to miss this place," Casey said to the poodle that had been glued to her side. He sensed something was wrong.

"Are you ready?" Brock walked through the door to the loft.

Casey nodded as she stood up. "All I have is the trunk and this one bag."

Brock made short work of loading her trunk and bag into his truck. They dropped Ladybug off with Kay Lynn—she was familiar and would love the Labrador like her own while Brock was gone. Taylor had wanted to accompany her back to Chicago, but she finally conceded that Brock had more freedom to travel at the moment. Taylor did, however, meet them at the airport to say goodbye.

"Call me as soon as you land. I hate that I'm not going with you." Taylor hugged her for a fourth time.

Clint was standing away from them holding Penelope. His collarbone was healed and he was contemplating his next move career-wise. This was the first time Casey had seen Brock and his stepbrother together in one place for more than a couple of minutes.

"Let me see my beautiful niece for a minute." Casey took Penny in her arms and hugged her and kissed her sweet-smelling skin.

"Thank you for taking such good care of my sister, Clint," she said to her brother-in-law before she gave Penny one last kiss on the top of the head and handed her back to her father.

"You get yourself squared away right quick." Clint pulled her in for a hug.

"That's the plan," she reassured him.

Taylor had tears in her eyes, even though Casey had explicitly told her sister *no tears*. Taylor wiped the tears off her cheeks and looked as if she was trying to rein in her emotions.

"Nick is picking you up from O'Hare?" her sister asked.

"That's what Mom said."

Their brother, Nick, had just graduated from law school and was studying for the bar exam. He still lived in Chicago and would meet them at the airport and take them straight to their parents' house in Lincoln Park. Her father and mother insisted that she stay with them until her health improved and she was grateful. The idea of being alone in her tiny one-bedroom apartment while she treated the cancer didn't appeal to her at all.

She knew she had cancer. She believed the diagnosis, even though she would be paying close attention to the second opinion when she visited the gynecological oncologist. But she suspected that she was in shock—she hadn't cried. Not once. She had systematically figured out the next steps she needed to take and then put her plan in motion. Perhaps her brain was giving her a break—perhaps her brain knew that home was the better place to have an emotional crisis.

"Thank you, Brock." Taylor, for the second time in one week, hugged the ranch foreman.

And, miracle of miracles, Brock and Clint acknowledged each other, were civil and shook hands before the two couples went their separate ways. Casey managed to sleep on the plane ride back to Chicago—she had Brock's hand to hold and Hercules to share a blanket with. She slept until the steward announced their descent into Chicago O'Hare; Casey blinked her eyes to focus them as she put her seat back in the upright position. She secured Hercules in his carrier and then pushed the window cover up so she could see the lights of her home city as they approached.

"Back to reality," Casey said under her breath. "I sure didn't expect to be coming home like this."

Brock tightened his grip on Casey's hand. He couldn't have predicted this if he'd tried, but he was about to land in Chicago with the woman he loved. Casey wanted him to see her home safely and then head back to Montana. But that just wasn't going to happen. He wasn't about to drop her off and take off like nothing was wrong. What kind of man would he be if he did that? No—he planned on staying in Chicago for as long as he could manage. He had savings— he'd always been smart with his money. He could stay until Hannah was scheduled to return to Montana, and then he would have to go. He was hopeful that, by then, Casey's treatment plan and prognosis would be clear.

"Nick!" Casey spotted her brother standing near one of the baggage carousels. "Nicky! Over here!"

Her brother heard his name and looked their way. She waved her arm in the air. Nicholas, the middle child and all-around golden boy, had always been the star of the family and the apple of their mother's eye. Nick was handsome and athletic and had followed their father into law. If he weren't such a likable guy, he would be completely intolerable.

Casey introduced her brother to Brock; the two men shook hands and then they walked closer to the crowded carousel area to grab the trunk and other luggage. Nick had been his normal friendly, but formal, self. On the other hand, she was completely worried about how her parents would react to Brock. They were still reeling from Taylor marrying a professional bull rider who hadn't gone to so much as community college—and now their youngest was involved with a cowboy. For their mother, it would no doubt feel like an epidemic of some sort. Something wrong with them that needed to be cured.

Their bags showed up in one piece. They loaded all of them into Nick's late-model Jaguar XJ, and merged onto I-90 East to Lincoln Park.

"Nice graduation present," Casey said from the backseat.

"I was going to wait until I passed the bar exam—and then I thought, why not use it as incentive to *pass* the bar?" Nick flashed her a smile in the rearview mirror.

"How's Mom doing with all of this?" she asked her brother, and he knew exactly what she meant. Their mom was a pathological drama queen; she was famous for making gigantic mountains out of microscopic molehills. Give her something like her "baby" having cancer to chew on? She could subsist on this kind of tragedy for years.

"She's already seen her shrink, her internist and located a support group for parents of children who have been diagnosed with some form of cancer."

"And Dad?"

Nick met her eyes quickly in the rearview mirror again. It was always a mystery to them how their father had lasted for so many decades with their mother.

"He's glad that you're going to be staying with them until this gets sorted out. How are *you* doing?"

"I'm okay…" She lifted her shoulders up and then dropped them down with a shake of her head. "I mean, I have cancer—so that stinks. But besides that, I'm okay."

Casey's parents' house in Lincoln Park was a display of wealth the likes of which Brock had never experienced before. The house was four stories tall, with floors of polished Italian marble, curtains made from velvet, crystal chandeliers and a double banister staircase that he'd only seen used in some of the fancier hotels he'd stayed at over the years. There were layers of crown molding in every room, marble fireplaces and rooftop terraces with views of downtown Chicago. Brock hadn't often felt out of place in his life, but he sure as heck felt out of place here.

"I'm going to see that you're settled and then I'm going to head to my hotel—I made reservations at one of those extended-stay places." Brock's deep voice echoed up the stairwell leading to the second floor.

"Already planning your escape?" she asked him, only half in jest.

"I'm staying close by…"

As it turned out for Brock, he ended up staying even closer than he had anticipated. Her mother, Vivian Bartlett Brand, had floated down the curved stairwell in a flurry of diamonds and designer clothes and hugged her harder than usual before turning her attention to the tall ranch foreman. To her utter amazement, her mother took to Brock like she took to a new Louis Vuitton bag. Vivian insisted that Brock stay in the guest room, and if there was one thing that Vivian excelled at, it was getting her way with a man.

Her mother had one of the housekeepers on staff get Brock settled in the guest quarters while she accompanied Casey upstairs to the bedrooms on the upper floor.

"Let Leah do her job, darling." Her mother took her hand and led her out to a sitting area that overlooked one of the balconies.

"Come and sit with me." Vivian patted the spot next to her on a chaise.

Her mom wasn't often affectionate, but this was a rare occasion that Vivian put her arm around her shoulder and left it there for more than a quick second.

"Well…" Her mother gave her head a decisive nod. "They caught it early. You're going to be just fine."

Casey believed that. The doctor in Montana had assured her that it was at the early stages and the success rate of treatment was very high. If she was going to get cancer, it seemed that this was the better one to get. It was slower growing and hadn't reached the lymph nodes. Surviving the cancer wasn't her main concern—the recommended treatment was her concern.

"The doctor in Montana said that I might need to have a partial hysterectomy." Casey looked at her mom and, for the first time since the diagnosis, she actually felt tears forming in the backs of her eyes.

"Well, just think. No more menstrual cramps." Vivian patted her leg with an upbeat lilt in her voice. "Besides—motherhood isn't everything it's cracked up to be, Casey. If I had to do it all over, I'm not so certain I'd choose it again."

* * *

"Are you lost?" Casey found Brock in the hallway leading to the cellar.

"I was." He had a bemused expression on his face. "How big is this place?"

"Four thousand square feet." She walked into his open arms.

They stood together silently, hugging each other tightly. Brock felt so warm and solid and safe. She was glad now that he had insisted on coming *and* staying.

"Are you hungry?" Casey linked her arm with his.

She already knew the answer—Brock could always eat. She took him to her father's fully stocked bar and then called up to the kitchen. The cook told her what was on the menu for the evening with options for other meals if the prime rib he had prepared didn't sound appealing.

Brock bellied up to the ornately carved mahogany bar. "It's like a hotel—I swear I've run into at least three people who work here."

"I know." Casey went behind the bar. "I think it's really embarrassing, but as long as it keeps Mom off his back, Dad lets her run the house the way she wants. Can I buy you a drink, cowboy?"

"I wouldn't be mad at a nice, smooth bourbon."

Casey poured them both glasses of one of her father's best bourbons. She leaned toward him, her glass extended.

"Here's to us," Casey toasted.

"To us." Brock touched his glass to hers. "Why don't you come over here with me? You're too far away."

She joined him on his side of the bar; he put down his glass so he could pull her into his arms.

He looked into her eyes. "I love you, Casey. I'm going to be here for you. That's a guarantee."

"I love you."

They kissed and held each other; they were tired from their day of travel and a bit disoriented from the drastic change of setting. Her parents' posh Lincoln Park mansion was a world away from Brock's modest Montana ranch.

"I'm sorry Mom roped you into staying here, Brock."

Brock kept one arm around her but freed up a hand so he could take another taste of the bourbon.

"I'm not worried about it. I'm closer to you—so it's okay. She's a well-preserved woman. I thought she was your sister. I really did."

Casey took a seat next to him. "She has a great plastic surgeon. Well-placed fillers and Botox."

"Uh—do you do that?"

"No." She laughed. "I'm sorry to tell you that I'm going to wrinkle. Not that I wouldn't—don't get me wrong. But I'm scared to death of needles. I really am. I've wanted to get a butterfly tattoo on my ankle since I was fourteen and I've never been able to do it. I've gone twice to get it done and both times—" she made a cutting gesture with her hand "—I chickened out."

Their conversation waned for a moment, then Casey looked at the ranch foreman's face lovingly. "My mom really likes you."

"Is that right?" he asked with a pleased smile.

"Yes." She nodded her head but her brow was wrinkled. "And it doesn't make a bit of sense. I've brought any number of very preppy guys with excellent pedigrees home and she picks them apart like I scraped them right off the bottom of the barrel. But for you? Vivian had nothin' but praise."

Brock winked at her as he finished off his drink.

"I don't get it. But, somehow…all of that—" she pointed to his cowboy hat and boots "—fits in with—" she gestured to her parents' opulent mansion "—all of this. Go figure."

Three weeks after arriving home in Chicago, Casey had been on a whirlwind tour of specialists and surgeons. A specialist confirmed her cancer type and stage; a partial hysterectomy with her ovaries preserved was the recommended course of treatment.

The hard truth—the undeniable truth—she would never be able to carry her own child. She would never know what it was like to feel a life growing inside of her. Brock was always quick to remind her, however, that a child with her dark green eyes and his height wasn't out of the question. Yes, they would have to find a suitable uterus to rent, but at least there was still hope. So, instead of having surgery straightaway, Casey opted to receive fertility treatments for two weeks to harvest her eggs. She despised needles—but she didn't hate them enough to risk losing the chance to have a child of her own one day. Once her eggs were harvested and frozen, Casey went in for surgery. Two days in the hospital and she was back at her parents' house for recuperation. Brock was with her every step of the way; he had made good on his guarantee.

"Hi…" Casey opened her eyes and looked for Brock in the room.

"Hey." Brock was sitting in a chair near the window. He stood up the minute he heard her voice and came to the side of the bed.

He leaned down to kiss her on the cheek. "How do you feel?"

"A little better, I think." Casey winced when she rolled onto her back. Her entire abdomen was still so sore from the surgery. "Are you packed?"

It was time for Brock to go back to Montana. Hannah would be returning home and he had to start thinking about getting her ready to go back to school. It was hard to see him go, but depending on her body, she could be healing for another month. She wanted him to get back to his life.

Brock sat down on the bed next to her, took her hand and kissed it. "I wish I could take you back to Montana with me."

"I know." Casey gave him a tired smile. "But goodness knows I have plenty of people around here to take care of me, and Hannah only has you."

"You know I'm comin' back for you, now, don't you? I'm comin' back to get you, bring you home and marry you."

"Well…I guess you're going to have to get around to asking me," she teased him.

"You just sit over there and look as pretty as you are and let me worry about the details," Brock teased her back. "And, once we're married, we're going to start working on having those babies I promised you."

Casey looked into the face of the man she had grown to love so deeply. There was a promise in his eyes that she knew he intended to keep. Maybe they wouldn't be able to conceive and bring a baby to term with a surrogate—but at least they had a chance.

"Brock…" She threaded her fingers into his fingers. "Thank you for getting me through the worst of this."

He kissed her hand again and then pressed it between his two large palms. "You're probably going to get sick of me saying this…but I love you, Casey. You're my best friend and I'm always going to be here for you. You and Hannah…that's my life, right there… Hannah and you."

Brock returned to Montana and took care of his daughter; he got her back into her routine, which was a challenge, and he got her back into school, which was yet another challenge. But the biggest challenge for the rancher was being without his woman. Yes, they talked on the phone, they saw each other through video chat, but he couldn't kiss her, or touch her, or hold her hand. He couldn't feel her warmth next to him in bed—he couldn't make love to her—there were too many miles between them. Too many miles.

"Brock!" Casey's sister waved her hand so he would see that she was already there.

He slid into the booth and ordered a coffee from the waitress.

"I appreciate you meeting me," Brock said to Taylor.

"I was surprised to hear from you. You said you needed my advice?"

He did need advice. He'd been trying to convince Casey to put in notice at her job and come back to Montana to be with him and Hannah. But no matter what angle he tried, she was resisting. He didn't doubt that she loved him—yet she always found a reason why they should postpone their reunion. For him, the time for them to get back to the business of being a family of three had long since passed. Taylor knew Casey better than anyone, and that included him for now. It wouldn't always be that way.

"You know I love Casey."

Taylor nodded. "I do know that."

"I want her here with me, Taylor. I want us to get married. But, no matter what I say, she's always got a reason why we've got to wait."

"She's concerned about Hannah…"

"I know she is, and God knows I love her for it…but Hannah misses her. And Casey's talking about working her contract and waiting until the summer to come out. Hannah will be in California with her mother then and we could be right back where we started—except now it's a year later."

"But what do you want from me?"

"Tell me how to get through to your sister, Taylor. Because I've run out of ideas and I want her with us. And so does Hannah."

Taylor studied him for a moment and then she said, "The only thing I can tell you is that Casey can really dig her heels in when she thinks she's right. If you want to convince her that you're ready and Hannah's ready, then you need to get your butt on a plane, go to Chicago and do some convincing in person."

Chapter Sixteen

Casey Brand stepped off the elevator into the reception area of the Signature Room. Situated ninety-five stories above ground level on Michigan Avenue in downtown Chicago, the Signature Room restaurant had the best views in Chicago and it was one of Casey's all-time favorite places to dine. No matter how many times she watched the sunset over the downtown skyline of her hometown city, it never lost its appeal.

Tonight was a special night—she had just received a clean bill of health earlier in the week from her gynecological oncologist and her parents were taking her out to eat to celebrate. She hadn't dressed up in a pretty dress in such a long time, so she gave herself permission to break out her Bloomingdale's credit card. Several hours of shopping later, she emerged with a fabulous cocktail dress that made her legs look longer than they were, her waist smaller than it really was and gave the illusion of an hourglass shape. Of course, shoes and a cute evening clutch to match were absolute necessities.

After working up a sweat at Bloomingdale's, Casey met her mom at her mom's favorite spa for a day of beauty. Her mom treated her to a deep-tissue massage, a manicure-pedicure, a facial, hair and makeup. The whole deal. By the end of her shopping excursion and spa day, Casey felt reenergized and ready to slip on her sassy cocktail dress and strappy, fabulous heels, and meet her parents at the Signature Room.

"Reservations under Angus or Vivian Brand," Casey said to the maître d'.

The gentleman located their reservation. "Right this way."

"Thank you."

Casey followed the man to one of the tables with a window view. She had asked that her father make an early evening reservation so she could see the sun set—sitting at a table at the top of the John Hancock Center was like having a window with a view of the whole world.

The gentleman stopped next to a table set for two and pulled out a chair for her.

"I'm sorry—we need a table for three."

"I apologize, ma'am—let me check into that for you. Please have a seat and I'll be right back."

Casey sat down and enjoyed the view while she waited. Out of the corner of her eye, she saw a man walking her way—she turned her head toward him.

"Brock…?"

The man walking toward her was Brock. Her ranch

foreman was dressed to the nines in a tailored black suit and a soft gray shirt with a beautifully matched tie. He was carrying a single red rose in his hand and he looked so tall and handsome and in control as he walked her way.

The look on Casey's face when she first spotted him in a place where she least expected to see him was worth all of the planning and preparation for this surprise dinner. He'd enlisted the help of Casey's family— he wouldn't have been able to pull this off as well, or as smoothly, if they hadn't agreed to be complicit.

Casey stood up and met him halfway—Brock hugged her tightly, not caring about the stares or the curious eyes. He only cared about holding the woman he loved in his arms again. She tilted her head back, her eyes shining with happiness and surprise—she kissed him lightly on the lips and then immediately wiped her plum-colored lipstick off his lips.

"This is for you." He handed her the rose.

"It's beautiful. Thank you."

Perhaps it was a cliché to love red roses, but they were her favorite flower. And Brock must have picked the biggest, reddest, most scented specimen he could find because it was one of the prettiest, most fragrant red roses she had ever received.

Brock held out her chair for her and then joined her at the table.

She immediately reached for his hand; there had been a small part of him that had worried about her reaction. Had she really been stalling their reunion because of Hannah—or was she using his daughter, consciously or unconsciously, as an excuse? But the love and acceptance he saw in her eyes scrubbed away his doubt. Casey loved him. It was there on her pretty, freckled face for anyone to see.

"I can't believe you're here." She leaned toward him.

"I couldn't wait any longer to see you."

She was wearing her long red hair down tonight, just as he had imagined it would be, and the green material of her dress only enhanced the loveliness of her wide green eyes.

"I've missed you." Casey put her other hand on top of their clasped hands. "I must think of you a hundred times a day."

Their waiter stopped by their table with water, took their drink orders and brought them the menus.

Casey didn't open her menu right away. "How's Hannah?"

"She's having a good year. She has a message for you."

Brock handed Casey his phone; she pushed the "play" icon on the video and smiled as Hannah's round face and wild brown curls came to life.

"Hi, Casey...it's Hannah. Hey—when are you coming back? I hope you like what's on the menu!"

Casey handed the phone back to Brock.

"She has the cutest face! I swear it's the truth."

Brock slipped the phone into his pocket. "She misses you."

Casey felt a twinge of sadness—she missed Hannah almost as much as she missed Brock. It wasn't this way before her summer break, but there were as many people in Montana to miss now as there were in Chicago—her aunt and uncle, her sister and niece, her cousins.

"I miss her."

"You don't have to miss her." Brock looked directly into her eyes. "You can see her every day whenever you want."

They had had this discussion so many different times in so many different ways—but the facts, as far as she was concerned, hadn't changed. On her end, she was under contract for one more year with her school and her kids needed her. But whenever she would bring this up to Brock, he would say, *I need you. Hannah needs you.*

On Brock's end, Casey felt strongly that Hannah needed time to adjust to her parents' divorce. She needed time and they needed to give it to her. Brock agreed with her completely, but they also *disagreed completely* about the timeline.

Brock must have seen her furrow her brow. "We have plenty of time to talk later. Right now, the only thing I want to do is enjoy a great meal and enjoy this gorgeous view."

"It is an amazing view, isn't it? You can see for miles."

Brock smiled at her. "I meant you."

Casey felt herself flush with pleasure. Brock always made her feel like the most beautiful woman in the room—he never so much as looked at another woman when they were together. He genuinely only had eyes for her.

"What looks good to you?" Brock looked at his menu.

Casey didn't pick up her menu.

"Aren't you going to look at your menu?" he asked her with an expectant expression on his face.

"Uh-uh." She shook her head. "I already know what I want. I have this menu memorized."

"They may have something new on the menu—something you may want to try."

"Nope. I've been thinking about the Scottish salmon all day. It's in-*credible*."

"Look at the appetizers…you may want something to start."

"Lobster bisque." She nodded. "Every time."

Brock had stopped looking at his menu; he was frowning at her in thought.

"Why are you looking at me like that?"

After a second of thinking, Brock picked up her menu and handed it to her. "Please look at the menu."

"Why do you want me to look at it so badly?" She laughed.

"Don't you remember what Hannah said to you in her message?"

Casey had to think back to the video, but then it hit her—Hannah had said that she hoped she liked what was on the menu.

With understanding dawning in her eyes, Casey gave him a suspicious look before she looked curiously at the menu. In the middle of the menu, a new dish had been added:

Meet Me at the Chapel for the Rest of My Life.
Marry Me, Casey.

Casey stared at those words printed on her favorite menu, blinking her eyes rapidly to stop tears from dropping into her lashes.

She looked up from the menu and Brock was no longer in his chair. He was kneeling beside her, in the now-crowded restaurant, holding an open ring box in the palm of his hand.

Casey's knees started to shake from the adrenaline being pumped all over her body by her rapidly beating heart. She had known that one day this proposal would come, but Brock had been so good at hiding his plans to fly into Chicago and surprise her, that there was no way she could have anticipated that the proposal would happen tonight.

Brock took her hand in his. "Casey Brand. If you'll let me, I want to spend every day of the rest of my life showing you how much I love you. Will you marry me?"

Casey didn't need to think about it—she already knew what she wanted to do. "Yes. I'll marry you, Brock."

Brock must not have heard her, because he asked her, "Was that a yes?"

Casey laughed and brushed some wayward tears from her cheeks. "Yes!"

Brock took the antique-inspired brilliant-cut diamond ring set in filigreed platinum from the box. Everyone within earshot or sight line of the table started to clap and cheer as he slipped the ring onto her left hand.

"I love you." She put her hands on either side of his face and kissed him.

"I love you more."

Brock had reserved a suite at a downtown hotel, so their engagement night was full of incredible views of downtown Chicago—first at the Signature Room and now at a suite at the Hyatt Regency. Brock had lit candles in the room so they could leave the curtains open and enjoy the twinkling of the city lights all around them.

Brock walked up behind her carrying a glass of champagne. "What are you doing?"

She made a pleasurable noise when her fiancé brushed her hair to the side to kiss the back of her neck.

"I'm sending everyone a picture of us at the restaurant after we got engaged."

Brock took her phone and handed her the glass of champagne. "That can wait."

She laughed easily. "Okay—you're right."

They toasted each other and drank the champagne, and then with the red and green and white lights of the city as their landscape, Brock wrapped his arms around her from behind and breathed in the scent of her perfume.

"I've missed this," he murmured into her neck.

She put her hands over his hands and leaned her head back to rest on his shoulder. "So have I."

Brock moved her hair over her shoulder so he could unzip the zipper. As he inched the zipper downward, he kissed her skin as it was exposed.

"Are you ready to try?" he asked.

She knew what he was asking—was she ready to try to make love for the first time after her surgery? The doctor had cleared her for sex and her stitches had dissolved. The changes on the inside of her body scared her, but she did want to try. She missed being connected to Brock in that most intimate of ways.

Brock slipped Casey's cocktail dress off her shoulders and it fell in a whisper of fabric to the plush carpet at her feet. She stepped out of the dress, standing now in her bra, panties and her strappy new shoes.

Casey turned in his arms; his hands felt hot on her bare skin as he kissed her lips and neck and the rounded tops of her breasts.

"You're so beautiful to me, Casey. So beautiful."

Casey ran her finger through his hair as he rested his head for a moment on her chest. When he lifted his head, she smiled a playful smile; she took him by the tie and led him over to the bed.

"You look very sexy in a suit, cowboy." She pushed him gently in the direction of the bed.

"You think so?"

Casey walked behind him and pulled his suit jacket off his shoulders. She ran her hand over his backside and gave it a little smack before she circled back around to his front side.

"Nice." Brock winked at her when she slapped him playfully on the backside. "Foreplay."

Casey gave him a little smile and tugged the tie knot loose. Brock let her have control for a couple of minutes, watching with admiring eyes while she untucked his shirt, unbuckled his belt and started to slowly unbutton his shirt one button at a time.

Brock grabbed her by the wrists and pulled her against his body. As she laughed at his impatience, the ranch foremen reached behind her and popped open her bra. He pushed the flimsy material out of his way so he could take her breast into his mouth.

She held on to his shoulders and rested her forehead on the top of his head. The feel of his warm mouth on her breast made her catch her breath.

Brock had a devilish glint in his eyes when he lifted

his head. He spun her around, cupped her breast with his hand and then slipped his fingers into her panties.

"Hmm," he murmured when his fingers found her. "Someone missed me, too."

Casey dropped her head back and moaned again. Brock knew how to make her body hum in the most sensual ways. She reached behind her and put her hand over the hard bulge in his half-unzipped pants.

Brock made a frustrated noise in the back of his throat. He quickly divested her of her panties—the only things she had on now were jewelry and her high heels.

Her fiancé stripped out of his clothes without fanfare; he'd lost some weight while they were apart. The ranch foreman—tall and burly and 100 percent male—was a thing of beauty as far as she was concerned.

"Do you want to take your shoes off?" Brock asked her.

Casey looked down at her sexy heels. "Actually—no. Why shouldn't I leave them on?"

"It's okay with me." Brock swept her off her feet and into his arms.

Casey laughed at the odd feeling of being carried naked. "Wait! The bed is *that* way!"

Brock ignored her and carried her over to the wide windowsill ledge that ran the length of the long wall of windows that maximized the view.

"What are you *doing*?" she squealed when he started to put her down.

"Something I've wanted to do since I saw this ledge." Brock put her down on it.

"It's cold!" she complained on a laugh.

Brock knelt down in front of her. "Shhh."

Casey looked over her shoulder—yes, they were in silhouette, but it was highly conceivable that someone out there in high-rise land could see her bare back and snow-white butt cheeks!

"Brock!" she tried to protest again, but he refused to listen. Her fiancé gently coaxed her knees apart, exposing her to his admiring eyes.

When he put his mouth on her—when she felt his tongue taste her, all thoughts of further protest drifted away on her moans of pleasure.

Brock wrapped his arms around her body and pulled her toward him. When she was ready, when she was wet and so sensitive and digging her fingernails into his shoulders, Brock took her to the bed.

"I love you, Casey." Brock lay between her open thighs.

She kissed him. "I love you."

As gently as he could, and with as much control as he could muster, Brock eased their bodies together.

"Are you okay?" he asked her. She was so hot and tight and slick; it was difficult for him to take it slow and gentle.

Casey was taken out of the sensuality of the moment into the fear of the unknown. Would her body react the same? Would it hurt? Would she be able to orgasm?

"Still okay?" Brock lifted himself up a little so he could look down into her face.

"It's a little sore." She was honest. "And I'm worried that I won't be able to…have an orgasm like I used to."

Brock stopped moving. "Baby—we're going to work this out together. If you can't have an orgasm the way you used to—then we'll have fun finding a new way."

His words reassured her and Casey started to relax

her mind and relax her body. Her rancher took it steady and slow—he was so patient with her.

"Are you coming?" Brock asked her in a husky voice.

"Yes," Casey said in a breathy voice, relieved that she could still have an orgasm.

"Damn," Brock swore. "I can't hold off any longer, Casey."

"Don't." She kissed his shoulder. "Don't hold back."

Casey held on as her man thrust into her faster and deeper until she felt his entire body tense above her and he cried out her name. After taking a minute to catch his breath, Brock opened his eyes and looked at her. They both started to laugh.

"We've still got it." Brock smiled proudly at her.

"Yes, we do." Casey was pleased, as well. Her maiden voyage with her remodeled female plumbing had been a total success.

After a quick shower, they got back into bed and drank another glass of champagne.

"It was okay for you?" Brock ran his finger over the four small scars on her abdomen from the surgery.

Casey pulled the sheet over her legs and curled her body toward him. "It was a little sore at first, but after we got going, I forgot all about it."

"Good." Brock kissed her left hand and then looked at the new ring on her finger. "We're engaged."

Casey admired her engagement ring—it was a stone that was modest in size but large on quality. It was bright white with lots of fire.

"We're engaged," she repeated.

"Do you like your ring?"

"Oh, Brock…it's such a beautiful ring! I couldn't have picked out a better ring for myself."

"I did have a little help," he admitted.

"Taylor?"

He ran his finger over the stone that had taken a decent chunk of his savings to buy.

"I should call her and thank her."

Brock took her glass from her to put it on the night table. He pulled her close and kissed her on the lips.

"Tomorrow." Brock wrapped his arms around her and held on so tight. "Tonight, my love…tonight is only for us."

* * * * *

Looking for more of the Brand family?

Don't miss out on Nick Brand's story,
the next book in Joanna Sims's
THE BRANDS OF MONTANA *series,*
THANKFUL FOR YOU
coming in November 2016 from
Mills & Boon Cherish.

MILLS & BOON®

Cherish™

EXPERIENCE THE ULTIMATE RUSH OF FALLING IN LOVE

A sneak peek at next month's titles...

In stores from 8th September 2016:

- **A Mistletoe Kiss with the Boss** – Susan Meier *and* **Maverick vs Maverick** – Shirley Jump
- **A Countess for Christmas** – Christy McKellen *and* **Ms Bravo and the Boss** – Christine Rimmer

In stores from 6th October 2016:

- **Her Festive Baby Bombshell** – Jennifer Faye *and* **Building the Perfect Daddy** – Brenda Harlen
- **The Unexpected Holiday Gift** – Sophie Pembroke *and* **The Man She Should Have Married** – Patricia Kay

---

Just can't wait?
Buy our books online a month before they hit the shops!
www.millsandboon.co.uk

Also available as eBooks.

916/23

MILLS & BOON®

EXCLUSIVE EXCERPT

Emma Carmichael's world is turned upside-down
when she encounters Jack Westwood—her
secret husband of six years!

Read on for a sneak preview of
A COUNTESS FOR CHRISTMAS
the first book in the enchanting new Cherish quartet
MAIDS UNDER THE MISTLETOE

'You still have your ring,' Jack said.

'Of course.' Emma was frowning now and wouldn't
meet his eye.

'Why—?' He walked to where she was standing
with her hand gripping her handbag so hard her
knuckles were white.

'I'm not very good at letting go of the past,' she
said, shrugging and tilting up her chin to look him
straight in the eye, as if to dare him to challenge her
about it. 'I don't have a lot left from my old life and
I couldn't bear to get rid of this ring. It reminds me of
a happier time in my life. A simpler time, which I don't
want to forget about.'

She blinked hard and clenched her jaw together
and it suddenly occurred to him that she was struggling with being around him as much as he was with
her.

The atmosphere hung heavy and tense between them,

with only the sound of their breathing breaking the silence.

His throat felt tight with tension and his pulse had picked up so he felt the heavy beat of it in his chest.

Why was it so important to him that she hadn't completely eschewed their past?

He didn't know, but it was.

Taking a step towards her, he slid his fingers under the thin silver chain around her neck, feeling the heat of her soft skin as he brushed the backs of his fingers over it, and drew the ring out of her dress again to look at it.

He remembered picking this out with her. They'd been so happy then, so full of excitement and love for each other.

He heard her ragged intake of breath as the chain slid against the back of her neck and looked up to see confusion in her eyes, and something else. Regret, perhaps, or sorrow for what they'd lost.

Something seemed to be tugging hard inside him, drawing him closer to her.

Her lips parted and he found he couldn't drag his gaze away from her mouth. That beautiful, sensual mouth that used to haunt his dreams all those years ago.

A lifetime ago.

MILLS & BOON®

18 bundles of joy from your favourite authors!

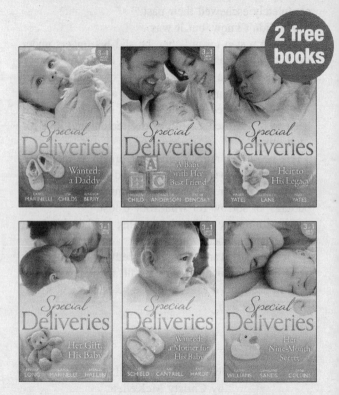